A Question of Judgement

A Question of Judgement

SARA KEAYS

QUINTESSENTIAL PRESS

Published by Quintessential Press Ltd.
8 Strutton Ground,
Westminster,
London, SW1P 2HP.

ISBN 1–85138–000–0

Typeset, printed and bound
in Great Britain at
The Bath Press, Avon

Contents

Foreword

My daughter Sara has had my entire support in the preparation of this book.

I deplore the behaviour of people in public life and in the media which has made it necessary.

Hastings Keays

24 October 1985

'I like people who talk straight, no jargon, no fudging.'

So said the Prime Minister, Mrs Margaret Thatcher, in an interview for the *Mail on Sunday*, 3 February 1985. Yet few people can have demonstrated greater mastery of the art of 'fudging' than the Prime Minister in her handling of the Parkinson/Keays Affair.

The scandal broke on 6 October 1983, with the publication of a statement by Cecil Parkinson, then Secretary of State for Trade and Industry. He announced that he had had a 'relationship' with me, that I was pregnant by him and that, in spite of having told me of his 'wish' to marry me and given me an 'assurance' that he would do so, he had decided to remain with his wife and family. This statement, to which I had reluctantly given my consent, was itself a classic piece of fudging, as the Prime Minister herself was well aware. However, it paled into insignificance when compared with what followed.

Cecil's refusal to acknolwedge in that statement the extent and the seriousness of our relationship should have been a warning to me. If I could have foreseen the events that followed its publication, I would never have given my consent to it. I did not realise that the Prime Minister's desire to sustain him in office in the face of mounting pressure for his resignation would lead to our love affair being portrayed as a mere 'dalliance' and my pregnancy as the unfortunate result of a minor indiscretion on his part—intolerable lies that struck to the very core of my character. Nor did I imagine—it was inconceivable to me—that Cecil would tolerate, even connive at, the assault on my reputation.

To begin with, 10 Downing Street parried questions from the media about the Prime Minister's knowledge of the matter and Cecil's Cabinet appointment with assertions that it was a purely 'private' matter. The fact that this 'private' matter, and the wording of his statement, had been the subject of urgent discussion with his Cabinet colleagues only hours before was concealed. The public were to be persuaded that all that needed to be said on the matter had been said in his statement.

Then, during the week that followed, a disinformation campaign was mounted by 10 Downing Street to shore up his position and counter the pressure for his resignation. The same thing was done at the Conservative Party Conference in Blackpool, where attempts were made to bolster his reputation at the expense of mine. There were people in the Conservative Party who believed that by blackening my name they could kill off awkward questions from the media about Cecil Parkinson's conduct and the Prime Minister's judgement.

Questions about what he had told the Prime Minister, and when, were smothered in a mass of conflicting information. Lobby correspondents were fed a steady diet of 'facts' about the affair that had caused Cecil this unfortunate embarrassment. The disinformation campaign paid off and a week after his statement he was emerging as the unfortunate victim of a scheming woman who had tried to trap him into marriage by 'deliberately' becoming pregnant.

On the Thursday evening, 13 October 1983, I issued a statement to *The Times* to try to put a stop to the smear campaign. I withheld facts which I knew would be highly damaging to both the Prime Minister and the Conservative Party and said only as much as I believed would be necessary to defend my reputation against further attack.

Cecil's resignation was inevitable because of the discrepancies between his statement and mine, because he had omitted significant details and concealed the extent of our relationship. Furthermore, I had exposed the inaccuracies of the pronouncements that had been made on the subject by 10 Downing Street. But all that was soon forgotten. Within hours the public were being told that Cecil's resignation had been forced on the Government solely by the publicity. My statement was dismissed by the media as an act of revenge by a 'woman scorned'.

There were many people in the Conservative Party who wished to divert public attention from the truth. What better way of doing so than by traducing me? They were largely successful. The story was re-written, with me as the villain of the piece. Cecil, and by association, the Government and the Conservative Party were portrayed as my unfortunate victims. The day after my statement was published the *Daily Express* reported from the Conservative Party Conference that:

> The verdict among Tories is that Miss Keays was determined to bring Mr Parkinson down and had the ammunition, which she used, to destroy him.

There were public expressions of dismay at the 'hypocrisy' that had caused his downfall. His former Cabinet colleagues gave television interviews, expressing their sorrow at his departure from Government and saying that, had the matter been kept 'private', he would have been able to survive the scandal. In one such interview, Norman Tebbit accused me of reneging on an undertaking that I would remain silent on the matter. I had given no such undertaking and in no circumstances whatsoever would I have done so.

The belief that it was solely the publicity—and that I had caused it—which had brought about Cecil's downfall, soon set like concrete. However, not one word of my statement was ever challenged by him, the Prime Minister or anyone else, although strenuous efforts were made to discredit it by means of the 'Lobby' system of off-the-record briefing of the media.

Within hours there was an army of experts available to volunteer 'facts' to the press to 'prove' that my 'version' of events was untrue. None of these knowledgeable individuals was prepared to reveal his or her identity, but this did not deter the press from publishing their anonymous accusations.

As a result of these accusations, it is now widely believed—it has certainly been stated publicly time and again over the past two years—that Cecil Parkinson was brought down by my statement and that I issued it out of a desire for revenge on my former lover. No matter that the opinion had been expressed during the previous week that it was only a question of time before he would have to resign, that pressure on him would become intolerable as the birth of our baby drew nearer.

The only events perceived to be of significance were those which occurred in the week from 6 to 14 October 1983, culminating in his resignation. The events that had led up to this extraordinary episode were obscured by skilful briefing of the media and eventually buried altogether. Those who wished to avert questions about the Prime Minister's judgement made much of her loyalty and compassion for Cecil Parkinson—a colleague in distress. The matter was talked of in terms of 'humbug' and 'outdated' values. There was no mention of duty, or integrity, hitherto considered fundamental to British public life.

Loyalty was the new watchword; compassion the greatest virtue. But there was to be none for me or for my family, whose loyalty and discretion the Prime Minister and the Conservative Party neither recognised nor deserved.

It caused me great anguish that my family was exposed to months of odious and unnecessary publicity solely because the Prime Minister and Cecil Parkinson were determined that he should continue in office. It was repugnant to me to have to issue my statement, but I had no other means of defending myself.

It occurred to no one, apparently, that I could not defend myself without embarrassing the Prime Minister and without being accused of vindictiveness and malice.

Had those been my motives and had I indeed wished to cause embarrassment, I could have done so to great effect during the General Election campaign.

I hope it will be recognised from my father's correspondence with the Prime Minister and from the subsequent conduct of myself and my family that, far from wanting to embarrass the Government, we behaved with the utmost discretion and kept silent in the face of gross provocation. Had my position and that of my family been considered at all—had Cecil behaved less selfishly and the Prime Minister less arrogantly—both his family and mine could have been spared a great deal of suffering. Had he and the Prime Minister acted differently, his statement and the events which followed it could have been avoided. Certainly I would not be writing this book.

I was derided for saying in my statement that I considered I had 'both a public duty as well as a duty to my family to put the record straight'. The *Guardian* called it 'portentous flummery' and 'little more than a scream of pain'.

Although it is hard to write about events which have affected me so personally and so painfully, I do believe they have more than merely personal significance and that my account of them should be published. I do believe that integrity is of equal importance to public and private life and that you cannot sacrifice personal honour to political expediency without being both personally and politically devalued.

My wish to defend myself would be sufficient reason for writing this book, but it is not the only reason. I wish also to expose the double standards applied within the Conservative Party, their hypocrisy and the sham of their talk of equality and fairness.

It was not enough that the occasion of the Conservative Party Conference in October 1983 had been used to launch a smear campaign against me. They wished apparently to put an end to my political career and to prevent me from applying for Parliamentary vacancies, although I had been on the Party's Approved List of Candidates since November 1982. Perhaps they hoped that I would be too preoccupied to notice, or so dismayed by my recent experiences as to let the matter drop. Instead of dealing openly and straightforwardly with me, they have been deceitful and evasive. It has been put about that I am an embarrassment to the Party. If that is the case, it is because I defended myself against the Party 'machine'. So much for the Party which supposedly champions the rights of the individual.

Nor did they stop there, but certain people highly placed in the Government attempted to put pressure on other members of my family in order to prevent them from speaking out in my defence, even privately.

I had let it be known that I would say more if the attacks on my reputation continued, but it soon became apparent that those who had been blackening my name would go to almost any lengths to do so and that there were those in the media willing to assist them in their task. What hope had I of defending myself if even the so-called reputable press gave greater credence to the accusations of people too cowardly to be identified than to the facts contained in my personal statement to *The Times*.

I decided that I must publish a detailed account of the events that led up to Cecil's resignation. It was not a decision I took lightly. I was nervous of the task and easily persuaded myself that it would be better to wait and to review a very painful series of events from a greater distance in time. I have no doubt that I will be attacked yet again by the people who reviled me for my statement and accused me of destroying Cecil's career. I can only say, however, that this book is concerned just as much with those in the Conservative Party leadership who chose to interfere in the matter and who tried to discredit me as a means of protecting themselves.

I also wish the facts to be available to my daughter. During the past two years, many people have presumed to advise me as to the consequences of my actions for my daughter. They have expressed their extreme disapproval of my doing anything that might harm the reputation and career of her father, on the grounds that she would hold it against me, even hate me for it. The same people expressed no concern at the consequences for her of the destruction of her mother's reputation.

I hope that those journalists who wrote at such length about the Parkinson/Keays Affair when they knew so little about it will take the trouble to read this book. I found, as others have before me, that many journalists do not allow ignorance of the facts to stand in the way of a story. I hope they will recognise that there were many occasions when they presented fiction as fact, perhaps sometimes unwittingly, and were too hasty in their judgements. In their defence, they may plead that they were misinformed and deliberately misled, but I hope they will be as ready to admit error as they were to pass judgement.

If judgements are to be made, let them be based on the facts, which I shall try to set out fully in this book, rather than the half-truths and downright lies that have circulated since October 1983.

Part One

Love affair

Background

When Cecil Parkinson's statement was published on 6 October 1983, the media wanted information in a great hurry and perhaps it was merely the desire to be first with a story that made some reporters so careless. Many of their errors were trifling, and on occasions quite funny, but some were most offensive. Unfortunately it is invariably the latter which stick.

Some reporters went to extraordinary lengths to try to obtain information about me and my family. They could get none from us so they tried anyone else who might possibly be able to help and offered them huge sums of money. We were living in a state of siege at the time, with a horde of reporters camped outside the house, and it was only later that I heard about their attempts to buy information and the contempt with which these were met by local people. It was distressing to be the cause of such behaviour and I was touched by the sympathy and kindness shown to me and my family by the people of Marksbury and neighbouring villages, who suffered considerable nuisance and disruption of their lives as a result of the media invasions of October 1983 and January 1984.

It would appear that some of the reporters either swallowed whole anything they were told, without bothering to check its accuracy, or, when no facts were available, they manufactured them. It should have been quite easy to ascertain, for example, when I started working in the House of Commons, but few of them got even that right. Some went to the lengths of finding out where I had been to school and the kind of family I came from. If such information was of interest then, perhaps I ought to give it here, if only to correct the record.

The members of my family mentioned in this book are my parents, Colonel and Mrs Hastings Keays, my brothers William and Tom, their wives Cheryl and Georgina, my twin sister Elisabeth and her husband Richard Dalton, my sister Flora and her husband Roger Giles.

My father's age ranged from 70 to 80 (he was then 78) and some reporters liked to refer to him as my 'octagenarian' father. For most of them he was a 'wealthy landowner' whose 'imposing mansion' was variously placed in Wiltshire, Avon, Somerset and Dorset. His former regiment was supposedly the Royal Engineers, when in fact it was REME. My younger sister, Flora, was usually at least two years older than I, to her chagrin, and her husband, Roger, was on one occasion referred to as her father-in-law. He said that if he had aged as much as that, it should be put down to press harrassment.

It was said that I came from a 'privileged' background and that I would have no worries about bringing up my child on my own because my 'wealthy' parents would provide for me. My parents were far from wealthy and had a hard financial struggle bringing up their five children. My father would hardly have been able to support me and my baby on his Army pension, even if I could have contemplated such an arrangement. But these facts would not have fitted the kind of story such journalists wanted to write.

If by 'privileged' they meant being part of a very close-knit and loving family, then I am privileged indeed. I cannot imagine how I would have coped with the events of the past two-and-a-half years had I not had my father and my brothers and sisters to help and encourage me. They made light of the publicity and the unwelcome attentions of the reporters who hounded them for months. They were cheerful and uncomplaining. There were occasions, especially in the weeks leading up to and just after the birth of my baby, when I was utterly dependent on them for my privacy and peace of mind.

I suppose it was the size of Winsbury House, with its five acres of land, which led reporters to conclude that its owners were wealthy. In fact my parents managed to scrape together just enough money to buy the house from the Church in 1947, on a large and burdensome mortgage. Having cast my father as a wealthy landowner, the press went on to inform their readers that he had bought me a cottage on the edge of his 'estate' where I could live in seclusion with my child. The fact that I bought the cottage myself would not have fitted into the picture the press wanted to create, so it was disregarded.

My parents had long periods of separation imposed on them by my father's career, but it did not diminish their devotion to one another, or to their children. My father served in the Regular Army for 27 years. He left the Army in 1957, anxious to obtain a job in industry which would enable him to continue working until his five children were educated. He did not retire until the age of 72 and throughout his working life he was obliged to spend a great deal of time away from his family. After he left the Army his job required him to live in London and he could be with us only at weekends and on holidays. It was not until after I had grown up and left home that I realised how much my parents had put into the happiness of their children. But they never made us feel that they had made sacrifices for us and we lived the happiest and most carefree existence imaginable.

Similarly, it was only as an adult that I came to appreciate the great qualities and strength of character of both my parents. In the past two years my father has been a constant source of strength to me and I have been filled with admiration for him. Would that those who have maligned us had his integrity.

My mother, who died in 1981, was a talented artist, and her pictures, most of which hang in Winsbury House, are a constant reminder of her and of all the various stages and important events in the life of the family. It is an indication of her character, and her dedication to her art, that she did so much work and of such a high quality, while bringing up a large family. The only occasions when we ever saw her unhappy were when family crises or illness prevented her from painting. She was a wonderful person and we all adored her.

My parents were both forceful personalities, with strong convictions, but at the same time tolerant and forward-looking. They were both well-read and keenly interested in the arts. They resisted our requests for television, and encouraged us to read and to discuss any topic that interested us. Family conversation, including sometimes heated argument, was one of the features and pleasures of family life, although as children we found it advisable not to remain too long sitting round the kitchen table, or we were liable to find that my mother had put up her easel in the corner of the room and was painting us.

My sisters and I went to Clifton High School in Bristol—one press article said my twin sister and I were separated so that the staff could tell us apart and that I always felt that I had 'drawn the short straw' with the subjects I had chosen, because Elisabeth went on to university and I did not. We were indeed very alike but we were not separated and there was no question of 'drawing straws'. Certainly I was disappointed that I did not go to university, but the truth of the matter was that I had not applied myself sufficiently to my studies and although I had a good array of exam results my grades were not good enough to gain me a university place. I had long discussions with my parents about what I should do. I had no burning ambitions, only a keen interest in politics, which was the subject I had wished to read at university. My parents, anxious to see me with some means of earning a living, urged me to do a secretarial course. I agreed very reluctantly. Elisabeth went on to Oxford and in no time at all I had finished my secretarial training and had to think about getting a job. My younger sister, Flora, had left school and was about to start a Pre-Diploma course at the Camberwell School of Art, so we went to London together in September 1967 and set up home in a rather gloomy flat in Kensington. I hated those first weeks in London. The prospect of secretarial work in some dreary office depressed me. The only job which appealed to me was one which would enable me to learn more about politics and government and which might lead eventually to a parliamentary career. I had sought the advice of our local MP, Paul Dean, who had suggested that I see Miss Lewis at Conservative Research Department, then in Old Queen Street, Westminster. I did so, only to be told that I ought to get some secretarial experience first. If so, she said, I might be able to get a job as a Member's Secretary in the House of Commons. I was disappointed, but was persuaded that some experience was necessary for such an important job. Later, when I started working in the House of Commons, I realised that this was not the case and that a college-leaver with common sense and a capacity for hard work could master the job as quickly as someone with secretarial experience.

I spent two years doing a variety of secretarial jobs. In March 1970, I decided to call on Miss Lewis again. She remembered my earlier visit and said that it just so happened that she knew that Bernard Braine, the Member for South-East Essex, needed a secretary. She rang him up and I went straight over to the House of Commons to see him. A few days later he offered me the job and I accepted. My political career made its tentative beginning when I started work at the House of Commons in April 1970.

In November 1970, a friend who was also working in the House, and who wanted to take an extended holiday overseas, asked if I would stand in for her. I gave up my job with Bernard Braine but when the temporary job, with Charles Morrison and Ian Gilmour, came to an end in April 1971 I could not immediately find another. I asked John Marling, who ran the Conservative Whips' Office for many years and knew just about everything about the House and everyone who worked in it, to let me know if he heard of any Conservative Member requiring a secretary.

Two weeks later I received a telephone call from Ralph Howell, the Member for North Norfolk, who wanted a part-time research assistant and had heard I was looking for a job. I was far more interested in doing political research than in dealing with constituency correspondence and was delighted when he offered me the job. However, it was only a part-time appointment and it was essential, if I was to earn a sufficient income, that I find another Member to work for as well.

On 25 May I had to meet Ralph in the House to discuss some work he wanted me to do. Afterwards I called in at the Government Whips' Office to see John Marling again. He was talking to a man whom I did not recognise. As I entered the room, John said to his visitor, "This is the girl for you".

That was how I met Cecil Parkinson. He had been elected to Parliament only six months earlier in the by-election in Enfield West following Iain Macleod's death. He had been talking to John Marling about advertising for a secretary when I entered the room. I had, by then, been working in the House for a year and he was still a new enough Member to be impressed by my apparent knowledge of the place. Two days later he offered me the job—my diary reveals that I was very pleased that he offered me a salary of £26 per week—and I started working for him on 2 June 1971.

Our love affair

No journalist ever succeeded in finding out when my love affair with Cecil began, but many of them did not allow such ignorance to deter them from claiming to know and from passing on this and other 'facts' to their readers.

When I met Cecil I was 23 and he 39. Our love affair spanned nearly twelve years. However, those who read this book hoping to find an intimate account of it will be disappointed. I would have preferred to deal only with the events of May 1983 onwards, but decided that I must give some account of our relationship in order to show that it was not a mere 'dalliance', a 'sad and silly blunder', but a long-standing, genuine love affair.

Cecil was the only man with whom I had ever been in love. I had, until I met him, entirely conventional views about marriage. I hoped that I would one day meet the 'right' man, marry, and have a family, but all that was way off in the future. I had never imagined that I would have an affair with anyone, let alone with a married man. My life was full and enjoyable. I was by then thoroughly settled in London and most of my friends were there. I had been working at the House of Commons for a year and loved it. I was at that happy stage where all the wonderful things in life seemed to be just ahead of me. I was young enough and optimistic enough to believe that I could simply live in the present and let tomorrow take care of itself.

Inevitably, unhappiness and doubt crept into the relationship, on my side at least. I loved him and wanted a commitment that he was unable or unwilling to give me. In March 1974 I told him I wanted to end the affair. There had been a great deal of tension between us during the General Election campaign the previous month, and he agreed that we ought to part company. Two weeks later, when I had already been interviewed for and offered another job, he suddenly poured out his feelings for me and begged me not to go. I believed that he truly loved me and for the first time felt I could hope for future happiness with him. Had I been more determined, I would have extricated myself from the affair then. I told myself that I had genuinely tried to leave him, but, looking back, I have to admit that my attempt was half-hearted. It did, however, mark a fundamental change in our relationship. We were very much in love and spent more and more time together.

For the next three years I was very happy. My life was hectic and exciting and the months flew by. Gradually, however, all my earlier anxieties began to re-assert themselves. I could not shut out of my mind the thought that perhaps he was content to keep things just as they were and that we would never marry. He was doing well in politics, his work was very demanding, and our affair made up for the shortcomings of his domestic arrangements. Whatever the stresses of such a life, it was probably bearable for him. But it was becoming increasingly unbearable for me. I wanted so much to marry him and have his children. More and more of my friends were married and having families. Those who were not had interesting and challenging careers. While I was happy with Cecil I had been able to put up with the limitations of my job. As my unhappiness about our relationship increased, so did the awareness that I was missing out on a career. I felt increasingly that I must develop my own abilities and try to pursue a political career of my own.

By the end of 1976 I was very unhappy. Cecil understood the reason and was loving and attentive. He tried to make me happy by giving me the most lavish presents. At the beginning of 1977 he paid for me to have a skiing holiday. For my birthday that year he gave me a car, and in September we had a brief but wonderful holiday together in New York. We stayed at the Plaza Hotel, which seemed to me the last word in luxury, and visited my sister Elisabeth and her husband Richard, who were then living in New York, Richard having been posted to the UK Mission to the United Nations.

Although we had some very happy times together that year, I still could not shut out the thought that I must inevitably break away from him if I were ever to have any chance of meeting anyone else and marrying. I was by then 30 and felt that my chances of ever having a family of my own were slipping away. My career prospects were equally limited unless I left him. I did not want to leave the political world, but it now seemed unavoidable. I did not want to leave London as most of my friends were there and I was reluctant to give up the unfurnished flat in Marylebone which I had had the great good fortune to find in 1974. I knew that if I moved out of London, or went abroad, if I ever returned to live in London again I would be back in bedsitterland.

Then, at the end of 1977, came an opportunity to achieve the independence and freedom of action I wanted so desperately. My brother, Tom, had been working overseas for some years and wanted to put his savings into a property. He proposed that we buy a house together, which would give me a permanent home in London and him a base to come back to when on leave. A joint purchase was also the only means by which either of us could then aspire to a property in London. In December 1977 I found just what we were looking for, a house in a new development south of the Thames called Temple West Mews, just a mile from the House of Commons. I wanted it from the moment I saw it. It was a little modern box of a house, but light and airy and set in a quiet and attractive courtyard. Tom was in England briefly over Christmas and the New Year and we looked at the house together on 4 January. He liked it as much as I did so we made our offer. It was accepted and that afternoon Tom flew back to Lagos. I had three anxious months before we completed the purchase at last in April 1978.

It was wonderful to have my own home and I got enormous pleasure out of decorating and furnishing it. More importantly, if I worked overseas for a year or two, I had a home to come back to in London. I had talked to Cecil often about leaving. I do not think he really believed me. He hoped, I think, that we could continue with our existing arrangement indefinitely. Much of the time we were very happy, but there were many occasions when I was deeply depressed. I loved him wholeheartedly and wanted nothing more than to spend the rest of my life with him. He had said many times that he wished he could marry me, but I no longer believed that he would. He was doing well in politics, Mrs Thatcher having made him an Opposition spokesman on Trade, and it was likely that he would be given a Ministerial appointment in the next Conservative Government. If that happened, he would not want to have any upheaval in his private life.

Hardest to bear was the secrecy of our relationship, having to maintain an appearance of total normality at work when I was often preoccupied with my feelings for Cecil. I had been working in the same office, with the same people, for years and was sure that any strain between Cecil and myself would be apparent to them. And the strains were beginning to appear. What I had been prepared to put up with before, when it had been outweighed by my happiness and the general excitement of my life, I had come to detest. I loathed the deceptions which our affair entailed. I made up my mind that I would leave after the next General Election, which was bound to be held some time during the next year, and that I would go abroad. In my heart of hearts I knew that I had to go away. It was useless to try to end the affair and at the same time continue to work in politics. It was hard to have to leave the House of Commons, to cut myself off from friends and from my life in London, but it seemed to me that I had no choice.

The General Election was held on 3 May 1979. The Conservatives were returned to power. The following Sunday Cecil telephoned me to say that Mrs Thatcher was appointing him Minister for Trade. I was thrilled for him, but sad for myself, believing that it put an end to my hopes that we would marry. Soon after the election I told him that I would leave at the end of July, when the summer recess began and his workload would be lightest. I had no clear idea what I would do, but resolved to go abroad for several years and start a new life. I thought I would try to find a job with the European Parliament or Commission, or with the United Nations, but there was so much work immediately after the election that I had no time to do anything in the way of job-hunting. Then, in June, quite by chance, I heard of a possible vacancy in the office of the President of the European Commission, Roy Jenkins. One of his two personal assistants was leaving to get married. I wrote immediately to ask if I might be considered for the job.

It was said in the press in October 1983 that it was Cecil who had decided that we should part company and that he had found me the job in Brussels, but it was

I who ended the affair and I found the job myself. In May 1979, when I told Cecil I was leaving, he agreed it was the right course. Later, however, he did not want me to go, and right up to the last moment I believe he hoped I would change my mind.

My final weeks at the House were hard to bear, but I was determined to stick to my decision and to leave at the end of July. I had told all my friends there that I was leaving because I felt it was time for a change of scene and I was anxious to appear happy at the prospect of going. It was very difficult to get through those last days without my unhappiness being apparent. Moreover, I still had not heard whether I would even be interviewed for the job in Brussels. I was leaving on the day the House rose for the summer recess, Friday 27 July, and Cecil and I met to have dinner together for the last time on the Thursday evening. In spite of our attempts at cheerfulness, we were a miserable pair. He left early the following day having promised that he would not get in touch with me again. We had agreed that there could be no half-measures: we must not see each other again. It was an agonising decision for me and I believe for him too. I had never seen him so wretchedly unhappy.

A fresh start

The next two months were miserable. In the hope that I would get the Brussels job—and in any case I was determined to get a job somewhere in Europe if that failed—I enrolled for an intensive French language course at the Institut de Français in Villefranche. However, they did not have a vacancy until October.

August dragged slowly into September and at last I heard from the Commission and went to Brussels to be interviewed by Roy Jenkins on 20 September. Four days later his Chef de Cabinet, Crispin Tickell, rang to offer me the job and I accepted. I was very pleased. At last I knew what I was going to be doing, at least for the next year. The job was to start on 10 December. My time, which had seemed so empty for the past two months, was fully occupied once more.

I spent a month at Villefranche, returning on 27 October with all the arrangements for my move to Brussels still to be made. I was staying in London that weekend in order to visit my twin sister Elisabeth, whose third child had been born while I was in France. I was at home at Temple West Mews on the Monday morning when the telephone rang. To my great surprise, it was Cecil, ringing from Luxembourg. He asked me not to hang up on him, saying that he knew he was breaking his promise but he just had to speak to me. He said that he wanted to talk to me about something very important and asked if I would agree to meet him. All my firm resolve melted away. I was thrilled to hear his voice again and longed to see him. He asked if I would meet him for lunch, saying that he could come back on a flight to Northolt with one of the Defence Ministers and be in central London by two o'clock.

I agreed and we met at a restaurant in Victoria. I was there waiting for him and feeling very tense when he hurried in soon after two o'clock. I remember thinking how well he looked and that he did not seem to have suffered from our separation. He was rather strained to begin with and I wondered what he wanted to discuss with me. I was not expecting what followed. He said that he knew he had promised not to get in touch but he could not leave it any longer, he wanted to ask me if I would marry him.

For years I had longed to hear him say that. I was overjoyed. I remember little of the rest of our conversation, only that I was tremendously happy and elated and that, of course, I said yes. That week was wonderful. He came to see me every day and we talked about the future. My only regret was that I had accepted the job in Brussels, but he said that I must be patient as it would be some time before we would be able to marry and that it would do me good to have a complete change of scene. His Ministerial job would require him to travel a great deal over the coming year, but he would see me whenever he was in Brussels for Council meetings and we could meet in England for weekends. He said that we would start our new life together when I came back from Brussels at the beginning of 1981.

It was said in the press in October 1983 that Cecil had asked me to marry him while I was still working at the House, that he had 'offered' to leave his wife in order to marry me, but that he had then changed his mind and that it was as a result of that decision that I had left Westminster for Brussels. It was said that he had ended the affair and that I had tried to keep it going after he had changed his mind about marrying me, all of which was the reverse of the truth.

I went to Brussels somewhat reluctantly at the beginning of December, but was excited at the prospect of my new job. I felt I could put up with anything now that I knew that Cecil and I were going to be married. The time passed very quickly, the first three months being particularly demanding, with my knowledge of French being sorely tried. The contrast with my work at the House of Commons could not have been more marked. I was an 'agent temporaire', like many of the staff of the Cabinets of the various Commissioners, but bound by the same bureaucratic rules of the Commission as the permanent staff, the European civil servants.

Cecil telephoned me every week and I saw him whenever he came to Brussels for Council meetings and on the occasional weekend in London. I felt that the year would soon pass and was enjoying learning about the EEC, even if what I learned was in some respects rather depressing.

Then, on 17 March 1980, my father telephoned me with the shattering news that my mother was incurably ill with cancer. She had been admitted to hospital the previous day for what we thought would be a minor operation. My father said that the disease was far advanced and that the surgeon believed she would live for only another three or four months. I returned home four days later and visited her in hospital. We were advised that it would be better for her not to know that she had cancer and we all tried to continue life as normally and as cheerfully as possible. The strain for all of us was very great, but especially so for my father.

My feelings about being in Brussels were transformed overnight. I wanted to spend as much time with my mother as possible and to do what I could to help her. I obtained compassionate leave from the Commission and was able to stay at home for over a week to nurse her when she came home from hospital. Fortunately, there was a Commission holiday in April and I was able to go home again for another ten days.

The next few months were very difficult. I wanted to give up my job and be at Marksbury with my parents, but my father believed, and we agreed, that we should do our best to carry on our lives as usual. I knew that my mother would have worried if I had abandoned the job and come home. I returned to England virtually every weekend, sometimes flying, sometimes driving back and catching a late ferry at Ostend or Calais, arriving at Marksbury at around four in the morning. It was extremely tiring and if I could not get a cabin for the crossing I usually found that I could not quite complete the journey without stopping to sleep for a short time. I would leave Marksbury again on Sunday evening, drive to Dover and take the overnight ferry to Ostend, so that I arrived in Brussels on Monday morning with about an hour to spare before going to the office. Each time I left Marksbury I wondered whether I would see my mother again. Although she was so ill and often in great pain, she never complained but was always cheerful, amusing, and interested in everything and everybody around her. She continued painting and sketching whenever she felt well enough. She had to go into hospital regularly for chemotherapy, which always made her feel dreadfully ill for a few days but, to our delight, her health slowly improved. By the summer, she was a great deal better and was able to do some gardening and drive a car again.

Cecil and I met whenever we could. He was travelling all over the world, but came to Brussels frequently. He always had a Private Secretary with him and sometimes a Press Officer as well, so that if I met him for a drink at his hotel he would usually ask them to join us, believing that it was sensible to meet openly and treat it as entirely natural for him to meet his former secretary for a drink or lunch. He was always booked into the Europa Hotel, which was where visiting British Ministers usually stayed, but I do not think he ever actually slept there as he would come to my house, which was only about five minutes walk away, and return to the hotel early in the morning. Sometimes he came to Brussels solely in order to see me, catching the last flight from Heathrow at night and returning by the first flight from Brussels the next morning. He was also able to spend one or two weekends with me in Brussels and we would go for long walks in the country or sit in my rather overgrown and overlooked little garden. Generally, if we met for weekends, we would meet in London. Tom and I had decided not to let the house while I was in Brussels so that we would both have somewhere to stay in London when we were home on leave.

During the long Commission holiday in August, Cecil suggested that we have a holiday together in the Bahamas. He was making a Ministerial visit to South America at the beginning of the month, so I went on to the Bahamas ahead of him. Ten days later he met me in Nassau and we had a blissful few days together, staying at the Ocean Club on Paradise Island. It was a brief but very happy interlude in a rather trying year. On our return to England, he drove me to Marksbury and called in to see my parents, as he had done on other occasions in the past. It was a glorious summer day and they were sitting in the garden. I was very pleased to see that my mother looked so much better. Cecil kissed her and asked how she was. I left the three of them walking in the garden and went indoors to make coffee for Cecil before he drove on to Cornwall to join his family, who were on holiday near Padstow. I felt uncomfortable on such occasions and I am sure my parents did too. However, they knew of our intention to marry and what anxieties they felt on the subject they kept to themselves for my sake. Cecil knew all my family and was quite open with them about his feelings for me.

My remaining four months in Brussels passed quickly. I was greatly relieved by the remarkable improvement in my mother's health and looked forward to starting a new life with Cecil in the New Year. I went home for Christmas at Marksbury, unaware of the bombshell that was about to burst upon me.

On 30 December Cecil telephoned me and asked me to meet him in London the next day. We arranged to meet for lunch at my house and I drove to London, looking forward eagerly to seeing him again. He arrived looking anxious and tired. Half way through lunch he suddenly said that he could not marry me after all, that his family problems were insurmountable and that he could not leave his wife. It was so totally unexpected that I could hardly believe it. I could not understand how he could have come to such a decision so suddenly. I was very upset and angry, believing that he must have been thinking of this for some time and yet been afraid to tell me. How could he have waited until a week before I left Brussels for good to tell me that I was coming back for nothing? He had destroyed any chance I might have had of starting a new life and new friendships abroad by allowing me to go on believing that he wished to marry me. Also he knew that I had turned down the offer of two good jobs in Brussels, either of which I could have taken if he had informed me of this decision a few weeks earlier.

There is no point in dwelling further on that meeting. I drove to Brussels to complete the remaining five days of my job, which were concerned with arrangements for the hand-over to Jenkins' successor as President, clearing the office and packing up my belongings at my house in readiness for the move back to London. It was a dreary and depressing task and I returned to London on 6 January 1981 feeling utterly miserable, without a job and without a purpose to my life.

Despair and new hope

Eight days later my mother was admitted to hospital in Bath for a minor operation. She returned from hospital after only two days and seemed to be recovering quite well.

On 21 January 1981 I went to London to meet a friend who had come over from Brussels. The following day Cecil came to see me at Temple West Mews. He said that we could not just stop seeing each other and wipe the slate clean without any further conversation. He wanted to know what my plans were so that he could help me, both financially and in finding a job. He proposed to give me some money to enable me to buy out my brother's share of our house, to give me some security for the future. I said that he would not need much imagination to realise that I had no plans at the moment and that if I had, I would not be telling him what they were. I was very angry and sceptical of his wish to help, which sounded more like a sop to his conscience than anything else. But for him, I would not have moved back to London. I had spent the whole of the past year believing in him and now my future was a complete blank. The only thing I could think of was that I had to go far away. Seeing him again made me extremely unhappy. I went home to Marksbury, hoping that I would be able to clear my mind and make a firm plan for the future.

I arrived home to find that my mother had become very ill indeed as a result of a post-operative infection. She was in great pain and in need of constant nursing. For several weeks my sisters and I took it in turns to look after her. During February her health slowly improved and as I had more time to think about myself, I became increasingly unhappy and anxious. I spent the next few weeks writing job applications but with little enthusiasm for my task and even less success.

From time to time Cecil would come and see me, but such occasions only made me more unhappy and we had frequent disagreements. On Friday 6 March, he asked me to have dinner with him after his constituency 'surgery' in Borehamwood. He drove into London and collected me from Temple West Mews for a late dinner at the Carlton Tower Hotel. He stayed the night with me and left early the following morning to drive out to the constituency for a 'surgery' in Potters Bar. I heard the door close behind him and then, a moment or two later, he was running back into the house, shouting up the stairs that his car had gone. I rushed down to him. He was frantic, saying that his car must have been stolen and that he had completely forgotten that he had left two despatch boxes in the boot. He had been driven out to his constituency the night before and had transferred the boxes from the government car to his own before driving into London to see me. It had been very late when we got home after dinner and he had forgotten all about them.

It was an appalling moment. A Minister is not supposed to allow his despatch boxes out of his sight and a safe is installed in his home in which the boxes or their contents can be locked overnight. The consequences for Cecil, and possibly the Government too, if the boxes got into the wrong hands, were dreadful to contemplate. He said that he must notify the police immediately but did not wish to reveal to them where his car had been parked when it was stolen. It seemed to me that he would have no choice but to tell them, but he was adamant that he could not do so, saying that if the boxes were not found it would be the end of his political career, and that was quite bad enough without revealing his affair with me as well. I drove him over to his flat in Cambridge Street, just a few minutes north of the river and he rang the police from there. They assumed that the car had been taken from Cambridge Street and he did not enlighten them. The next twenty-four hours were a nightmare. He was not even sure what papers the boxes contained, not having had a chance to go through them, but his Private Secretary reassured him that they contained no Cabinet papers or other secret material.

At lunch-time on Sunday, to my great relief, Cecil rang me to say that the car had been found. It was badly damaged, the thieves having used it as a source of spare parts for another vehicle, but the despatch boxes were still intact in the boot, although one of them apparently had marks on it as if someone had tried to force the lock but had given up the attempt.

Cecil told me that he had to see the Home Secretary, as he was obliged to inform him of the incident. He still felt that his future hung in the balance but when he saw Willie Whitelaw on Monday morning he was greatly relieved at his response. Although critical of Cecil's lapse, he was also sympathetic, saying, apparently, "There but for the grace of God would go a great many of us" which was no doubt quite true. But there was one Minister at least who would never make the same mistake again. It was a most nerve-wracking and unpleasant weekend, not least because of Cecil's attitude towards me. The incident had really driven home to him the risks he was taking and he blamed it on his involvement with me. I could understand his anxiety about what had happened, but was hurt by his reaction to it.

He came to see me a week later and tried to make amends, saying that he had been under a great strain. I was well aware of that but felt that I could not take any more strain myself and I told him that I did not want to see him again. He knew that I was going to the United States at the end of the month to visit friends. I said that I did not know when I would come back and that in any case I would look for another job overseas. I made him promise not to get in touch with me again.

I felt a great sense of failure and regretted having allowed Cecil to continue our affair when I could perhaps have got over it while I was in Brussels. I regretted my weakness in seeing him after he had told me he would not marry me after all. I felt no enthusiasm for my trip to America and would have preferred to go home to Marksbury, but did not want my mother to be worried about me. When Cecil had broken the news to me that he was not going to marry me after all, I had been unable to keep my feelings to myself and had told her. She was deeply sympathetic and anxious about me and I did not want to burden her further.

I spent a month in the States. My friends urged me to stay longer, but I was anxious to see my mother again. I was also running out of money and worried about finding a job.

I returned home on 24 April to find that my mother's health was much improved and that my father was arranging to take her to Venice for a holiday. They had been there five years before and had always wanted to go again. They urged me to go with them, but I had to look for a job. Elisabeth decided to go for the first few days and I said that I would look after the children while she was away, something which I always enjoyed.

Soon after my parents returned from Venice, my mother's health began to deteriorate rapidly. We knew that she often felt dreadfully ill, but she never complained and continued to try to lead a full and active life. As her health worsened, what little desire I had to go overseas again vanished. I wanted only to be at home to look after her.

I stopped trying to find a permanent job. Instead I bought an electric typewriter and advertised in the House of Commons that I was available for temporary work, which I could do from my home. There was no shortage of work as MPs are always looking for temporary secretarial help, especially in the summer when their secretaries are away on holiday. If I worked really hard I could get most of it done in three or four days and could be at Marksbury for the rest of the week.

Elisabeth too wanted to be at home so she and Richard decided to move to Winsbury House for the summer. They wanted my mother to have as much quiet and rest as possible, and rather than stay in the house, they hired a huge portable cabin of the kind that is used on building sites. It was delivered on a massive transporter which could only be got into the paddock after several feet of the wall had been knocked down to make the gateway wider. After lengthy and impressive manoeuvring, the cabin was at last deposited at the top of the paddock close to the house. My brother Tom put in a cable to supply it with electricity from the house and the children settled down to a somewhat unusual camping holiday. They adored it and my parents got great pleasure out of having them close at hand. Flora's children came up from their home in the village every day to play with their cousins. The weather was glorious and they spent most of the time out of doors.

During June and July, family life settled into an even routine. I continued to do temporary work for various MPs, usually going to London late on Monday night and returning home on Thursday night for a long weekend. It was tiring and something of a struggle financially, but very worthwhile. Although there was a great underlying sadness to the life of the family, we treasured the time we could spend with my mother. I admired her more than ever.

On Monday 13 July something happened to upset the tenor of my life once more. I arrived in London very late at night, having work lined up for the next four days. At about one o'clock in the morning, when I was just about to go to bed, I was startled by the sound of knocking at the door. It was Cecil. I had not seen him since the middle of March when he had promised he would not come near me again. He said that he had heard I was working in the House and just had to know how I was. I said that he could see for himself that I was fine. Actually I was in a turmoil of conflicting feelings, of which anger got the upper hand. He left after a few minutes. I was undermined and upset by his unexpected visit. Two days later he telephoned and apologised. He said that he had had rather a good dinner that night and had decided on the spur of the moment to come and see me. He said that he could not bear knowing that I was in London and not being able to see me. A week later he came to my house again. I could not bring myself to turn him away, but it was a miserable evening, which ended in a bitter argument.

In August he went to the Bahamas for a holiday with his family. I went to Marksbury, feeling angry with myself for having had anything to do with him. At least when I was at home, I had to force myself to think about other things. Each day was very full. It was hardest when I had to go back to London to places and work which reminded me of the past.

The work slackened off in August and I spent more time at home. My mother's courage was impressive. She knew by then that she had not long to live, but remained calm and cheerful, continuing to paint whenever she felt strong enough. On 5 September Elisabeth and Richard returned to London as the children would be going back to school. My mother was very ill at times and my sisters and I had established a rota so that one of us would always be at home to look after her. Flora was there every day, as she lived in Marksbury, and Elisabeth and I were anxious to share the nursing with her.

On Monday 14 September came the news of Mrs Thatcher's Cabinet reshuffle in which Cecil was appointed Chairman of the Conservative Party.

At the end of September I was offered a permanent job in the House. Peter Brooke, the Member for the Cities of London and Westminster South, who was then a Conservative Whip, wanted a full-time secretary. It was very tempting, as I was finding the hand-to-mouth existence of temporary work a great strain. I explained my difficulties and he said he would have no objection to my taking long weekends if I felt I could get the work done. I accepted and it was a relief to have a regular income, though the job was very demanding.

October dragged slowly by. My mother was often in great pain and it was agonising to be able to do nothing to make her better, but only what we could to make her days happy. She was as perceptive as ever. One day she said that she knew that I had been preoccupied and unhappy for some time and asked if I had seen Cecil again. I told her what had happened. She was very critical of him and urged me to have nothing more to do with him, saying that he was weak-willed and that she doubted his ability ever to extricate himself from the mess his private life was in. I could not bear her to be upset and worried about me. I was afraid she was right about Cecil. I did not believe he would try yet again to resume our affair, but if he did, I would refuse.

A week later he came to see me. I told him that I did not wish to see him and that he was being very unfair to me, knowing that my life could not be much more difficult than it was then, and that I simply could not cope with any additional unhappiness. I said that if he truly loved me, he would leave me alone. He said that it was because he loved me that he had to see me. He was very tender and reassuring, begging me to believe that he truly loved me and wanted us to be together more than anything in the world. He said that his personal life had been fraught with difficulties, which was why he had not been able to keep his promise before, but that in due course these would be resolved and he would give up politics after the next election, when he would be able to marry me, if I still wanted him and would agree to wait. I believed him. I know that I emerge from this account no better than he does, that I too was weak-willed. But I loved him and longed for the companionship and happiness that we had had in the past. In spite of all that has happened since, I still believe that he meant what he said then, even if his circumstances and his feelings eventually changed. I do not believe that he was deceiving me or that the love he felt for me was not genuine.

I could not see him very often over the next few weeks, but I derived great comfort and support from the occasions when we could meet and from our frequent telephone conversations. He was deeply sympathetic, knowing how I adored my mother and what anguish we were all suffering. It was a great relief to be able to talk to him and he helped me through that difficult time.

It seemed impossible that life could become any more difficult than it already was, but it did. At the end of October, my sister-in-law, Cheryl, William's wife, was admitted to hospital with a digestive problem. For several days she was very ill and in great pain. Two days later, my father had a bad fall. He damaged his wrist and I took him to the local hospital, where he had to wait a long time for his arm to be X-rayed and put in a plaster cast. The following day, my mother went into hospital, staying overnight for further chemotherapy. I returned to London to try to catch up with my work.

Two days later, on 5 November, Flora rang to say that my mother was much worse and I drove home immediately. Her doctor prescribed a powerful drug to ease her pain and make her last days more comfortable. She never once complained, even though we knew that she had some very bad moments, but was calm and dignified to the very end. On Thursday 12 November 1981, with all the family gathered round her, she died.

We experienced a sense of relief that her suffering was over, but felt our loss acutely. For my father it must have been terrible. The rest of us had the preoccupations and hopes of our own lives to carry us forward, but he had lost the person with whom he had shared his life for fifty years and the feeling of emptiness and loneliness must have been so hard to bear. I was filled with admiration for the fortitude and determination which he showed following my mother's death. He remains a devoted father and grandfather, taking as great an interest as ever in his family, especially in his grandchildren who adore him, and has ensured that Winsbury House continues to be a beautiful and happy place around which the life of the whole family revolves.

We were drawn even closer together as a family by my mother's death and stayed at Marksbury whenever we could so that my father should not be alone all the time. Christmas that year was a sad occasion but 1982 brought new happiness. At the beginning of February my brother Tom got married. He and his wife Georgina moved to Marksbury to live with my father for a few weeks while house-hunting in the West Country. Three weeks later Elisabeth and Richard's youngest child, Arthur, was born.

Although these events brought happiness and a feeling of optimism to all of us, they also sharpened my own feelings of frustration and impatience. I felt very much that I was just marking time and that my future with Cecil was at the mercy of events over which I could have no control. The anguish of the past two years had affected my attitude to everything, and especially to my life with him. Every moment that I could spend with him was precious and I was impatient for a resolution of our problems. He knew how much I wanted to have children and how much he was asking of me to wait so long for us to marry. I was happy for him that his career was going so well. I was prepared to wait and accepted that we would not be able to marry until some time after the next election. He understood that if I became pregnant I could not contemplate an abortion. One day he told me that he was making provision in his will, lest he should die and I be left alone with a child to look after. My mother's death was still so much in my thoughts that such talk upset me.

However, I was happier at that time than I had been for many months. I lived my life almost entirely around his and shared in the excitement of seeing his political career develop. The past two years had been difficult for both of us. While he was Minister for Trade he had had to do an enormous amount of travelling all over the world and we had both been under considerable pressure. Although he was now a member of the Cabinet, with more onerous responsibilities, we were able to meet more easily and far more frequently.

There were occasions when I felt depressed by the continued need for secrecy and longed for a normal life. We had some stormy times together, but I was generally very happy and believed that he was too. His life was full, his job as Party Chairman being very demanding. The interest I derived from talking to him about his job made up for the lack of enthusiasm I felt for my own.

Falklands

Suddenly, at the beginning of April 1982, the comparative tranquillity which I had enjoyed with Cecil for the past three months came to an abrupt end with the Falklands crisis. There had been speculation for some time about the activities of Argentinian scrap merchants on the island of South Georgia. Then, on the night of Thursday 1 April, our Ambassador to the United Nations warned the Security Council that Argentina appeared to be about to mount an invasion of the Falklands. It was also reported that we were about to send a small task force to the South Atlantic to deter Argentina from any such action. Cecil had stayed with me at Temple West Mews that night and had been about to drive to Cambridge the following morning when we heard the news of an emergency meeting of the Cabinet concerning the Falkland Islands. He left in a state of some anxiety lest anyone from 10 Downing Street had been trying to get in touch with him.

I went to my office at the House of Commons. At eleven o'clock that morning Humphrey Atkins, then Lord Privy Seal, told the House that he was unable to confirm the rumours that the Falklands had been invaded. It was a day of intense speculation and considerable embarrassment for the Government. It was not until the evening that the Foreign and Defence Secretaries, Lord Carrington and John Nott, were able to confirm that the Islands had indeed been seized by the Argentinians that morning. There was widespread anger at the failure of the Foreign Office to give warning of Argentina's intentions and criticism of John Nott's Department for their lack of preparedness. The following day was equally extraordinary, with the House of Commons sitting on a Saturday for an emergency debate on the crisis, John Nott struggling through his speech in the face of furious criticism from both Conservative and Opposition Members.

Cecil was meant to be staying with me the following night, Sunday 4 April, but rang to say that he had to be available to speak to the Prime Minister later that evening and asked if I would go over to his house in Pimlico instead. When I arrived he explained that Mrs Thatcher was seeking the views of the Cabinet on the question of whether or not Lord Carrington should resign as Foreign Secretary. Cecil asked what I thought and I said that it seemed to me that Carrington would have no choice but to resign and that John Nott would have to do the same. The country was in a furore over Britain's humiliation by Argentina and was badly in need of reassurance of the Government's determination and ability to deal with the crisis. Cecil said that Carrington had told the Prime Minister that he believed he should resign, but that she did not wish him to do so. In the event, the weight of Cabinet opinion was against her and not only Carrington, but also Humphrey Atkins and Richard Luce resigned from the Foreign Office. It seemed to me remarkably inconsistent that John Nott was able to cling to his perch, but Carrington could not. That evening became particularly memorable for me because of its interesting parallel for Cecil and myself in events eighteen months later.

I did not see him for the next three days. On Wednesday 7 April he arrived at my house very late, having been at the Commons for the second debate on the Falklands. He said that Francis Pym, the new Foreign Secretary, and John Nott had made good speeches. There was to be a Cabinet meeting the following morning and he left early saying that he would meet me for lunch. However, at lunch-time he rang from 10 Downing Street to say that it was impossible for him to get away. From then on his life was frantically busy. As a member of the Inner or War Cabinet, with Willie Whitelaw, Francis Pym and John Nott, he became one of the Prime Minister's closest advisers. He was plunged into the thick of the political and diplomatic turmoil that followed the invasion and was under enormous pressure throughout the crisis. I feared that it would become impossible for him to find time to be with me. However, to my delight he came to see me regularly, regardless of the difficulties and the strain he was under, often arriving very late and weary after meetings of the Inner Cabinet. Far from being cut off from him, I felt more closely involved in his life than ever. He had been deeply sympathetic to me over my mother's death and it had been a great comfort to be able to talk to him. It made me very happy that I should now be able to share his anxieties and preoccupations. It was a nerve-wracking time and I felt it a great privilege to know so much of the events behind the scenes. I cared as passionately as anyone that the Task Force should be successful and watched the official news bulletins on television avidly, with my awareness of the dangers heightened by what Cecil told me of the background to these momentous events.

The sudden eruption of the crisis and its inexorable escalation into war, without apparent warning, were appalling. For the men of the Task Force, the days of anticipation of battle must have been dreadful. While the political arguments and international negotiations continued at a frenzied pace, the Task Force was getting closer and closer to its destination. General Haig had embarked on his famous shuttle between London and Buenos Aires in his attempt at the impossible: a settlement that would satisfy both Britain and Argentina. For all the public discussion of settlement proposals, it was clear from what Cecil told me that the Inner Cabinet, like most of the population, privately believed that war was unavoidable.

On Sunday 18 April, Cecil came to see me very late and rather angry. It was the only time I heard him make a serious criticism of the Prime Minister, for whom he had great admiration, being deeply impressed by her courage and determination. He was infuriated by an exchange he had had with her at a meeting of the Inner Cabinet with the Chiefs of Staff. When he had expressed his concern about the risks attendant on a particular course of action, one of several under consideration, she had rounded on him with words to the effect that there was no room for faint-hearts in the Inner Cabinet. I thought it a very telling incident. If the Prime Minister's closest colleagues could not feel free to express their opinions to her absolutely frankly, they could be of no use to her at all. When I next saw Cecil, he had put the incident behind him. The rift with the Prime Minister had been only temporary and eventually he became her close confidant.

One of the things I found most interesting about my conversations with Cecil during the Falklands War was what he revealed about the different personalities of his fellow members of the Inner Cabinet and their preoccupation with the presentation of their decisions to the rest of the Cabinet and to the country. In fact they presented a remarkably united front, but that was probably due either to the toughness and determination of the Prime Minister, or to a realisation that there were really only two choices: to fight the Argentinians and drive them off the islands, or to concede sovereignty. The latter would have been political suicide. There was no third option, unless someone was able to come up with a miraculous proposal that would have satisfied both countries. The politicians and media pundits who held forth about such a third option were only putting off the moment of decision whether to fight or concede sovereignty.

The most extraordinary feature of the Falklands crisis was how quickly it was all over and receding into history, although the euphoria lasted long afterwards. The brilliant achievement of the Task Force enabled the Government to recover from the humiliation inflicted on them by the invasion, for which they had been totally unprepared. What could have been a disaster was turned into a triumph and Mrs Thatcher was lauded for her resolute leadership, earning the admiration of the public and of even the most critical members of her own Party. It was interesting, however, that the differences of opinion in the Cabinet which had been smoothed over during the crisis, began to make themselves felt again immediately it was over. I was surprised by what Cecil had said during the crisis about Francis Pym, whose public pronouncements at the various stages of the war had shown him to be a forceful and effective Foreign Secretary. Pym was apparently the odd man out in the Inner Cabinet and by the time the Falklands crisis came to an end it was apparent that his days as Foreign Secretary were already numbered.

Bermondsey

In August Cecil went to the Bahamas with his family for a much-needed holiday. I hated it when he went away and August was always rather a dreary month. However it gave me time to take stock of my career, or rather my lack of it.

For a long time I had nursed the ambition of a political career of my own. A number of MP friends had urged me to apply for the Conservative Party Candidates' List and to try to get adopted as a Parliamentary Candidate. Cecil had approved of the idea, but I had so far done nothing about it, being totally wrapped up in his career and content to put all my efforts into helping him. He had warned me that it could take years of determined effort to get adopted as the candidate for a winnable seat and I decided it was high time I made a start. I hoped that he would continue his political career after we were married, even though he talked often of giving up, and I wanted very much to be involved in politics in my own right, especially if it transpired that we had left it too late to have children.

I was finally spurred into action when the Bermondsey Conservative Association, of which I had become a fairly active member, announced that they were looking for a candidate. I knew that they would probably consider only people from the Conservative Central Office Approved List, but I lived in the constituency and it was too good an opportunity to miss. Not being on the Candidates' List, I could not apply through Conservative Central Office, but wrote directly to the Chairman of the Association, saying that I would like to apply for the vacancy. At the same time I wrote to Sir Anthony Royle, then Vice Chairman in charge of Candidates at Central Office, saying that I wished to put my name forward for inclusion in the Approved List of Candidates. When I had been working for him temporarily at the House of Commons the previous year, he too had urged me to apply, saying "We need good women in the Party".

For the benefit of those not familiar with the Conservative Party's procedure for the selection of Parliamentary candidates, I should explain that it is customary for any Conservative Association in any constituency seeking a candidate, whether for by-election or a general election, to notify the Candidates' Department at Conservative Central Office, who circulate details of the vacancy to all those on their Approved List, specifying a strict deadline for applications. The

Candidates' Department has on their files a potted biography of each candidate on the Approved List and supplies the local Association with particulars of all those who have applied for the seat. Competition for constituency vacancies is intense, even in Labour strongholds, where a win by the Conservative candidate would require a massive swing from Labour. If the vacancy is in a 'safe' Conservative seat, or a 'marginal' constituency, several hundred candidates will apply.

The choice of candidate is given to a Selection Committee comprised of members of the constituency Conservative Association. They study the particulars supplied by Central Office and interview perhaps thirty or more candidates, eventually arriving at a short-list of three or four from whom they make their final selection. The candidate selected by the Committee is then proposed for adoption at a full meeting of the Conservative Association, or as many members of that Association as have been persuaded to attend. In some constituencies, the Selection Committee produces a short-list of candidates and the final selection is made by the Association as a whole.

The only circumstance in which a candidate who is not on Central Office's approved list can apply for the seat is if he or she lives in the constituency and applies directly to the Association as an unofficial candidate. It is extremely rare for such candidates to be selected. Furthermore, although it is not publicly acknowledged, Central Office frequently 'advises' the constituency about those who have applied for the seat—as I know from personal experience. Many Associations take a strongly independent line, but there is no doubt that Central Office can usually exercise considerable influence. It is a weakness of our Parliamentary system—as serious, in my opinion, as any of the arguments about voting methods—that potential Members of Parliament, whose duty it will be to represent the interests not just of their supporters but of all their constituents, are selected by a small group of Party activists from a list approved by Party headquarters. The whole process is kept as secret as possible.

Acquiring the Central Office 'seal of approval' is the first hurdle for a would-be Conservative MP. The competition is stiff at all times. Even between General Elections, Central Office will receive a continual stream of applications and will have several hundred names on its Approved List. As a General Election approaches, hundreds more will apply. Getting on to the List is a lengthy procedure. The aspiring politician writes to Central Office and is asked to complete a detailed questionnaire, which requires full personal particulars: marital status, children, religion, education, employment, political interests and experience, speaking ability, work done for the Party, and the applicant's reasons for thinking that he or she would make a good MP. The applicant must provide the names of three referees, which should, if possible, include an MP and a constituency Chairman. Having fulfilled this daunting task, the would-be candidate then waits anxiously while Central Office sends further questionnaires to the three referees, who have to answer searching questions about the applicant's character, Party loyalty, past record and experience, political knowledge and awareness, speaking ability and anything else the referee cares to add. I duly completed an application form for Central Office and was told that I would be notified in due course whether they wished me to go before a Parliamentary Selection Board.

I did not see Cecil for six weeks as I went on holiday myself at the beginning of September. I was longing to see him again and to tell him the exciting news that Bermondsey wanted to interview me. He was in the thick of preparations for the Conservative Party Conference in October, his first as Chairman of the Party. I was surprised by the lack of enthusiasm with which he greeted the news that I had applied for Bermondsey, but did not discuss it with him as he was anxious to talk to me about the speech he was to make on the first day of the Conference, which was to start the following Tuesday. There had been many times over the years when he had tried out his speeches on me and I had taken the role of critical audience, interrupting him and asking awkward questions. I always enjoyed going through a speech with him, especially if I was then able to hear him make it on the day. That year I could not go to the Conference until the Wednesday, but was able to watch him on television at home.

I was nervous about my interview and put hours of thought into my speech. I should have liked to talk to Cecil about it, but had been unable to speak to him privately during the past week because of the Party Conference. My interview was set for the evening of Tuesday 12 October. Late that afternoon Cecil rang me. To my utter dismay he rang not to wish me luck, but to express doubt about the wisdom of applying for the seat. He thought that if I were adopted, I was likely, as a by-election candidate, to be the subject of considerable media attention and there was a serious risk that my name would be linked with his. I was astonished and very upset by his attitude. What was it that he expected me to do? He wished I would withdraw my application. I said that I could not possibly do so and that in any case I thought his fears were groundless as I would be up against stiff competition and that my chances of getting selected were pretty slim. I never wished to do anything that would jeopardise his career, but at the same time I thought the risk he imagined was nothing compared with those he had taken earlier, especially when a member of the Inner Cabinet. I was perplexed by his attitude and went to my interview feeling anxious.

In fact, it went better than I had expected and I was delighted to be told that I had got through to the final selection, at which three candidates were to be considered. Cecil came to see me late that night, anxious to know how I had got on. He seemed to have accepted that I was determined to do my best to win the selection. The final interviews were held the following Monday, 18 October. I came so close to success. I gained the same number of votes as another candidate, Peter Davis, but, after a second vote, he was selected. It was a disappointment, but I was very pleased to have been runner-up and felt that, for a first attempt, it had not gone too badly.

A week later, Bob Mellish, Labour MP for Bermondsey, announced that he was retiring before the next General Election, which would mean a by-election in the near future. The following morning, the Chairman of the Bermondsey Association, Miss Betty North, rang me to say that Peter Davis had withdrawn as the chandidate, saying that he had not expected to have to fight a by-election and that it would be impossible for him to take the necessary time off from his job. Betty was annoyed that the Selection Committee should have gone through the lengthy process of selecting a candidate only to have him drop out when he learned that he would have to fight a by-election rather than a General Election. Furthermore, he had informed Central Office rather than the local Conservative Association of his decision and a press officer at Central Office had taken it upon himself to inform the press of Davis' resignation without first consulting the Bermondsey Executive.

Betty then said that she was ringing me on behalf of the Executive Committee of the Association to propose that I take over the candidature. I was delighted. I said that I should be honoured to become their candidate but that it was important that I should not be presented to the constituency or the media as a second-best candidate. If Central Office were as clumsy in their handling of the matter as they had been over Davis' resignation, it could do our campaign great harm. Betty said that she was going to telephone the Party Chairman to complain about Central Office's handling of Davis' resignation and that she would also talk to him about how they would handle my candidature. She rang again soon afterwards to say that Cecil had urged the Association to do nothing further without first discussing the matter with Central Office and had asked her to go and see him that afternoon.

When Betty rang me again that evening it was to say that at the meeting at Central Office, it been had proposed that the constituency start the whole selection process again from scratch and that Central Office write again to everyone on the Candidates' List, inviting applications. They proposed that the vacancy should be open for applications for one week only and that a further selection should be held immediately afterwards. Betty said that Bermondsey Executive had decided that they must be guided by Central Office and had agreed on this course of action. She added that I would be on their short list for the final selection and asked if I would therefore submit another formal application for the seat. I did so immediately. All other applications, of course, were made through Central Office.

For a week I waited to hear at what time I would be interviewed. By Thursday, with the selection meeting due to be held the following evening, 12 November, I was concerned that I had received no notification from the Agent of the time of my interview. When I telephoned her, she was very embarrassed. To my amazement, she said that they were not going to interview me after all. She thought Betty North had told me and suggested I telephone her. I did so. She was even more embarrassed and awkward than the Agent. She said that Central Office had advised them not to include me in the short list, the 'Central Office view' being that it would be better to have a man as their candidate in a tough seat like Bermondsey and that in any case, Cecil had told her that they had 'better things' in mind for me. A similar line had been taken by the Central Office representative who had attended the meeting of the Bermondsey Executive the previous Tuesday evening, 2

November. As a result they had decided not to include me in the re-selection process.

I had been offered the candidature only to have it withdrawn because Central Office persuaded the constituency that they should go through a complete re-selection. I had been assured that I would be interviewed with the final short list and asked to re-apply. Not only had they been persuaded not to consider me at all, they had not even had the decency to tell me.

As for Cecil's intervention, it was incredible that he could do such a thing and do it, moreover, behind my back. I had spoken to him virtually every day over the past fortnight and he had given no indication of what he had done. I had bowed to his superior judgement when he assured me that a full re-selection was advisable and had talked to him about what I would say at my interview. And he had allowed me to go on anticipating the interview and hoping for success, knowing that I had already been dropped.

I could say nothing of this to Betty and contained my feelings as best I could. However, I did point out that I had re-applied for the seat only because they had urged me to and that I thought it extraordinary that no one had troubled to tell me that they had decided to drop me from the selection altogether. She was very apologetic. She said that it was impossible for them to ignore Central Office's advice, tempted though they were to do so on many occasions, as they would be looking to Central Office for a great deal of help during the by-election campaign. She said that Cecil had said some very complimentary things about me to her and that she was sure I was destined to find another and more winnable seat. I could not be angry with her when she had clearly been misled, but I was deeply disappointed. It was altogether a shabby business.

Later that evening, when I challenged Cecil with what Betty had told me, he did not deny it, but kept telling me over and over again that he had done what he did for my sake, that he had acted with the best intentions and with my interests at heart. He said that I would be wasted in Bermondsey, where the Tories would be hopelessly defeated in the by-election, and urged me to apply for other seats, saying that he would do all he could to help and advise me. I was sceptical. It would have been a challenge to fight Bermondsey and I had wanted to do it so much. I did after all live in the constituency, something which I doubted any of the other applicants for the seat had been able to claim. As for the idea that a man would do better than a woman as the candidate, it was as ridiculous as it was offensive and I said so.

The following morning he rang me and pleaded with me to believe what he had said the night before and to forgive him. Eventually I did so. If the reader wonders how I could have believed him, when he had hurt me so much before, I can only say that he was very convincing, that I wanted to believe him and that, if love is blind, it was never more so than in my case.

In any event, life was sufficiently hectic at that time for me to be unable to dwell for long on the incident. A week later, I attended a two-day Parliamentary Selection Board. Forty-eight candidates are assessed by each Selection Board, in a series of tests over two days, the assessors being members of the National

Union of Conservative Associations and Members of Parliament. It is a gruelling process. The assessors make their decisions immediately afterwards and the candidates are notified within a few days.

On 24 November, to my great satisfaction, I receiveed a letter from the Secretary of the Conservative Party's Standing Advisory Committee on Candidates, informing me that I had been successful and that my name had been added to the Approved List of Candidates. If I would be so kind as to pay my subscription to the Party's literature service (to which Candidates are required to subscribe) I would thenceforth be notified of any Parliamentary vacancies that occurred. I felt a great sense of achievement. It was only the first hurdle, but I could put the disappointment of Bermondsey behind me and look forward to applying for other constituencies.

That evening I was working late at the House and Bernard Weatherill looked in to my office to ask if I would like to go to a meeting which he was addressing in one of the Commons Committee Rooms. I had first met him when Cecil became a Junior Whip and he had been Deputy Chief Whip. He was now Deputy Speaker of the House of Commons. I worked in a room along the corridor from his office and had talked to him from time to time about my political ambitions. He had been very encouraging. He was addressing a meeting of the 300 Group, whose principal objective was to see more women elected to Parliament, their wish being to have an equal membership of men and women in the House of Commons and he thought I might like to meet them. It was an interesting meeting, but I came away feeling less sympathy with the Group than I had expected. Although I agreed with them that we ought to have far more women MPs, it seemed to me that they should be elected on personal and political merit, not because some quota of either sex had not been adequately filled. If I were ever elected to Parliament, I wanted it to be on my merits, rather than as a 'statutory woman'. I was to acquire considerably more sympathy for their objectives later, when I realised from personal experience just how heavily the dice are loaded against women.

At the beginning of December, I was asked by Channel 4 Television if I would be interested in contributing to their *Comment* programme which follows the evening news. I would have to write a test piece and read it in front of a television camera. If I came up to scratch, they would ask me to write and present a *Comment* one evening in the New Year. It meant condensing the view one wanted to put across into a three or four minute speech, so I went along to their studio on 17 December in some trepidation. However, they approved of my performance and said that I would be hearing from them in the New Year.

The year which had begun so sadly had proved eventful and exciting. There was a general feeling of optimism in the family as we gathered at Marksbury for a far happier Christmas than the year before. Tom and Georgina were expecting their first child in three months' time. Tom had started a new job which would take them to Nigeria for the next two years. My brother-in-law, Richard, was awaiting the outcome of his application for the candidature of their home constituency, Richmond, in Yorkshire. If he were successful, he would give up his career in the Foreign Office. In the meantime, he and Elisabeth were expecting to be posted overseas the following spring. Whichever course they followed would be challenging and stimulating.

I was very happy and I think Cecil was too. He was under increasing pressure of work, with the prospect of a General Election some time the following year, but was enjoying his job. For my Christmas present he had paid for me to have a holiday with relatives in South Africa. I wished he could come with me. When I left London it was cold and dark. I arrived in Cape Town on New Year's Eve on a glorious summer afternoon. I was elated at the prospect of the coming year and felt that I was on the brink of an exciting and happy future. Not in my wildest imagination could I have anticipated the extraordinary experiences I was to have in 1983. I had a wonderful holiday and returned to England blissfully unaware that I was soon to be plunged into a long ordeal.

Election fever

On my return from South Africa Cecil told me that an early General Election was looking increasingly likely. Within a few weeks, the speculation about dates started. In the hope of getting adopted by a constituency in time for the election, I started applying for seats.

At the beginning of February 1983, I was asked to do the *Comment* programme by Channel 4 TV and had the somewhat unnerving experience of seeing myself on television, little knowing that I would be repeating the experience before long in very different and distressing circumstances.

One by one the constituencies I had applied for sent back polite rejections. Then at last I heard that I was to be interviewed by the new constituency of South Hams in Devon. In the meantime, my brother-in-law, Richard had gone through the first selection in Richmond and had been shortlisted. It was a hectic time. The Bermondsey by-election was to be held on 24 February and I was doing my bit to help with canvassing in the evenings. Then my father became very ill and caused the family great alarm. Elisabeth and I took it in turns to go home and help Flora, who was looking after him. To our great relief, he gradually recovered.

The Conservative candidate was heavily defeated in the Bermondsey by-election. Cecil asked me if I were not glad that I had not fought the seat. It was still a sore point with me, but I had to agree that I would probably have done no better.

On Saturday 12 March, I went to Totnes to be interviewed by the South Hams Selection Committee. On the same day, Richard went for final interview in Richmond. I came away from mine feeling that I had not given as good an account of myself as I should have done and knowing that I was up against stiff competition from more experienced candidates, including some former MPs. I was disappointed, but not entirely surprised, when I received a letter informing me that I had been rejected by the Committee.

Richard did very well in Richmond, having got through to the final short-list of three, but was beaten by Leon Brittan, to the great disappointment of the family. Richard would now continue his career as a diplomat and would be taking up his new post in Oman in May. Elisabeth and the children would join him in August and we would only see them on occasional home leave.

As speculation about the date of the General Election increased, Cecil's programme became increasingly demanding. He travelled all over the country, giving pep-talks to constituency workers and ensuring that the Party machine was ready for an election campaign.

There being no other constituency vacancy for which I wished to apply, I decided that the time had come to sell my house. I had been thinking of doing so for some time and Cecil agreed it would be sensible. Since 1978, the rates had increased rapidly and were becoming a major financial burden. In 1982 I had put it on the market only to withdraw it again because of the lack of interest. When the 1983 rate demand arrived, I decided to put it on the market once more and to look for a house in Battersea, near Elisabeth and Richard's London home.

There was great excitement in the family when Tom and Georgina's first child, Maria, was born on 25 March. A week later the House of Commons rose for the Easter Recess and I went home to Marksbury for a few days to see my new niece. I was despondent about selling my house, thinking it would take a long time to find a buyer and having so far failed to find a property that I liked in Battersea.

Ten days later my father rang me in London to say that he had been visited by a neighbour who wondered whether any member of our family would be interested in buying his cottage. Various members of the family had talked in the past of buying the cottage if it ever came on the market, because of its proximity to Winsbury House. Richard had already suggested that if I did not find a house straight away, I should move into theirs. They were leaving for Oman shortly and would much prefer to have a member of the family living in the house rather than let it. The cottage would be a good investment for the proceeds of the sale of my house and I could let it for the time being and make Elisabeth and Richard's house my home while they were abroad. I had the good fortune to find a buyer for my house almost immediately and to have my offer for the cottage accepted a week later.

Cecil, in the meantime, was becoming increasingly preoccupied with preparations of the Conservative Party Manifesto for the General Election. He told me that he hoped that the Prime Minister would go to the country early in the year rather than later. The economy showed signs of improvement and he believed that Mrs Thatcher should capitalise on that success and the feeling of confidence following the Falklands War.

Then the local government elections took place and were a resounding success for the Conservatives. The pressure for an early election was on, but Cecil told me that there was a split in the Cabinet and in the Party generally over when Mrs Thatcher should call an election. He was in no doubt that it was in their interests to go to the country soon.

The following Sunday, 8 May, he came to see me after a long meeting with the Prime Minister and other members of the Cabinet at Chequers and told me that the date of the election had been set for 9 June. It was announced the following day and Parliament was dissolved four days later on 13 May.

I was relieved that the election had been called at last, although disappointed to know that I would see Cecil only occasionally over the next few weeks. He was under considerable pressure, it being his first election as Party Chairman, and anxious to see the Party do well. I wanted it to be a success as much as he did and only wished that I could help him during the campaign.

Turning point

On the day of the dissolution of Parliament I went to France for the weekend with Flora and Roger. The trip had been planned for some time and I had promised to go with them to act as their interpreter. The main object of our trip was to enable Flora, who had started keeping goats two years earlier, to see the process for making goat cheese being used by a very successful producer near Sancerre. My knowledge of French was stretched to its limits by the technicalities of cheese-making and we had a hilarious but interesting visit to the cheese factory. We left Sancerre on the Saturday afternoon, intending to spend the remainder of our weekend visiting some of the chateaux of the Loire valley. That night we stayed at a beautiful hotel close to the river in the ancient walled town of Beaugency.

I awoke the following morning feeling rather unwell and not in the least like sightseeing. As the day wore on and the feeling of nausea persisted, I realised that I might be pregnant. By the time I returned to London on Monday, I was convinced that I was and a test the following morning confirmed it. I sat at home for a long time, thinking about this momentous change in my life. It was what I had wanted for so long. But, of all the times when it could have happened, why did it have to happen then? How would Cecil take the news? And when was I going to be able to tell him? I didn't even know where he was at that time. All I knew was that he was in the thick of an election campaign and that it would be impossible to speak to him. I just hoped fervently that he would ring me soon.

That week was very trying. As each day passed and still he did not ring me, I became more anxious. To make matters worse, I was still working for Peter Brooke and was supposed to be doing my bit to help him in the election campaign. In one way it was a good thing that I had to go to his constituency office each day and deal with his correspondence as it kept my mind occupied. At the same time, I was feeling very sick and finding it difficult to concentrate. The work, which before would have held my interest and attention, now seemed unimportant.

Saturday 21 May 1983

On Saturday morning, Cecil rang me at last. He was speaking on the telephone in his government car while being driven into London. I was wary of talking on such a line and simply said that I had something very important to tell him and must see him straight away. He guessed immediately what it was and arrived at my house within the hour. How I wished we could have talked in different circumstances. He had very little time and there was so much to say. To begin with he was reassuring and tender towards me, wanting to know how I felt and saying that he would look after me. Then he sat down and was silent for a moment or two. When I saw the expression on his face my feelings of relief and happiness gave way to a ghastly sense of impending disaster. He said, "You are not thinking of having the baby are you?" It was dreadful. I told him that of course I was going to have it; he had always known that I would. He protested that it was madness for me to have the child, that it could not have come at a worse time. He begged me to have an abortion, saying that if I had the baby, I would destroy his career.

It was the worst moment I had ever experienced. I was shattered by his reaction. I had known that he would be alarmed and upset by my news. It was a very difficult time for him, as he was under tremendous pressure from the election campaign. But I had not expected this. There was more to come. He said that I had better understand that he would never marry me and that if I had the baby he would never have anything to do with me again and never wanted to see the child.

I was appalled. So that was how he really felt. His talk of marriage had been a sham. He did not love me and probably had ceased to love me a long time ago. Nothing that I could say or do would make him feel differently. I said that I was glad he had told me his true feelings and that I could not imagine anything worse than his marrying me if he didn't love me, but that I was going to have the baby, no matter what he said or whatever else happened. After some very bitter exchanges, he left.

It was shattering to have to face the fact that he no longer loved me, but I had to accept it and to tell myself that it was better to know now. But why had he lied to me? Why had he allowed me to go on believing that he loved me and wanted to marry me? Why had he told me so often that he wanted to give up politics when it was clear now that his Ministerial career was all-important to him?

Hardest to bear was his attitude to our baby. It appalled me that he should urge me to have an abortion, knowing how abhorrent the idea would be to me and knowing how much I loved him and wanted his child.

Sunday 22 May 1983

The next day he turned up at my house in the evening without warning. He apologised for the things he had said the previous day and I thought that perhaps he had come to terms with the situation. But he had not. After a time he reverted to the same theme, urging me again to have an abortion. It was hateful and very distressing. I repeated that nothing would change my mind. He said that I would finish him politically if I had the baby, as enough people knew about us for speculation that he was the father to be inevitable, and I would destroy his marriage as well as his career.

I had had enough. The feeling of despair brought on by his initial reaction gave way to intense anger. His new-found concern for his marriage struck me as hypocritical and insincere. It was his desire for political advancement that lay at the heart of his reaction to my pregnancy. If his career were more important to him than anything else, he should have left me alone. I hadn't asked him to come back into my life, or to say that he wanted to marry me. I had suffered greatly because of him in the past. If I succumbed to his pressure for an abortion I wouldn't be able to live with myself. I told him that I was not going to sacrifice our baby's life to his political career; nor was I going to conceal from the child or from my family the identity of the father. If he didn't want to marry me, so be it, but I would have the baby.

He accused me of using the threat of a scandal to try to force him to marry me. It was intolerable that he could say such a thing. How could he believe it? I still loved him in spite of everything but I would never have wanted him to marry me just because I was expecting his baby, especially if he did not want the child. I would prefer never to marry, than to be married in those circumstances. I said that if there were a scandal, he must share the responsibility for it. Furthermore, he must inform the Prime Minister. It seemed certain that we would win the election and he could not accept an appointment in her new government and keep her in ignorance of his circumstances. Even if I could keep my pregnancy a secret, a birth was impossible to conceal. And why should he feel that he had a right to carry on his life as if nothing had happened and expect me to hide away for ever? I was not going to lie about the identity of the father of my child, or worse, risk having it suggested that I did not know his identity.

I was certainly not going to conceal the truth from my family. How did he think they would react? He knew them all well, especially Elisabeth and Richard and my brother, Tom. Did he think they too would expect me to conceal the identity of my baby's father? They thought he had behaved badly towards me in the past. They would think the worst of him now. As for my father, I couldn't bear to think what his reaction would be. I told Cecil that he was expecting far too much of everybody and must face up to his responsibilities. It was one thing to have decided that he did not love me after all—and I was glad to have found out then rather than later—but it was quite another to expect my family to concur in a lie about the identity of the father of my baby, simply so that he could continue his political career unhindered. He was expecting them to do whatever he asked in order to protect him, when he clearly had no intention of doing anything to protect me.

As he himself had just said, there would be talk. Too many people knew about us or would have guessed at our affair. If there were a scandal, did he think that my family would not wish to defend me, that we would tolerate whatever gossip or rumour occurred, simply because he wished to have a post in the Government?

I did not believe that he would allow such a situation to arise. In the event, all my worst fears were to be realised. However, when, nearly five months later, I was finally driven to make a public statement, I did not reveal the pressure that Cecil had put on me to have an abortion, or that he had to be made to tell the Prime Minister, or the extent to which he imposed on the decency and loyalty of my family, without showing any such consideration for them in return.

He did not seem to be able to think the thing through. I thought that he was exaggerating the long-term harm to his career. It was certainly unlikely that Mrs Thatcher would want him in her new government until any scandal had subsided, but it would be only a temporary check to his career, not the end of it.

He would not for a moment consider telling the Prime Minister. He said it was ludicrous and that if he did tell her he could kiss goodbye to any hope of further appointment. He was furiously angry with me and stormed out of the house.

During the three weeks up to Polling Day, he continued to try to get me to agree to have an abortion, ringing me up late at night or early in the morning, and coming to see me. Those three weeks must have been awful for him; for me they were almost unbearable. Throughout, I had to carry on with my work. I was helping Peter Brooke in his election campaign and Peter, thinking that I would have time to spare and would find the work interesting, had told Robin Cooke MP, who was running the Prime Minister's office in the House of Commons, that perhaps I could help deal with some of her election correspondence. Fortunately I was able to arrange to do some of that work from my home, but it was a considerable strain having to go to the House at all and try to carry on life normally. To make matters more difficult, completion of the sale of my house was imminent and I had relations staying with me. But for my sisters, in whom I had confided, I do not know how I would have got through that time.

Wednesday 1 June 1983

It was my thirty-sixth birthday and it turned into a truly awful day. I was feeling very sick and exhausted and had told Peter Brooke that I would do my work at home and take it to his office in the afternoon.

Cecil had left me in peace for two days but he rang me that morning. He wished me a happy birthday and said that he wanted to come and see me. He arrived clutching a bouquet of roses and I thought at first, as I had thought on each occasion that he had come to see me in the past fortnight, that he had accepted my decision and wanted to make peace. Once again he pleaded with me to end my pregnancy. Perhaps he didn't realise just what he was doing to me and what anguish I was suffering. He said that I was going to destroy his career and his family's happiness as well as his own. He asked me to consider whether it was right to set the life of one person against the lives of four others. I was only too aware of the consequences for everyone, but how could he ask me to make such a choice? I begged him to leave me alone. I was beginning to feel that if anyone risked being destroyed by this dilemma it was I.

That evening I moved from Temple West Mews to Elisabeth and Richard's house in Battersea. I had intended to move soon after the election, but I wanted to avoid Cecil. Elisabeth and Flora came to London for the night and helped me move some of my belongings. I was extremely unhappy and it was a great comfort to have them with me.

The following morning I awoke in an agony of doubt. Was I being selfish and doing the wrong thing? Would Cecil always hate me for it? Each time he came to see me I hoped that he would have come to terms with it. But each time he renewed the pressure on me to have an abortion. He had painted an appalling picture of the consequences for himself, his family and the Party. Perhaps I was being selfish and ought to agree to what he asked. I felt frantic. I was so distraught that Elisabeth and Flora were alarmed and took me to see a doctor. He talked to me for a long time and eventually I felt calm. He said that I must concentrate my thoughts on the future with my baby and put all other considerations out of my mind. He was right of course, but it was easier said than done. Elisabeth wanted me to go to Yorkshire and stay with her for a while so that Cecil could not get in touch with me. I couldn't simply abandon my job, but on the Friday evening, 3 June, I drove to Yorkshire to spend the weekend with her. I had two days of complete rest and returned to London on the Sunday evening.

The following day he tracked me down once more. He said that he had been very cruel and that he was terribly sorry, but he felt he was being torn apart by the problem. He accepted that I was determined to have the baby and he understood why. He wished that it had not happened and that although he cared deeply for me, what was happening to us now would destroy everything. He did not feel that he would be able to love the child because of what this dilemma was doing to him and that he could not marry me: the other considerations were too important. It upset me dreadfully to hear him, because I believed he had truly cared for me. He wanted to know if I would agree to go away and start a new life abroad, saying he would provide whatever money I needed and we could both start afresh. This new pressure was terrible. Why should I go away? Why should I cut myself off from my family and friends? I did not see why it was necessary. I begged him to face up to his responsibilities. Quite apart from having a duty to inform the Prime Minister, it was grossly unfair of him to put me in the position where, if he remained silent, I would be held responsible for any scandal simply because I had refused to have an abortion or to leave the country.

We had another bitter argument. Again he said that he would not tell the Prime Minister, and he did not see why it was necessary. He said that I was being totally unreasonable and that plenty of politicians had had scandalous private lives without their public careers being affected. The Prime Minister was considering appointing him Foreign Secretary and he hoped that one day he might lead the Party. He said that I was asking him to give all that up, adding that I should consider the effect of my actions on the child, who would hate me for destroying his or her father's career. He seemed not to give a thought to the consequences for my reputation and career.

I asked him whether he had thought what it would mean for my family, especially Elisabeth and Richard. If Cecil were right about his post in the new government, how did he think Richard would feel? As a member of the Diplomatic Service, he would be in the extraordinary position of knowing that his sister-in-law was about to give birth to the illegitimate baby of the Foreign Secretary? Was Cecil expecting that he too would keep the matter secret? Did he really believe that Richard could compromise his position as a diplomat, and do such a thing solely to protect Cecil's political career? He could not answer me.

Wednesday 8 June 1983

Elisabeth and Flora were very concerned that Cecil had again been to see me. Elisabeth rang him at Conservative Central Office to insist that he must leave me alone as she was worried about what he was doing to my health. Shortly afterwards he rang her back and said that he would very much like to talk to her in person and asked if she could come to London. She agreed to do so and he met her at King's Cross station at lunch time on Wednesday 8 June. He had asked if I would agree to meet them both after they had their talk, so at two o'clock that afternoon I came home from work to wait for them. They arrived a few minutes later, having had a long and apparently heated conversation. It was not until much later that I learned what they had said to one another. Cecil said that they had had a talk and he had something to say to me.

He apologised for having put such pressure on me, saying that he wished that I were not having the baby, but had accepted that nothing would change my mind. He said that I had destroyed any chance we had of happiness together and that he would not marry me. Nor would he ever have anything to do with me or the child. I was infuriated that he should have dragged Elisabeth to London simply to say that, and I told him to go. After he had gone, I was terribly upset and angry. Elisabeth tried to comfort me, saying that I was to do everything I could to put him out of my mind and that the family would look after me. She was going home to Yorkshire that evening and urged me to go and stay with her as soon as I could.

Polling Day: a solemn promise

The following morning I left the house early to go to Peter Brooke's office. The election campaign was virtually over and there was not a great deal of work that I could do on Polling Day. That afternoon I went to the House of Commons to return my typewriter and files to my office and then went home to pack some clothes, intending to drive to Yorkshire to stay with Elisabeth. I got home at about a quarter to four. I could hear the telephone ringing as I approached the house and I hurried in to answer it. To my dismay, the caller was Cecil. "Thank God I have found you," he said. "Please don't hang up. I've something very important to say. Please just listen." I did so.

He said that he had come round early that morning, but I had already left and my cousin, who had answered the doorbell, could not tell him where he could find me. He said he had been frantically trying to track me down all day. He said that he knew he had behaved dreadfully towards me and begged me to forgive him. He said that he loved me very much and that I must try to make allowances for the fact that he had been desperately worried. He said that the Prime Minister had sent for him, that he would be seeing her in a few minutes and that he as going to tell her everything. If I could forgive him and still loved him, he wanted to marry me.

I was amazed and very sceptical. Why the sudden change of heart? Was he asking me to marry him just so that he could tell the Prime Minister that everything was going to be nicely tidied up? I did not believe that he really wanted to marry me and I said so. He begged me to believe him, saying that he knew he had behaved abominably, but that he had come to his senses and hoped that I would be able to forgive him.

He said that he was due at 10 Downing Street in a few minutes and there was not time to explain everything then, but that he would ring me again very soon. He said that he was sure that the Prime Minister would not want him in the Government, but that that was just too bad and he accepted it. There were so many things I wanted to ask him, but there was not enough time. I was worried about how he would feel towards our baby and wondered whether we could ever really be happy together. He said, "Please trust me, Sara" and assured me that we would 'work things out somehow' and that we would be happy if that was what we both wanted. We had a hurried and anguished conversation. He implored me to believe him and of course I wanted to do just that. Even now, I think he did mean what he said then, but I suspect that pressures that he was unable to resist were put on him later. I simply cannot believe that he was lying to me then.

He repeated his question, "Will you marry me?" I asked if he really meant it. "I give you my solemn word of honour," he said. He even said he would put it in writing if I did not believe him. I laughed. "Don't be ridiculous" I said, "your word of honour is good enough for me." He sounded happy and relieved. He promised to ring me immediately after he had seen the Prime Minister, but I said that I was leaving soon to drive to Yorkshire, so he said he would ring me at Elisabeth's that night.

After he had rung off, I sat on the stairs going over and over in my mind what he had just said to me. I was exhausted and nervous, but at the same time elated. He did love me and we were going to be married after all. Looking back on that moment now, I know that I must appear naive and gullible. What I know and feel now does not alter what I felt then. I loved him and I believed him.

I rang Elisabeth and told her what had happened. She was astonished and very sceptical. She sounded worried and urged me to leave soon. When I joined her in Yorkshire just after ten o'clock that night she greeted me on the doorstep with the news that Cecil had rung her at about six o'clock to say that he had spoken to the Prime Minister. Elisabeth said that he had sounded very happy and had asked her to reassure me that everything was going to work out. He said that the Prime Minister had asked him to take the post of Foreign Secretary in her new government. I could not help wondering how we were going to cope with the inevitable scandal, but was so relieved that I put such thoughts out of my mind.

Shortly after I arrived, Cecil rang again to repeat to me what he had told Elisabeth. He sounded so happy. He was at pains to reassure me about the future, saying that there would be difficulties, but that we would get over them. We would be married and he was sure we would be happy. He said that the Prime Minister had been very kind and understanding and he was very excited at the prospect of his new job. He could not talk for long but promised to ring me again the following day.

The election results had started to come in and Elisabeth and I sat up very late watching television. The forecast was a handsome victory for the Conservatives.

Part Two

Trust misplaced

Cecil's call from 10 Downing Street

Friday 10 June 1983

Friday morning was an oasis of calm after the ordeal of the previous three weeks, but now that I had time to think over the events of the previous day, I began to wonder how a scandal could be avoided. Did Cecil intend that we should be married before the baby was born? Whatever happened, a scandal seemed inevitable. I was very surprised that the Prime Minister had decided to make him Foreign Secretary in spite of what he had told her. Clearly she could not have been unduly worried by it. Cecil had sounded so pleased and happy when he rang me the previous night that everything must be all right. If he and Mrs Thatcher thought it would all work out, then there was no need for me to worry. Even so, I could not help feeling anxious and hoping that Cecil would ring me again soon. I did not go out of the house, for fear of missing his call. At four pm that afternoon he telephoned.

He sounded so different from the previous night. I had expected him to be thrilled with the spectacular election result. Instead he sounded very subdued. He said that he was ringing me from 10 Downing Street. He was talking very quietly. He said, "I have just had the most ghastly meeting with the Prime Minister. She showed me your father's letter. It was terrible. He said some terrible things about me." I didn't know what he was talking about. What letter? "Your father's letter to the Prime Minister", he said. Sudden realisation of what had happened hit me. It was a ghastly shock. I cried out to Elisabeth who rushed upstairs to me. Cecil was trying to comfort and reassure me, saying that everything was going to be all right. "It's awful, but we'll work it out." He said that of course he would not now be Foreign Secretary, but that he would be having another post in the Cabinet, as yet to be decided. He said that he could not talk any longer and that he would ring me again that evening.

I sat on the window seat in Elisabeth's room, staring out at the landscape, while she told me what had happened. I could hear the children outside the door. They had been told to go downstairs, but must have felt the tension and were clamouring to be allowed in.

Elisabeth described the mounting anger she and Flora had felt during the past two and a half weeks, as Cecil had tried every means to get me to agree to have an abortion; how they had stood by helplessly, not wanting to interfere, but desperately anxious to protect me. She told me how Cecil had appealed to her to help, asking her to meet him in London, saying "Lizzie, please help me sort this awful problem out". She wanted to help, but had realised from what he had said at their meeting, and in his telephone call to her on the morning of Polling Day, that all he was trying to do was to buy some extra time, to put off the moment when he would indeed have to 'sort out' what he was going to do. Finally she and Flora had decided that my father must be informed straight away. And of course she was right. I knew, as she spoke, that what had happened had been inevitable and that my father and my sisters had acted entirely correctly. I felt bitter regret that they should have been put in that position and acutely embarrassed that Cecil and I should have been the cause of it. If only Cecil had faced up to his responsibilities sooner, my father would not have been driven to intervene. I did not question his right to do as he did and I respected the principles which motivated him.

Elisabeth wanted me to understand what had happened but at the same time did not want to distress me with an account of what Cecil had said to her, or of my father's feelings on the matter. After all, she knew how much I loved Cecil and I had convinced her that his proposal was sincere. I so clearly believed him and wanted to marry him; she could not bring herself to tell me just what he had said to her. She asked if I understood that their actions had been motivated by concern not solely for me, but for the whole family, but added that if Cecil truly loved me and did indeed want to marry me, the whole family would accept him and stand by him.

It was not until much later that she told me what Cecil had said to her during their conversation in Battersea Park, how he had tried to persuade her to use her influence with me to get me to agree to an abortion; how, when she refused point blank to do anything of the kind, he asked if she would persuade me instead to go abroad. She had cut him short angrily, saying that he must leave me alone, that the family would not want him to have anything to do with me if that was how he was going to behave. Finally, she had delivered an ultimatum, saying that he must face up to his responsibility, that a scandal was highly likely and that if he did not tell the Prime Minister, one of her family would.

At nine o'clock the following morning, Polling Day, (not long after calling at her house in Battersea, looking for me) Cecil had telephoned her in Yorkshire. He said that he *would* tell the Prime Minister but that he would *not* do as Elisabeth had asked and tell her that day. He said that *he* would choose when she should be told and that he would hate us for the rest of his days for what we had done to him. Elisabeth repeated what she had said the previous day: either he told the Prime Minister on Polling Day, or the family would do so for him. He refused. He warned her that she would live to regret having brought bad publicity on her family and concluded by saying that any further communication with him must be through his solicitors.

Elisabeth had telephoned Flora. They were by then convinced that Cecil's sole concern was to protect his career and that he wanted nothing to get in its way. If he intended to delay informing the Prime Minister, it could only be because he wanted to be sure of securing a government appointment before doing so. And just what exactly was he going to tell her?

His talk of bad publicity for the family clinched matters for them. If there were to be any publicity whatsoever, my father must be prepared for it. Flora went immediately to Winsbury House and told my father that I was pregnant. She told him how Cecil had behaved towards me and what he had said to Elisabeth. It must have been a great shock to my father and very worrying for him. I wished it had been possible for me to be there to tell him myself.

Both he and my mother had shown Cecil consideration and understanding. For my sake and because they had believed that he intended to marry me, they had accepted him warmly, in spite of their grave reservations. I could well imagine my father's outrage at Cecil's behaviour and his determination to protect me. Without any warning he had been plunged into a very worrying and potentially damaging situation and had little time in which to act. A scandal was inevitable, whatever Cecil's intentions. Not only did my father wish to protect his own family from such a scandal; he was also concerned about its consequences for the Prime Minister.

My father's first letter to the Prime Minister

Elisabeth told me that my father had telephoned her as soon as he had heard the news from Flora and had said that she was to do nothing further, that it was for him to deal with and that he would write to the Prime Minister immediately. Elisabeth said that he was very worried about me. Later he told me how thankful he had been that Cecil was not going to marry me and how relieved he was that I had refused to have an abortion.

On the morning of Polling Day, my father and my sisters knew nothing of Cecil's change of heart. All they knew was what he had repeated to Elisabeth: that he did not wish to marry me, he wished to have nothing to do with me or the child, and wished I would emigrate. Furthermore he had finally agreed to inform the Prime Minister only because of the likelihood that the family would do so for him, but that he was gong to take his time about doing so.

While my father wrote his letter to the Prime Minister, Elisabeth arranged for a courier from Bristol to go to Winsbury House by eleven o'clock to take the letter to Downing Street. He was instructed to deliver the letter into the hands of the Prime Minister or her Private Secretary and no one else. My father made a copy of his letter and Flora witnessed it.

The following is the text of his letter to Mrs Thatcher:

Winsbury House
Marksbury
Bath

9 June 1983

Dear Mrs Thatcher,

It is with the deepest regret that I am obliged to write to you to tell you that your Party Chairman, Mr Cecil Parkinson, has behaved in a truly scandalous manner towards my family, and that his behaviour, in my opinion, renders him totally unfit to hold any public appointment.

My daughter Sara commenced working for him as Secretary and Personal Assistant some ten years ago when he was first elected to Parliament.

He appeared to become deeply enamoured of Sara early in their association, and some five years ago he came to see my late wife and myself to tell us he was in love with Sara and intended to divorce his wife and marry her. Not long afterwards he told Sara that it had become impossible for him to do this and that he had, for some undisclosed reason, changed his mind. However, he continued to pursue my daughter in spite of our very determined efforts to get the whole situation terminated.

Since he became Chairman of the Party he has become more than ever persistent in his pursuit of Sara, to an extent which has made her life and ours truly wretched. The pressure he has applied upon Sara has greatly increased recently to an extent which made it seem that he now intended marriage. This morning I have heard that Sara is now pregnant by him.

On the ground that his career will be damaged he has applied enormous pressure on her to have an abortion but I am glad to say she has totally refused.

We have urged Parkinson to avoid scandal for the Government and to resign but this he is reluctant to do, and I am therefore driven to the unhappy expedient of writing to you myself.

Yours sincerely

H de J Keays (Colonel Ret'd)

Elisabeth asked me to imagine how she had felt when I had rung her from London at 4 pm on Thursday to tell her that Cecil had changed his mind and begged me to marry him. If the Prime Minister had not yet received the letter, she would do so at any moment. At 6 pm Cecil had telephoned her to say 'I have told the Prime Minister and she *has* offered me the job of Foreign Secretary'. He had even joked with Elisabeth about being Richard's new boss. So the Prime Minister was making him Foreign Secretary in spite of everything. Elisabeth was amazed and wondered just what Cecil had told the Prime Minister, and whether she could indeed have received my father's letter.

As I listened to Elisabeth going through the events of the last two days, I was filled with horrible doubts. Why had Cecil asked me to marry him? Had he really meant it? Just what had he told the Prime Minister? Had he told her the truth? He couldn't have done, otherwise why had she asked him yesterday to be Foreign Secretary, only to change her mind today when she saw my father's letter? And even if he had meant what he said to me yesterday and really did love me, how would he feel now?

I said to Elisabeth that I was filled with doubt about marrying Cecil, that I feared he had only asked me because he had been made to tell the Prime Minister and thought that she would look more favourably on him if he had decided to 'do the right thing' and marry me. Elisabeth said, 'Let's get this absolutely clear. At *no* time has he been under any pressure from *us* to marry you. Do you really think that, after the way he behaved to you before, we *wanted* him to marry you? But if he does truly love you and you want to marry him, then you know that we will all stand by you.'

In the light of all that has happened since, I am glad that my father did write to the Prime Minister. His correspondence with her is proof that she did have the facts on Polling Day or the following day and bears out what I said in my statement to *The Times*.

I became increasingly agitated as I waited for Cecil to telephone me again. However, when he rang me that evening, he was very reassuring. He said that he had got over the shock of being confronted with my father's letter and that he understood why he had written as he did. He said that it had been a very humiliating experience for him, but that we would get over it.

As for the job, he was disappointed that he would not after all be Foreign Secretary, but very pleased that Mrs Thatcher had said that she still wanted him in the Government and would give him an important post, possibly merging two departments into one. He said he would ring me again and let me know. In the meantime, he told me not to worry and reassured me that we would work out our problems and be very happy together.

Saturday 11 June 1983

On Saturday evening Cecil telephoned to say that he had had another long talk with the Prime Minister and that she had asked him to head the combined departments of Trade and Industry. He was pleased with the appointment, saying that it would be a very big job and a considerable challenge. Furthermore, the Prime Minister had told him that the post of Foreign Secretary would be his after a year or eighteen months 'if all went well'.

He asked me to give him time to work things out in his own way and to choose the right time to tell his wife and family. He was concerned that we should do everything we could to keep my pregnancy a secret for as long as possible. He urged me to give up my job at the House immediately after the election and to stay out of sight for the time being. I said that of course he could have all the time he needed to sort things out but I did not think I could quit my job without any warning. It would be unfair to Peter Brooke and I thought it would also look decidedly odd if I just walked out without notice. We agreed that I should give in my notice the following week and leave at the end of June.

Cecil then said that he was going to telephone my father immediately to try to straighten things out with him. He rang me again shortly afterwards to say that my father had been very brusque with him, which was hardly surprising in the circumstances, but he had reassured him of his intentions towards me. When I rang my father a little later he sounded tired and it was distressing that he should have been put through so much anguish on my account.

In view of what happened later, it is appropriate to quote from my father's diary note of his conversation with Cecil that night:

> **Saturday 11 June 1983**
> Cecil Parkinson phoned me at 10.15 pm. He said that the Prime Minister had shown him my letter of 9th June 83.
>
> He said he was to be the new Minister for Trade and Industry. He wished to assure me that he intended to do the right thing by Sara and that he intended to look after her and their child. I was unenthusiastic about this statement and he said "I am not a rat Colonel Keays—you are speaking to your future son-in-law."
>
> He appeared somewhat put out by my attitude and said "You know what the news hounds would do about this."

My father said that he had indeed been brusque with Cecil and that he had been sceptical of his protestations of love for me.

I shall never know at what point Cecil decided he did not wish to marry me after all. I cannot believe he had already decided then. If he had, his telephone call to my father could have been made with only one object: to buy time for himself. I do not believe that it was. The following October, however, political commentators in the press said authoritatively that the Prime Minister had told Cecil that he could have a job in her new government, *only* if he stayed with his wife. This has never been denied and casts an interesting light on the Prime Minister's role in the matter.

The Prime Minister replies

On Sunday afternoon I drove back to London. That same day the Prime Minister wrote to my father.

The letter was written in her own hand and was remarkable, not so much for what it said as for what it did not say. It could scarcely have been briefer:

Chequers
Butler's Cross
Aylesbury
Bucks

12th June 1983

Dear Colonel Keays

Thank you for your letter of 9th June. I understand that since then you have spoken to the person concerned.

Yours sincerely

Margaret Thatcher

My father concluded that she regarded the matter as closed. When Cecil came to see me later that week he said that Mrs Thatcher did indeed regard it as closed and as evidence of this she told him that she had burnt my father's letter on the sitting-room fire at Chequers on Sunday 12 June after writing her reply. Cecil was pleased. He too wanted to put the matter behind him. I shared his optimism and his belief that we would be happy together.

His new job kept him extremely busy and for the next few weeks we could meet only once or twice a week. He was under considerable pressure of work and obviously worried, but he gave me no cause to doubt his intention to marry me. I myself was preoccupied with moving house and finishing my job at the

Commons. The sale of my house was completed on 22 June, the day of the State Opening of the new Parliament, and I left my job a week later. I told friends at the House of Commons that I had bought a cottage in the West Country which I wanted to do up and that it was a wonderful opportunity to take a break from work. I was indeed looking forward to it.

The work on the cottage was going to cost at least £16,000 but Cecil said that he would provide the money in due course and that in the meantime I should go ahead with the work. We did not yet know when we would be able to live together, but Elisabeth and Richard had said that we were welcome to live in their house until we had made other arrangements, as they would be abroad for the next three years.

When I left the House of Commons at the end of June, it was with none of the heartache I had experienced in July 1979. Although there were difficulties immediately ahead of us, and the risk of scandal, these could not mar the happiness I felt at knowing that I was going to be married to Cecil and have his child.

I could not see him very often in July, although we met on most of my visits to London. He had said that he thought it advisable for me to stay in the West Country but I still had matters to attend to in London and had also to see my doctor from time to time. Cecil had asked me to have private medical care and to keep the arrangements for my confinement secret.

Cecil said that he did not think he could break the news to his wife until after the Party Conference in October, when he would be standing down as Party Chairman. She had worked very hard during the election and he felt he owed it to her to leave it until after the conference and all the post-election celebrations were over. He was going ahead with a family holiday in the Bahamas in August that had been arranged some months before, but I hoped he would decide to tell her on their return. I had agreed that he should have such time as he needed, but I could not help becoming anxious about the delay. I had done as he asked and given up my job. I had tendered my resignation as a governor of two schools in Bermondsey and dropped out of all the political and social activities that had hitherto been part of my life in London. I had also cut myself off from all but a few very close friends and was living as quietly and discreetly as possible. I now had no income but had some substantial bills to meet; Cecil had promised to provide me with money. I had reminded him about this on two or three occasions. Knowing that he was about to go abroad, I asked him again and he apologised, saying that if I would give him a note of my bank account he would arrange for £5,000 to be sent direct to my bank. I was somewhat baffled to receive notification from the bank a few days later that they had credited my account with a cheque for £5,000 from AJ Mathew. The name meant nothing to me. I asked Cecil about it and he explained that he had asked his secretary, Angela Mathew, to send me a cheque on her account and that he had reimbursed her.

After all he had said about the need for discretion and secrecy, I was very suprised that he could do such a thing. I would have expected him to have asked his solicitor to send me the money, as he had done on other occasions. I felt very uneasy and wished he had sent the money himself.

He was leaving for the Bahamas on 5 August and the last time we would be able to meet before his departure was in the evening of 2 August, when we had dinner together. He was rather preoccupied but we had a happy evening together and arranged to meet for lunch in London on 30 August, the day after his return from holiday.

I wished that he did not have to go away, but he needed a holiday and I had plenty to keep me occupied for the next three weeks, getting the building work started on the cottage.

Incident with the *Daily Mirror*

Tuesday 23 August 1983

On Tuesday 23 August, I drove to London. I had a dental appointment that afternoon and was to see my obstetrician, Mr Kenney, the following afternoon for my next check-up, being in the twentieth week of my pregnancy. I was only going to spend one night in London, possibly two if I felt too tired to drive home on the Wednesday evening. At 7 pm on the Tuesday evening the doorbell rang. I was not expecting visitors, but was lying on the sofa watching television. I opened the door to find two men, total strangers, one of whom stood to one side, as if to let the other do all the talking, facing towards him rather than me. This, I learned afterwards, was because he wished to conceal from my view the machine with which he was tape-recording the conversation. The other individual was a stout middle-aged man, with a pushing, somewhat aggressive manner. "Miss Keays?" he said. "Yes." "Mr·Brooke's Secretary?" I hesitated: I was no longer Peter's secretary, though I had been until just a few weeks ago. While I was wondering who on earth these men were, the stout one said, "May we come in?" and started forward. I was instantly on my guard and asked who they were and what they wanted. He said they were from the *Daily Mirror*. I asked to see their identification, which they produced. The spokesman, adopting a somewhat confidential manner, said that they had something rather important to discuss with me and that they had better come inside. I told him that they certainly could not come in and that whatever they had to say they could say it on the doorstep.

He said "Is it true that you are pregnant by Cecil Parkinson?" The asking of such a question by a total stranger disgusted me.

I cannot now remember word for word my conversation with them, except that I asked him how he dared to ask me such a question. Using a veiled threat which is typical of a certain kind of journalist, he said "But it's all over Fleet Street. My Editor thought we ought to discuss it with you."

"You disgust me," I said, "I wouldn't discuss anything with you. Please go away." He made a couple more attempts to get me to talk and then they withdrew.

I shut the door and leaned against the wall feeling very anxious and angry. How did they know? Who could have told them? How had they found out where I was living? I remembered an odd telephone call at around 6 pm. When I answered, a male voice said "Sara?". I said "Yes" and he immediately hung up. No doubt it was one of the men from the *Daily Mirror* checking whether I was at Elisabeth and Richard's house. But how did they know I was living there, and how did they know the number, which was listed under Richard's name, not mine? Someone had given them some very specific information.

Only a moment or two had elapsed since their departure. I suddenly thought of my father and my sister. I telephoned Flora at Marksbury immediately, but as I was telling her what had happened, someone knocked at her door. She asked me to hold on for a moment and when she came back she said "It was someone wanting Roger. I said he would find him at the farm." As I continued with my awful news, she realised that it might have been a reporter who had called on her. Our first concern was to get in touch with my father and to warn him. I hung up so that Flora could ring him.

I was waiting anxiously to hear from her when the doorbell rang again. I sat motionless for a moment, thinking that the men from the *Daily Mirror* must have returned, then crept along the passage to the front door and looked through the peep hole. I could see a man standing on the doorstep, but his face was in shadow and I mistook him for a next-door neighbour. I opened the door and immediately realised my mistake. He was holding a camera and before I could shut the door there was a flash and he had taken a photograph of me. This further violation of my privacy filled me with revulsion and heightened my feeling of impending disaster.

I suddenly felt very alone in that empty house. I took the telephone off the chest in the hall and carried it into the sitting room, closing the door behind me, in case a reporter should lurk on the doorstep to try to overhear my conversation. I felt they were capable of anything. Just what lengths they would go to I was soon to find out.

I was meant to be meeting a girlfriend for supper but before deciding what to do about that, I rang Flora again. Our fears had been justified, but she had been too late to warn my father. It was a warm summer evening and he had been in the kitchen garden, hoeing a path. Two men had called at his house. Having rung the doorbell in vain, they had walked around the garden until they found him. He was somewhat surprised to find two strangers approaching him in the recesses of his garden. One said "We are looking for Colonel Reay. Can you tell us where we can find him?" He replied "I don't know anybody of that name. I am Colonel Keays. What do you want?" They did not beat about the bush. "Is it true that your daughter is going to marry Cecil Parkinson?" How I hated my father being troubled by these people at all, let alone asked such a question. He said "If you you wish to know anything concerning my daughter, I suggest you put your questions to her." "But this is a matter of national importance" said the spokesman, adding something else about national security, "and it's got to be sorted out." "Then I suggest you push off and sort it out somewhere else" was my father's response. They left.

I told Flora about the photographer sneaking a picture of me and said I had just noticed a large estate car parked on the other side of the road, and I was certain that the two men sitting in it were watching the house. I thought of calling the police and saying that there were suspicious characters lurking outside, but decided that, if they were reporters, they might try to use the incident against me in some way. Later I regretted my decision. Had I called the police I might have been spared an awful ordeal.

It seemed ridiculous to stay out of sight, like a prisoner in my own home, just because some reporters had called on me and might be waiting outside. After discussion with Flora I decided to keep my supper engagement. I left the house and as I got into my car, which was parked right outside the door, the engine of the car opposite started up. It was facing up Albert Bridge Road, towards the river; mine was facing in the opposite direction. I drove down to the traffic lights at the junction with Prince of Wales Drive and looking in my driving mirror, I saw the estate car turning round to follow me. The traffic lights changed just as I went through them and the blue car was caught. I turned off Prince of Wales Drive and lost them.

I met my girlfriend as arranged and over a hamburger supper in Pimlico I told her of my predicament. I had known her since my early days working at the House of Commons. Like the true friend that she is, she said immediately that she wanted to help me and suggested that I stay the night at her house. I pointed out that I hadn't a change of clothes with me for the following day and that in any case, if I was to abandon the house in Albert Bridge Road for the time being, there were things there that I would have to collect. At the same time, if the reporters saw me leaving with a suitcase, they would be more determined than ever to follow me. I did not want them to follow me to her house, or when I went home to Marksbury.

We decided that we could take most of the things I needed out of the house in a couple of carrier bags. We drove to Albert Bridge Road, hoping the coast would be clear but to my dismay, the watchers had returned. The estate car was back where it had been before, but this time it was facing the other way, towards Prince of Wales Drive.

I parked outside the house, on the corner of a driveway which runs alongside it, so that I could turn the car round without difficulty when we left and go back over Albert Bridge.

We went into the house, turned on a lot of the lights and drew the sitting room curtains. We went downstairs to the kitchen to make ourselves some coffee and were sitting there, with the curtains drawn, when suddenly we heard the faint sound of footsteps outside the kitchen window. Someone, presumably from the estate car, had come into the front garden and was standing beneath the front steps by the basement door. From then on, we talked in whispers. We went upstairs and assembled the things I would need to take away with me.

At about eleven o'clock, leaving various lights on so that it would look as if I were coming back, we left the house and walked casually to my car, chatting and trying to look as if we were unaware of the watchers. As we got into my car, the engine of the estate car started up. Both cars were facing in the same direction, down Albert Bridge Road towards the traffic lights at the corner of Prince of Wales Drive. I glanced over at the estate car and realised that there was another car, a white saloon with one man inside, also starting up, which was parked bonnet to bonnet with the estate car. As I pulled out of my parking space, the white car roared into action, mounted the pavement on the far side of the road and drove along it a short distance until it could get out from behind a row of parked cars. It then turned sharply into the road and roared back towards us, stopping almost alongside me and facing the same way. At the same time, the estate car pulled out of its parking space on the other side of the road.

Suddenly I felt frightened. The white car had pulled up so close to me that the driver must have intended that I should know what he was doing. Who on earth was he? Perhaps these people weren't reporters after all. I was alarmed and anxious to get away from them. I backed my car into the alley to turn round and drove off in the direction of Albert Bridge. The road was clear ahead of me and the lights were green. As I sped through and swung right onto the Embankment, I could hardly believe it possible, but when I looked in my driving mirror, the white car was right behind me. Somehow the driver had managed to do a U-turn and catch up with me in time to get through the lights before they changed. I was thinking hard where I could go for help and to get free of my pursuer. At that moment, I thought there was only one. I looked in my driving mirror again and was horrified to see the estate car coming up behind me as well.

It was bad enough to be followed at all, but it was the middle of the night and these people, whoever they were, were chasing me as if they were determined to stop me. They stayed as close behind me as they could and were changing places with one another every few moments, so that I would see the white car behind me, then a few minutes later the blue estate car. I drove faster, although I knew I was breaking the speed limit. I dreaded the thought that I might have to stop at the traffic lights at the Chelsea Bridge junction. There was little other traffic about and I did not know how I would get help if my pursuers trapped me at the lights. Fortunately these stayed green and I shot through and on down the embankment towards Westminster. I was meant to be heading for my girlfriend's home in North London, but had decided by then that I must go to the police and was trying frantically to think where the nearest police station was. Then I realised we were close to Rochester Row. We were by then in Grosvenor Road, heading towards the Vauxhall Bridge junction. At that moment, the big estate car pulled out and began to overtake me; at least I thought it was going to overtake. It pulled alongside and I glimpsed the face of the man in the passenger seat. He was laughing. The white car was right behind me. The estate stayed alongside me although there was no traffic ahead of me. I was really frightened and decided to take the next turning left, which was only fifty yards ahead. Just beyond it was a pedestrian crossing. The estate car was still alongside me, driving very close indeed, but I was determined not to be made to pull over. He must suddenly have realised that he had an urgent decision to make about the island in the middle of the crossing which we were fast approaching. He had either to drive past it on the wrong side of the road, or hit it, or force me to move over, or drop back. Clearly he had no intention of dropping back and I was not going to let him make me pull in—knowing that it would be a simple matter with two cars for them to force me to stop altogether. He evidently didn't like the remaining options and there was a loud bang as our cars collided. I was very frightened and very angry. My companion must have been terrified. I braked hard and turned left, leaving the estate car sailing on down the Embankment. I felt very shaky but somehow I managed to keep going to Rochester Row Police Station. The white car was right behind me. There was no other traffic in Rochester Row and I said to my girlfriend, "I am going to pull across the road and stop right in front of the police station. Run in ahead of me and get help." The white car pulled up a few yards down the road and waited.

I was in a very agitated and anxious state of mind as I went into the police station. I felt that terrible problems were closing in around me. Just a few hours earlier the press had burst into the comparative tranquility of my life and shattered it with their offensive and bullying behaviour. I hadn't been able to warn Cecil and didn't know how I was going to do so. A scandal was imminent and I had experienced the awful things the press were capable of doing to maximise it. I was shaking with fright at the ordeal I had just been through and suffering from a bad attack of nausea. I was going to the police for help and protection and yet I knew that they would have to ask me awkward questions about what had just happened.

The police acted swiftly and, as we were ushered into a little room to explain matters to a sympathetic Sergeant, another officer went straight out, and got the particulars of the driver of the white car.

The Sergeant who interviewed us was very kind and efficient and got the facts straight with the minimum of fuss and embarrassment. Of course, he asked me why these men were chasing me and who I thought they were. I told him that I had reason to believe they were reporters with the *Daily Mirror*. Why? Because they had called on me earlier in the evening and I thought they had been watching the house. Why were they hanging round and why would they want to follow you? That was a tricky question; I could not lie to him, but told him as little as possible. In any case, I was heartily sick of all the deception and I had no idea what my pursuers might say to the police. I told him that it was to do with the fact that I was pregnant and that they wanted to know the identity of the father. Why would his identity be of such interest to them? I was reluctant to answer but he pressed me. I explained that it could cause embarrassment in political circles. I said that I was well aware that I had driven from the scene of an accident without stopping, but had come straight to them because I was so frightened. That was an understatement. By now I was suffering quite a reaction to the experience and felt very upset. We were given cups of tea and told that we need be in no hurry to leave, but I was already worrying about how we were going to get away if these frightful men were still hanging about.

An officer came into the room and reported something to the Sergeant, who informed me that I was quite right, my pursuers were from the *Daily Mirror* and the driver of the estate car had reported the incident at another police station.

While we were making our formal statements an officer went out and drove my car round behind the police station into Vincent Square. We waited a little longer to be sure that the reporters had given up and then were escorted out by a back door to the station yard, where we got into a police car and crouched down in the back. We were driven to where my car was parked and, at last, satisfied that the coast was now clear, and full of gratitude for the police officers who had assisted us, we drove to my girlfriend's home. We arrived there at one o'clock in the morning feeling exhausted. I could not sleep. How was I going to get in touch with Cecil to tell him what had happened and warn him that reporters might be waiting for him on his return from the Bahamas? I had an idea that one of his daughters had remained in England and I was worried lest she too might be questioned. I was afraid that I had not acquitted myself well that evening and that he would be critical. It is easy after the event to think how one might have handled such a situation better. I was worried about my medical appointment next day, wondering whether the *Daily Mirror* also knew that I was going to Mr Kenny—they seemed to know so much already. I could not bear the thought of being followed again.

I was worried too about other consequences of the evening's events and what the police would decide to do. Strictly speaking, I had committed an offence in not stopping at the scene of the accident; and what would they do about the *Daily Mirror* reporters?

Later, when I was asked by the police whether I wished to pursue the matter, I decided not to do so, believing that the newspapers would use any court case as an opportunity to get as much information as possible about Cecil and me. I was an anxious as he to minimise any scandal and knew that he would be appalled at the prospect of such publicity. It was possible as well that any court case would occur at the time of, or soon after, the birth of our baby. So I decided to let the matter drop, little knowing that the matter would receive publicity anyway, not least because a public-spirited citizen chose to make a complaint to the Press Council about the behaviour of the *Daily Mirror* reporters, even though I had chosen not to make a complaint myself. One of the most galling aspects of the whole incident for me was the decision of the Press Council to pursue the matter even though I had said expressly that I did not wish to make a complaint and declined their request to make a statement. I knew that, if I became involved in the matter, Fleet Street would climb in on the act, at a time when I was doing everything possible to avoid further publicity. Nevertheless, the Press Council went ahead. The right to confidentiality which they can afford a complainant was denied me because they treated me as a third party rather than the victim, and their findings—which resulted merely in a half-hearted reprimand of the *Daily Mirror* that they 'were not justified' in following me—were based on the statements of the reporters, including an allegation that my car had swerved and hit theirs, and a tape-recording, allegedly of their conversation with me, but made secretly. To add insult to injury, I was not allowed to hear the tape-recording and was not notified of the Press Council's findings until some time after they had given it to the press.

It does not surprise me that the Press Council is considered by many people to be an ineffective body, more inclined to look after the interests of Fleet Street than to protect the citizen.

Wednesday 24 August

The following morning I telephoned Cecil's solicitor, Clive Lewis, who was a very good friend of his. Through Cecil I had got to know him quite well and his firm had acted for me for a number of years. He was not at his office. It was desperately important that I get in touch with Cecil and I asked one of his partners to get an urgent message to Mr Lewis asking him to ring me. At last, by mid-morning, I spoke to him and told him what had happened. He agreed that we must warn Cecil immediately and said that he would get a message to him asking him to telephone. He could not ring him direct as there was no telephone where they were staying. We agreed that I would go to Mr Lewis' office at 2 pm in the hope that I would be able to talk to Cecil myself.

I sat in Mr Lewis' office that afternoon, waiting for Cecil's call. Mr Lewis had managed to speak to him already and had put him in the picture, but I was very anxious to speak to him myself. When at last I spoke to Cecil, I was surprised at how calmly he seemed to have taken the news. I was even more surprised when it became clear that he had his wife with him while he was talking to me. Then I realised that he must have told her about us and I was greatly relieved, having been afraid that he might put it off still longer.

I said that I was afraid the *Daily Mirror* would be lying in wait for him on his return and urged him to alter his travel plans. He told me not to worry about that. His chief concern was that his parents and his father-in-law might be bothered by the press and he was anxious to warn them. He said that he had informed the Prime Minister's office of the incident and that he would be in touch with me as soon as he returned from the Bahamas. He urged me to leave London as soon as possible and to stay out of sight. He wanted to know where I would go. I was not sure, but said I would let Mr Lewis know. I told him that I had an appointment with Mr Kenney and that I felt too exhausted to drive home that day. I was not even sure that I ought to go home as I could not bear the thought of my father being bothered by the press on account of my being there.

Mr Lewis was very kind to me. He offered me the use of the appartment behind his firm's offices, beneath which there was a garage where I could conceal my car. I thanked him, but said I had already arranged to stay the night with friends and I left their telephone number with him in case of any further developments. As the *Daily Mirror* reporters would recognise my car if they saw it, I agreed that it was better not to use it for the time being and I locked it away in his garage.

I thanked Mr Lewis for all his help and walked up Harley Street to Mr Kenney's consulting rooms. I was so exhausted that I fell asleep in the waiting room in the few minutes before my appointment. Mr Kenney was, as always, very reassuring, telling me that the baby was doing all right, which was all that mattered and that I must try to keep calm and take each day as it came. I was increasingly appreciative of the encouragement and advice that he gave me over the ensuing months and very thankful indeed that he was taking care of me. He helped me through some very difficult times. I spent two nights with friends, staying out of sight and resting.

Friday 26 August 1983

I was relieved to hear from my family that there had been no further press enquiries. They urged me to go home and I was only too glad to do so. I collected my car from Mr Lewis's garage and drove to Marksbury hoping that there were no reporters keeping an eye on Winsbury House. The coast seemed to be clear when I arrived and I locked the car in the coachhouse staight away.

To my dismay, Roger and Flora reported that they had heard from a friend that there were rumours circulating locally, that someone had been asking questions about me in the neighbourhood and that there had been talk about me and 'a politician'. We were all very worried about this. All my family behaved very discreetly and were anxious to help Cecil and me through these difficult months.

I knew that Cecil was arriving from the Bahamas on Monday, the August Bank Holiday, and I waited all that day and all the next for him to ring. Before he went on holiday we had arranged to meet that Tuesday for lunch and I had been looking forward so much to seeing him. Now all I could do was wait, in vain, for a telephone call from him.

I was becoming very anxious at not having heard from Cecil. Flora and Roger suggested that I get out of the house and try to relax. It was the last day of their children's summer holiday so we decided to take them on an outing. I had given Clive Lewis Flora and Roger's telephone number in case he couldn't get me at home. Flora and I took the children to Weston-super-Mare and they had donkey rides on the beach. The tide was so far out that the water was barely visible in the haze and we had a long trudge, getting muddier and muddier, before we reached it. As an outing it seemed to Flora and me something of a flop, but the children appeared to love it.

On our return, Roger told us that Mr Lewis had telephoned to say that Cecil wanted to meet me the following day. I spoke to Mr Lewis myself later in the evening. He proposed that we meet at his office, but was anxious that neither of us should be spotted going there. He suggested that I arrive early, go in by the back entrance and wait in the apartment. Cecil would come to the main office entrance half an hour later. I agreed and Mr Lewis suggested that I drive straight to the mews behind his office and put the car in the garage. He would meet me there.

The bitter truth

I drove to London and arrived in good time for our rendezvous. I parked in Mr Lewis's garage and sat in the car waiting for him. At two o'clock he appeared and took me up to his flat. He left me to return to his office, saying that he would bring Cecil up as soon as he arrived. I sat and waited. Cecil was very late. I tried to read but could not concentrate. Then I heard footsteps on the stairs and they came into the room. Mr Lewis left us together, saying that he would come back later.

Cecil was very suntanned and thinner than when I had last seen him four weeks previously. He looked tense and anxious, which was hardly surprising, in view of recent events. He did not embrace me but sat down and said nothing for a moment. I wished him happy birthday and said that I had no present for him as I had been unable to go shopping, for fear of being tracked down by the press. He wanted to know if I thought I had been followed to Mr Lewis's office, but I was sure I had not. Then he asked how I was. I was all right, I said, but I was still feeling awful about what had happened with the *Daily Mirror* people and was very worried about what they might do next.

There was another pause, then he said that he'd had a ghastly time during his holiday, that his wife had confronted him, saying that she knew about us and that I was pregnant and wanted to know what he was proposing to do about it. He said "We talked for a long time and we decided that the most important thing was the family".

For a moment I thought he was talking of him and me and our baby, but I knew in the same instant that that was not what he meant at all. He added, "We have decided that we must keep our family together".

I could hardly believe what I was hearing. The realisation of what he was saying was frightful.

He made no apology to me, no reference to what had happened in June, to his having begged me to marry him. He expressed no regrets at what he had done. He was remarkably matter-of-fact about everything and seemed to be taking it so calmly, at least so it seemed at that moment.

I was shattered. For how long had he been deceiving me? Had anything he had said to me been sincere?

Then he reverted to the line he had taken before Polling Day, reproaching me for not agreeing to have an abortion, saying that I had tried to destroy his career and his marriage, but that I was not going to succeed. He said he never wanted to see me again or to have anything to do with the child. He even referred to a conversation he had mentioned to me soon after Polling Day that he had had with Ian Gow, the Prime Minister's PPS.

I well remembered Cecil telling me how, on the Saturday after the election—the day after she received my father's letter—the Prime Minister had suggested that he and Ian Gow have dinner together as she felt that Gow could give Cecil some good advice. What he had not told me then, but enlightened me with now, was that Gow had been very critical of me, saying that if I had really loved Cecil I would either have had an abortion or gone abroad, and not have jeopardised his career. Cecil added that Norman Tebbit had also told him that he would be a fool to chuck up a promising career for me. I was so repelled that I couldn't speak.

At that moment, Mr Lewis came into the room. He could see how upset I was and asked if he could do anything for me. I was very curt with him. All I wanted to do was to get away from them both as quickly as possible. Cecil did not want me to go, saying that he wanted to talk to me about providing money for me and the baby. I felt sick with disgust and anger. Mr Lewis said that I must have legal advice and asked if I knew of a lawyer to go to. He handed me a piece of paper with something written on it, saying that it was the name of a very good firm which he was sure could help. I crumpled it up. I felt that he must have known all along what Cecil was going to do and I spurned his offer of help. Mr Lewis was saying that he did not think I should drive when I was so upset and Cecil said that he wanted to know what I was going to do, but I left. I couldn't bear to be with them another moment.

It was only when I had been driving for a little while that I was able to think and all the awful questions filled my mind. How long had he been deceiving me about his feelings? Why had he asked me to marry him and when had he decided that he was not going to? If his wife really had confronted him, as he put it, who had told her? And who had told the *Daily Mirror*? I wondered why they had not tried to question Cecil and why they had approached me while he was on holiday, as they would have known he was? Cecil had said nothing about the press and how I should deal with them if they reappeared. And where should I go? I decided in the end to go to Elisabeth and Richard's house again. I did not want to go home to Marksbury until I had had time to think things over; I was too upset to go anywhere else.

I felt betrayed and utterly alone. I couldn't understand Cecil's behaviour and I found his coolness and lack of regret extraordinarily callous. He seemed to feel no concern at the ordeal I had been through with the press on his account. I had been through a great deal for him, and would have endured anything for his sake. Now I realised that he felt no similar desire to protect me. I wondered how he could have waited until two days after his return from holiday before doing so, knowing how anxious I was.

I sat up late that night thinking things over and wondering what was going to happen. What *was* I to do if the *Daily Mirror* dug up any more information, if anyone talked to them? After all Whitehall leaks like a sieve, and 10 Downing Street is no exception. How many people in the Prime Minister's office knew about my father's letter and how many others like Gow and Tebbit had Cecil talked to about his personal problems? Whoever had given the *Daily Mirror* the information was out to make trouble for me. Was someone trying to frighten me off, scare me into having an abortion or leaving the country? What happened to me would be of no concern to anyone except me and my family, particularly now that Cecil had finally decided not to marry me.

There were things he had not mentioned that afternoon which I needed to know. What was he going to tell the *Daily Mirror* or any other newspaper that started asking questions? What was he going to do about his job? Was he going to resign? Had he told the Prime Minister? I had to know what the repercussions were to be for me and my family and I had to tell my father so that we could decide what we were going to do about any press enquiries and how we were going to cope with the scandal.

At about eleven o'clock that night I finally telephoned Cecil. I said that I needed to know what he was going to say to the press if questioned. Was he going to acknowledge that he was the father of my baby? Had he told the Prime Minister? Was he going to resign? He retorted that that was none of my business. I said that it was my business, that my family would have to decide what to say to the press if they were badgered by reporters, and that I had a right to know what he intended to say. He hung up. A little later he rang me back. He did so several times. Eventually I took the telephone off the hook.

I was unable to sleep for some time. At around two-thirty in the morning, I telephoned Elisabeth and Richard knowing that they would be starting their day, it being then six-thirty in the morning in Muscat. Elisabeth and I talked for a long time. I said that I had not yet told my father and knew that I must warn all the family. I was feeling very upset about the consequences for the family of any scandal and anxious to decide how we were going to deal with the press. Elisabeth comforted me and reassured me, saying that I was not to worry about the family who would all be right behind me. I said that I would talk to my father in the morning and ring her again and she promised to stay close to the telephone all day. At last I was able to sleep.

Early the next morning the telephone rang. It was Cecil again. What he said in that and several other calls to me that morning was extraordinary. He said some dreadful things: that I had done everything possible to keep our relationship going, that I had tried to blackmail him into marrying me, and more besides. I was very angry, protesting vehemently that he knew that what he was saying was untrue. He was very sarcastic and said that it was time that I lived in the real world (whatever that meant) and that I had better get a solicitor soon as from now on all dealings with him must be through his solicitor.

I thought I heard the sound of another person on the line and said so. He then said "I have no secrets from my wife; she has been listening in to all these conversations".

Part Three

Betrayal

My father's second letter to the Prime Minister

Friday 2 September 1983

I didn't want to hear another word and took the telephone off the hook. I had to think what to do and I had to get legal advice. I could no longer go to Clive Lewis. I felt angry and upset about the previous day's events and I believed then, quite wrongly I think, that he knew in advance what Cecil was going to do. I was not prepared to trust him and go to the solicitors he had suggested. I was very worried. Ever since my experience at the hands of the *Daily Mirror* reporters I had felt anxious, afraid that the story might break at any moment and other reporters appear at my door. At least at that time I felt I had had Cecil's support, that it was something we would face together: now I felt completely alone and increasingly alarmed. That Cecil could have said such dreadful things to me—and with his wife listening in on the conversation—totally undermined me.

All I could think of was that I wanted to get out of London and go home, but I could not bear the thought of my father's anxiety. I rang Elisabeth and Richard again and they suggested that I telephoned Messrs Iliffes, a firm of solicitors, who could recommend a firm to act for me. Mr Sweet of Iliffes said that his firm could deal with the matter and two hours later I met him and his partner, Mr Wicks, in their London offices in John Street. Then came the painful business of explaining my circumstances to them. We talked for about an hour—it seemed much longer—and I said that Cecil had promised to provide for me and for the baby, and that my principal concern was what I should do if the story broke in the newspapers: we should be ready to deal with the press and to make a statement should it prove necessary. They said they would immediately see Clive Lewis, so I returned to Battersea, feeling by this time barely able to stand, I was so tired. I lay down for a while and telephoned Flora, who urged me to come home as soon as possible. I had told Mr Sweet and Mr Wicks that I would await their call and in due course they rang to say that they had had a brief, amicable meeting with Clive Lewis, who had repeated his client's assurances about financial provision and would be writing in due course with proposals. All that remained for me to do was to pack up whatever belongings I might need—not knowing when I would be able to come to London again—and drive home. The journey was a great effort, but it was an enormous relief to be back at Marksbury. That Thursday and Friday seemed the blackest days of my life. Yet there were others just as bad, if not worse, still to come.

When I arrived home, my father told me that he had written to the Prime Minister again. He was disgusted at Cecil's behaviour and appalled that a man who could behave so unscrupulously should hold public office of any kind. He considered that, in view of Cecil's refusal to disclose the facts to the Prime Minister, except under pressure, he had no option but to write to Mrs Thatcher a second time. He was very concerned about her position and the likelihood that the press would expose the matter. He wrote to inform her of the press enquiries (he did not know, as I did, that Cecil had informed 10 Downing Street about the incident with the *Daily Mirror*) and to warn her of the imminent scandal. After all, it was only nine days since the *Daily Mirror* reporters had invaded the privacy of his home. He expected similar onslaughts from other papers at any moment. He also fully expected Cecil either to offer to resign or to be asked to do so by the Prime Minister.

I did not ask to see my father's letter and I certainly had no objection to his writing. I considered that he had both the right and the duty to do so. He showed me his letter the following week when the reply came.

My father wrote to her, on Friday 2 September, as follows:

Winsbury House
Marksbury
Bath

2 September 1983

Dear Mrs Thatcher

It is with regret that I am obliged to refer to my letter to you of 9 June concerning the scandalous behaviour of Cecil Parkinson towards my daughter Sara Keays, and your reply thereto dated 12 June when you said that you understood that Parkinson had spoken to me on the matter in the interim.

Parkinson did indeed speak to me on the phone on 11 June. He then assured me that he intended to marry Sara, that he would ensure the greatest possible care of her and of his child by her to be born next January. He gave a solemn assurance of this to Sara as well and said he had told *you* also. He asked Sara to quit her job to preserve confidentiality. This she did and all members of my family have co-operated in order to give him time to resolve his problem.

He returned a little while ago from holiday with his wife. He spoke to Sara in his solicitor's office in the most disgusting terms.

He said he most certainly would not marry her and he would not acknowledge his unborn child. He accused Sara of blackmailing him with intent to ruin his career.

Sara is now without employment and her future is a matter of grave concern to me. She is being harrassed by the press, without any support from Parkinson, and has been forced to go into hiding to prevent an untimely release of the facts. I am being pursued by the press also and have held them off with difficulty.

I think you must agree the situation is now intolerable. We have briefed a solicitor to watch over my daughter's interests and to prepare a statement for the press.

The chief purpose of this letter is to warn you that a public scandal must be regarded as imminent. This situation is definitely not of our seeking but in our view it is essential that the parenthood of Sara's child should be acknowledged, but I have no wish that she should marry the man.

Yours sincerely

H deJ Keays

On the Sunday, 4 September, I drove to Devon to spend a few days with friends. Monday was a beautiful, warm and sunny day, memorable for being one of the few tranquil days that I had throughout my pregnancy. We walked along Putsborough Sands to Woollacombe and I managed to put my problems aside for a few hours.

On Tuesday afternoon they returned with a vengeance. First I had a call from my solicitors, saying that they understood that my father would be receiving a reply from the Prime Minister the following day. I had not taken them into my confidence about this correspondence, considering it unnecessary for them to know—it was after all my father's private correspondence—and I considered also that the fewer people who knew about it the better, for everyone's sake.

Unfortunately Cecil had told his solicitor about the correspondence and he in turn had assumed that Iliffes also knew. They were agog to know what my father had said and what reply he received. I explained that the correspondence had no bearing on my instructions to them—at least as matters stood then. In fact I never did show them the correspondence: it was never necessary to do so.

It was hard to convince them of this at the time, probably because of the nature of the message they had received from Mr Lewis. I think the wording of that message, which Mr Wicks relayed to me over the telephone, is significant. I made a shorthand record of all telephone conversations at this time—a habit acquired from working as a secretary for many years, which in fact proved very useful as the negotiations over the wording of Cecil's statement to the press were conducted almost entirely by telephone. Sometimes I tape recorded such conversations as well. This is what Geoffrey Wicks said to me:

> "I had a telephone call this morning from Mr Lewis who told me that a meeting took place last night between Cecil Parkinson and the Prime Minister, but I have not been given any indication as to what the outcome of that meeting was. I have been authorised to say that the Prime Minister apparently took the view that the one thing that was particularly important to their conversation was the contents of your father's letter, which she considered to be of great significance. Everything is going to turn on your father's letter and the reply which has been sent to him by the PM, which was sent to him last night."

It was clear that the Prime Minister wished us to believe that she regarded my father's letter very seriously. However, her reply which we received the next day bore little comparison to this roundabout telephone message. I do not see, even now, how 'everything' was supposed to 'turn' on my father's letter and her reply. Her reply didn't even refer to the chief points of his letter.

I had a second telephone call, this time from Peter Brooke, who had obtained the number from my father and who was ringing to express his concern on hearing about the incident with the *Daily Mirror*. I was aghast that he should know about it. He told me that he had heard from John Stradling Thomas, the Welsh Secretary and a Cabinet colleague of Cecil's, who had been told by the Chief of Police in the Palace of Westminster. He in turn had been told by the police at Rochester Row. I felt certain that it would now be only a matter of days before the whole of Westminster knew. I trusted Peter, who was most solicitous and anxious to help, but I wondered who else might have acquired the information along the way. My fears were justified—two days later I heard from a friend in the House that a lobby correspondent had told him that there was a scandal imminent concerning a 'junior minister'. I decided to return home immediately and got back to Marksbury late that night.

The Prime Minister replies

Wednesday 7 September 1983

The Prime Minister's reply arrived the following morning. When I came downstairs my father was reading it. He handed it to me without a word. This time her reply was typewritten. It was rather longer than her first, but again was remarkable for what it omitted as much as for what it said. She expressed no concern whatsoever about the likely scandal—that did not even merit a mention. Neither did she express any concern about my father's position. Indeed, by concentrating her reply on a matter which he had not asked her to consider, she appeared to attribute another motive to him altogether. It was even too much for her to thank him for writing to her, let alone for maintaining confidentiality.

The following is the full text of her letter:

10 Downing Street

5 September 1983

Dear Colonel Keays

I have today discussed with Mr Parkinson the contents of your letter of 2 September, which I received on my return to London this afternoon.

He is deeply distressed by the pain and anguish which he has caused to your daughter, to you and to your family, as well as to his own.

He does not accept *all* that you say in your letter.

He has assured me, however, that he will make full and generous provision for your daughter and for the child, and I understand that he has given instructions to his solicitors to that effect.

I am sure that you will agree that it is the welfare of your daughter and her child which is of paramount importance. I sincerely hope that the arrangements which are to be made will ensure that that is so.

Yours sincerely,

Margaret Thatcher

By ignoring my father's stated purpose in writing, which was to warn her of the imminent scandal, was she presuming in her last paragraph to tell him what his priorities in the matter should be? Her letter did not contain a single expression of her own view of the matter. Indeed, she seemed to be writing in the capacity of spokesman for her Minister. Just what was it in my father's letter that Cecil, and by implication the Prime Minister, disputed? Why did they not specify it?

The attentions of the press which we had already suffered did not even rate a mention in her letter. She could not deny the truth of what my father had said about the press enquiries. Cecil had told me over the telephone from the Bahamas that he had informed 10 Downing Street about the incident with the *Daily Mirror* and it was evident from Peter Brooke's call to me that at least one other member of the Cabinet knew about it.

I wonder what the Prime Minister expected us to say or do if we were questioned again. Was I to say 'No, I'm not pregnant'; or 'Yes, I'm pregnant but I can't tell you who the father is'; or simply 'Yes, you're quite right. Cecil Parkinson is the father. He had promised to marry me but now he's gone back on his word'. I had told the *Daily Mirror* reporters nothing. I could have answered their questions. What would have happened then?

I was deeply disappointed by the Prime Minister's apparent indifference to the discretion and loyalty which my father had accorded her. We thought it extraordinary that her reply was concerned only with financial arrangements between Cecil and myself. Indeed it could just as well have been written by his solicitor. She did not address herself to the far more important question of the likely exposure by the press. If she had given any consideration to it, clearly she was not concerned with our position. That was one of the most galling aspects of her behaviour, and Cecil's, throughout. They were only ever concerned about themselves. Surely my family also deserved some consideration?

When the scandal broke the following month, much was made of Mrs Thatcher's loyalty to her friends. It was exploited to the full by the Party Conference and extolled by the media. Her 'loyalty' and her 'compassion' were used to excuse any errors of judgement she had made in her handling of the matter. But she showed no compassion to me or to my family: our loyalty and our discretion were of no significance to her.

A form of words

Five weeks were to elapse between my meeting with Cecil on Thursday 1 September and the publication of his statement to the press on Thursday 6 October. They were five very long and unpleasant weeks. A scandal was imminent and we were powerless to avoid it. Each day seemed to lead inexorably to the eruption of publicity in October. Yet it could have been avoided or greatly reduced had Cecil and the Prime Minister acted differently between Polling Day and 1 September. Even after 1 September there was still time.

Friday 9 September 1983

On Friday afternoon, a week after our first meeting at Iliffes' offices in London, Geoffrey Wicks came to see me at Marksbury. The first thing he told me was that Clive Lewis felt unable to act for Cecil in the matter, because he had previously been my solicitor also, and that Farrer & Co were now representing Cecil. I was relieved about this, as I liked Clive and his withdrawal from the matter removed the unpleasant suspicion I had felt that he had known in advance what Cecil was going to do.

The chief purpose of Wicks' visit was to familiarise himself with the background to the problem by going through the history of my relationship with Cecil. Time and again during the ensuing weeks I was to be upset at having to discuss with solicitors very personal details of the past twelve years. I realised that they were bound to ask such questions, but I hated the endless discussions which occurred over the next four weeks, even with my own solicitors, about whether or not Cecil had really intended to marry me. I had believed he loved me and wanted to marry me and I therefore had the right to expect any public statement about the matter to acknowledge that fact. Wicks and I talked for about an hour, at the end of which I thought he had a better understanding of the matter. I had not liked talking to him about it but he had assured me it was necessary. I hoped that he was now well armed for discussions with Cecil's solicitor.

It shocked me that in just over a week since Cecil's announcement that he was not going to marry me, we had moved so far apart. Whatever was going to happen, I could do nothing about it and I would never know how much of the twelve years of what I had thought was a devoted and loving friendship had been an illusion.

After Wicks had gone, I sat and talked for a long time to my father and Flora. As always they were understanding and did everything they could to help me. Throughout the weekend, I thought about what should be done. My instructions to my solicitors had been to assist me with the preparation of a possible press statement by me should one prove necessary. I expected at any moment further press enquiries at my father's home, where I was now living, and I wanted to do whatever was possible to spare members of my family from embarrassing questions.

Monday 12 September 1983

There were more than three weeks of negotiations before Cecil's statement was issued on the night of Wednesday 5 October. These began at 2.30 pm on Monday 12 September when Wicks had his first meeting with Cecil's new solicitor, Sir Matthew Farrer. I am going to describe the negotiations in some detail because it is the only way I can refute the allegations made against me in various newspaper articles and elsewhere following Cecil's resignation that I had insisted on his issuing a statement on behalf of us both, and that I had broken my word in issuing my statement to *The Times*.

I hope it will be clear from the following account of the negotiations between solicitors first that the proposal that Cecil issue a statement was put forward by his solicitor, and second that I refused to give any undertaking that I would remain silent. It was unthinkable that I should ever give any such undertaking. I could hardly give up my right to protect myself and my baby and I also refused to be drawn into any arrangement which would smack of my having been 'bought off'.

The negotiations were very detailed and involved many telephone conversations. Virtually nothing was put down in writing by the solicitors, and I was obliged to make a full note of our conversations so that I could give my approval or otherwise of every proposal that was put forward.

I had asked Mr Wicks to put forward no proposals on my behalf, but to have an exploratory meeting with Sir Matthew, in order to find out what his client proposed to do. Wicks telephoned me immediately afterwards. He said they had discussed the matter 'without prejudice' for an exchange of ideas and that

> Farrer felt that from the child's point of view it was important that there should be a public statement at an early date. He had drafted a few words very roughly. He was not aware of the extent of the relationship, or how long it had gone on. He probably had not had much of a discussion of the history of it with his client. He (Farrer) seems to feel that time may not be on our side, although perhaps they had been hoping the problem would just go away. He thinks something should be sorted out in the next two to three days at the most.

> The statement would be nominally from his client with contemporaneous. statement from you. Farrer regards it as absolutely imperative that everybody concerned agrees to say nothing. On the financial side, Farrer would not be drawn on the sort of figures they had in mind. He said he had no idea at the moment. He would like information from me in form of headings under which provision has to be made ...

Wicks read me Farrer's 'very rough draft':

> In order to dispel rumour that is now circulating, I wish to make the following statement. I have been involved in a relationship with another woman other than my wife and as a result this person is now pregnant. I have decided that I am remaining with my family and have so informed the other lady concerned. I very much regret the situation and will naturally provide whatever financial support is required for the lady concerned. I think it appropriate in the circumstances to tender my resignation from office etc.

Wicks added that obviously the last part of the statement would not be Farrer's responsibility. To cap it all, it was proposed that I issue a separate statement simultaneously with Cecil's, identifying myself as the woman concerned.

Finally, Farrer said that his client would give a written undertaking that he would never see the child. I told my solicitors that I did not want, nor would I accept, any such document. Cecil had made it clear to me that he never wanted to have anything to do with me again and would not wish to see the child, but I had not sought any such undertaking and I had no wish for our child ever to think that I had.

As for the proposed statement, it was admittedly a very rough draft, but it was totally unacceptable and repugnant to me, conveying as it did the impression that Cecil had had a passing affair with another woman (not even worthy of mention by name) who had unfortunately become pregnant. The suggestion that I consent to such a document and then obligingly identify myself as the woman concerned was astounding. I told Wicks that I would never give my agreement to such a proposal. I said that whatever else happened, any public statement whether by Cecil or by me on the subject would have to make clear that our baby was conceived in a relationship of many years standing and that I had believed that we would marry. I told Mr Wicks then, and was to repeat the point on almost every occasion, that I was prepared to try to co-operate with Cecil on this, but that there were issues involved on which I would *never* compromise and if Farrer was not prepared to recognise that, I would issue a statement of my own and would disregard Cecil's interests entirely.

My insistence that any statement should indicate the true nature of our relationship and my belief that Cecil intended to marry me proved to be the sticking point all the way through the negotiations. It was only with the greatest difficulty, and because I was totally determined, that the statement which was eventually issued included any reference at all to Cecil's having asked me to marry him. I mention this meeting and Mr Wicks' report of it because it shows clearly the following important points:

— That the other side and his client considered a statement to be essential and were the first to propose that one be issued;

— That they wished it to be issued as soon as possible;

— Cecil had either tendered his resignation to the Prime Minister or was intending to do so; or at least, Farrer thought that was Cecil's intention.

Tuesday 13 September 1983

The following day I drove to Chesham to see Mr Sweet and Mr Wicks at their offices there. I was prepared to issue a statement myself if necessary but had drafted one to be made by Cecil, should he wish to make one on behalf of us jointly. I had read this to Wicks over the telephone on the Sunday evening and now asked him to put it to Farrer. It was duly read to him over the telephone and was as follows:

> In order to bring to an end the speculation and rumour concerning myself and Miss Sara Keays, and to prevent further harrassment of Miss Keays and her family by reporters, I wish to make the following facts public.
>
> I have had a relationship with Miss Keays over a number of years and had told her of my wish to obtain a divorce from my wife in order to marry her. I know that Miss Keays allowed our relationship to continue because of her belief in our eventual marriage.
>
> Miss Keays is now five months pregnant and I am the father of her child. Although I gave her an assurance that I would marry her and also told members of her family of my intentions, I have recently informed Miss Keays that I am no longer able to keep my promise. I greatly regret the distress this has caused to Miss K and her family and have told her that I wish to acknowledge the child and to make full financial provision for both herself and the child.
>
> Both Miss Keays and I wish it to be known that neither of us, nor any members of our respective families will be prepared to answer questions from reporters on this subject.

Farrer's reaction was most unfavourable. He thought it went 'too far' though in what way he did not say, and read Wicks his own draft, which I rejected immediately as it made no mention of Cecil's having asked me to marry him. I insisted that Wicks obtain his assurance that he would put my draft to his client. I then drove wearily into London to stay at Elisabeth and Richard's house and await developments. That night Wicks rang to say that Farrer had reported that in no circumstances would Cecil refer to having promised to marry me, or to having broken that promise.

Wednesday 14 September 1983

Mr Wicks rang me to say that the gulf between us and the other side over the wording of a statement was enormous and probably unbridgeable. Farrer would not budge from the line he had taken the previous day. Wicks said that Mr Sweet was on his way to London for a meeting with Farrer at 11 am, the main object of the discussion being financial matters, adding that 'Farrer feels it is important that guidelines should be laid down at this stage whilst everybody has sufficiently good intentions towards each other'.

What neither Mr Wicks nor I knew then was that Mrs Thatcher had decided to replace Cecil as Party Chairman and that an announcement would be made that afternoon that John Selwyn Gummer had been given the job. I suspect that great pressure was being put on Cecil and Farrer to get a statement agreed as it must have seemed inevitable that the press would start asking awkward questions about why Cecil was being replaced *before* the Party Conference.

Wicks said that he and Farrer had concluded that agreement on a statement seemed impossible. He told me that it looked as if Cecil was going to go ahead and issue a statement without my consent. "I said that all I could ask him [Farrer] to do in the circumstances was to let us know, if possible in advance, what they were going to say and when and how they were going to say it." It was agreed that if I decided to say anything myself, we would let them know.

At 2 pm Wicks rang me again: "The up-to-date situation is that whilst Jack Sweet was on his way up to London I had a further call from Matthew Farrer, who said he had had yet another go at the statement because he was so desperate to try to find, if possible, a formula which could be acceptable to both of you, acknowledging that it went considerably further than they wished to go, but not as far as we wanted to go".

Wicks and I talked for some time, but as Farrer would accept only the very slightest changes to what he had already proposed and was not prepared to include anything which would show that I had believed Cecil was going to marry me, I flatly rejected it.

At 2.30 pm I rang Wicks back and said that he should tell Farrer the following:

— If he published his statement as at present drafted (by Farrer) I would dissociate myself from it;

— I would feel no obligation to refrain from comment;

— I would feel obliged to defend myself and that it would be necessary for me to indicate the true nature and extent of our relationship;

— I would certainly not be able to prevent other members of my family from speaking out if they feel it right and necessary. I pointed out that we had been restrained so far because we wanted to give him the opportunity to do the right thing.

— I said that I had hoped that Cecil would feel that the least he could do, having behaved so shabbily, would be to try to protect me from further harrassment of the kind I had already suffered and to prevent further damage done to my reputation.

Wicks duly delivered my message to Farrer and rang me to tell me the following: "I have spoken at some length with Farrer. He was aghast at the prospects which were opening up. He made one or two attempts at possibilities of compromise but I made it plain in quite emotive terms the extent to which you feel the emotional relationship has not been fully explained in any way. I have set out the tremendous harrassment you have sustained and said that you are now at the end of your tether. I have also made clear that there is no desire on your part to be awkward."

I then had a conversation with Mr Sweet who expressed concern about the situation and said that Farrer had told him that there would be an announcement that afternoon that Cecil was standing down as Party Chairman and that there was great concern about this.

He said that the discussion of financial matters was 'wide open', but added: "Returning to the statement: my feeling is that if the statement that goes out is not either a joint statement or one which is simply confirmed by you, i.e. if there is any question of disagreement, it will be very bad for both of you."

I felt under terrible pressure. Wicks was sympathetic but I got the feeling that Sweet thought I was being unreasonable. I told Wicks that I didn't see any point in any further discussions with Farrer—we had reached stalemate. I was sure that as soon as the announcement of Cecil's replacement occurred the newshounds would be hot on my trail, so I told him that I would go home to Marksbury. He agreed that I might well be bothered by the press but said that he was not going to be by a telephone all evening, although I could get him after 11 pm if I wanted to speak to him.

I hastily got ready to leave London. I rang home to tell my father that I would be coming home that evening and he said that my brother William had suggested that I get away from all the pressures and spend the following day with him. They were all worried about the effect the endless arguments were having on me and I was only too glad to agree to a day off. I told Wicks that I would not be available for most of the following day, but would ring him some time in the afternoon. I set off for Marksbury at 5 pm and heard the announcement on my car radio that John Selwyn Gummer had taken over as Party Chairman. It was a great relief to find when I arrived home that there had been no press enquiries and it began to look as though Gummer's appointment had made scarcely a ripple on the public pond.

Thursday 15 September 1983

William had proposed that I accompany him to Dorchester Fair to buy some sheep, and we set off early in the morning. It was a complete change for me and very restful. Not even the torrential rain could spoil my enjoyment of the day. We had to queue in the market office to pay for William's purchases and by the time we had done that and then put his very wet and rather dejected looking sheep into the trailer, it was getting on for four o'clock. I had promised to ring Wicks and Sweet. When we found a telephone box, there was a queue for it. When I got through to Wicks at four o'clock he was most indignant and said he had been trying to get hold of me for hours. I thought that was a bit much, especially as I had told them I would not be available all day. I wondered why there was this sudden urgency. He said that in conversation with Farrer the suggestion had been made that Cecil and I and our respective solicitors should have a meeting at Farrer's office. I do not know who had proposed this, but I flatly refused. I did not wish to see Cecil.

I had been alternately pressured and kept hanging about by the telephone in the last three days and now I was being asked to go to London again. I did not believe that any useful purpose would be served by such a meeting with Cecil and Farrer. Indeed, I feared that I would come under pressure to agree to what they wanted. Wicks said he thought I ought to consider the suggestion of a meeting and asked me not to dismiss it out of hand. He seemed to think it was a good idea, and that we should try every possible course in order to reach agreement with the other side. He did not seem to understand my scepticism about the worth of such a meeting or how much I detested the very thought of it. He asked me not to make a hasty decision and I agreed to ring Wicks when William and I got home.

William's reaction to the latest proposal was the same as mine. He also thought it would be bad for me to have any more emotional upheavals. Certainly I often felt exhausted and was easily upset. Both conditions are associated with pregnancy but I was getting more than my fair share of them and longed for peace and quiet. I was also increasingly anxious about getting my cottage ready before the baby was born.

As agreed, I rang Wicks when I got back to William's house soon after 6 pm. I told him that I would not agree to a meeting, that there was such a gulf between us and the other side on the question of a joint statement as to make further discussions pointless, and that from now on I would act independently and issue a statement in my own name when I thought it necessary. Wicks said he was going to speak to Farrer again and would ring me back. I waited for his call. When he rang it was clear from what he said that there had been a fundamental change in attitude by Farrer and, presumably, his client. Having pressed us very hard for the past three days to agree a joint statement, he had suddenly put the brakes on that idea. From now on he and Cecil were to carry on as though we had all the time in the world to resolve the problem. Gone were the expressions of anxiety from Farrer about getting a statement out quickly.

Wicks said: "I eventually got through to Farrer. He said that, in anticipation that that might be the position, (i.e. that I would 'go it alone') he has been looking for the next possibility, because he is anxious, in the interests of both of you, to find a way in which the ordeal of too much publicity can be avoided."

Of course they were very keen to avoid publicity—weren't we all. What had happened was that Cecil believed his replacement as Party Chairman had been effected without the *Daily Mirror* putting two and two together and coming up with a bright answer. I was not impressed by Farrer's talk about the 'interests of both' of us and the 'ordeal' of publicity as there had never been any expression of concern from him or his client at the treatment I had received from the *Daily Mirror* reporters and the possibility of further similar incidents. It seemed to me that all they were worried about was whether Cecil's political position would be damaged. Damage to me and my family was apparently of no concern to them.

Wicks continued: "It is proposed that he should issue his statement and you should issue yours. It follows on from what he said to Jack Sweet last night that each side will in effect agree in advance what the other will say." (Sweet did not report to me about the conversation with Farrer which Wicks had mentioned, so I have no note of what was said.)

I did not see how we were going to agree each other's wording when we had not been able to agree a joint statement. They still refused to acknowledge that Cecil had asked me to marry him. I had been prepared from the outset to make concessions: they had offered none. I knew that to make a statement at all was going to put Cecil in a very bad light. The whole exercise was odious, but there was a point of principle on which I would not compromise and it seemed impossible to make them understand it. I wanted him to acknowledge—for the baby's sake—that I had believed we would marry. I did not want it spelt out in detail and any reference to the circumstances in which he had asked me for the second time to marry him was both unnecessary and open to the worst misinterpretation for both of us. It was for that reason that I had worded my draft in the way that I did. I felt that what I had asked was less than I could have asked: I never said that he ought to acknowledge how many times he had asked me to marry him and therefore how many times he had broken his promise.

The only possible argument in favour of a meeting was that Cecil might better understand my wishes and my intentions than he would through our intermediaries. At the same time I was afraid that any meeting would be used to persuade me to agree to something which was in Cecil's interests and not mine and I could not bear the thought of any such discussions in front of our solicitors. I felt intense frustration. Wicks asked me not to rule out the idea of a meeting but to think it over and discuss it with him again the next day. When I got home to Marksbury I thought for a long time about what I should do and what could be achieved by a meeting with Cecil.

Friday 16 September 1983

I had a bad night and awoke feeling very nervous. I was not sure what to do.

There were many times during the weeks of discussion between solicitors when I was beset with doubts. Sometimes it seemed, because the *Daily Mirror* had done nothing yet, that perhaps it would be best to do nothing and simply wait until the time when the scandal finally leaked out—as it seemed inevitable that it would—and deal with it in whatever way seemed best. Then the telephone or the doorbell would ring, and I would be very alarmed, albeit unnecessarily, and would decide that I could not go on as we were, that we had to be prepared and that Cecil and I had to be in agreement. Perhaps I felt so nervous because I was pregnant and that in other circumstances I would have felt stronger and more determined about dealing with the press.

I still had not made up my mind about a meeting but when I spoke to Wicks he said that he thought the discussions were tending to become 'adversarial' and that a meeting would be helpful, although he understood my feelings about it. After some discussion, I agreed very reluctantly to go to Farrer's office the following Sunday evening.

Last meeting with Cecil

Sunday 18 September 1983

The meeting with Cecil and Farrer was to take place at 7.30 pm and I had arranged to meet Geoffrey Wicks at the Waldorf Hotel in Aldwych at 6 pm. It had seemed a convenient place to meet for a talk before going to Farrer's office, which is only a short distance away in Lincoln's Inn Fields.

I left Marksbury at around 3 pm and had a tiresome drive into London in the thick of the Sunday evening traffic. I managed to park in Aldwych opposite the hotel and found that Wicks was already there waiting for me. The hotel lobby was very busy and the only seats we could find were in the middle of a crowded hall. Conversation was difficult, not least because I felt very nervous and was consumed with regret that I had agreed to the meeting with Cecil. I do not remember much of our conversation; all I could think about was getting the meeting at Farrer's over.

We left my car in Aldwych and Wicks drove me to Lincoln's Inn. The square was deserted. We pulled up in front of a building which looked equally deserted and was in darkness except for a light in one window on the first floor. Farrer was waiting for us just inside the entrance. The building was chill and gloomy. Farrer and Wicks exchanged some pleasantries about the journey, but I noticed that Farrer did not meet my gaze. He seemed scarcely to look at me, something I was to notice several times during our meeting. As we mounted the dimly-lit stone staircase I felt as if we had embarked on some furtive and underhand mission.

Farrer's room was more brightly lit, but rather depressing in appearance. Cecil was standing there, looking very casual and relaxed in his blue blazer and grey slacks. I could see that he was in fact very tense, but he seemed to glow with health and animation and looked out of place in these dreary surroundings. I felt there was something utterly unreal about our being there. All my anxieties came back to me in a rush and I knew that I should not have come. There was going to be an argument about some words on a piece of paper that were supposed to explain—wipe away—all the private things between us over the past twelve years. How could an hour's meeting in some solicitor's office possibly help us?

And what was it all for? To satisfy the curiosity of an uncaring public? To try to keep a political image shiny bright? The only thing that was real to me was the fact that I was going to have a baby.

Farrer offered us all a drink. We sat down at a table so that Cecil and I were facing one another. Farrer took charge of the discussion— in fact he did most of the talking throughout the meeting. He had a document in front of him, their draft of a statement to be made by Cecil. I was given a copy.

An argument developed almost immediately. It concerned the following passage:

> For some years, I have had a relationship with Miss K who is expecting a child of which I am the father and for whom I am making provision.
> During that relationship, I told Miss K that, if my present marriage were brought to an end, I would marry her. I subsequently decided that I could not bring to an end my own marriage and I so informed Miss K. My relationship with Miss K is now ended finally.

They were determined there should be no indication of the extent or significance of the relationship, nor of what I had believed it had meant to both of us.

Farrer's draft continued:

> My wife, who has been a great strength to me, and I are determined that our marriage will continue and that we shall keep our family together.

This was to be followed by a political passage, unspecified, and an expression of regret for the distress caused to me and my family, his family and his colleagues.

I suppose that I should have been grateful that it was a big improvement on their first effort. What sickened me was the sentence:

> During that relationship I told Miss K that, if my present marriage were brought to an end, I would marry her.

It was untrue. It made it sound as if marriage had only ever been a remote possibility, something that *might* happen if luck was on my side and his marriage conveniently came to an end. What Farrer was proposing made it sound almost as if the matter had been left to some outside agency, some third party to bring to pass.

> I subsequently decided that I could not bring to an end my own marriage

left out the important point of *when* he made that decision. And of course, it did not say anything at all about how many times this had happened. I had not intended that it should, but I had expected him to be honest about the intentions he had expressed towards me (and which he had repeated to other members of my family).

Farrer said that there should be a final paragraph to the statement, which he had not included in the draft, to the effect that nothing further would be added to it—in other words that neither Cecil nor I, nor any member of our respective families would say anything on the subject. I said emphatically that I would not agree to such a paragraph, that I would not give up the right to protect myself if the need arose and I certainly would not try to bind my family to silence. My family had already afforded Cecil support and discretion that he did not deserve and I did not see why any of them should undertake to remain silent, no matter what happened. Wicks backed me up and said that I could not be expected to give such an undertaking.

Farrer tried to turn the discussion back to the main points of his draft, but I was beginning to feel that I could not cope with any further argument. I could not bring myself, in front of Wicks and Farrer, to remind Cecil that he had begged me to marry him, and sought me out, had done everything he could to keep the relationship going; that he had broken his word, deceived me and betrayed my confidence to his wife. I could not bring myself to mention the points I had thought of before the meeting, especially as I was in effect having to make them to Farrer. I could not talk to a stranger about my feelings for Cecil. The only way in which I felt able to deal with the points that mattered to me was by referring to the words on the piece of paper in front of me, by keeping the discussion as neutral as possible. I could *not* talk about what Cecil had or had not said to me during the past four years; it was unbearable. I pointed out that their wording gave a false impression of the relationship and said to Cecil that he knew it did. When I referred to the notes I had made and my own draft, Farrer raised objections. He insisted we could discuss only his draft. He conducted the meeting as if I were asking concessions of them and they were doing me a big favour, when their sole object was to try to justify, even excuse, Cecil's behaviour so as to prevent damage to his political career. They seemed to have forgotten that the statement became necessary only because he was determined to continue his life as if nothing had happened.

Discussion seemed pointless. There were a number of long silences. Cecil said almost nothing, leaving Farrer to do the talking for him. What it boiled down to was that Farrer was prepared to rearrange the words on their piece of paper, but not to add anything to them which would indicate the significance and extent of the relationship.

I felt extremely upset and frustrated. I humiliated myself by shedding tears and was angry that I should have revealed my feelings in front of Farrer. From the outset, his manner towards me suggested disapproval, even dislike of me. He was reluctant to meet my eye and his response to my reference to Cecil's promises of marriage was scornful.

Referring presumably to the proposal of marriage which Cecil made on Polling Day he said, "But in what circumstances was this offer of marriage made?"

That did it. My pent up anguish burst out. I turned on Farrer and said "*Offer* of marriage? Did you say offer? Tell me, when you wanted to marry your wife, did you *offer* her marriage? Did you send her some carefully-worded legal document, saying that if she were a good girl and came up to your high standards, then one day you might *offer* to marry her? Or did you long for her, *beg* her to marry you?"

Cecil burst out laughing, which must have infuriated Farrer who said indignantly, "That was quite different. An offer of marriage given under duress is meaningless". I felt such anger that I did not trust myself to speak. Duress? There had been none. Cecil was never under *any* pressure from me or from any member of my family to *marry* me, only to face up to his responsibilities and to come clean with the Prime Minister. In fact my family were relieved that we did not marry. As for his so-called offer of marriage, after what had happened during the previous three weeks, I would not have accepted when Cecil asked me on Polling Day to marry him, if I had not believed he were sincere. He knew that to have been the case and I despised him for not saying so.

Farrer's mention of duress disgusted me. If anyone had been under duress it was I when Cecil had put such pressure on me to have an abortion. Remembering all that I had gone through during those agonising three weeks before Polling Day, and then Cecil imploring me to believe him and begging me to forgive him and say that I would marry him, I felt utter contempt for the line that he and Farrer were now taking.

Did Cecil really want me to think that his word of honour and his passionate declarations of love were utterly meaningless and that they had been given under duress? I had never exerted any. I would neither have been able nor have wished to do such a thing. I would rather never be married, than marry someone who did not love me. The argument seemed all the more extraordinary to me because I thought that Cecil himself would have preferred to have shown himself to have been a loving and sincere person, even if he were unable to go through with his promise to marry me and had ceased to love me. We had had a love affair lasting nearly twelve years. To pretend that it was one-sided or shallow, quite apart from being very cruel, seemed to me to present him as callous and insincere. I could not understand how he could bear to be seen in such a light.

As for the financial consideration, I did not want to have anything from him. I felt that he was trying to buy me off—particularly after the line taken by the Prime Minister in her letter to my father—and the idea revolted me. Later on, my family and my solicitors insisted that I would need money from him, not least for our child, and a settlement was agreed.

All that mattered to me then was that Cecil should acknowledge that he was the father and that our child was the product of a genuine loving commitment to one another, not of a casual affair. I could not bear to argue with some solicitor about whether Cecil had genuinely wanted to marry me, whether his promise of marriage had been sincere. No-one except Cecil and I could know what it was like, what was said. I resented the fact that he was determined to do all the talking, almost as if Cecil was not to be trusted with me, whereas I was expected to speak up for myself and justify my objections to their proposed statement. I felt that I could not take another minute in that room. I said that I saw no point in continuing and that I wished to leave.

Cecil then spoke. Apart from greeting me when Wicks and I arrived and enquiring after my health, it was the first time he had spoken. He said "I am sure that if our solicitors would leave us to discuss this privately we could sort something out". Farrer was having none of it. He got to his feet and said he and Cecil would withdraw to leave Wicks and me to have a discussion. When they had left the room, Wicks said "Cecil obviously wants to speak to you alone, although I don't think Farrer wants him to. How do you feel about it? Do you want to talk to him privately?" What I wanted more than anything was to get away from there, away from all of them and to be alone. I said that I did not think we were getting anywhere and he agreed. I really felt too upset anyway and didn't think I could cope with a conversation with Cecil. We got up and Wicks went out into the corridor to find Farrer and Cecil. I got the impression that they had reached the same decision. In any event, there was no further discussion and Wicks and I left them to their deliberations.

Awaiting the storm

Monday 19 September 1983

I felt utterly exhausted in the morning, having had a very bad night. As I lay in bed thinking about the previous evening, I was alarmed by a sudden pounding, bursting feeling in my chest and neck, as if my heart were racing. It passed off within a few seconds, leaving me feeling limp. I got up and eventually forgot about it.

I telephoned Wicks and told him that I was not prepared to go any further with the negotiations, which the previous evening had shown to be a waste of time. I did not see why I should have to agree to anything with them. As I had told Wicks many times before, I was quite prepared to face the problem without Cecil's co-operation and to take independent decisions about what the press should be told. Wicks was not at all happy about this and urged me to give them more time, his view being that it was infinitely preferable that Cecil should make a statement for both of us. I agreed eventually to wait one more day and see what they said.

Not long afterwards I experienced the same horrid sensation that my heart was doing overtime, almost as if I had, by a supreme effort, narrowly avoided some ghastly accident. At eleven o'clock I went to see my GP. He said that I was suffering from 'panic attacks', caused by anxiety and exhaustion. There was no cause for alarm, but I should try to take everything more calmly and get as much rest as possible. Armed with a prescription for mild sleeping tablets I went back to Elisabeth's house. It was easier said than done to try to be calm and get more rest. Ever since I had known I was pregnant I had been under a considerable strain, first plunged into despair, then filled with renewed hope, only to be cast down again. I had worked through a General Election campaign, which is exhausting at the best of times, wound up my job, and moved house. I had had enough of solicitors. I seemed to be forever having to drive back and forth to London from Marksbury, wondering at all times when I would be pounced on again by the press. While all this was going on the birth of my baby was drawing nearer and I was supposed to be supervising alterations to the cottage that would be our home. There were times when I felt I could hardly take any more.

I had my next appointment with Mr Kenney on Thursday morning and was also supposed to be starting a course of antenatal classes on the Wednesday afternoon. I could not face another long car journey and decided to stay in London until Thursday afternoon. On Monday evening I spoke to Wicks on the telephone. He said: "I spoke to Farrer late this afternoon, but to no great purpose. He has not spoken to his client since last night. He has been turning the statement round and read to me what he put down. I could not read it over to you if I tried because it is in a form which I don't think you will approve of. Farrer also said that the original idea was that you were being severely harrassed and that we had to do something jolly quick, but that the pressure is off for the moment."

My reaction to that was that the 'original idea' was not ours, that it was Farrer, and presumably Cecil, who had been so anxious to get a statement out quickly. I was quite sure that their sudden about-turn was not made with *my* interests uppermost in their minds and that the truth of the matter was that Cecil, and no doubt the Prime Minister, wanted to do nothing until after the Party Conference, if ever. Cecil probably hoped, as he had on other occasions, that the problem would somehow be taken out of his hands and resolved without action by him.

Tuesday 20 September 1983

I rang Wicks to ask him to make the following points to Farrer:

—Cecil has had long enough to show good intentions towards me. He has said he intends to acknowledge his paternity of the child and *now* is the time to do that, not when the baby is born. I want to be able to settle down and lead a normal life and not to have to deal with scandal and questions when the baby is born.

—He may think it is 'quiet' at the moment, but I am being damaged by rumours and speculation about my pregnancy, which is now quite obvious.

—It is very unfair to me and my family that we should be under this pressure.

Wicks forestalled me by saying: "Yesterday I spoke to Farrer again who said that he had been trying his best, as far as he was humanly able, to find a form of words which went to meet what he felt you wanted in the statement and which nevertheless was something he could get his client to agree to. His new draft is as follows:

> "'To bring to an end rumour concerning Miss Sara Keays and myself and to prevent further harrassment of Miss Keays and her family, I wish, with her consent, to make the following statement.
> "'I had a relationship with Miss Keays over a number of years. Miss Keays is now expecting a child due to be born in January of whom I am

the father and for whom I am making provision. During our relationship I told Miss Keays of my wish to marry her, but despite having given that assurance I subsequently decided I would not leave my wife and family. My wife, who has been a great strength to me, and I are determined that our marriage will continue and that we shall keep our family together.'

"Then there was to be a 'political' paragraph, the contents of which Farrer either did not know or would not reveal. The statement would continue:

> "'I regret deeply the distress that I have caused to Miss Keays and her family, to my own family and to my colleagues. Both Miss Keays and I wish it to be known that neither of us nor any member of our respective families intend to make any further statement about this matter and will not be prepared to answer questions from the press about it'."

It was hardly an improvement on what Farrer had proposed on the Sunday evening. I would not agree to it. It implied that Cecil and I had ended our love affair and then the baby had been conceived, after he had decided he would not marry me, which was quite untrue. Wicks asked me to think about it. I had written the whole conversation down in shorthand, as usual, and said that I would look at it carefully, but that I didn't see how I could agree to it. Wicks said:

> "I do advise you, as your lawyer and objective assistant at this moment that if we could find an acceptable form of words that I felt said enough to protect you, I still believe that that must be in your interests. If you could tell me in an hour or two whether you are able to either accept it as it stands or put forward some proposals that I could go back with, that is a good thing. I feel that the statement in the form in which I am looking at it does not say anything which reflects adversely on you. It is short on detail and does not contain all the nuances of the relationship, but I feel if you were to associate yourself with that statement it would do you no harm in the legal sense."

I said that I would think about it and ring him back, but that one thing I positively would *not* agree to was to say that I would *never* make any statement on the matter myself. I reminded him that hitherto he had agreed that Cecil had no right to expect my family, and my father in particular, to agree to say nothing. I said that it was desirable to indicate that we would not be prepared to answer questions from the press, but that I had *never* said that I would not make a statement. Indeed, throughout all the negotiations so far I had reiterated my intention to say something publicly myself if I felt it necessary. Wicks agreed, saying that I must retain the right to protect myself if necessary. I said I would telephone him in due course, when I had had time to go through Farrer's draft thoroughly. When I rang him back at 6 pm it was to say that I could not agree to what Farrer proposed, for the following reasons:

—The phrase 'I had a relationship ...' followed by 'Miss Keays is now expecting a child ...' implied that I had become pregnant *after* the relationship had ended, which was untrue.

—That untruth was repeated in the next sentence of the statement which again implied that I had become pregnant *after* he had told me that he would not leave his wife after all. It also made it sound as if his decision had been made quite some time ago, rather than *after* I had become pregnant.

—I could not agree to anything that suggested that our baby had been conceived after we had ceased to be in love.

—I proposed that that particular paragraph should read as follows:

> I *have* had a relationship with Miss Keays over a number of years and had told her that I wished to marry her. I know that she allowed our relationship to continue because of her belief in our eventual marriage. Miss Keays is expecting a child [deleting the phrase 'due to be born in January'—I did not wish the date to be announced to the press] of whom I am the father and for whom I am making financial provision. Despite my assurance to Miss Keays that I would marry her, I have subsequently decided that I will not leave my wife and family. The relationship is now ended.

—I told Wicks that we must know in advance what the 'political' paragraph contained before we agreed to the statement.

—I said I found the reference to the distress to his 'colleagues' hard to believe. How could their distress (if they felt any, which I doubted) compare with mine, or his family's?

—I repeated that I would not forego the right to make a statement myself, that I had to retain the right to defend myself against things that might be said about me following Cecil's statement and therefore the final paragraph should be amended to read 'neither of us nor any member of our respective families will be prepared to answer any questions from the press about this statement.' On this last point I told Wicks that I wanted to be absolutely sure of my legal position if the statement were made as I had amended it, so that I could not be said to have given up the right to make a statement myself if I wished to. This point was of great importance to me and I was reassured by Wicks on a number of occasions that my right to speak was unfettered by the wording we had proposed. As for my family, I knew that they would co-operate with me fully and would never say or do anything to harm me or to interfere with anything I agreed with Cecil, nor have they ever done so.

I went through the statement again with Wicks, word by word, so that he had my revised version of the second and final paragraphs accurately and he said he would go back to Farrer and put the amendments to him. There was nothing more to do now but wait, something I spent a lot of time doing during the next two weeks.

Wednesday 21 September 1983

Flora rang me to say that there was a piece in the 'Peterborough' column of the *Daily Telegraph* about Cecil saying that it was unfortunate that Mrs Thatcher had chosen the previous Wednesday to promote John Selwyn Gummer to the Conservative Party chairmanship when the agenda released yesterday for the Party Conference in October had a photograph of Cecil under the caption 'Chairman of the Party'. The article was not itself particularly significant but I wondered whether it would prompt the *Daily Mirror* into action. It enhanced my feeling that exposure of the scandal was imminent.

In the afternoon I went somewhat apprehensively to my first antenatal class which proved very enjoyable and provided much-needed relief from the strains of recent days. It was reassuring to be with other expectant mothers and to be reminded that it was a time to be happy, that we should simply concentrate on learning how to relax and to master the breathing techniques that help one through labour. I had booked into a course of eight classes but unfortunately was able only to attend the first two. After the affair with Cecil became public it was impossible to go again.

Wicks rang me at six o'clock that evening to say that he had no news for me. He said: "I spoke to Farrer this morning and passed the thing on to him. I rang him just before lunch, when he was tied up. I rang again just after lunch and he was going to ring back, but did not. I rang him again about 4 pm. I don't think he is giving me the run-around. On the other hand, I would not swear that they are not perhaps now going to adopt the attitude that they should let us sweat a bit. He says he is unable to make contact with his client. He also says that he regards the possibility of them accepting your second paragraph as remote." I asked whether he thought that what we were getting all the time was Farrer's view of what Cecil ought to think, or what Cecil actually thought himself. Wicks said "Farrer is saying that his views are those of his client".

Thursday 22 September 1983

I had another appointment with Mr Kenney. I had had further 'panic attacks' and was worried about the effect of all the strain on my baby. I was also nervous about taking sleeping pills but was finding it very difficult to sleep at night. He reassured me about everything and said the baby was doing well. He told me to try to concentrate on the future with my child, who would bring me much happiness. It was the thought of my child that kept me going and made everything else seem bearable.

When I got home at lunchtime I rang Wicks. He had no news. He said "I spoke to Farrer at 1.30 pm but he said that he had not spoken to his client. He is trying to get hold of him but he [Farrer] will not be available at all this afternoon and therefore will be unable to get hold of Parkinson until early evening. He said there was no realistic likelihood of their being in agreement. I have said that as far as we are concerned we have run out of time and patience and I will be speaking to you with a view to our deciding what to do."

At 8.45 pm that night Wicks rang me to say that he had heard from Farrer who had spoken to his client, and it appeared that we were not going to reach agreement. He said, "They are just not prepared to agree the sentence which you included [about my belief that we would eventually marry], nor indeed the little bit that went before it. They would very much have preferred, for everybody's sake, but particularly for yours, that we agreed Farrer's wording, but they are ready to accept that the likelihood of this being agreed is non-existent.

"I am not expecting to speak to him again, except that he has said that if we are going to issue a statement, they would like to know when and how, for a very good practical reason that if a reporter says anything to him or his client, he wants to be sure that they are not just dealing with somebody who is purely 'kite-flying'."

All that I had endured for the past eleven days of negotiations had been for nothing. I said that I thought we should prepare ourselves to issue a statement. Wicks was very unenthusiastic about this and urged me to do nothing precipitate. I said that I didn't know what he thought I was about to do, but that at that moment, if reporters were to arrive at my door, I saw no reason why I should not tell them *exactly* what had happened. However, I agreed to do nothing for the time being and told Wicks that I was going home to Marksbury.

I discussed the matter at length with my father, and with my brother William, and Flora. They were very sceptical of Cecil having any honourable intentions towards me and thought that I was right to prepare myself to go it alone on a statement. However, once I was back in the secure surroundings at Marksbury and out of reach of the press I felt very inclined never to venture forth again and reluctant even to think about what I should do if approached by the press. I had detested the arguments with Farrer and despised Cecil for his refusal to acknowledge the truth about our relationship. At other times I would feel terrible regrets for such thoughts and would feel sorry for him. At least I would have our child; it seemed to me on those occasions that he would be left with nothing worth having.

Whenever the telephone rang I would think it must be for me and I didn't want to go near it. I didn't want to have to speak to a solicitor ever again; I was sick to death of going over and over these ghastly sets of words.

Monday 26 September

Sweet had said he wanted to talk to me about the financial negotiations. When I spoke to him on Monday he began by talking about the arguments over the statement, a subject on which he and I had never agreed. He said: "My feeling is to do nothing. I cannot see from your point of view the need for a statement to be made either by you or by him. In any case they seem to be more anxious than we are to make a statement." That had always been the case, but I did not believe that my interests had played a part in their decision and I felt very strongly that Sweet was quite wrong to believe that *no* statement by either of us was necessary. It was a view he expressed on a number of occasions, although he never had any advice as to how I should deal with any further enquiries.

On the subject of finance, Sweet said that he had had a 'very open-ended discussion' with Farrer and that he thought he and I ought to have a meeting to talk about the kind of provision that should be made. I agreed to meet him at Elisabeth and Richard's house on Wednesday 28 September.

Wednesday 28 September 1983

Sweet arrived at 11 am. We talked generally about such things as the cost of the medical care I was having and the expected cost of the confinement [I was having private care at Cecil's insistence] and the likely cost of schooling.

Sweet then turned to the matter of the statement and repeated his view that it would be better to say nothing at all. He then handed me the second page of a two-page memorandum which Wicks had written to him on the subject. Sweet urged me to study it and to consider what Wicks had said very carefully as they were very much opposed to my issuing any statement myself, which they considered could only harm me. I said I would look at it and he left.

The memo, or at least the part Sweet had left with me, concerned the point which Wicks referred to as the one 'upon which we were all falling apart', being my wish to have included in Cecil's statement the phrase:

> I know that she only allowed our relationship to continue because of her belief in our eventual marriage.

Wicks said in the memo that he had consistently expressed the view that

> from a *public* point of view, I believe that the omission of those words does her no harm at all.

He went on to say

> nobody who has not been a party to the conflict about their inclusion or exclusion would have any reason to think about that particular point and the inferences to be drawn from what is included in the statement are in my view fully sufficient to cover Miss K.

I quote from this memo because it shows my inability to get across to all concerned *why* I was so anxious that any public statement about my affair with Cecil should show *my* feelings about it. After all, I was not asking him to say what he felt about me, or admit to his several changes of heart. I knew that any statement would provoke a storm of comment in the media and that, if Cecil were determined to ride it out and stay in office, he and/or others in the Government would be anxious to play down the significance and extent of the relationship. I may seem to be labouring a point I have touched on already, but it is hard to express the strength of my feelings that it was very important, for my baby's sake more than my own, that I should not appear as a woman whose pregnancy was merely an unfortunate accident. After Cecil's dishonourable behaviour towards me in the past four months, I felt that he might well allow my reputation to be sacrificed in order to save his own. Subsequent events, and media comment on the matter in particular, proved that my fears were fully justified. It was precisely because this point was not included in Cecil's statement that it was possible for the smear campaign against me to take hold.

Wicks' memo went on to say that "it now appears to Miss K, and rightly so I feel, that the other side are by implication saying that they do not even believe her when she says she believed that marriage was in prospect". He said that whilst he appreciated my feelings, he could not see what good bringing this point out "and having a slanging match" would do. He said that even if there were to be a private slanging match, "there can be no possible reason for having a public slanging match". This last comment was most offensive, especially the use of the words 'slanging match'. It was the last thing I would go in for, privately or publicly, and I could not see why my insistence on the inclusion of a particular sentence in Cecil's statement would cause a *public* argument. Indeed it was the exclusion of that sentence and the smear campaign that was successfully built up afterwards that forced me to issue my own statement and so to provoke public discussion of the matter.

On several occasions Sweet had expressed the view that if I made difficulties over the wording of any statement, I could jeopardise any financial settlement. He may have been right and no doubt as my lawyer he had a duty to point this out, but I cared far more about the effect on my reputation of any public pronouncement Cecil made than I did about how I was going to make ends meet in the future. I cared passionately that Cecil should acknowledge the relationship we had had.

Having reached stalemate with Farrer and Cecil and, at the same time, having Wicks and Sweet very forcibly telling me that I ought to agree to what Farrer had proposed, I hardly knew what to do. It is exceedingly difficult, in a situation of that kind, to stick to your own judgement in the face of opposition from professional advisers. I felt very isolated. I discussed my anxieties frequently with my family but at the same time, I could not ask them to advise me what to do. Also none of us knew just what was going to happen, what kind of public reaction there would be when the news broke. Was I being over-anxious? Perhaps I ought to be guided by Wicks and Sweet. In the end, I agreed to a compromise. I refused to agree to what Farrer proposed, but decided to go along with Wicks and Sweet and not to issue a statement of my own, at least for the time being.

As a result, nothing happened for the next few days. I spoke to Wicks and

Sweet once or twice, but they had nothing to tell me. Sweet said that he thought that he and I ought to have another meeting when he had seen Farrer, which he was arranging to do. I went back to Marksbury, and returned to London the following Sunday evening, 2 October, expecting to meet Sweet on the Monday or Tuesday.

Tuesday 4 October 1983

All pressure from the other side to agree a statement had ceased and I was sure they would not want to say anything further about it until the Conservative Party Conference—now only a week away—was over and done with. I was lulled into a false sense of security, believing that I had at least a week's respite from the arguments. My comparative tranquillity received a severe jolt when a friend rang me from the House of Commons on Tuesday afternoon to say that she had had a telephone call from a reporter who wished to know where he could contact me. She had said that she did not know where I was. There could only be one possible reason why a reporter should want to get in touch with me. However, no one called at the house and the only telephone calls I received were from my sisters. I tried to put the matter out of my mind and went to bed.

Cecil's statement

Wednesday 5 October 1983

I had not set my alarm clock and was awakened by the telephone. It was Marcus Fox, the MP for Shipley and a friend of Cecil and myself for some years. He said "I'm sorry, Sara, it's bad news, I'm afraid. Have you seen *Private Eye*?" I had not. He proceeded to read out a piece from the magazine which was clearly libellous. Eventually a full apololgy was published in *Private Eye*, but I was very upset at the time.

I rang Cecil's Private Office at the Department of Trade and Industry. A member of his staff answered. When I asked to speak to him, I was told that was not possible. I gave my name and said that I had to speak to him immediately. The line went dead for a moment or two and then I was told again that he could not speak to me. I said, "If you have your Minister's interests at heart you'll put me through to him immediately. Tell him that the press are after me." I was put through to Cecil.

"Have you seen *Private Eye*?" I demanded. "I've just been talking to Matthew Farrer about it." he said. He expressed no regret, no concern whatsoever for my feelings at being the subject of this scurrilous article. I told him that Marcus had just rung me and I said, "If you don't do something about it, I will. You've got until midday to decide whether or not you are going to issue a statement and if you won't, then I will."

He said that his solicitor would speak to mine. It was the last conversation I had with him. He has never made any attempt to speak to me since then, nor I to him.

Early in the evening Marcus telephoned me to say that he had been asked to go and see the Chief Whip, John Wakeham, and that Downing Street was in a turmoil over Cecil's statement.

The arguments over the wording of the statement went on all day and into the night. We wrung some slight improvements out of the other side. They agreed to alter the tense and the phrasing of part of his previous draft in such a way that it no longer sounded as if Cecil had decided some time before I became pregnant that he no longer wished to marry me. They also deleted from the final sentence the phrase which would have barred me from making a statement myself. But that was as far as they would go. They would *not* agree to include *anything* that would show that I had allowed the affair to continue because I had believed that he intended to marry me.

I was exhausted and could not face any more discussions of individual words and phrases, when the spirit of the statement was fundamentally wrong and put such a gloss on his conduct. Wicks was adamant that what was now proposed was the best I could hope for and advised me to agree to it. I asked him to read it over to me again so that I could check my note of it and be sure I knew what I was being asked to approve. I had had so many different versions read to me over the telephone and none of them, with the exception of the draft Farrer had produced at the meeting with Cecil on 18 September, had ever been put in writing, at least not to me.

Wicks read the statement to me once more:

> To bring to an end rumour concerning Miss Sara Keays and myself and to prevent further harrassment of Miss Keays and her family, I wish, with her consent, to make the following statement.
> I have had a relationship with Miss Keays over a number of years. She is expecting a child due to be born in January, of whom I am the father, and for whom I am making financial provision.
> During our relationship I told Miss Keays of my wish to marry her but, despite having given that assurance, I subsequently decided that I would not leave my wife and family. Our relationship has now ended.
> My wife, who has been a source of great strength to me, and I are determined our marriage will continue and we shall keep our family together.

At this point there was to be what Farrer had termed a 'political paragraph'. Then the statement continued:

> I regret the distress which I have caused to Miss Keays, to her family and to my own family.
> Both Miss Keays and I wish it to be known that neither of us nor any member of our respective families will be prepared to answer any questions from the Press about this statement.

The only alternative open to me was to refuse to co-operate further with Cecil and issue a statement of my own. Wicks was vehemently opposed to my doing that and urged me to agree to Cecil's statement.

In the end I decided that it was the lesser of two evils. I told Wicks that I would give my consent to it, provided that I had also approved the 'political' paragraph and provided that Farrer gave an undertaking that the statement would go out that night.

At nine o'clock, Wicks rang me to say that a difficulty had arisen in that Cecil had to discuss the wording of the statement with a number of his Cabinet colleagues. Wicks said he doubted whether the statement would go out that night, but he was waiting for Farrer to ring him again. I said that the statement *had* to go out that night and that if I did not receive an assurance within the next hour that it would, my consent would be withdrawn and I would issue a statement of my own.

The news that Cecil's 'colleagues' were taking a hand in the matter worried me. Powerful forces were ranging against me and I felt increasingly isolated. Cecil's colleagues would care even less than he if my reputation had to be sacrificed to enable him to remain in office. The thought of them discussing the matter was repellent. They ought to have been appalled that such discussions were taking place at all.

I had had the misfortune to fall in love with a married man and to believe his declarations of love and his solemn promises. He was the only man I had ever been in love with, yet already it was being put about—thanks to *Private Eye*—that I was promiscuous and that the identity of my baby's father was in question. My reputation was about to be thrown to the wolves and all Cecil and his colleagues cared about was that he should remain in office and protect himself.

Wicks rang me again shortly before ten o'clock and said that, on the advice of his Cabinet colleagues, Cecil wanted to make a slight alteration to the wording of the statement. They proposed that he should say that he was 'of course' making financial provision 'for the mother and child'.

They also wanted to combine the second and third paragraphs into one which would read:

> During our relationship, I told Miss Keays of my wish to marry her. Despite my having given Miss Keays that assurance, my wife, who has been a source of great strength to me, and I decided to stay together and to keep our family together.

I wondered which of his colleagues had advised these changes—the Prime Minister? Norman Tebbit? What did they think they achieved? Or were they merely trying to delay the statement so that it would miss the Press Association's deadline for that night. Wicks said that he thought the new paragraph was better from my point of view than the previous two, but I did not agree with him.

Wicks then said that he also had the 'political' paragraph, which read as follows:

> I have made a full disclosure to the Prime Minister, who has asked me to continue in my present position as Secretary of State for Trade and Industry.

I thought that was putting a nice gloss on what really happened, but if it was so important to them, they could have it.

Wicks urged me to give my consent to the statement. I was distrustful of the intervention of Cecil's colleagues and asked Wicks if he thought that we really had had the last alterations. He said he was sure we had.

Reluctantly I gave my consent to the statement on the understanding that it went out immediately. Wicks said he would ring Farrer straight away and would let me know when the statement had gone out. I sat in the hall waiting for the telephone to ring. Shortly after eleven o'clock Wicks rang to say that the statement had been given to the Press Association. So the news was out and there was nothing I could do now but take the consequences. It was a relief to have reached that moment at last. I telephoned Flora and told her. We debated whether or not to telephone my father, but knowing that he would have been in bed for some time, we decided that Flora would tell him early the following morning.

Part Four

Propaganda

The storm breaks

6 October 1983

At a quarter to six the next morning I awoke with a start at the sound of loud banging on the front door, followed by incessant ringing of the doorbell. I got out of bed and peeped through the slits in the window blind to see a group of people on the path below and on the pavement just outside the gate. Some were carrying cameras. They were staring up at the house and I stood to one side of the window, nervously staring back and hoping that I was not visible to them.

When I telephoned my father, Flora answered. She said that my father had been awakened in the middle of the night by a call from the *Daily Mail*. She and Roger had also been disturbed by the press during the night and Marksbury was now thick with reporters who were going from house to house trying to obtain information. There were cars parked all along the main road and Winsbury House was beseiged by reporters. They did not remain at the gate, but walked round to the back of the house and tapped on the windows in the vain hope that she or my father would go out and speak to them.

My brother William came over from his home to fend off the more persistent and intrusive reporters, some of whom felt quite at liberty to roam about the garden, presumably hoping to overhear something or sneak a photograph through one of the ground-floor windows. My father had prevented that by drawing all the curtains and shutters. The house has the great advantage of being on a hilltop so that the watchers at the gate were looking up at the windows rather than into them.

To try to put an end to the incessant ringing of the doorbell, William went out and told the waiting reporters that the family would not be commenting on Cecil's statement and that there was no point in waiting. He assured them that I was not there and was not expected, but they continued to wait.

Meanwhile I sat in my bedroom in London, wondering how long it would take the reporters outside to decide they were wasting their time. I had got back into bed and put the radio on to hear Cecil's statement being given as the first item of news. I was hungry, but reluctant to go down to the kitchen in case I was spotted. In any case I had not intended to stay in London for more than one or two nights and had little food in the house. I did not relish the prospect of leaving. By 9.30 am there were so many people outside the house that I was nervous of being jostled as I left. I could imagine the kind of photographs they wanted, to show how pregnant I looked and the state of my emotions. I did not feel I could face it.

Another problem was the telephone. It rang incessantly and I had to wait ages for an opportunity to ring home. As soon as I put the telephone down it would ring again. At one point, thinking it had gone silent at last, I picked it up to make a call to my solicitors only to find someone on the line.

The longer I put off my departure from the house, the less able I felt to deal with the situation outside. In desperation I telephoned a close friend and asked if she could help. I described the scene outside, but she assured me that did not bother her and that I could expect her within half an hour. She also urged me to stay with her for a night or two but I was afraid that I would lead reporters to her house and said that I would go to Marksbury. Although I was nervous about being pursued down the motorway it was preferable to staying where I was and I longed to be in the bosom of my family. I rang Wicks and told him that I was proposing to leave and he said he would come over to be on hand to deal with questions from over-zealous reporters. It was by now nearly lunchtime and we agreed that they would come to the house at around 2 pm.

Just before my visitors arrived, all the reporters outside the house vanished as if someone had sounded an alarm. I couldn't believe my good fortune. Having checked again that the coast was clear, we left immediately. My girlfriend had to go back to work but gave me a key and told me to go to her house and said she would join me that evening. We weren't spotted by reporters as we left, so I was able to get there without being followed. At last I could relax and take stock of what was happening. It was a great relief to have escaped the press and to have some time to prepare myself for their next onslaught.

It was a strange sensation to hear my name on every news bulletin. Elisabeth and Richard's house was shown on the television news with a reporter saying that I was not there, but was believed to have gone into hiding, when I had probably been there at the time they took their film.

I rang Flora who described the scene in Marksbury. The village was still heaving with reporters, their cars and television vans, and there was a substantial gathering of people at the bottom of the drive of Winsbury House, all presumably awaiting my return. Reporters had called at Flora and Roger's house at regular intervals throughout the day and had followed Flora up the lane when she took the children to school and back again when she collected them in the afternoon. She said they must have taken hundreds of photographs of her and the children but that, fortunately, Lucy and Emma seemed oblivious of the cameras and all the attention they were getting. My father had remained indoors, ignoring the ringing of the doorbell and the telephone, except for calls from members of the family, who would let the telephone ring a certain number of times, then hang up and ring again. Later even that was to prove impossible. My father wanted to know whether I was all right and when was I going home. I rang him and said that I thought it would be better for everyone if I stayed where I was for the moment and let the dust settle a bit before I came home. I did not realise then that the press were prepared to camp on his doorstep for weeks and that there was no way I could avoid them if I wanted to go home.

Wicks came to see me at 7.30 that evening and said that he had been inundated with calls from the press who wanted to know where I was. He had said that I was staying with friends and that he did not know when I would go home. They wanted him to let them know when I was likely to reappear. I said that he should tell them nothing and that we would review the situation the next day.

It was not until that evening, when I saw the day's newspapers, that I realised that Cecil's statement had been changed after I had given my agreement to the wording. It appeared that the 'political' paragraph which had exercised the minds of his Cabinet colleagues had been deleted. I checked all the newspapers. Most of them had the statement in full, or with the final paragraph in reported speech. None of them quoted the 'political' paragraph, which we had been told would read:

> I have made a full disclosure to the Prime Minister, who has asked me to continue in my present position as Secretary of State for Trade and Industry.

I wondered why it had been omitted. Was it because Mrs Thatcher knew, from my father's correspondence with her, that Cecil's 'full disclosure' had been made with great reluctance?

The media were in a state of great excitement about Cecil's statement. Almost all the newspapers carried it in full. Most of them also reported a statement made by a spokesman for 10 Downing Street soon afterwards who said that the Prime Minister knew of Mr Parkinson's statement, but took the view that

> This is a private matter. Mr Parkinson is a member of the Cabinet, doing a good job, and the question of resignation does not and will not arise.

There was as yet no editorial comment.

The Downing Street statement showed incredible nerve. How could the Prime Minister insist this was a private matter when she had known since 24 August of the enquiries made by the *Daily Mirror*? From the moment they acquired their information, the matter ceased to be a private one. In any case, even if someone had not tipped them off, there had always been a serious risk of a scandal.

The London *Evening Standard* that day said:

> Rumours of Mr Parkinson's relationship with Miss Keays had been current for some time in Whitehall and the House of Commons. One national newspaper was known to be working on the story, but the first public intimation came in the current issue of the magazine *Private Eye*.

It was interesting that the *Daily Mirror* made no attempt to claim advance knowledge of the story. Was it a bad conscience about their behaviour towards me that made them so unusually modest? I noticed that they had on their front page the picture sneaked by the photographer on that unforgettable evening in August. That was the last time I wore the dress shown in the photograph and in any case I was certain no-one had photographed me since then.

Wicks was reported as saying that the decision to issue the statement so soon after the *Private Eye* piece appeared was 'purely coincidental'. That was rather stretching the point.

Just a 'private matter'

Friday 7 October 1983

It was a great relief to be out of the reach of any reporters and to have time to think about what I should do. I could not impose on my friends indefinitely and sooner or later I had to go either to Marksbury or back to Battersea. I wanted very much to go to Marksbury, but I did not want to cause my family any more distress than they had already suffered. When I telephoned Flora she said that the place was still seething with reporters, so I decided to stay where I was for another night at least. I had promised to ring Wicks, but put it off until I had read the newspapers, a depressing exercise.

It was clear from the newspaper comment on Cecil's statement that the 10 Downing Street spokesman, presumably the Prime Minister's Press Officer, Bernard Ingham, had been hard at work. No doubt he had started preparing the ground before the statement was published. In any event, the pronouncement from 10 Downing Street the previous day seemed to be having the desired effect. If the Prime Minister had known all the facts and regarded it as a strictly 'private' matter, then there was no reason for anyone else to have any doubts.

Under the headline PARKINSON TO RIDE OUT STORM, the *Daily Telegraph* said:

> The Prime Minister and Mr Parkinson ... were determined last night that he should try to survive the disclosure of an affair with his former secretary without having to leave the Government.
>
> Mrs Thatcher made it clear she did not regard it as a matter for dismissal or resignation. ...
>
> The Minister, now reconciled with his wife and family, indicated that he wanted to remain in office unless the situation became intolerably embarrassing for the Prime Minister and the Government.

The fact that the situation was bound to become intolerably embarrassing for us was something that was never mentioned then or at any other time. The *Daily Telegraph* continued:

> The Prime Minister, who had known of Mr Parkinson's situation for some months, took the view that it was a private matter requiring no action from her. Mr Parkinson told Mrs Thatcher about Miss Keays's pregnancy some months ago, although 10 Downing Street and his department would not say exactly when. He offered to resign if she wanted him to. But she said he should stay. There were official denials yesterday of the suspicion that Mr Parkinson's affair had led to Mrs Thatcher's replacing him as Party Chairman last month with the surprising choice of Mr John Selwyn Gummer. Mr Parkinson told a few other Cabinet Ministers about his affair recently. It had been hoped that details would not leak out.

He had told at least one Cabinet colleague, Norman Tebbit, before Polling Day and Ian Gow, then the Prime Minister's PPS, also knew about it in June. I would have thought that the hope that details would not leak out was faint indeed.

It was interesting to see how much information the newspapers were given and how much was being concealed from them. They were being told that the Prime Minister had known 'for some months' but precisely when she had been told was not revealed.

The Times reported:

> Downing Street emphasised again that the Prime Minister viewed the matter as 'private' and it was stated that Mr Parkinson would still be addressing next week's Conservative Party Conference ...

The Times was, as far as I know, the only newspaper to raise the question of security and I wondered whether the idea of mentioning it originated with their reporter or the spokesman for 10 Downing Street.

> The Prime Minister may have been informed of Mr Parkinson's long-standing affair with Miss Keays by either the Home Secretary or the Director-General of the Security Service at the time of the minister's inclusion in the Falklands war cabinet last year ... Neither Downing Street nor the Home Office was willing yesterday to be drawn on the possible security aspects of Mr Parkinson's affair ...

The article went on to quote Lord Denning's report on the Profumo affair in 1963 and said:

> given that Mr Parkinson had access to the most sensitive military and diplomatic information at the time of the Falklands crisis, the Security Service would have had special cause to ensure that the particular circumstances of Mr Parkinson's relationship were understood by the Home Secretary, then Mr William Whitelaw, or by the Prime Minister.

I found the comparison with the Profumo affair most objectionable. In any case, if the Security Services had indeed notified the Home Secretary or the Prime Minister of Cecil's involvement with me throughout the Falklands War, and if they thought I was a security risk, should not something have been done about it? I could have taken comfort from the assumption that they did not regard me as a security risk, if it had not seemed more likely that they did not actually know about our affair.

The Times said:

> The fact that Mr Parkinson's resignation was not required is therefore seen as a measure of Mrs Thatcher's undoubted liking and respect for one of her own inner circle in the cabinet.

The Times was at variance with all the other newspapers I saw in saying that Mr Parkinson had *not* offered his resignation.

The *Daily Mail*'s banner headline asked the important question: WHEN DID MAGGIE KNOW? with the following, by Gordon Greig, Political Editor:

> Was Cecil Parkinson suddenly replaced as Tory chairman last month to avoid an open party scandal and save his political neck? This was the crucial question being asked last night following his disclosure of his love affair with his ex-secretary. If he was, Mrs Thatcher's behaviour towards one of her favourite ministers begins to look more suspect. It is now clear that if Mr Parkinson, the Trade and Industry Secretary, had still been party boss, there would have been no option for him but to resign in disgrace from the post. ... if it is proved that the affair was the motive for Mr Parkinson being switched, then Mrs Thatcher's claim that the case is a personal matter and not a public one could become untenable.

The answer is very definitely that it *was* the likelihood of a scandal that caused his replacement. Cecil had told me in July that he would go to the Conference in October as Party Chairman—he was looking forward to it as the General Election victory meant it would be a celebratory occasion—but that he would stand down soon afterwards.

The Guardian said confidently:

> The Prime Minister knew about the affair Mr Cecil Parkinson was having with his ex-secretary when she replaced him as the chairman of the party. This was confirmed last night by senior Tory sources who were left in no doubt that Mrs Thatcher was anxious to limit the damage Mr Parkinson's affair would do to the party's image as the defender of the family. Mrs Thatcher gave her emphatic support to the Trade and Industry Secretary by making it clear that she would not be expecting his immediate resignation ...

And later in the same article:

> Mr Parkinson is understood to have told the Prime Minister before the summer recess that he wanted to step down from the chairmanship, to reduce the load of carrying two senior posts.

They did not know that he had intended to step down *after* the Conference, not before.

Another article in the *Guardian* carried the interesting remark 'Last night it emerged that the two had never lived together'. I wondered who had inspired this confident assertion? Cecil? Someone at 10 Downing Street? And what difference was it supposed to make? But this remark was nothing in comparison with the extraordinary 'facts', which 'emerged' in the press over the next few days.

I was interested to note that, by the following day, the *Daily Mail* had dropped its question about when the Prime Minister knew and I wondered what had persuaded their Political Editor that it was no longer important. Presumably the determined efforts of the 10 Downing Street spokesman to play the whole thing down.

Why did the *Daily Mail* consider that the scandal would have been greater and that Cecil would have had no option to resign had he still been Party Chairman? Surely a Cabinet post is as important as the chairmanship of a political party?

The *Daily Telegraph* said:

> There were official denials yesterday of the suspicion that Mr Parkinson's affair had led to Mrs Thatcher's replacing him as Party Chairman last month with the surprising choice of Mr John Selwyn Gummer.

The Downing Street 'spokesman' must have been very busy.

The *Daily Express* had an article by their Political Editor, John Warden, which said:

> Shamed Tory Minister Cecil Parkinson last night was ready to ride out the storm over his love child—thanks to the unshakable loyalty of Mrs Thatcher. She has saved his job in the Cabinet; and helped save his marriage to his distressed wife Anne.

Warden's article continued:

> It was revealed that the Prime Minister has shared his secret for months, possibly even since the June General Election. This explains why she resisted pressure for his resignation when the scandal broke yesterday ... Mrs Thatcher had long ago decided to stand by him, and accept whatever damage it might do to the Government ... Many Cabinet colleagues now believe the Prime Minister promoted him in full knowledge of the scandal in his life.

How right they were.

> If so, it confirms that her loyalty to him is of the most special kind.

How special, indeed. I had to keep reminding myself that the press, like everyone else, had been misled and that if they had been in possession of the facts they might have reacted differently.

I noticed that the *Daily Mirror* still had not revealed that they had had the story before anyone else and it gave me some satisfaction to think that, if not actually ashamed of their actions, they were at least worried.

The Times' editor wrote loftily:

> It is only legitimate to discuss the Parkinson affair because Mr Parkinson has made it so. He could have stood pat on the principle that his private life was not the concern of others beyond his family and friends. That would have been a perfectly respectable position and should have commanded respect. He did not. By making a statement in the early hours of yesterday morning he put his private life into the public domain ...
>
> This is unfortunate for a number of reasons. It is unfortunate for his family and for Miss Keay's family ... It is unfortunate because it has inevitably put the Prime Minister and her colleagues on the defensive, over a matter which should be of no concern to the Government.

The Editor of *The Times* was not to know (I assume) that the *Daily Mirror* had set its hounds on me in August and it was likely that the matter would be brought into the public domain from that moment. However, he appears to have overlooked the fact that the *Private Eye* piece had ensured that the matter would be discussed publicly whether Cecil made a statement or not. I assume the Editor of *The Times* would not deny my right to have taken legal action over the *Private Eye* article.

Furthermore, it was not Cecil's statement which put the Prime Minister and her colleagues 'on the defensive', but her decision that he should remain in government.

The Editor of *The Times* then posed the question whether it was necessary for Cecil to reveal those details of his private life. Again it is a question of whether it was preferable that he should be the one to do it, or whether he should have waited for a newspaper to do the job for him.

The Editor went on:

> It is undeniable that it would have been politically more convenient for the Prime Minister if Mr Parkinson had resigned as a result of this accouncement ...
>
> Politically that might have been more convenient, but there was no political necessity for it ... The Prime Minister is a hard political taskmaster but she is a loyal friend, particularly to fellow-politicians

> in personal trouble. In this case her loyalty is assisted by the fact that the episode has in no way impaired Mr Parkinson's ability to carry out his function as Secretary of State for Trade and Industry.

The Prime Minister evidently considered that it had impaired his ability to do the job of Foreign Secretary.

Political necessity and convenience seem to have been the only considerations of importance to politicians and media commentators alike. It did not appear to occur to any of them that the decision that Cecil should remain in office was a selfish one and unnecessary one. Was he really supposed to have been politically indispensable? If he had refused an appointment in Mrs Thatcher's Government in June, he would have spared his family and mine a great deal of suffering and would have emerged, in my opinion, as a more courageous and compassionate person; and he would no doubt have returned to the Government by now.

The editors of *The Times* and other newspapers could be forgiven much of the high-minded nonsense they wrote at that time because they were not in possession of the facts. What I could not forgive was remarks such as that made by the Editor of *The Times* in his final paragraph in which he said 'Mr Parkinson has made a sad and silly blunder'. An affair of twelve years duration—the press knew from Cecil's statement that it had lasted 'a number of years'—can hardly be deemed a blunder, which suggests something casual, even inadvertent. Silly it might have been, but to have been silly for twelve years hardly fits with the Editor's assertion that 'the episode has in no way impaired Mr Parkinson's ability to carry out his function as Secretary of State for Trade and Industry.'

Perhaps it was merely my pregnancy that the Editor of *The Times* thought was a sad and silly blunder. At least he spared me the insult handed out by other newspapers of suggesting that it was arranged by me as a plot to trap my unfortunate lover.

The leader in the *Daily Telegraph* was headed SHE IS RIGHT and began:

> When a senior member of the Cabinet runs into a private difficulty which overnight becomes public property, a heavy burden immediately falls on the Prime Minister of the day.

You would think from this that Cecil's life had otherwise been running without a hitch until he suddenly encountered this problem. He did not 'run into' his 'difficulty'. It had been with him for a long time. Nor was the matter suddenly dumped in the Prime Minister's lap at the time the matter became public property. She had known about it for almost four months and had plenty of time to decide what best to do about it. I presume the Editor had read his own front page on which it said that the Prime Minister 'had known of Mr Parkinson's situation for some months'.

The Prime Minister had not made her decision hastily or, if she had, there had been plenty of time for her to reflect on it and rescind it afterwards. Furthermore, she knew of the impending scandal in August, when Cecil had informed her of the visit I had had from the *Daily Mirror* reporters. She knew of the negotiations between our solicitors. She knew of his promises to marry me and, most important, that there had been no pressure on him to marry me. She knew in September, if not much earlier, of his decision to brerak his promise. It would seem that she condoned, even approved, his behaviour. That, and her lack of consideration for my family, certainly does not square with her professed belief in fairness and straight dealing, or her reputation for compassion.

Be that as it may, the Editor of the *Daily Telegraph* considered that Mrs Thatcher had made 'a sensible assessment' and that 'the hardest and most responsible part in this has fallen to the Prime Minister'; with both of these statements I heartily disagree. The Editor said that 'Her harshest critics could hardly assail her personal integrity'. I dare say he knows Mrs Thatcher a great deal better than I do. I had never been one of her harshest critics: on the contrary I had admired and supported her. I can only judge her integrity in the light of her treatment of me and my family, in which it fell short of the standard accorded to her by the Editor of the *Daily Telegraph*. He concluded his editorial by saying 'She has declared her support for Mr Parkinson and her desire to keep him in her administration. Is anyone else in a very strong position to tell her she is wrong?' I was, as were other members of my family, but we did not.

The *Guardian* editorial said 'There should be no question of Mr Parkinson resigning (now or later) and Mrs Thatcher's quick gesture of support does her credit'.

The *Daily Mail* editorial said:

> This most attractive of politicians has fallen headlong into the trap which lies in wait for every unwary MP and Minister in the corridors of Westminster. The bizarre working hours, the long absences from home, the aphrodisiac of power—these are the notorious perils.

I assume this bilge was written by a man. I find it extraordinary that men should write about themselves in such terms. Are they really so weak and so easily trapped? Do they really consider themselves to be without will and incapable of exercising judgement, and blind to these so-called perils? Or are they perhaps masochists? If men really are so incapable of self-control and judgement in the corridors of Westminster, then how many of them are fit to represent us? I am heartily sick of the portrayal of women as predators and the idea that men are capable of constancy only when the subject of their love is frequently on hand to refresh their memories. If such descriptions are valid, they must apply equally in the reverse. It must be just as often the case that women are beguiled or ensnared by men, as the other way round.

The way the MP's lot is described nowadays, I wonder how men and women in other professions, such as the Armed Forces, who really are obliged to endure long periods of separation, remain married at all.

The *Daily Telegraph* that day carried an article in much the same vein, by Tony Conyers, who said:

> Most experienced MPs will view Mr Parkinson's adultery with his secretary as a lapse brought about by the long arduous hours they are all expected to work ... The many pressures include long hours, all-night sittings, separations from wife and children, and the desire now and then to break away from the claustrophobic world of politics. [Isn't it a wonder that so many men seek careers in politics?]

The *Daily Mail* had an article by Paul Johnson about THE PRIME MINISTER AND HER FALLEN IDOL in which he wrote:

> Margaret Thatcher has every right to feel she has been grievously let down by Cecil Parkinson. [So had a number of other people.] ... he was engaged in conduct which could not be publicly avowed, of which he knew Mrs Thatcher must strongly disapprove, and which ran directly counter to the whole spirit of the mission she had entrusted to him. His behaviour was hypocritical and unworthy of her trust.

In mitigation of this he said:

> ... Cecil Parkinson did not attempt to brazen things out. He did not lie to colleagues, his solicitors and the House of Commons. He did not make his Prime Minister look an idiot, out of touch with life. Obviously up to a certain point, Parkinson hoped to get away with it. More fool he.
>
> But there came a time when he did summon the courage to go to 10 Downing Street, confess the truth to Mrs Thatcher and throw himself on her mercy.
>
> This had the enormous advantage that when the moment came—as was almost inevitable—for the Press to break the story, Mrs Thatcher was prepared, psychologically and in other ways. She had already made her decision and was able to announce it in advance of the screaming headlines.

Some of the credit for that goes to my family for not speaking out publicly about Cecil's behaviour. Contrary to what Paul Johnson and the rest of Fleet Street had been led to believe, Cecil *did* attempt to brazen things out. He had to be made to tell the Prime Minister. If he did not lie to the people Johnson mentions, he certainly lied to me, to my father and to other members of my family. Why? He did not have to say he wanted to marry me in order to be able to tell the Prime Minister of his difficulties, unless he thought she would hold a shotgun to his head and order him to 'do the decent thing'.

Paul Johnson finished his article by saying:

> ... Mrs Thatcher is in the best position to know all the facts and to weigh them and I, for one, am prepared to trust her judgement.

I had trusted her judgement, as indeed had the rest of my family. We do so no longer.

Having depressed myself with the newspapers, I spoke to Wicks and Sweet on the telephone.

Wicks said that they were being bothered with continual requests for information from the press about me, in particular about when I would 'appear in public'. I did not know what to do about it. During the day, I heard references on radio and television to my having 'gone into hiding', which made me sound as if I were guilty of something. I had to make a decision soon whether to go home to Marksbury, or back to Elisabeth and Richard's house, as I could not stay where I was indefinitely. I decided that I would go back to Battersea on Saturday. I could not face the ordeal of being pursued down the motorway to Marksbury and I thought that I would simply draw more reporters to my father's door, where there was already a substantial number waiting. Wicks asked me what I wanted him to tell the media. Should he say that I was going back to the London house? I did not want to attract attention to what I was doing but on the other hand I did not want him to lie to them. I certainly did not want to be portrayed as having some reason to hide. I told Wicks that if he were asked, he could say that I was going back to London on Saturday. Later I was told that the BBC were annoyed that they 'had not been told' when I was going home, as if we had a duty to inform them. They were not told because they did not enquire. ITN knew because they rang Wicks.

I spoke to Flora that evening and she said that she did not think I should be alone in London and that she and Roger would drive up the following morning and accompany me to Battersea. Wicks said that he too would accompany me, to fend off questions from reporters.

'Why Maggie stood by Parkinson'

Saturday 8 October 1983

Flora and Roger duly arrived, followed soon afterwards by Wicks, and we decided on a plan of action. I had to take my car to London and Wicks said that he would follow me in, leave his car north of the river and accompany me to Albert Bridge Road in my car. Flora and Roger would follow us.

When we arrived in Albert Bridge Road, there was no parking space near the house, so that we had to walk some distance. We could see a throng of reporters waiting for us. As we approached, a reporter looked round and spotted us. Immediately there was a stampede towards us, cameras clicking and all of them asking questions at once. We made it to the gate and headed for the steps. I made some non-committal answers to their questions, "No, I would not comment on Cecil's statement", and, "Yes, thank you, I feel fine", and we had made it to the front door. We went downstairs to the kitchen where Roger promptly drew the curtains. He and Flora had brought provisions and we set about getting ourselves some lunch.

We had scarcely sat down when the telephone rang. It was someone from the ITN crew outside who said that unfortunately their microphone had not worked properly and would we mind going out and coming in again, so that they could do a retake? Flora had answered the telephone and said, "Yes, we would mind, very sorry". After all, they had their bit of film and we felt sure they would add words of their own anyway. We took the telephone off the hook, so that we could enjoy our lunch in peace.

Flora then handed me a large bundle of letters which had arrived for me at Winsbury House. They were from relatives and friends wanting to comfort and reassure me. I had not thought about the reaction of people who knew me to Cecil's statement. I had been so preoccupied with getting through the past few days and with everything that had been said by the media, that it came as a shock to realise the effect Cecil's statement must have had on friends and relations. I was even more surprised to find that there were even some letters from total strangers. It was very touching that people who knew nothing about me, except what they had read during the past two days, should want to express their sympathy and should take the trouble to write. I received many such letters over the ensuing months. Later I also received some unpleasant letters, of the 'poison pen' variety, just before and just after the birth of my daughter, so my father and sisters took to opening my mail for me. But the great majority of the letters I received were very kind and I derived much comfort from that. Many were from women who had been similarly let down but who had not had the protection and support of a loving family that I have had.

Amongst the letters that Flora handed me there was one which was in a class apart from the rest. At first glance it looked rather odd, two pages closely typed in capital letters. In any case Wicks was about to leave, so I put the letter on one side to read later.

Wicks asked me what I thought he should say to the waiting reporters as he left. I did not think he should say anything, but he disagreed. He thought that as we had allowed them to know when I was going to Battersea we ought to be prepared to answer some of their questions, although he would not be saying anything about the statement. I said that he could tell them that I was fine, but that I would feel even better if they would go away, but I did not in any circumstances want him to express an opinion on anything that had happened or to appear to be expressing mine.

Flora and I stood in my bedroom and peeped through the bamboo blind to watch Wicks leave. He descended the steps from the front door, followed by Roger, who was going to drive him to where his car was parked, and then they stopped. Wicks had his back to the house, so we couldn't see his face and we couldn't hear a word of what was said. The reporters were clustered round him, cameras clicking, microphones at the ready. Roger was standing slightly behind him. We couldn't see his face either, but could tell he was impatient from the way he was jiggling his car keys in his hand.

I was very anxious about having anyone speak for me or about me. I thought he was spending too long with them. I willed him to leave, but still he lingered. At last we saw the reporters stand aside to let him and Roger through. Flora and I waited anxiously downstairs for Roger to return, so that we could hear what had been said.

To my dismay, it appeared from the reports in the papers the following day that Wicks had taken a rather sentimental line with the press. I don't know why he did not simply say 'No comment' to such questions as whether or not I intended ever to see Cecil again. I never wanted the press to know how I felt or did not feel about anything and certainly did not want anything said which revealed any kind of emotion on my part.

When Roger returned, we ensconced ourselves in the sitting-room, having first drawn the curtains. They remained drawn until I left for Marksbury three days later.

I was glad to be alone at last with Flora and Roger and to have a chance to talk freely about all that had happened over the past few days. We also looked through Saturday's newspapers, some of which reported mounting pressure in the Tory Party for Cecil's resignation, others that the majority of Conservative backbenchers supported his decision to stay.

The *Daily Telegraph*, the *Daily Mail* and the *Daily Express* were supporting the pro-Parkinson line. The *Daily Mail*'s banner headline read WHY MAGGIE STOOD BY PARKINSON. The *Daily Express* front page said IT'S BUSINESS AS USUAL AS PARKINSONS STEP OUT, and the *Daily Telegraph* THATCHER TOLD BY PARKINSON BEFORE ELECTION. Downing Street had succeeded in glossing over what really happened and must have been pleased to see how the story was turning out.

The *Daily Telegraph* said:

> Mrs Thatcher knew about Mr Cecil Parkinson's affair with his former secretary before she promoted him to the post of Secretary for Trade and Industry, Cabinet colleagues revealed yesterday.
> They said Mr Parkinson learned during the General Election campaign that Miss Sara Keays was expecting his child. He offered to resign as Paymaster General and Conservative Party Chairman after the election, but the Prime Minister told him she wanted him to remain, according to other Ministers.

The *Daily Telegraph* article continued:

> Yesterday 10 Downing Street still refused to discuss when Mrs Thatcher first learned of the affair, or when she decided to change the party chairmanship.

Then comes the first mention of a lie which was repeated time and time again in various newspapers, and which was an important part of the propaganda exercise:

> But Cabinet colleagues said Mr Parkinson went to her immediately it was confirmed that Miss Keays was pregnant.

This theme was enlarged in the *Sunday Times* of 16 October and by other newspapers. A key part of the propaganda was the assertion that Cecil did not know that I was definitely pregnant until shortly before he saw the Prime Minister on Polling Day, and that he immediately offered to resign.

I knew that phrases such as 'Cabinet colleagues revealed' and 'according to other ministers' were used to conceal the fact that the information came either from the Prime Minister's aides, or from Cecil himself. Those familiar with Westminster know of the off-the-record briefing of Lobby Correspondents by the Prime Minister's Press Officer and by Ministers themselves and will recognise such phrases for what they are, but I am sure that millions of newspaper readers are regularly taken in.

The *Daily Telegraph* reported that:

> Mrs Thatcher's demonstration of support looked yesterday to be having its desired effect of minimising hostile reaction from the Conservative Party throughout the country.

> Mrs Thatcher and her colleagues yesterday began final preparations for the party conference in Blackpool next week, hoping there would be a rallying-round Mr Parkinson there in recognition of his role in masterminding the Tories' General Election campaign.

The Times had a front page article headed PARKINSON GIVEN OVATION AT DINNER and quoting Ian Gow, the local MP, as praising the 'notable courage of the Secretary of State, who may have wanted to go to ground this week, in fulfilling the engagement which he made several months ago'.

The Guardian said:

> The Prime Minister was told three months ago that Miss Sara Keays, aged 36, was pregnant by Mr Parkinson, aged 52, the Trade and Industry Secretary. She decided that he should give up his post as Chairman of the Conservative Party because it would reflect on the party as a whole, but there was no reason for him to stand down from the Cabinet.

This was further confirmation of the Prime Minister's view that the Party Chairmanship is a more important post than that of a Cabinet Minister.

What none of the press knew was that she had intended to make him Foreign Secretary. Clearly the scandal was too great for a Foreign Secretary to survive, but not for a Trade and Industry Secretary.

Furthermore, it was not three, but nearly four months ago that the Prime Minister had been told. The same article said:

> Mrs Thatcher remains convinced that it would be wrong to sack Mr Parkinson from his government post over an essentially private affair. She is hoping it will blow over during the party conference ... and party workers are expecting a wave of sympathy for Mr Parkinson when he speaks on Thursday ...
>
> Tory backbenchers from all sections of the party were inclined yesterday to give Mr Parkinson the benefit of doubt ...

The *Daily Mail*'s Political Editor, Gordon Greig, had a front page article under the headline WHY MAGGIE STOOD BY PARKINSON. It showed that Mr Greig, too, had been fed a number of lies that were to become an important part of the smear campaign against me and had been told that Cecil had told the Prime Minister on Polling Day that he was *not* going to marry me, and that I had put pressure on him to make a public statement.

The article began:

> Mrs Thatcher did know of Cecil Parkinson's love affair before she gave him a major promotion four months ago.
>
> But she still felt honour-bound to reward the man who, as Chairman of the Conservative Party, had just helped her win the biggest election victory in modern times.
>
> Yesterday, as Mrs Thatcher's anger grew at the way the story has

> backfired, it became known that the two met at Downing Street within hours of the June 9 landslide and discussed the growing crisis inside the Parkinson household ...

The phrase 'it became known' is one of Fleet Street's ways of saying that Lobby Correspondents were being informed, strictly off-the-record, probably by the Prime Minister's Press Officer, Bernard Ingham.

> Mr Parkinson made it clear to the Prime Minister that he had changed his mind about marrying 36-year-old Sara and was going back to patch up life with his family.

This is the reverse of what he told me and my family.

> According to Cabinet insiders, Mrs Thatcher is said to have been happy with this assurance and also with Mr Parkinson's promise that he was making proper provision for Miss Keays and their child.

Mr Greig had dropped the line he had taken only the previous day when he had said:

> ... if it is proved that the affair was the motive for Mr Parkinson being switched then Mrs Thatcher's claim that the case is a personal matter and not a public one could become untenable.

Now he wrote:

> Yesterday, as more details of the long-running affair circulated at Westminster, the Prime Minister's anger at the way the story is developing had reached an incandescent level in private.
> Ministers are desperately hoping it will all blow over before next week's Party Conference ...
> MPs have noted two other points to emerge in the cascade of gossip.
> First Mrs Thatcher moved Mr Parkinson from the Tory chairmanship 24 days ago in an effort to limit the damage. ...
> Second, Mr Parkinson is said to have been under some pressure from Miss Keays to make a public statement about their relationship.
> Although this may not have squared with his own belief and that of the Prime Minister that the affair could be kept private, the announcement late on Wednesday pre-empted the story exploding in the middle of the Party conference with even more fearful repercussions.

Little did Mr Greig and his fellow journalists know that it was Cecil, through his solicitor, who proposed that a statement be made. They had been desperate to get something agreed before Gummer's appointment in Cecil's place as Party Chairman but when they thought they had got away with it and thrown the press off the scent, they went cold on the idea. All I had asked was that he make up his mind whether he would issue a statement on behalf of us both, or leave me to speak for myself.

An article in the *Daily Express* showed that their Political Editor, John Warden, had also been misled by his sources. He had doubtless been talking to the same person as Mr Greig, although his 'facts' differed slightly from those printed in the *Daily Mail*. Under the headline MAGGIE WAS TOLD OF LOVE BABY BEFORE POLL he said:

> Mrs Thatcher knew of Cecil Parkinson's affair with his ex-secretary at the height of the General Election campaign. Mr Parkinson gave her his news before Polling Day ...

This was untrue.

> But Mrs Thatcher threw her powerful weight behind her most loyal supporter, rejected his offer (to resign) and later even promoted him to his present post as Trade Secretary. ... When he did resign as Tory chairman, it was because of the excessive workload in the run-up to next week's Tory Party conference ...

In the evening, I remembered the strange letter which Flora had brought with the bundle of mail from Winsbury House. I read it through carefully with growing unease. The writer described himself as a former mercenary and gave detailed personal information about himself, including his criminal background. He then said that he had been approached on 15 September and asked to undertake a campaign to discredit me by linking my name with those of two MPs in addition to Cecil Parkinson.

I showed the letter to Flora and Roger and we read and re-read it, wondering whether it could really be true. I did not want to believe it, but to dismiss it as a hoax. However, the writer had been very quick off the mark with his letter and was at pains to make me understand that he would not impart any information about the matter to anyone except me, or except on my specific authority, and that he did not wish any kind of benefit, material or otherwise, to accure to him from his approach to me.

I realised that it might be an attempt to draw me out in some way and trick me into some action that would compromise or discredit me. In any case, there was nothing I could do about it then. I felt I had more pressing problems to deal with, not least the reporters who were still waiting outside the house and showed no signs of leaving.

Just a 'warm-blooded man'

Sunday 9 October 1983

The *Sunday Express* had a front page article headed SCANDAL TORY GETS FRESH BACKING which said:

> Mr Cecil Parkinson, the Trade and Industry Secretary, faces the Tory Conference in Blackpool this week confident he can continue his Ministerial career and that he has the support of the vast majority of his colleagues.

It would appear that someone 'close' to 10 Downing Street, or Cecil himself, had inspired this article because it contained the usual references to unnamed 'friends' and to facts that had 'emerged'.

> Friends talk of the large number of messages of understanding received by Mr Parkinson since he cleared an atmosphere of thickening rumour with his dramatic admission about his relationship with his former secretary, Miss Sara Keays.
>
> Their thought is that the Tory Party will respond to Mrs Margaret Thatcher's lead in regarding the matter as entirely private.
>
> It also emerged this weekend that the Prime Minister has not in the least changed her position and her confidence in Mr Parkinson as a valued member of the Cabinet.
>
> The trust between Mrs Thatcher and her Minister is complete, it is said. There is no question of Mr Parkinson being asked to resign and his own suggestions that he should do so have been turned down.
>
> There is also a growing recognition that in taking the course he did Mr Parkinson may well have made the situation more difficult for himself. . . .
>
> The hope among Mr Parkinson's well-wishers is that those who at the moment might be inclined to be critical will come to appreciate that he stood by his family and chose, in the end, to meet matters head-on.

Also on the front page was a photograph of me, underneath which it said that I 'emerged from hiding last night ...'.

The editorial was headed TWO LOYAL LADIES, referring to Mrs Thatcher and Mrs Parkinson, and said:

> Even in the depths of his personal and political misfortune, Mr Cecil Parkinson has two reasons to be profoundly thankful this weekend.
> His wife Ann is standing loyally by him. ...
> His boss Mrs Margaret Thatcher, is standing by him too. ...
> Who then dares to be so smug or so self-righteous as to kick Cecil Parkinson now he is down, when two such remarkable women stand up so bravely for him?

Fleet Street was pulling out all the stops to play the Downing Street tune and drum up support and sympathy for the unfortunate Cecil. The base note that day was played by John Junor in the *Sunday Express* who wrote:

> ...Of course he has brought it all on himself. Like many another warm-blooded man before him he has been a fool. But will I have Women's Lib and the Equal Opportunities Commission on my back if I ask just one question? In this day and age does any 36-year-old lady become pregnant unless she deliberately sets out to do so?

The few voices raised in opposition were faint by comparison. the *Sunday Times* front page headline read TOP TORIES TELL THATCHER: SACK PARKINSON. The article beneath began:

> Senior Conservative MPs are planning to send word to Mrs Thatcher this week demanding the resignation of Cecil Parkinson, the Trade and Industry Secretary. The official line by Government and Party spokesmen is that the question of Parkinson's resignation does not arise, but a cross-section of Tory MPs yesterday insisted that it does—and that it must. Speaking privately, MPs gave clear warning to Mrs Thatcher and Tory Central Office that they regard Parkinson's affair with Miss Sara Keays, and his statement last week, as extremely damaging. They intend to make their views known at this week's Tory conference in Blackpool.

The editorial said:

> ... The Parkinson affair will test Tory tolerance, never generous on moral matters at the best of times, to the limits. ... it is by no means certain that Mr Parkinson has chosen the wisest course. His determination to brave it out will be sorely tested in Blackpool, whatever the displays of public solidarity. His chances of survival are helped by Mrs Thatcher's loyalty to one of her own and very successful ministerial creations. But there are many in the party and the country who think the more honourable course for Mr Parkinson would have

been to have kept his promise, gone for divorce and married his pregnant mistress. Many Tories are also bound to think that he would have done the more decent thing by his party if he had resigned and gone to the backbenches, possibly to return in a few years when the embarrassment has died down. If Mrs Thatcher detects such strong sentiments at Blackpool she may well reconsider her support, and ask Mr Parkinson to go. That would bring the political implications of the affair cleanly to an end. No great political weight should be attached to it ...

The *Observer* had an article on its front page which included a piece by the 'Political staff' who wrote:

> At Blackpool, warm tributes to Mr Parkinson for his work as Tory Party Chairman in the election victory are expected from both the Prime Minister and the new chairman, Mr John Gummer.
>
> The disclosure that Mr Parkinson's offer to resign was rejected by Mrs Thatcher before the election appears to have defused calls in the party for his sacking though a number of MPs believe his Cabinet post is rapidly becoming untenable. ...
>
> But they believe that the Prime Minister's support means that he will be able to ride out the affair despite disquiet in some constituency parties ...
>
> Some Tory backbenchers concede that in the light of the affair it would have been impossible for him to continue as Party Chairman but they argue there is no reason why he should not continue as a senior Minister.
>
> His position has undoubtedly been strengthened by the Prime Minister's willingness to face criticism from her own party for refusing his resignation.

The Editor of the *Observer* was one of the few people to grasp the essentials of the matter:

> ... Even the Prime Minister can hardly expect one firm assertion from her—that the question of Mr Parkinson's resignation 'does not and will not arise'—to dispose of everyone else's doubts on the matter. ... Even more to the point, when exactly did she know? Before Mr Parkinson became Party Chairman? Clearly not. Before she propelled him spectacularly into the Falklands War Cabinet? Probably not. Before she replaced him as Party Chairman with the irreproachable Mr Gummer? Common sense suggests that she must have done. Such questions are not just 'a private matter', especially when they are raised by public statements from Downing Street ... Mrs Thatcher owes it to her Conservative colleagues, at the very least, to come clean about the party chairmanship. Was the timing of the change—too late for inclusion on the printed conference

> agenda—provoked by her sudden knowledge about the affair, or about the baby, or by the fear that it might all leak to *Private Eye*. If so, doesn't it seem rather odd that different standards should apparently be expected of a party functionary than of a Cabinet Minister? And if, as is now commonly assumed, Mr Parkinson has forfeited all chance of ever being Prime Minister, then the nation is, in fact, acquiescing in one code of conduct for a person who heads a Cabinet and another for those who merely sit in it. . . . When all the posturing and moralistic twittering are over, however, there are more important things in life—for Mr Parkinson and those nearest to him, including his unborn child, than whether he sits round a Cabinet table or not.

The *Sunday Telegraph* had a front page headline DOUBTS GROW OVER FUTURE OF PARKINSON. It said:

> Concern was mounting among senior Conservatives last night that Mr Cecil Parkinson might be forced to resign as Secretary of State for Trade and Industry because of continuing dissatisfaction in the party over his affair with his former secretary, Miss Sara Keays.
> Mrs Thatcher's hopes that the matter would quickly blow over were dashed yesterday when Miss Keays appeared in public for the first time since the affair became known last week.

Were they suggesting that the matter would have 'blown over' if I hadn't 'appeared in public'? To have continued to go about my normal life without being seen by the press and photographed would have required a miracle. Interestingly, no-one ever questioned the right of the Parkinsons to appear in public, or the propriety of Cecil's off-the-record briefings of the media.

The article also said:

> Mrs Thatcher's personal support for Mr Parkinson and her desire that he should remain a member of the Government was reaffirmed by Downing Street aides last night. It is also echoed by a number of MPs, including Mr Parkinson's Cabinet colleagues, who argue that difficulties in his private life should not be a cause for resignation.

The Editor of the *Sunday Telegraph* editorial plucked at his readers' heartstrings with:

> The sadness of Mr Parkinson's fall from grace is a reminder to all who live in the public eye that they exercise power only at a price. In his case, the price is exacted in painful publicity for him, and those close to him, over a private disaster. . . . Mr Parkinson's own clouded future can best be left to himself and his Prime Minister: life can be agonising for public figures, and casting the first stone is not a commendable activity.

The *Mail on Sunday* had its readers reaching for their hankies; its front page headlines said: NEW ANGUISH FOR PARKINSON AS LOVER SPEAKS (to give the false impression that I had given interviews to the press) and CECIL IS ON THE BRINK OF QUITTING, above an 'exclusive' article by Peter Simmonds, about whom I shall have more to say later. He wrote:

> An anguished Cecil Parkinson was last night torn between a fervent wish to retire from public life and Mrs Thatcher's insistence that he faces his critics at this week's Tory Party conference. A key factor in Mr Parkinson's continuing doubts over his Cabinet position was the unexpected appearance in public yesterday of his former lover, Sara Keays ... The new burst of publicity has upset his plans for riding out the storm and he is now distraught. Friends fear that the unanticipated new pressure will re-kindle his personal wishes to quit the Cabinet and retire to private life ...

Alongside this article was a photograph of me with the headline SARA PICKS UP LIFE AGAIN and further down another headline SHE'S SO GLAD THE SECRET IS OUT NOW which was in quotes so as to give the impression that it was a remark made by my solicitor. It was said that I had 'emerged from hiding' the previous day. Peter Simmonds' article was continued overleaf and said:

> The new pressure on Mr Parkinson came as newspapers and television reporters gathered ... in Battersea after being alerted to Miss Keays' imminent return.

It was rubbish, of course, but it soon became clear that the media, encouraged no doubt by Downing Street, believed that I was out to embarrass Cecil. The press had not been 'alerted' by me or by anyone else. They had pestered my solicitors who had said quite truthfully that I would be going home on Saturday. In fact I was told later by a neighbour that reporters had called at the house every day so they would have witnessed my arrival whatever Wicks had said.

Simmonds' article continued:

> Miss Keays and her solicitor, Mr Geoffrey Wicks, disappeared into the house, but only after pictures of the pregnant Miss Keays were taken.

This made it sound as if I had wanted to be photographed, whereas I had hurried to the house from my car while the photographers had trotted backwards ahead of me, photographing me from every angle. I did not stop and pose for them.

Simmonds continued:

> Mr Wicks reappeared shortly afterwards and issued what was termed an informal statement.

He did nothing of the kind. He stayed for lunch. The reporters waited outside and he answered some of their questions as he left.

Simmonds promoted the lie that I had broken an agreement not to say anything by the following sentence:

> The issuing of this statement is known to have surprised senior Tories, who had read the initial statement issued by Mr Parkinson on Wednesday which specified that neither he nor Miss Keays nor their families would be prepared to answer further questions.

His statement had indeed said that and we had stuck to it. I had told Wicks that he could, if asked, tell the press that I was well and just wanted to be left in peace and quiet to get through the rest of my pregnancy without further strain. I wondered who gave Simmonds the idea in the first place and who had encouraged him to write such an article.

The other front page article was also continued overleaf and quoted me as saying 'in a faltering voice':

> Neither I nor my family want to comment about what happened. Nothing has changed.

They got the quote almost right, but my voice did not falter, it was nearly drowned out by the barrage of questions from reporters. Then I was alleged to have been asked if I would give my side of the story and to have replied 'I don't think it would be wise'. I was asked no such question and made no such response.

I couldn't help wondering, as I read this rubbish, whether they had actually had a reporter there, or whether they had simply decided what message they wanted to put across and made up a suitable story to convey it.

Peter Simmonds also had a hand in the centre page article headed PUBLIC SMILES, PRIVATE TEARS: HOW FATE FORCED CECIL PARKINSON, THE TORIES' MR CLEAN, TO REVEAL HIS STORMY LOVE AFFAIR.

The entire article was written in an authoritative, knowledgeable tone, to ensure that the reader would not question the accuracy of its 'facts'. It was full of semi-educated guesswork dressed up to look like inside knowledge of the matter. I suppose that Mr Simmonds and his colleagues scraped together whatever information they could from Cecil's 'colleagues', Fleet Street gossip and anyone they could find who would speculate about the affair. Most of it was sentimental and sensationalised rubbish. It began:

> Fate had marked out Wednesday 5 October, as a black day in the calendar of Cecil Parkinson's life. It was the day when his private and public lives were doomed to crash headlong into one another ... Parkinson the politician was a golden man ... He was the most influential and powerful man in Mrs Thatcher's Britain. His destiny seemed [sic] to become the next Prime Minister. Parkinson the private man did not enjoy a life so charmed ... He was troubled by a daughter who took heroin and by his lack of love for a wife who was devoted and loyal. And the woman he did love demanded so much.

For eight years these public and private lives weaved themselves in and out of one another's paths. [Eight years? What were they talking about?] Sara Keays was a young secretary in Westminster when the promising new MP for Enfield arrived in the Commons in 1970. She was 23 when she became his secretary ... [Right at last, but not for long.] Their affair began three years later ... It was a relationship of extremes ... After seven years Sara Keays could stand no more. In 1980 she left the country to let things cool down ... [I went abroad in 1979.]

I could go through the article picking out error after error. There were many like it in other newspapers but this one is a particularly good example of such irresponsible journalism.

Another article on the same page said:

> While the gentleman and his wife are cast in traditional roles, Miss Keays' behaviour is open to interpretation ... the baby arrives at the very end of the affair. ... Ambitious and well-off young women of 36 do not have babies by accident. In the age of the Pill and easily available abortion they choose to have them.

The *Sunday Telegraph* also had a front page headline MISS KEAYS IS 'UNLIKELY' TO SEE PARKINSON and an article with the following about Geoffrey Wicks:

> He said he could not comment on whether Miss Keays felt let down by Mr Parkinson or on what financial provision had been made for her. "Her only interest is to remain well and calm for the sake of the baby."
>
> Asked if Miss Keays had any plans to see Mr Parkinson, Mr Wicks replied: "I certainly wouldn't have thought so".
>
> Later he added: "There is nothing riddled with long-term implications in what I said. I didn't mean she will never ever see him again. I interpreted the question as meaning in the immediate foreseeable future."

The *Observer*, had a photograph of me going home to Albert Bridge Road, with an article underneath headed SARA WON'T WANT TO SEE CECIL AGAIN.

The *Sunday Mirror* had an article which was as infuriating as that by Peter Simmonds in the *Mail on Sunday*. However, whereas Simmonds may have been deliberately misled and have made some genuine errors, I knew that the *Sunday Mirror* piece was at least inspired, if not actually written, by a reporter who had angered my brother William with his offensive and persistent questioning. My brother and his family were badgered daily by reporters, who even tried to extract information from his children. While most reporters would accept that neither William nor his wife were going to speak to them, the man from the

Sunday Mirror who called on them on the Saturday was so persistently rude that William had eventually to tell him in very forceful terms to go away.

Under the headline SARA STILL LOVES HIM—SAYS BROTHER was an 'exclusive' story. I wondered whether these reporters had felt confident that they could write whatever they liked because I was unlikely to defend myself, in view of what Cecil had said at the end of his statement about our not answering questions from the press.

I knew instantly that the report was a fabrication. William, like the rest of the family, never told the press anything, but in any case it was unthinkable that he would have used the words attributed to him. The article began:

> The jilted mistress of Tory Minister Cecil Parkinson is still in love with him, her brother claims. Mr Bill Keays ... said "I think she is besotted by him".

The *Sunday Mirror* also put some extraordinary remarks into the mouth of my solicitor:

> Sara ... was said by her solicitor, Mr Geoffrey Wicks, to have 'taken the publicity very badly'. He went on, 'She is numb with shock and wants a few days' breathing space before deciding what her next move should be'.
>
> Mr Wicks revealed that Sara had made an arrangement with the 52-year-old former Tory Party chairman never to speak out about their affair. He said 'My client signed an agreement not to talk publicly about this business. That agreement was drawn up between ourselves, representing Miss Keays, and Mr Parkinson's solicitors. I am certain Miss Keays has no intention of breaking it.'

I could not imagine Wicks describing me as being 'numb with shock'. While that was merely rather funny, the paragraph about my signing an agreement was a lie that must be exposed. The article went on, under the headline HE TRIED TO COOL THE AFFAIR:

> Unlike Sara, her close relatives and friends have broken their silence ... One close friend of Sara claimed that Mr Parkinson had her transferred to a job at the Common Market HQ in Brussels. The friend said: 'It was an attempt to end his affair, but it didn't work. She was always popping back to London.'

It was a complete fabrication and I felt that these remarks by 'friends' originated with Cecil, or someone close to him. Other papers followed suit and a few days later it was being said in Blackpool at the Conservative Party Conference that Cecil had 'tried to cool the affair' and had sent me to Brussels.

The *Sunday Mirror* editorial was headed WHY DID HE TELL? and asked:

> If it is a private matter, as Mrs Thatcher says, why make a public statement? The paragraphs in *Private Eye* were only a hint. The rest of the press knew, but was silent.

Did the Editor of the *Sunday Mirror* think that it did not matter that the paternity of my baby should be called into question? Other media commentators had said the same thing, that it was not necessary for Cecil to make a statement, that the matter could have been kept quiet. Surely I had a right to defend myself, and my baby? If Cecil had not said anything, I certainly would have done. Even if I had merely sued *Private Eye*, the matter would have come out. In doing so, I would have identified Cecil as the father of my baby. Like everyone else, the Editor of the *Sunday Mirror* looked only at whether it was necessary for Cecil to say anything. My reputation did not matter.

Then there was the bizarre claim by the Editor that 'the rest of the press knew, but was silent'. Oh noble Fleet Street. He overlooked the fact that someone, possibly from the *Daily Mirror*, was determined that the story should get out and therefore gave it to *Private Eye*. The Editor's idea of keeping silent on such a matter presumably means not writing about it in a newspaper, but that it is perfectly acceptable for it to be Fleet Street gossip.

Furthermore, was I really to believe that he was unaware of the activities of the *Daily Mirror* in August when the two papers are run under the same roof by the same publishing company?

Also in the *Sunday Mirror*, was an article by Woodrow Wyatt headed WHY MAGGIE FORGAVE PARKINSON which was about Mrs Thatcher's compassion and loyalty to her friends 'even when they give her problems'. Like so many other people, Wyatt was ready to give us his emphatic views on a matter about which he knew almost nothing. He wrote:

> ... Mr Parkinson could have got a divorce and kept his promise to marry Miss Sara Keays. No-one would have thought the worse of him. ... Finally he decided to stay with his family. Who can say that was not the more honourable course? Yet it is suggested that Mr Parkinson behaved badly in doing so. That is because Miss Keays is about to have his baby. ... Miss Keays is 36 years old. Her affair with Mr Parkinson had been going on for a long time. She must have known the risks of pregnancy.

He could just as well have written: 'Mr Parkinson is 52. His affair with Miss Keays had been going on for a long time. He must have known the risks of pregnancy. Why didn't he leave her alone?' Instead, he went on:

> Lloyd George fathered several illegitimate children. But in his days the Press didn't tell everyone about it. So he became a magnificent war-time Prime Minister. Now every peccadillo of public figures is paraded for our entertainment.

Lucky Lloyd George. He wasn't found out, so his 'peccadillos' didn't matter. He went on to become a 'magnificent' Prime Minister. What happened to the women and their children, I wonder? They do not rate a mention of course.

Woodrow Wyatt's view was just as narrow-minded as that of John Junor of the *Sunday Express*. For them, men who have extra-marital affairs must be treated with indulgence because they are simply 'warm-blooded' chaps who can't help their 'peccadillos'. Theirs are but trifling and forgiveable sins. Women, on the other hand, are expected to be careful, cool-headed and calculating. For the Junors and the Wyatts of this world, it is now the woman's responsiblity to ensure that a baby is not conceived.

If the man has the misfortune to be found out, he will be forgiven his little blunder. The woman, on the other hand, is seen as calculating, even destructive. How dare these people make such assumptions? Or was someone directing their thoughts along this path? Who, for example, had told Fleet Street that the baby had 'arrived at the end of the affair' and that Cecil had 'tried to end' the relationship?

I knew that I could not deal with all the wildly inaccurate things that were being said about me and that, if I tried to refute such lies as they arose, the newspapers concerned would have a field day at my expense. However, I was determined to try to put a stop to the suggestions that I had signed an undertaking, as the *Sunday Mirror* alleged, 'never to speak out' about the matter. I did not believe that Wicks had said this. The disparity between the *Sunday Mirror* report and those of other Sunday papers bore this out. Wicks said that he too was annoyed about the article but that he did not think we should do anything about it. I very much wanted him to refute the allegation. But both he and Sweet advised against it.

Sweet said that they couldn't possibly deal with *all* the press inaccuracies about me. I pointed out that I was not asking them to do that, only to deal with the allegation about an agreement. There was no such agreement and I was determined that that should be clearly understood by the media. I rang him repeatedly that day and pointed out that if we did nothing about the *Sunday Mirror* article, other newspapers would repeat it the following day and the next thing would be an allegation that my silence had been bought. He said that I was attaching too much importance to the matter.

I was under a great strain and the difficulties with my solicitors were the last straw. The press were still waiting outside and we preserved our privacy only by keeping the curtains drawn. It was hard not to feel trapped and harrassed. Late that night Sweet telephoned me to say that they had had a telephone call from the Press Association asking for confirmation of what had been said by the *Sunday Mirror* as a number of papers were likely to carry the story the following day. It was being asked whether the money Cecil was providing was conditional upon my signature of this agreement—in other words, had my silence been bought? Sweet said that they had therefore told the Press Association that there was no truth in the story and that I had not been paid to keep quiet.

I was very relieved, though annoyed that the story had been denied only because the Press Association had asked my solicitors for confirmation. I pointed out to Sweet that what I had feared had in fact been about to happen—that the story had been in circulation that I had been bought off, and that he could have spared me a great deal of anguish and anxiety if he had carried out my instruction earlier in the day. He did not comment. That day marked a significant deterioration in my relations with my solicitors.

Flora and Roger had to return to Marksbury that night and I watched their departure from my darkened bedroom. There was still a crowd of reporters waiting outside and cameras clicked and flashed as Flora and Roger left. The reporters stayed on and it looked as if they were prepared to wait indefinitely. One or two of them started pressing the doorbell again, but it had run down by this time and I had not rewound it, so instead they knocked on the door from time to time. I ignored them and eventually they gave up.

‘The question of resignation does not arise’

Monday 10 October 1983

The knocking on the door began again at around 6 am, as did the telephone calls. Once more I felt obliged to stay at home. My solicitors had said they could not check all the newspapers, so I would have to do it myself and I asked a friend to get them for me. They reported mounting pressure for Cecil’s resignation.

The *Daily Telegraph* had a front page headline GRASS-ROOT ANGER OVER PARKINSON:

> As Conservatives prepared for this week’s party conference, Mrs Thatcher last night remained resolute that Mr Cecil Parkinson, Trade and Industry Secretary, need not resign.
>
> Soundings suggested that her attitude is supported by senior Conservatives, but ‘grass roots’ opinion among constituency party officials showed a weekend swing to the view that Mr Parkinson should go. Some local officials said he should submit his resignation today.

As for Cecil himself, the *Daily Telegraph* reported that:

> friends said he would definitely fight on to remain in office.

In another article, they claimed that:

> On Saturday, Miss Keays’ solicitor, Mr Geoffrey Wicks, issued a statement expressing for the first time his client’s views of the matter.

He did not issue a statement, nor did he express my views on anything. He simply agreed that recent months had been a strain for me and said that I wanted to be left alone for the sake of my baby.

It was yet another example of journalistic error creating ‘facts’ that would be used against me.

The Times had a front page article headed CHANCE OF PARKINSON SURVIVAL DWINDLES which said that ‘more of his colleagues were privately critical of him' and that 'he appeared to be protected only by the Prime Minister's firm support'.

It also said 'A common view yesterday was that Mr Parkinson would survive the Conservative Party conference, which starts at Blackpool tomorrow, and perhaps for some weeks longer ...' However, both Cecil and the Prime Minister were determined he should stay and a further statement was issued by 10 Downing Street. *The Times* reported:

> Downing Street said last night, "There is absolutely no evidence to support the suggestion that Mr Parkinson is about to resign. There is no change in the position. The question of resignation does not arise."

Enormous publicity was given on television and radio as well as in the newspapers, to the fact that he was to be interviewed on Monday evening on BBC Television's *Panorama* programme. This must have been the most widely publicised programme of the entire week. In the *Daily Mail*'s television page it was given top billing in the *Pick of the Day* column.

The Times wrote of the *Panorama* programme:

> His readiness to face, if not to answer, challenging questions was seen last night as evidence that he and the Prime Minister still believe that the present storm will subside ...
>
> It is now known that he told her the full facts for the first time at Downing Street after the polls closed on general election day June 9. [This is not true: he saw her at 4 pm and clearly did not tell her the full facts.] The Prime Minister thanked him for his services as Party Chairman and his role in the campaign and raised the question of his further promotion.
>
> Mr Parkinson said that he could not accept advancement without her knowing that a child was to be born in January to his former secretary and that the whole history was bound to become public. She took her decision to promote him in that knowledge.

I am sure this is untrue. Why otherwise did she react as she did when she received my father's letter the following day, and tell Cecil he could no longer be Foreign Secretary?

The *Guardian* also reported the Downing Street statement. Under a front page headline WHISPERS SPLIT PARTY:

> The ministerial future of Mr Cecil Parkinson hung in the balance last night amid conflicting claims of political pressure for his resignation and public and private expressions of sympathy and support.
>
> Mrs Thatcher reiterated her support for Mr Parkinson last night with a statement which said: "There is absolutely no evidence to support the suggestion that Mr Parkinson is about to resign. There is no change in the position. The question of resignation does not arise."

> His colleagues in the Government, aware of claims of a growing clamour for his resignation, do not believe he will take such a step in the near future . . .
>
> Mr Parkinson will be in a position to make his own intentions clear tonight with his confirmation that he will keep an engagement to be questioned on political matters on BBC Television's *Panorama* programme. He has also agreed that he will answer a question on his private life in the course of the interview with Mr Fred Emery.
>
> The Secretary of State for Trade and Industry seems unlikely to be prepared to discuss his relationship with Miss Sara Keays . . . but he has clearly decided that it is appropriate to acknowledge the situation.

The *Daily Mail*'s banner headline was PARKINSON DEFIES HIS CRITICS, the *Daily Express* had PARKINSON STAYS SAYS MAGGIE, the *Sun*: DEFIANT CECIL TO RIDE OUT SCANDAL.

The attacks on me under the cover of 'friends' of Mr Parkinson 'say' began to appear. The *Daily Mail*'s article by Gordon Greig, Political Editor, was a good example:

> The Cabinet life of Cecil Parkinson was hanging by a thread of goodwill from Mrs Thatcher last night, but he was fighting back against a gathering campaign of whispers which threatened his political future.
>
> He is determined to see his personal crisis through, whatever the critics say, and hold on to his job as Trade Secretary . . .
>
> Tonight he is to be interviewed on BBC Television's *Panorama* programme and doubtless the affair will be raised . . .
>
> Mr Parkinson's friends claim that, given the circumstances, he has acted properly and that politically it would have been easier if he had sought a divorce and married his former secretary instead of withdrawing his offer to do so and remaining with his wife . . .
>
> Mr Parkinson's friends are infuriated that the reports of criticism are coming from Tory supporters who are not prepared to be named. They believe the whispering campaign is being inspired by rivals . . .
>
> Miss Keays had for some time been pressing for their situation to be made public before Mr Parkinson's dramatic statement late last Wednesday night.
>
> On Saturday she further upset the Parkinson family by making a public statement of her own through her solicitor.
>
> Mr Parkinson's friends are also continuing to ask how a 36-year-old woman in this day and age should become pregnant after such a long affair if she did not want to be . . .

I suppose the reader was intended to think that I must have got what I wanted out of the affair, so what did it matter if he broke his promise? Who were these 'friends' I wonder?

> Another problem is that if Mr Parkinson remains in public life, the baby would become a celebrity at birth, but unless the anguish for his family becomes intolerable—or Mrs Thatcher feels she has made a mistake in protecting a favourite who made a fool of himself—then Mr Parkinson is ready to ride the storm.

It never seemed to occur to anyone to wonder what would be the effect on my family of his determination to remain in office.

The editorial in the *Daily Telegraph* was headed CAN YOU FORGIVE HIM? There was no doubt where the Editor's sympathies lay. His editorial was nauseating. Of course, he was not in possession of the facts and I could have forgiven some of the nonsense he wrote, but for his offensive suggestion that the scandal could have been avoided by my having an abortion.

His whole purpose was to persuade his readers that such wrong as Cecil had done was not really so very great, certainly not great enough to justify his resignation.

He began by referring to Cecil's statement as 'unusually candid'. In what way was it 'unusually candid', I wonder? In comparison with other such statements? Had there ever been any? In fact, Cecil's statement was far from candid, omitting as it did such crucial facts as when and how many times he had asked me to marry him.

The Editor then set out to prejudice his readers against me, referring to my return home on Saturday as if I had intended it to provoke newspaper comment:

> The only event of note was Miss Keays's return to London over the weekend. She said almost nothing on that occasion [implying that I had said something about the matter on another occasion] but her photograph provided a useful peg for detailed, if speculative, accounts of the affair in the Sunday papers. More than anything else, this reflected the public's prurient interest in scandalous goings-on among prominent people and the competition among newspapers to satisfy it. That is how scandals feed upon themselves.

It is the media, the press in particular, who display this 'prurient interest'. I was not aware of any members of the public waiting outside my London home, or at my father's house. I was not followed about by members of the public, only by reporters and cameramen. No doubt they all believe that they merely 'reflect' public interest, when, in reality, much of it is actually whipped up and sustained by the media, the press especially.

He continued:

> But we have no reason to regard this process as the considered judgement of public opinion which should impel Mr Parkinson's departure.

Indeed not. How can public opinion be measured, or accurately 'reflected', by any newspaper, or television or radio programme? Having nailed his colours firmly to the Parkinson mast, the Editor tried to persuade his readers to do the same. He set out to do so by refuting the three 'moral judgements' which he said had been 'advanced'.

The first—'the most severe'—was that:

> Mr Parkinson should resign because he committed adultery. We disapprove of adultery. But should it ruin an otherwise unblemished career?

The Editor clearly thought not, saying that such an argument would put an end to other public careers.

It was his next 'argument' that incensed me.

> Then it is said that not the adultery, but the embarrassing fact that it resulted in a pregnancy is the issue. But the moral logic there is that a quiet abortion is greatly to be preferred to a scandal.

In what way could 'logic' be 'moral'? How dare he mention abortion at all, let alone put it forward as an option. The very idea that an abortion could be preferable to a political scandal was shocking. What was almost as outrageous was that the Editor could suggest that it could be an option. Did he believe that an abortion on such grounds would be legal? The Editor's only comment on his extraordinary 'argument' was:

> That hardly seems a moral advance.

The third 'argument' concerned Cecil's broken promise of marriage. The Editor dismissed this as follows:

> Certainly, no such promise should have been given (though it was apparently prompted by genuine feeling rather than a cynical wish to deceive). [How could he presume to know what feelings had prompted it?] But it was right not to keep it. It is a very eccentric morality that a husband's promise to his mistress should take priority over his responsibilities to his wife and children ... Mr Parkinson might have suffered less public opprobrium if he had quietly made the wrong choice. He therefore deserves greater credit for making the right one.

What sophistry. According to this twisted argument, every one of the thousands of married men and women who has fallen in love with someone else and obtained a divorce in order to marry that person, is following a 'very eccentric morality'.

He concluded that:

> Properly understood, then, [what a nice touch—if you did not forgive Cecil as he had done, it was because of your insufficient understanding] the moral argument points to a punishment short of resignation *and that if he did have to resign* Mr Parkinson will have been sacrificed less to morality than to appearances.

To my delight, Elisabeth telephoned me from Muscat that night to say that she was coming home for a few days to be with me and to lend her support to the family. She was catching a flight in a few hours' time and would be with us by eight o'clock the next morning. I proposed that we went to Marksbury soon after her arrival and said that I hoped Roger or William or both of them might come to London to take us home as my departure might be quite difficult, the house still being under siege by reporters.

Late in the afternoon someone calling himself John and claiming to be a friend of mine, telephoned to say that I 'ought to be told that Parkinson had just resigned' and claiming that this information emanated from the Cabinet Office.

Whoever he was, he was a stranger to me and I was suspicious of his 'information'. Of course it was a hoax, as I had suspected, no doubt a reporter hoping to trick me into making some unguarded comment.

In Blackpool, the Party was rallying round the leadership's 'Back Parkinson' campaign. That evening the London *Evening Standard* had an article by Robert Carvel under the headline THE STRAIN BEGINS TO SHOW alongside a photograph of 'grim faced' Mr Parkinson. He wrote:

> Top Tories gathering in Blackpool for their Party Conference made a mighty and well-orchestrated attempt this afternoon to put the lid on the Parkinson scandal. [He referred to John Selwyn Gummer] trying to steady Party morale after the shock waves which hit it in the aftermath of Mr Parkinson's confession that Miss Keays is expecting his baby.
>
> Senior Tory MP Edward Du Cann ... joined in the 'rally round Cecil' move which had the Prime Minister's full backing.
>
> "I give full marks to any man who keeps his family together," said Mr Du Cann. [Why should it be a matter for praise?] "I think there has been too much talk of this affair ..." He added, "The old English vices of hypocrisy and humbug have reigned almost supreme. For the sake of the child that is to come, I think it should stop now."

That, to me, was the ultimate in hypocrisy and humbug. I do not believe Du Cann has ever been concerned about my child.

Panorama programme

Cecil's interview with Fred Emery on the *Panorama* programme was being given star billing by the media. There were frerquent references to it on television and radio throughout the day and it was clearly the hot topic of conversation amonst Tory delegates in Blackpool, the general view being that his television performance would decide his future.

Not surprisingly, I too watched the programme. I thought it contemptible of him to agree to be interviewed when he had said in his statement that neither of us would answer questions from reporters about it. Much was made of the fact that he would not be prepared to talk about his statement, but all the questions and his answers stemmed directly from it. He seemed to think that, provided he did not actually mention me by name, he would have kept to his declared intention of not answering questions on the subject. If it had been the case, as he did his best to convey, that he was bound by an agreement not to answer questions, he should not have appeared on the programme at all and so allowed such questions to be put to him. By allowing them to be asked at all and phrasing his answers in the way that he did, he was able to convey the impression that he had given his word to me that he would say nothing and was therefore maintaining a dignified silence, while what he actually achieved was to underline or subtly alter certain features of that statement.

What he said in that interview, coupled with what he was telling the media in off-the-record, unattributable briefings had a profound effect on their subsequent comment and more important on their attitude to me.

Fred Emery began the interview by appealing to the sympathy of the viewer with "These are difficult times for you, Mr Parkinson."

> EMERY: Let me start by asking you, on the eve of the centenary Tory conference, do you agree that you've done enormous damage to the Party's image?

> PARKINSON: I would agree that, having worked for two years very hard to get the Conservative Government re-elected this event has caused a great deal of disappointment and a great deal of concern

among people. [I wonder precisely what he meant by 'event': our affair? My pregnancy? His statement?]

EMERY: Were you replaced as Chairman of the Party at short notice as a precaution against all this coming out before the conference, because you could hardly have gone there as Chairman?

PARKINSON: No. That wasn't the case ... It had always been understood that I couldn't combine the two jobs and that I would be leaving the chairmanship and a new chairman would be appointed. [Untrue.]

EMERY: The central question is whether you can continue in office now as the overlord of two ministries, trade and industry. Now I know the Prime Minister is backing you but will you continue, or will you resign?

PARKINSON: Yes. I will continue. I intend to continue in office and I've had literally hundreds of letters from people all over the country. I've had over 70 letters from colleagues in Parliament all of them urging me not to resign and I've had 26 letters which have said to me they thought I ought to resign.

EMERY: When did you tell the Prime Minister? Was it before or after the election?

PARKINSON: I am not prepared to discuss that. I have had a number of conversations with the Prime Minister and they remain private conversations between her and me. But I have kept the Prime Minister fully informed. [Now, perhaps, but not at the outset.]

EMERY: But is it true, as the Editor of The Times reported today, that you first told Mrs Thatcher of the facts at Downing Street after the polls closed on General Election day?

PARKINSON: I've just told you that conversations between myself and the Prime Minister are a private matter and I don't propose to discuss when I had them or what I said to her. But she has been fully informed.

EMERY: Did you offer at that time to resign?

PARKINSON: I am not prepared to discuss that.

EMERY: Did you offer at any time to resign?

PARKINSON: I am not prepared to discuss that. That is a matter between myself and the Prime Minister. But I would just make one point, that the Prime Minister appoints all ministers and that if I ever ceased to be an asset and became a liability to the Government and the Prime Minister felt so, then of course I would leave immediately.

EMERY: Given that the Prime Minister decided not to make it public why did you put out a long statement in the middle of the night? Why did you choose four months later to make public what many people would understand was a totally private matter?

PARKINSON: If you read the statement it explains why it was made and it gives the full facts, and ends with the sentence that neither I nor the other person's family intend to make any further statements. I am not free to make any further comments. [His statement did not give the *full* facts and he implied that we were legally bound to silence, which was untrue.]

EMERY: Do you understand when people say that your political campaign was hypocritical?

PARKINSON: I don't accept that at all and in fact I would say that all the actions which the Government has taken since the election have been strictly in accordance with the manifesto.

EMERY: You now face a difficult test at the Party Conference. If there were to be a groundswell of opinion—contrary to the letters that you have mentioned here tonight—that made it difficult perhaps for you to do your job, would you then consider resigning?

PARKINSON: I don't intend to resign and I don't intend to say anything which reinforces the sort of wild stories which were put about at the weekend of me tottering towards resignation. They were written by people who hadn't spoken to me—they were entirely fiction. Of course one of the problems is that the other parties to the statement and myself have kept our words and therefore there has been huge speculation based on nothing.

EMERY: Mr Parkinson, thank you for answering those questions.

It is hard to describe my feelings as I watched the programme. There was no denying that it had taken guts to go through with the interview, but I was sickened that he should have done so and by the gloss he had given to events. The answers he had given to some of the questions were dishonest. I wanted to believe that he had been put up to it, that the Prime Minister had insisted that he go through with it because she had stuck her neck out so far to support him and perhaps that is what happened.

His interview was the principal item of news that night and it was clear from the comment on the interview that it was already having the desired effect.

He had reinforced the Downing Street line that what had happened was private, between him and the Prime Minister. He had stressed that the statement had told the full facts, when it had not, and that he had kept the Prime Minister fully informed. His audience were given the clear impression that he had made a clean breast of things and that the Prime Minister had at all times been fully informed. In refusing to answer the question as to when he had told the Prime Minister and whether he had offered to resign he implied that he was prevented by some agreement with me from answering and, if that were not sufficient, it was a private matter between him and Mrs Thatcher.

He had implied that all that needed to be said on the matter had been said. He had been able to appear to be maintaining a dignified silence on matters which were of no genuine public concern.

There was also lengthy television coverage and analysis of the reaction of Tory delegates at Blackpool, including a discussion on the BBC Newsnight programme. His determination to remain in office received strong support from senior Conservative MPs, Party officials and delegates at Blackpool. As if the performance of du Cann had not been enough, the Party and the media were treated to the unedifying spectacle of Sir Russell Sanderson, Chairman of the National Union of Conservative Associations, diverting attention from questions that could have embarrassed the Prime Minister and the Party by appealing to delegates for sympathy for their 'friend' who had 'fallen on hard times'. He spoke with sadness, as if Cecil had met with some tragic accident. He paraded loyalty to a fellow-member of the Party, which in this instance was synonymous with loyalty to the Party leadership, as their finest ideal.

The Party standing by its friends

Tuesday 11 October 1983

Cecil's Panorama interview had tremendous press and radio coverage the next day. He was praised for his courage and his handling of his 'ordeal'. Much was made of his determination to carry on and the public declarations of support for him by the Party in Blackpool.

I thought over the events of the past four months, of how he had betrayed me, the Prime Minister's role in the matter and her response to my father. I thought of the struggle I had had to ensure that Cecil's statement made any acknowledgement of the true facts, and how, even so, he had managed to gloss over what had happened.

Just as he had been praised for his candour in making that public declaration of his 'problem', now he was being congratulated on his courage for answering questions on television. Certainly it had required nerve, but he did have the full weight of the Downing Street propaganda machine behind him, and it had been softening up public opinion for the past five days. Cecil and the Prime Minister had rewritten the facts ably assisted, albeit unwittingly, by the media. It had taken only five days of fudging to transform him into a noble, even heroic figure, and to portray me as a calculating, scheming woman who had tricked my lover into making me pregnant, who had got what she deserved out of the affair—because after all, if I hadn't really wanted the baby, I could have got rid of it. Such a simple solution.

Roger met Elisabeth at Heathrow and they were with me by about 8.30 am that morning. Elisabeth caused a certain amount of confusion amongst the waiting reporters, some of whom rushed up to her and addressed her as Miss Keays. She was looking remarkably sprightly considering she had had only a couple of hours sleep and a nine hour journey. It was wonderful to see her again and we had a lot to talk about while we waited for William to arrive in the afternoon. He had to get from his home near Shepton Mallet to Bath to catch a train to London and would not be arriving until about three o'clock. Roger too had had a short night and we were a rather tired trio that sat in the kitchen catching up on one another's news. Elisabeth was somewhat behind on developments as English newspapers are at least a day late in Oman.

She had seen for herself the avid group outside the house and Roger described the scenes in Marksbury, which was still crawling with reporters, and the way Flora and he and the children were constantly followed and questioned.

I told her about the Panorama programme and the excruciating remarks made at Blackpool by Sir Russell Sanderson, Du Cann and others; how the Party was standing by its 'friends'. I did not then know what lengths they would go to in order to protect their 'friends'.

The *Daily Mail* had PARKINSON: I WILL NOT QUIT and their Political Editor, Gordon Greig wrote:

> Cecil Parkinson last night faced up to the public ordeal of a live television interview about his affair with his ex-secretary ...
> The immediate reaction from Tories, gathering at Blackpool for their conference, was applause for the dignified and unflinching way Mr Parkinson answered questions about the impact of his domestic crisis on his political career ...
> He could have cancelled or asked for the interview to be recorded, with the right to censor anything harmful.
> Instead, Mr Parkinson chose to confront his problems head on by doing the interview live.

PARKINSON BRAVES TV ORDEAL said the *Daily Telegraph* headline, with the following report:

> Mr Cecil Parkinson, Trade and Industry Secretary, said last night that he would not resign. He made his position clear during his first television interview since he confessed to having had an affair with his former secretary.
> Although he looked pale and appeared to lack the confidence he normally displays on television, Mr Parkinson gave an overall impression of quiet dignity.
> At Blackpool, where Tories were gathering for their annual conference, there was strong support for Mr Parkinson staying in office.

They reported, as did most of the papers, that he had avoided mentioning me by name, although he had come close to it once, and had referred to me as 'the other person'. I had wondered as I watched the programme why he had done this. Was it in the hope that the less my name was mentioned, the sooner it would be forgotten? It seemed an odd way to refer to me when we had had an affair for twelve years, but perhaps it was motivated by the same feeling which prompted him, in answering Emery's question about whether he had damaged the Party's image, to refer to it as 'this event', as if it had been but a fleeting affair.

As I had feared, Cecil's remarks on the *Panorama* programme had caused the re-emergence of the suggestion that some 'deal' or agreement had been made between us and that this was the reason for our refusal to comment.

The *Guardian* front page by their Political Editor, Ian Aitken, contained the following:

> Mr Parkinson seemed to tell Mr Fred Emery, his interviewer, that he had done some kind of deal with Miss Keays. That deal, it appeared, required none of the people involved in the triangular affair to say anything more than had been included in Mr Parkinson's original midnight statement last week.

Mr Aitken then referred to Mr Emery's question as to whether Cecil would change his mind about resigning if there was a groundswell of opinion at the Tory conference suggesting that he should depart.

Mr Parkinson replied:

> "I do not intend to resign, or to say anything to reinforce the wild stories about me tottering towards resignation ... One of the problems is that the other parties to my statement, as well as me, have kept our word and therefore there has been huge speculation based on nothing."

The *Daily Star* said of the *Panorama* interview:

> He said he was unable to talk about the affair. This was taken to mean that legal agreements between his solicitor and Miss Keays's solicitor barred Mr Parkinson from public debate about their relationship.

It was certainly to Cecil's advantage that such a view should gain credence. It meant that he could choose exactly how much he would say on the subject and could plead this 'agreement' if any awkward questions arose. It would also put me in the wrong if I decided I had to say something myself. I had already had such accusations made against me in the press, although I had said nothing.

It was clear from Tuesday's papers that there was a swing away from the previous day's view that his resignation was unavoidable. Now the line he had taken in his *Panorama* interview was widely reported—that he would stay on unless he 'ceased to be an asset' to the Government. It was being heavily reinforced by the Party.

The Political Editors of the *Guardian* and the *Daily Mail* had almost identical paragraphs.

The *Guardian* under the headline TORIES SIT TIGHT ON PARKINSON CRISIS said:

> The Prime Minister and her senior colleagues in the Tory hierarchy have made it clear that they intend to sit on the lid of the Parkinson affair in the belief that it can be held down until the head of steam

> subsides. [But Mrs Thatcher was hedging her bets, it seems, as the article continued] ... Party chiefs are in no doubt that, if the pressure keeps up, Mr Parkinson will eventually have to go.

The *Daily Mail* said:

> But this favourable verdict [for his *Panorama* interview] may not cool down the speculation about his long-term survival.

And later in the same article:

> As Mrs Thatcher arrived in Blackpool, the Party hierarchy was trying hard to put the lid on the Parkinson scandal.

The Times was way out in front of the field with a front-page headline PARKINSON'S AFFAIR COST HIM FOREIGN SECRETARY'S POST. It was said that:

> Mrs Thatcher decided soon after the election not to appoint Mr Parkinson as Foreign Secretary after he had made his position clear.

Reporting from Blackpool, where they presumably received their information, Julian Haviland and Philip Webster wrote:

> Mr Cecil Parkinson would have been Foreign Secretary but for his affair with his former secretary.
>
> It was the post he most wanted, and Mrs Margaret Thatcher gave him a positive indication several weeks before the General Election that he was her preferred choice. She had already resolved to dismiss Mr Francis Pym.

That is exactly what Cecil himself told me early in the election campaign. However, the article went a little awry in the next paragraph, which said:

> The picture changed within an hour or two of the polls closing on June 9, when the Prime Minister and her successful party chairman discussed his future. Mr Parkinson then told her for the first time how he was placed, and her immediate response was that he could not, after all, take over the Foreign and Commonwealth Office.

I wonder who fed this disinformation to *The Times*. Cecil spoke to the Prime Minister at 4 pm, not after the polls closed, but he could not have told her 'how he was placed'. When he rang us later that night it was to express his relief at having spoken to her and his delight that she had asked him to be Foreign Secretary. It was only the next day, when she received my father's letter that she changed her mind, as Cecil told me himself when he rang me from 10 Downing Street.

The Times article also said of the Prime Minister:

> Her determination that Mr Parkinson should not resign or be forced out of office is founded in part on the fact that, in losing the senior and coveted post of Foreign Secretary, he has already paid a high price for his indiscretion.

Yet again, our love affair was being passed off as something trivial, a mere 'indiscretion'.

It was said that not all members of the Cabinet had been aware

> until recently of that sequence of events. But, those who were, appreciate the Prime Minister's staunch support of their colleague, and hope that the Conservative Party will demonstrate that they share that view when the party's annual conference opens in Blackpool today.

Such a story could only have originated with a source very close either to the Prime Minister or to Cecil himself. I wondered how many other reporters were being misled with half-truths and carefully re-arranged facts.

The Times published several letters that day under the heading MR PARKINSON AND THE MORAL ISSUE. One in particular, from Miss Mary Kenny, showed the extent to which many people, herself included, had believed without question the Government's propaganda. She wrote that:

> Mr Cecil Parkinson has behaved with honour and honesty in admitting responsibility for a pregnancy and defending that responsibility.

She suggested that others in similar circumstances had pressed women into having abortions without the public being any the wiser, and said that Cecil, his wife and I should be commended for the 'dignified way in which this very human problem has been faced'. She concluded:

> Men who tell the truth and face their responsibilities are, in my view, far more worthy of public office than men who take the easy way out. I trust Cecil Parkinson more for having done the brave thing.

Also widely reported were the remarks made by Sir Russell Sanderson, Chairman in Blackpool on the eve of the Conference:

> We in this party do not turn out friends just like that even when they go on hard times. It is when hard times come that you know who your friends really are. My reaction from the area chairman is that some people, particularly some sections of the Press, seem to think that because Mr Parkinson has fallen on hard times, and he has, we should all denigrate what has happened and throw him over. That is not the way we do it in this party.

What utter nonsense. Fallen on hard times indeed. Was it our affair or my pregnancy that was to be regarded merely as a tragic accident? Nowhere did I see any sign that this remark had been met with any of the ridicule or contempt it deserved. The party was quite determined to turn me out and to do so in the most underhand and cowardly way possible. But no doubt they have a scale of values for their 'friends'. He was a Cabinet Minister and I was merely a candidate—a fact that was kept very quiet, it being preferable to have me referred to in the press as just 'a secretary', or better still, his 'ex-secretary'.

And since when has the Conservative Party placed a higher value on personal and party loyalty than on public honour, duty and integrity?

It was evident that strenuous efforts were being made in Blackpool to shore up Cecil's position and that a major public relations exercise had been mounted by Party officials and by his colleagues, at the behest of the Prime Minister. Later I was told that she had been appalled by the press reports of a split in the Party and mounting pressure for Cecil's resignation, and that the campaign to save him had been pushed into top gear on the Monday as MPs and delegates began to arrive in Blackpool. The *Panorama* programme had been given the maximum possible build-up and it was hoped that a favourable reaction to it, together with appeals to the loyalty of Party workers, would silence any calls for his resignation.

I did not realise then that the entire Save Parkinson Campaign was dependent on the destruction of my reputation.

Besieged

Tuesday 11 October 1983

I was longing to get away from London. I felt as if I had been cooped up in that house for weeks. It was hateful having to keep the curtains drawn all the time and feeling anxious whenever the telephone rang. We had removed the doorbell altogether, so tired had we become of its incessant ringing. Even so, the waiting reporters knocked on the door regularly and pushed notes through the letterbox, appealing to me to come out on to the doorstep so that they could take photographs of me. They tried various ploys: one note pointed out that it had been raining hard and they were all very wet and miserably cold. If I would come out for just one minute they could take their pictures and could all go home. Another, from a Frenchman representing a Paris news agency, was quite witty and concluded with an appeal for mercy: his editor would assassinate him if he didn't get his story filed within the next hour; wouldn't I take pity on him?

Elisabeth and I packed a couple of suitcases—she had no winter clothes with her and I did not know how long it would be before I could come to London again—and went round locking windows and shutting up the house.

At half past three William arrived and the four of us then planned our departure. It was bad enough to have to face the horde of cameramen waiting outside but I had a horror of being pursued down the motorway, after the episode with the men from the *Daily Mirror*. William was to drive me in my car and the others would follow in Roger's car. We rang my father to tell him we were leaving and he warned us there was still a throng of people waiting at the end of the drive.

I was feeling very nervous. As we were about to leave, it suddenly occurred to me to check what personal letters and papers I had in the house. I went to my desk and hauled everything out and hastily checked round the house for anything else that might be important. Some items I locked in the safe; others I decided to take to Marksbury. I did not have time to make a very thorough check because a lot of my belongings were still in packing cases from the move from Temple West Mews and I could not remember what I had already moved to Marksbury. I did not know then just how thankful I would be a few weeks later that I had made that last-minute check.

At four o'clock we left the house. The reporters rushed forward firing questions at me while cameras clicked from all directions. They wanted to know where I was going and we had decided that we were less likely to be pursued if we told them, so I simply said, "I am going to visit my father".

It took only a few moments to walk to my car but we were totally surrounded all the way and I was amazed to see the reporters pushing and shoving for the best position. One man tripped backwards off the pavement just as we reached the car and others simply squashed him against the vehicle in their desire to get as close to me as possible. They continued to click away even after I had got into the car, pressing their cameras against the windows. It was so idiotic that I would have burst out laughing but for the fact that I knew the press would love to have been able to show me treating it all as a huge joke.

As we drove away I saw the reporters dashing off to the cars and I wondered how many of them would follow us. Elisabeth and Roger were close behind. We had agreed that we would not drive fast, again because I was so nervous about being pursued. By the time we had reached the motorway I had relaxed—we weren't being followed, or so I thought. Then we realised that we had hardly any petrol and signalled to Roger and Elisabeth that we were pulling into Heston service station.

To my chagrin, as William was filling the tank, a car pulled up behind us and a photographer got out. William asked him politely to leave us alone and, surprisingly he did. He only wanted to follow us, he said, did we mind? He was obviously going to follow us whatever we said, but at least he did not come and peer at me as I sat in the car.

We set off again and, sure enough, the photographer stuck close behind. When we pulled out into the fast lane, so did he. William was very good and calmed me with amusing conversation, so that our journey passed pleasantly enough, at least until we left the motorway at the Bath exit. We always take a short cut to Marksbury to avoid going through Bath and as we turned off the Bath road I realised that we were being closely followed by several cars. There was no doubt about it; they were right behind us all the way to Marksbury.

Winsbury House is on a hill, well away from the road and surrounded by trees, but you can see it from some way off. Below it, in a dip in the road there is a lay-by left when the old road was closed and a stretch of dual carriageway built. As we came along the dual carriageway I could see a throng of people at our gateway. My heart sank. Then the bottom of the hill and the lay-by came into view and I could hardly believe my eyes. There were cars parked all the way up the hill to the gateway and a police car and ambulance with blue lights flashing. Someone was being put into the ambulance as we passed.

Then the news-hounds saw us coming and started racing towards the house. We just beat them to it. My father was waiting for us. It had been a close-run thing for him too, he told me later. He had just been down to shut up the hens, thinking we would not arrive for a little while longer, when he heard the hubbub at the gate. He ran back to the house just as we arrived. If he'd been a little slower he would not have been able to get through the throng. We made it into the house just as they reached the door. Flora and the children were in the hall, but we could not stop there because of the glare of television lights shining through the windows of the front door, so we turned out the hall light and went through to the back of the house and into the kitchen. Roger and Elisabeth had got caught in the crush but managed to get into the house a few minutes later.

It was wonderful to be at home again, but so extraordinary to arrive in such circumstances. I noticed that all the shutters and curtains were drawn even at the back of the house, something we do only very rarely, when it is extremely cold. Flora explained that the gentlemen of the press had taken to prowling round the garden and even round to the back of the house, where they would tap on the kitchen window and call out to her.

Just then, she realised her children were missing and rushed out of the room. They were in the hall fascinated by the brilliant lights outside and all the people standing about. I heard Lucy asking her mother why she didn't answer the doorbell. As the days passed the children became somewhat uneasy about these people who followed them about all the time.

Only six days had elapsed since Cecil's statement was published, but the pressure had been on for such a long time that I felt as if we had been living this unreal existence for months. It seemed as if it would just go on and on, a long crescendo of intense emotion.

It was such an enormous relief to be at home and to see my father again. He was wonderful, wanting to comfort me and encourage me. I had all the encouragement I needed just being there with the family. We were all relieved at having run the gauntlet of the reporters and at having succeeded in maintaining our privacy. But it was hard to relax. However, life had to go on as before. William and Roger had given up a day's work to bring Elisabeth and me back to Marksbury and William had yet another journey ahead of him before he would get home. Flora and Roger had to get home to put the children to bed. It had been a very long day for everyone, but we sat in the kitchen and talked for a time, ignoring the doorbell, which continued to ring incessantly. William had spoken to the police outside the house, who explained that the ambulance had been called for a reporter injured in the rush, two cars having collided trying to bag a parking space. My father said that he would have known we had left London even if we had not telephoned. He had loooked out of an upstairs window to see reporters converging on the house as if a signal had gone up.

It was the first time we had had an opportunity for family discussion of the events of the past weeks and the extraordinary things that were being said by the media. We were all angry, my father especially, at the way the matter was being dressed up and at what we were having to endure so that the Prime Minister and her protégé could have their way. But that was nothing to my feelings later that evening when I learned how they were achieving their aim by blackening my reputation. The information came from what journalists would call 'an impeccable source'. Only a very few such trustworthy sources of information have remained available to me and I do not intend to reveal their identities. My informant said he could not be certain who was behind the smear campaign but thought I should know that I was being talked about in the most derogatory and damaging terms at the Party Conference in Blackpool. I was so incensed that I decided I must defend myself and that the only way to do so was by publishing a statement of my own. I made up my mind that night that I would publish the facts, no matter how unpleasant the task. I rang my solicitors and told them. They were vehemently opposed to the idea, but I was insistent that something had to be done and that I must discuss it with them. They agreed to come and see me at four o'clock the following afternoon.

The family urged me not to think about it any more and to go to bed. I was exhausted, as we all were, but found it difficult to sleep; I was so upset and so angry about the lies being circulated in Blackpool.

No end to the attacks

Wednesday 12 October 1983

It was so good to wake up at Marksbury. Even though the newshounds were still at the gate, and at the end of the paddock, peering at the house through binoculars, and the doorbell rang regularly all day, it was much easier to take than in London. The family did their best to make light of it as we sat in the kitchen discussing the day's newspapers. We still had the curtains drawn and talked quietly as we did not put it past some of the people outside to try to eavesdrop on our conversations.

My state of mind was not improved by Wednesday's newspapers. *The Times* had a front page article by Richard Dowden, headed MISS KEAYS NEARLY THE CANDIDATE about the selection of the candidate for the Parliamentary by-election in Bermondsey in February. He came so close to the truth of what had happened, but of course Central Office would have done everything possible to ensure that he did not find out the whole story. Dowden wrote that I had:

> narrowly missed becoming the Conservative parliamentary candidate ... after the local party executive was persuaded to reopen the selection process.
>
> Miss Keays had lost the nomination by one vote to Mr Peter Davis. A week after that selection conference, Mr Robert Mellish, the Labout MP, resigned, and forced a by-election. Mr Davis decided that business commitments prevented him from fighting the by-election and resigned.
>
> Some members of the local party executive, some sources say a majority, wanted Miss Keays to assume the candidature. However, at a meeting of the nine members of the executive on November 2, attended by the party agent, Miss Rose Freeman, and an official from Conservative Central Office, it was decided to go through a full selection process.

Richard Dowden's opening paragraph was correct: the local party executive was indeed 'persuaded' to reopen the selection process. What he did not know was that the persuading was done by no less a person than the Chairman of the Party himself. Richard Dowden's article continued:

> A short list was drawn up with three names: Mr John Maples, Mr Tony Patterson and Mr Robert Hughes. Mr Hughes, the eventual candidate, had been asked to put his name forward by Mr Ian MacLeod, the area party chairman. Miss Keays's name was not on that initial list but was added to it after the party had interviewed between 30 and 40 potential candidates.

My name was *not* added to the list and I wondered who had deliberately misled Dowden. Someone at Central Office, I was sure. Mr Dowden had evidently spoken to Mr Ian MacLeod in Blackpool and no doubt what MacLeod was reported as saying was correct. It was what he had left out that was important: that the Executive had been persuaded not to interview me at all, but to drop me from the reselection altogether.

I longed to put Dowden straight and tell him what had really happened, but I did not, even though he was one of the three people from *The Times* whom I saw the next day. All that mattered then was to put a stop to the lies circulating in Blackpool and being passed to the media.

The newspapers were full of reports of the support given to Cecil by the Party Conference. TORY CONFERENCE BACKS PARKINSON was the *Daily Telegraph*'s headline. *The Guardian* article headed TORIES CHEER ABSENT PARKINSON said that in his absence, he had received 'a spontaneous and prolonged ovation'.

It was said in some papers that only one dissenting voice was heard at the conference, that of Ivor Stanbrook MP, who said that Cecil was 'not only a self-confessed adulterer but also a damn fool' and that he should have insisted on resigning. He had also expressed disapproval of the attempts by the Party to 'rehabilitate' him. The papers reported that Stanbrook's remarks had infuriated the Party leadership and that he had been carpeted by Edward Du Cann.

An article by Lynda Lee-Potter in the *Daily Mail* said of me that I . . .

> could have deliberately got pregnant as the affair drew to a close, determined to establish herself once and for all as the woman in Cecil Parkinson's life.

It was infuriating, but I suppose I should be grateful that she did at least say 'could'. But where did she get the idea that the affair had been drawing to a close?

She also wrote,

> Her arrival at her sister's house, heavily pregnant in front of the hordes of photographers she knew would be there, was possibly deliberate and understandable.

'Possibly', note. It never occurred to her that there was no way I could go home, either to Elizabeth's house or to my father's (my own being at that time uninhabitable) *without* hordes of photographers seeing me.

My family and I could have had unlimited publicity and could have squeezed the last drop of sympathy out of the media and the public, if we had wanted to. We could have appeared in front of the photographers and indulged in public displays of emotion and so have ensured that the public were regularly reminded of our distress. We abhorred the publicity and did everything we could to avoid it and to keep our feelings and our views entirely private. Even so, I was accused of seeking publicity. The only thing that would have satisfied and silenced my critics would have been my total disappearance. There were those, I am sure, who heartily wished I were out of the way permanently.

The same article said:

> Promiscuity in the House of Commons is said to be not only rife but excusable because of the long hours, the onerous job, the unbelievable pressure.

She was writing about 'politicians' but it was galling nevertheless and reminded me of what I had been told the previous evening of the rumours about me.

Even more disgusting was a letter published in the *Guardian* under the heading VARIATIONS ON A THEME OF CECILIAN DEFENCE from a Diana Eden, who described herself as stunningly attractive, 37 years old and entirely without funds. She went on to declare herself willing to provide any Minister of the Crown with proof of his virility (meaning a baby, presumably) in return for 'a desirable country property, a life-long monthly cheque, and an assurance that he will *definitely* remain with his wife'.

I felt that morning that I had taken just about as much as I could stand and I longed to get out of the house and think about something else. I wanted so much to go and see my cottage. When Flora arrived that morning she had told me that the builders needed my decision on certain matters before they could go any further with the alterations and had asked if I would go and see them, but even if I went on foot, by way of the beechwalk, I was bound to be spotted by reporters. In addition to those watching Winsbury house, there were others waiting in the village who also called frequently at the cottage to question the builders. If I was followed about and photographed, I would no doubt be accused of another publicity stunt. I decided to leave it and sent a message to the builders saying that I would call and see them in the next few days.

I concentrated instead on what I should say in my statement and by the time Wicks and Sweet arrived at 4 pm. I had set out the principal points I wanted it to cover. I told them that I was determined to try to put a stop to the allegations that were being made against me and to publish the most important facts concerning Cecil and myself. I explained my reasons at some length and with care, as I knew from their remarks the previous evening that they were opposed to the idea. Even so I was amazed by the vehemence of Sweet's response. Wicks had expressed some sympathy for my feelings but he too was opposed to a statement.

My father and my sisters were present at the time, having come into the room a few minutes earlier to suggest that we all have tea. I glanced at my father and knew that he was shocked by Sweet's response to me. None of us said anything and our silence must have spoken for itself. Sweet elaborated: "You will ruin your reputation and lose any sympathy people might have for you".

Elisabeth, who was sitting next to me, told Sweet that he did not appear to understand what was being done to my reputation already. Sweet then said that he could not discuss the matter with members of my family present and that I would have to ask them to leave. I was inwardly seething. However, I had urgent decisions to make and must set aside such thoughts, so I suggested to my father that it would perhaps be better if they withdrew. When they had gone I told Sweet that I disagreed with his opinion of the consequences of my making a statement, and that it was not sympathy I was looking for, but justice. I told him that I had made up my mind and that I expected him to carry out my instructions. He refused. He said that they would not put out a statement for me. He did not produce a single legal argument against what I proposed. On all other aspects of the matter I considered myself as well qualified to judge the consequences as he and his partner. I decided, therefore, to proceed without them, if need be. I said to them: "it is my decision and it will be my responsibility. I will put out the statement myself and will relieve you of all responsibility for it. But I do need to know whether I may refer as I have to the incident with the *Daily Mirror*." I showed him the passage in my draft. After some argument, I persuaded them to do as I asked, but they said it would take time and they could not let me have an answer until the following day.

I called my father and sisters back into the room and told them what I had proposed. Elisabeth and Flora then produced tea for everyone and they and my father were hospitable and pleasant to Wicks and Sweet. The latter, perhaps to try to make everyone feel better, himself included, proceeded to describe the newspaper men who had been infesting their offices and who hoped that I would succumb to their ever-increasing offers for my story. Way out in front, apparently, was Rupert Murdoch's group. I had told Sweet at the outset that in no circumstances would I sell a story to any paper and I found the continual offers of huge sums of money offensive.

Eventually they left and my father and sisters then gave vent to their feelings. I have rarely seen my father as angry as he was at Sweet's behaviour. He was shocked at their apparent hostility towards me and their refusal to carry out my instructions.

It seemed to me that each day brought a new problem. It was like trying to carry a heavy load up a steep hill strewn with boulders. Not only was it a constant effort, but I was continually encountering difficulties. However, at least I knew now that I would have to write the statement myself and arrange for it to be published, but perhaps that was for the best. I had serious doubts about Wicks and Sweet's ability to deal with the press in any case.

I still had not decided just how to issue the statement, whether I should give it to the Press Association, or to one newspaper only, namely *The Times*. Nor could I decide when to issue it. I had wanted to do so that day, but Wicks and Sweet had rendered that impossible.

I prepare my defence

Thursday 13 October 1983

By Thursday the media and the Conservative Party, at least that part of it represented at Blackpool, had whipped themselves up to a pitch where all they seemed to be able to think about was how Cecil was going to perform when he addressed the Conference that morning. The Parkinson Affair had dominated the news throughout the week. It had been subjected to endless debate, analysis and speculation, to such an extent that it eclipsed all other political issues. Cecil's imminent appearance at the conference had been talked up to an even greater extent than the *Panorama* interview had been, so that, once again, it was not past conduct, but today's performance, on which he would be judged.

However, Thursday's newspapers also reported that the Party leadership was worried that it had gone too far with the 'Back Parkinson' campaign. The *Telegraph* headline said OVER-REACTION TO PARKINSON FEARED. The paper's Political Correspondent reported that some senior Tories had thought the scenes on Tuesday of the party conference applauding tributes to Cecil Parkinson were embarrassing. He went on:

> Mr Parkinson is to make his first appearance before the Conference today and the leadership's hope last night was that constituency representatives would again show him support but, with the wider electorate in mind, not to a degree which could be interpreted as condoning his affair.

They wanted to have it both ways, in other words.

An article in the *Daily Express* headed CECIL'S FAN CLUB WORRIES LEADERS contained the revealing sentence:

> Anxious Tory chiefs were wondering last night if they had been too successful in whipping up support for embattled Cabinet Minister Cecil Parkinson.

They also reported, as did other newspapers, that it was being recognised by the Party leadership that the 'Parkinson problem' would not 'fade away' as they had hoped and that he would find it increasingly difficult in the next few months to keep both his job and 'his credibility', but that 'the decision to quit or carry on will be for him alone'.

So Mrs Thatcher was trying, a little late in the day, to hedge her bets, so that if anything went wrong, the decision not to resign and its subsequent reversal, if it occurred, would be Cecil's responsibility alone.

The media still had Winsbury House 'staked out' and anyone entering or leaving was surrounded and questioned. Flora and Roger could go nowhere without their press escort. Neither Elisabeth nor I had set foot outside the house since our return on Tuesday night. The pressure on all of us was intense and by Thursday my feelings had reached a pitch that I can scarcely describe. The strain I had been living under for weeks seemed just to go on mounting. There was no escape from it. I was afraid of being too introspective, of caring too much about what was happening to me. I knew that the superficial reaction to what I was about to do would be that I had acted out of a desire for revenge. We are supposed to forgive them that trespass against us, but I did not see why I should take whatever they dished out to me and allow them to trample my reputation underfoot. No-one else was going to defend me—other than members of my family who would gladly have done battle on my behalf—even though a number of people in the Conservative Party could have done so. Such is the power of patronage that principle and integrity are outweighed for many by the fear of being passed over. Loyalty to the Party leadership has become their paramount concern.

I was filled with disgust at what was happening in Blackpool. I felt betrayed and I struggled with the thought that Cecil had connived at, or was even responsible for the smear campaign. I could not bear the thought that he could do such a thing and I did not want to believe it. I could not simply cast off the feelings I had had for him for so many years, but I could not escape the thought that he could have protected me, even if he had ceased to love me.

I was sickened by the media comment over the past week. It had been concerned almost entirely with the consequences for him, his family, the Government and the Party. There had been expressions of compassion and support for him. Now he was receiving praise for his courage and sympathy for him in his ordeal. It seemed not to have occurred to a single media commentator, certainly not to any of his colleagues, that he had acted selfishly. No-one had commented on what was being done to me.

It did not apparently occur to anyone that his decision to remain in office and his every action and utterance thenceforth would have repercussions for me and my family. Indeed, his future in office depended very much on us. We were baffled by the Prime Minister's apparent confidence that we would do and say nothing that would damage her. Why should any of us remain silent in the face of the lies that were going the rounds, especially when it had been suggested that my silence had been bought?

I had to try to put a stop to these accusations. For my child's sake as well as my own, I had to refute the rumours that I was promiscuous and had had a casual affair with Cecil.

I also believed, and still do, that as the matter had become the subject of intense public interest and debate, it was important that the truth should be told and the deceptions exposed. However, I was too careful in my choice of words. I pulled my punches, believing that I did not need to describe in detail what had happened, as the reader would already have sufficient information, and misinformation, to draw the appropriate conclusions.

My decision to publish a statement was the hardest I had ever had to take. Having taken it, I was faced with another, equally difficult: how, and even more important, when, was I to publish it?

In spite of all that had happened, I wished to give the Prime Minister the opportunity of distancing herself from the scandal and so reducing the harm to the Party. My father had always believed that we should do everything we could to minimise the scandal for the Government, which was the reason he wrote to the Prime Minister at all, and that it was Cecil's determination to remain in office that had dragged the Prime Minister into the mess. My father maintained that view in spite of the Prime Minister's insufferable response to his letters and her assertions that this was a private and not a public matter—an assertion which depended on his family's ability to resist media pressure and provocation and avoid the publicity attendant on the birth of my child. Looking back on that time, my family's sense of duty and concern for the Prime Minister and the Conservative Party was remarkable. By contrast, those for whom we were concerned appeared to have been motivated by self-interest. Knowing now how they totally disregarded the consequences of their actions for us, I feel great regret that I was not more outspoken.

That Thursday, however, I was agonising over how much I should say and *when* I should say it. I had wanted it over and done with already. Now I could not decide when it should be published. If I gave it to a newspaper that evening, it would appear on the last day of the Party conference, when the Prime Minister was to speak. Should I leave it until the weekend, or the following week? However, having decided to do the deed, I wanted to get it over with as soon as possible and, in any case, the Party had shown scant concern for my suffering.

I spent the greater part of the morning trying to put into words what I wanted to say. Flora and Elisabeth sat with me and from time to time I would read out a passage that I had been struggling with. They sat silently while I typed and then tore up page after page. They did their best to keep me calm, but I felt frantic. To make matters worse, I had tried to ring Wicks and Sweet, but was told that they were not available as they were in a partners' meeting which was expected to last all morning. I thought it extraordinary that they should both be unavailable at such a time, I wondered if they were discussing my intention to issue a statement.

Having drafted my statement, I could do no more until I had spoken to Wicks and Sweet about the point I had raised the previous day. I had to rest for a while and think about something else. I decided to go and see my cottage, something I had not been able to do for weeks, and it was just too bad if I was spotted. I knew that Cecil would be addressing the Party conference about then and I did not want even to think about it. Elisabeth, Flora and Roger came with me. We left by the back door and hurried out through the kitchen garden and into the beechwalk, doing our best to keep out of sight of the watchers at the end of the paddock with their binoculars and telephoto lenses. There were no reporters lurking at the cottage and we got in without being spotted, or so we thought. I spent an enjoyable half hour talking to the builders, though I was somewhat depressed at how slowly work seemed to be progressing. That was partly my fault, of course, for not having been there to approve various things. Then Roger said that we had company. We had either been spotted on our way down, or the reporters had decided to post a guard. There was nothing we could do about it.

There was a little group of them waiting as we left. We ignored their questions and hurried back to the house, but their cameras had clicked away furiously as we passed. Our appearance caused a flurry of interest and the doorbell rang repeatedly during the next hour or two.

When I finally spoke to Sweet I reminded him of our first conversation and the instructions I had given him then. As far as I was concerned, they had not carried them out. It was I who had monitored the press coverage and I who had done virtually all the drafting on my side during the negotiations on Cecil's statement. They had refused to deal with the allegations in the *Sunday Mirror* and had in the end only done as I had asked because the Press Association contacted them. Now they had refused to help me with a statement. I pointed this out to Sweet and reminded him that I was assuming full responsibility for the statement. I said that the very least he could do was to check the point I had raised with him the previous day. He said that they would deal with it when they could and that Wicks would ring me. I reminded him that we had had to take the telephone off the hook because it rang incessantly and we would not speak to the press. Eventually he agreed that I could telephone at the end of the afternoon and Wicks would have an answer for me.

After lunch I worked on my statement again. I still had not decided how to issue it. Should I give it to *The Times*, which might arouse the animosity of other newspapers, or should I give it to the Press Association? If I did the latter, I thought it likely that it would come out garbled, embellished or sensationalised, according to the way the paper concerned wished to present it.

If I decided to contact *The Times* and then failed to reach agreement with them on the form it should take, could I trust them not to talk about it? I did not feel I could trust anyone outside my family. We talked it over at great length and concluded that *The Times* was my best bet. I also thought that, if Wicks and Sweet let me down, *The Times* legal department would also check anything I was doubtful about.

At about six o'clock I telephoned Wicks. I had always got on better with him than with Sweet and was relieved that he did not try again to dissuade me. Nevertheless, there was a distinct chilliness to our conversation. He reassured me that the point I wished to make about being pursued by the *Daily Mirror* in

August was safe. I told him that I had not yet decided when or how I was going to issue the statement, but that I would of course let them know when it was going out.

I sat in the kitchen, thinking. I had to make up my mind whether I was going to contact *The Times* that evening or leave it for another day at least. I was very nervous. The family gathered round and we went through all the considerations once more. I thought suddenly, I can't bear another day of this, I'm going to get it over with.

I rang *The Times* and asked to speak to Richard Dowden. He had written a sensible article about the Bermondsey business. I told him who I was and asked for and received his assurance that whatever I said to him would be in strict confidence. I said that I was thinking of issuing a statement, that I had not made up my mind and that nothing I said to him was to be taken as any kind of undertaking that I would give my statement to them. I said that he would have to come to Marksbury that evening, accompanied by the two most senior members of *The Times* staff available, (he told me that the Editor, Charles Douglas-Home, was in Blackpool) so that any agreement we might make would be final. Half an hour later the arrangements had been confirmed and they were on their way to Marksbury. I had about two hours in which to produce my statement in its final form.

Part Five

In self–defence

My statement to *The Times*

I worded my statement with great care. I wanted it to be as unemotional and as concise as possible, and yet say enough to expose the charade of the past week.

My family had adhered scrupulously to the intention expressed in the final sentence of Cecil's statement not to answer questions from the press, even though it had been suggested by some that Cecil had bought my silence, while others had accused me of seeking publicity and of breaking an agreement with him. No such accusations had been made against Cecil, who had been constantly in the public eye and who had managed to appear to be maintaining a dignified silence on the subject while covertly adding to and embellishing his statement. In addition, his statement had been 'explained' and expanded daily by 10 Downing Street, by his Ministerial colleagues and by Central Office, with information that could only have been supplied by him. I know now that he also spoke to a number of journalists off the record.

He had used the *Panorama* interview, his participation in which had been given an enormous build-up, to encourage the view that he was a man of his word, that he had made a clean breast of things to the Prime Minister and kept her fully informed, and that there was nothing more that needed to be said. He had encouraged the belief that we were legally bound to silence, thus ensuring that I would be accused of acting dishonourably and of breaking a legal undertaking when I issued my statement, while he was able to appear to be maintaining an honourable silence.

The Downing Street statement that this was a strictly private matter was misleading: i) it was liable to become public from the moment the *Mirror* obtained their information; ii) the Downing Street statement was made in full knowledge of the incident with the *Mirror*, Cecil having informed them the following day; iii) even if the *Mirror* had decided never to use the information, I was not going to conceal the identity of my baby's father. I felt very strongly, as I had told Cecil, that the child had a right to know who his or her father was.

Downing Street had strenuously promoted the view that it was not a matter for resignation, that the question of resignation 'does not and will not arise'—in other words the Prime Minister considered that he had done nothing to require his resignation, so why should anyone else. Furthermore, it was repeatedly pointed out that she had known all the facts and it followed that, if she had decided to keep him on in full knowledge of those facts, then the matter could not be so very serious.

Cecil's statement and the disinformation campaign which had followed it had the desired effect of convincing people that he had only once asked me to marry him and that his promise had been given in circumstances in which, as the *Daily Telegraph* had said, it was not right to keep it. It had been alleged that my pregnancy had been an attempt to breathe life into a dead love affair.

The subsequent smokescreen of disinformation had succeeded in diverting attention from the questions which the media had raised at the outset, about what and when he had told the Prime Minister.

His statement had not been 'unusually candid'. Not only had the nature and extent of our relationship been concealed, it had been strenuously denied in off-the-record briefing of the press and had been passed off as a mere 'indiscretion' on his part. I was determined to show that my love affair had not been a casual 'fling', a mere sexual indulgence, and that he had not been 'cooling' the relationship, but had allowed me to believe that he intended to give up his political career and that we would marry.

Of most importance was that my statement should make clear that our baby was the product of a long and loving commitment to one another, and not, as had been alleged, the result of a casual involvement.

I wanted it to be obvious to the Prime Minister that I was holding back important facts about events during the election campaign and in particular on Polling Day and the day after, but was prepared to say more if the lies continued. I knew that much of the information given to the press emanated from sources 'close' to the Prime Minister. She might claim that she had nothing to do with it, that, like Henry II, she had not sent out her knights to do her dirty work for her and that they had translated her thoughts into action against her wishes. Whoever was responsible for the campaign to blacken and discredit me, Mrs Thatcher ought, at the very least, to have had grave misgivings about it. She appeared to have condoned it: a nod is as good as a wink to most journalists.

I debated whether or not to mention that Cecil had put terrible pressure on me to have an abortion. I was sickened by the memory of what he had said, but, in the end, I could not bring myself to refer to it. I thought that he might regret his behaviour later, after the baby was born, and that I should keep from my child the knowledge that his or her father had wished such a thing. Such sensitivity was shown by subsequent events to have been misplaced.

I was disgusted at what had been said on the subject of my pregnancy, that I had tricked him into making me pregnant as a last attempt to get him to leave his wife; that, if I had not wanted to have a baby, I would either have prevented the pregnancy or had an abortion. After what I had been through in May when he had used every kind of emotional blackmail to get me to agree to an abortion, I was revolted by the widespread belief that it had been an option. Not only was the idea abhorrent to me, but there would have been no *legal grounds* for it.

The *Daily Telegraph* and others had suggested that it was not the adultery that was the real cause of scandal, but the fact that it produced a baby. We had broken the Eleventh Commandment: Thou shalt not get found out. This was considered to be *my* fault, it being believed that I should have prevented the pregnancy, or having failed to do that, I should have had an abortion. It followed that it was my doing, not his, that a scandal had burst upon the Government. It also followed from this reasoning, apparently, that I must have wanted to get pregnant and therefore there was no injustice in what had been done to me. The whole of this 'case' had been wrapped up in the lie that he had tried to end the affair, but that I had done everything I could to keep it going and had 'tricked' him into making me pregnant. All the carefree, throwaway talk of abortion disgusted me, as did the recollection of the glib reassurance given by MPs, Cecil included, to constituents who were concerned about the Abortion Act, that it should be 'tightened up' to prevent abuses.

I had protested to Cecil that it was grossly unfair that it should be my refusal to have an abortion that would trigger the scandal, either when my pregnancy became obvious and questions were asked, or after the baby was born. That was why I begged him to tell the Prime Minister and why I hoped that he would not take a job in her new Government, but wait until after the baby was born and any scandal had subsided. That was why I so deeply resented the talk of his courage, his ordeal, and the Prime Minister's compassion , when their selfishness has caused me and my family so much suffering.

There was so much that I could have said that would have been very damaging to both Cecil and the Prime Minister, but I could not bring myself to say it. I wonder if any of those who accused me of being vengeful and vindictive will be honest enough to acknowledge the injustice of their accusations.

I was still not entirely satisfied with my statement when the men from *The Times* arrived soon after ten o'clock that night and I kept them waiting for about a quarter of an hour while I finished it. It read as follows:

> "I agreed for the sake of my family that we would not discuss with the press the statement made by Mr Parkinson last week. I hoped that it would not become necessary for me to say anything. However, I now feel that I have a duty to do so.
>
> On Friday 7 October, *The Times* said that 'Mr Parkinson has made a sad and silly blunder'. Like the Government, the editor believes this should have remained a 'private matter'.
>
> For the *Daily Telegraph* (Monday 10 October) 'the moral logic is that a quiet abortion is greatly to be preferred to a scandal'. I was not aware that political expediency was sufficient grounds for an abortion under the 1967 Act, quite apart from the fact that I could not have contemplated it.
>
> On Monday night, in spite of the understanding expressed in his statement, Mr Parkinson saw fit to answer questions about the matter in a much publicised *Panorama* programme. It appeared from that programme that the Prime Minister had been kept fully

informed and that the statement issued by Mr Parkinson contained the full facts.

The full facts have *not* been made public. Press judgement and public opinion have been influenced by inadequate information, speculation, and the Government's desire to restore Mr Parkinson's position—as someone else put it, to 'rehabilitate' him.

It has been implied:

1. that I tried to trap Mr Parkinson into marriage;
2. that I sought to destroy his reputation; and
3. that the matter should have remained private.

This last presumes that I should hide from public view and declare on the baby's birth certificate 'Father unknown' so casting further doubt on my reputation and denying the child his fundamental right to know the identity of his father.

According to the view expressed in the *Telegraph*, I should have sacrificed my baby's life for Mr Parkinson's career and the Government's reputation.

I wish therefore to make known the following chronology of events:

1. My baby was conceived in a long-standing, loving relationship which I had allowed to continue because I believed in our eventual marriage. It has been suggested that Mr Parkinson only asked me to marry him after I became pregnant, when in fact he first did so in 1979.

2. In May, when I knew of my pregnancy, Mr Parkinson decided he no longer wished to marry me.

I told him that, while I had to accept the fact that he was not going to marry me, I could not deny my baby his right to know the identity of his father.

3. I did, however, implore Mr Parkinson, during May and early June, to inform the Prime Minister because his name and mine were sufficiently linked in political circles for speculation to be inevitable and it was essential that the Prime Minister was made aware of the situation before forming her new Government. He would not agree to this.

4. On polling day, Mr Parkinson sought a reconciliation and asked me to marry him. I gladly accepted. He said that he was about to see the Prime Minister to inform her of our relationship and to tell her that he would be obtaining a divorce in order to marry me. That evening he told me he had so informed her.

He also told other members of my family of his intention. He asked me to give him time to arrange matters and to leave my job at the House of Commons, which I did at the end of June. I and my family assured him of our full co-operation and that we would give him such time as he needed.

5. On 5 August, Mr Parkinson went on holiday abroad with his wife and family, having reassured me of his intention to marry me.

6. On 23 August, I was visited at my London home by reporters from the *Daily Mirror* who demanded to know if it was true that I was pregnant by Mr Parkinson. At that very moment others from the same newspaper called on my father and younger sister.

Later that night, as I was driving a girl friend to her home, I was pursued by two cars which I believed to be driven by reporters from the *Daily Mirror*, who tried to force me to stop and one of their cars collided with mine. I had to take refuge in Rochester Row Police Station.

7. On 24 August, I informed Mr Parkinson, who was still abroad, of the incident with the *Daily Mirror*. I assured him that neither I nor any member of my family had told them anything, but I was concerned that the press would shortly confront him.

He advised me to leave London, which I did, and he said he would speak to me again on his return to England the following week. He gave me no indication that matters between us had in any way changed.

8. On 1 September, Mr Parkinson asked me to meet him secretly at an office in London, where he informed me that he had decided while abroad that he was not going to marry me after all. Later that day I telephoned him to say that I thought it essential that he should inform the Prime Minister.

9. I subsequently instructed solicitors with a view to Mr Parkinson and myself issuing a joint statement. In the ensuing weeks it became clear that other newspapers were pursuing the story and that it was being talked about in political circles.

10. On Wednesday 5 October, when I was informed of what had been published in *Private Eye*, I telephoned Mr Parkinson and told him that if he did not issue the statement which solicitors had been discussing for some weeks, then I would be obliged to defend myself.

Press comment, Government pronouncements, and the continued speculation about this matter have put me in an impossible position. I feel that I have both a public duty and a duty to my family to put the record straight."

If I had known the lengths to which the Party leadership would go in order to shore up the Prime Minister's and Cecil's position, and that they would do so entirely at the expense of my reputation, I would not have been so restrained in my statement. But it was not until some weeks later that I was told the detail of the smear campaign, the nature of the 'information' that was fed to selected editors and political journalists on 'lobby terms', so ensuring that the source of the information could not be revealed, and how similar information was passed to selected Party officials and delegates at Blackpool, the Party Conference being the perfect means of high-speed transmission of gossip and rumour. If I had known what Cecil and his colleagues would say to 'explain' his conduct, I would have held nothing back.

I could have said in my statement that our love affair had lasted nearly twelve years, that it had not begun to fizzle out, as some believed, but terminated abruptly on 2 September. I could have revealed the suffering that he had caused me by pressing me to have an abortion. I could have shown the gloss that his statement had put on the matter. I could have revealed his conversation with my sister, how, when he saw that he would never persuade me to have an abortion, he tried to persuade her to get me to go abroad, that he would provide whatever money it took to enable me to start a new life far away. I could have revealed the extent of his deception, not just of me but of my father. I did not reveal that he had refused to inform the Prime Minister, so that my father was driven to write to her himself.

Perhaps it will be appreciated now just how explicit and how damaging my statement could have been if, as so many people alleged, I had set out 'wilfully' to 'destroy' his career and if, as was also alleged, I had timed it so as to cause the maximum embarrassment and damage. Perhaps it will be realised now that, if I had indeed wished to embarrass the Prime Minister, how easily I could have done so by explosing her role in the matter and publishing my father's correspondence with her.

The Prime Minister has never done anything to redeem herself in my eyes. The campaign against me did not stop. Instead, she gave it her tacit approval with her public support for Cecil as her respected friend and colleague and with her open encouragement of the campaign for his reinstatement in the Cabinet.

Has she never felt any compunction about the consequences of her actions for me and my family? I dare say that some will consider that it is no part of a Prime Minister's function or responsibility to concern herself with such matters. I believe that she took on such a responsibility when she involved herself directly in the matter by questioning the truth of what my father had said and dismissing as irrelevant or unimportant the discrepancies between what he had written to her and what Cecil had told her. Not only did she expect the nation to endorse her very partial judgement of the matter, but she used her Government office and the Conservative Party 'machine' to persuade them to do so.

I walked through to the sitting-room carrying my statement and three carbon copies. My father, Elisabeth and Flora were sitting with our three visitors, who introduced themselves to me: David Flynn, Deputy Executive Editor, David Blake, Home Editor, and Richard Dowden, reporter.

I had been so intent on the writing of my statement that I had given little thought to what I would say to them. I noticed that Richard Dowden had a tape recorder beside him. I said that they were not allowed to make any recording and that I wanted their word of honour that anything I said to them was in strict confidence. Mr Dowden said that the recorder was not switched on and offered me the tape. I explained that I had written a statement, but that I had not decided finally how it was to be published, whether I should give it to them or let all newspapers have it through the Press Association, and that my decision would depend on whether they would agree to my stipulations. I said that I would tell them what I wished to do and that, if I reached an agreement with them, they could publish the statement, but that if at the end of our conversation I was not satisfied that we could proceed, anything I said to them was strictly confidential and was not to be used by them in any way. They gave me their word and I then explained my reasons for issuing the statement. I did not tell them any more than was contained in the statement itself, but explained that the way the matter had been presented so far was incorrect and misleading in certain important respects. I then gave them each a copy of the statement and waited while they read it.

I wanted so much to get it over and done with, but I still had doubts about when it should go out. I explained that, although I was determined to set the record straight, I wanted to do it in such a way as would cause the least embarrassment to the Prime Minister and the Conservative Party. I said that I was reluctant to issue the statement just before the Prime Minister's speech to the Party Conference which would look like a deliberate attempt to embarrass her and that I wondered whether it ought to be postponed, at least until the Saturday. They urged me to set aside such considerations and said that if I was going to issue it at all, whether I gave it to them or not, I should do so straight away.

I had already discussed with the family the possibility that I might somehow be prevented from publishing my side of the story. I decided that I had tried for too long to be considerate of the other parties to the matter and that I would delay no longer. In any case the arrival of *The Times* men had no doubt been noted by the reporters stationed at our gate (they had been there day and night for almost a week), who would have been alerted to the fact that something was about to happen. It remained only to set my conditions. I said that the statement was to be published exactly as it was, in full, without any additions or alterations, on the front page, without any comment and without any additional story about me or my family or the conversation we were now having. They assured me that those conditions would be met and said they would have to telephone their office with instructions to hold the front page. My final stipulation, which they also agreed, was that a copy of the statement should be transmitted to Cecil and to the Prime Minister immediately after it had gone to press, so that they received it before the newspaper was on sale, but too late to able to do anything to stop it.

Richard Dowden then telephoned the statement through to *The Times* from the telephone in the hall while I stood next to him, checking each sentence as he read it out.

At last it was over and I was almost overcome by exhaustion and reaction to the strain of the past two days. It was very late, nearly midnight, but I still had one more thing to do. As I had promised, I telephoned Wicks to let him know that I had given my statement to *The Times*. I also told him that I had asked for copies to be sent to the Prime Minister and Cecil and that they should be receiving them very soon.

I returned to the sitting room to find that Elisabeth had made sandwiches and coffee for everyone. We were all very tired and I was relieved when our visitors left soon afterwards, Richard Dowden having said that he would be staying the night at a hotel in Bath and that he would bring us copies of the newspaper in the morning, as the statement would have been too late for the West Country edition.

Furore

Friday 14 October

I slept well that night for the first time in ages, so much so that Elisabeth came into my room in the morning to see if I was awake, as she thought I ought to know that Cecil had resigned and that I ought also to be aware of what was being said about my statement. I could hear the sound of voices coming from below my bedroom window and she said that there were crowds of people outside the house and the doorbell was ringing almost continuously. I went downstairs to find that my father had closed all the shutters and drawn curtains in those windows which had no shutters. Elisabeth had even hung a cloth over the window in the back door, believing it possible that someone might try to shin over the wall into the yard. Roger and Flora arrived and said that driving through our gateway was now a hazardous undertaking, because there were cars parked along the main road for several hundred yards each side of the gate and that the reporters were blocking the gateway to stop any vehicle coming in, so as to question the occupants. Later they found that it was even more difficult to drive out because the crowd and the parked cars made it impossible to see whether the road was clear.

The circumstances of Cecil's resignation and what I had said in my statement were the subject of frequent television bulletins and endless analysis. The reports from Blackpool included film of Cecil, taken at his hotel in Blackpool, saying "I gave an undertaking and I kept it. Other people can answer for their own behaviour". But there was no 'undertaking', as he very well knew. As for the final paragraph of his statement 'that neither he, nor I, nor any members of our respective families would answer questions about it', it was evident that he, or someone acting on his behalf, had been briefing the press unattributably—on 'lobby terms'—all week.

In no time at all it was being said on television and radio that I had broken an 'undertaking', a 'legal agreement' and my 'word' by issuing my statement. There was a lot of rubbish talked about a 'woman scorned' and my having wreaked my 'revenge' on my former lover, but that was the kind of froth I had expected. The suggestion that I had broken my word of honour or a legal agreement was most objectionable.

Most galling of all was that the media had not picked up the important discrepancy between what they had been told by 10 Downing Street during the past week and what I said in my statement. When Cecil went to see the Prime Minister on Polling Day it was to tell her that he was going to marry me, *not*, as had been put about for the past week, that he had at one time wanted to marry me but had changed his mind.

Was it of no interest to the media that official information on the matter had been deliberately misleading, if not downright dishonest? In fact the media never apparently questioned the official line, or the surprising changes that occurred in it. Soon after my statement was published, the media were being told that what Cecil had told the Prime Minister on Polling Day was that he supposed he would 'have' to marry me and that she had 'advised caution' and had told him to think again.

If he had indeed said that to her, it made his conduct towards me and my father even more despicable and it raised serious questions about the Prime Minister's role in the matter.

As we sat and watched the television reports from Blackpool we heard the roar of an engine outside and peeped out of the back door to see a helicopter circling low overhead. It continued to fly round and round above the house for some time.

Richard Dowden arrived, as promised, with more copies of *The Times* than we could possibly need. He said the scene outside the house was amazing. A little later we saw it ourselves, on television. It was extraordinary to see the house and the mass of reporters in front of it, while we were sitting inside only yards from where they stood. With the pack at the door and the helicopter overhead, we felt as if we were under siege.

Dowden said that he had been asked to do a piece on the state of affairs in Marksbury and asked if he could have permission to bring in a photographer to take a picture of us. I said that he could not. I was determined, as were all the family, that the privacy of our home would not be breached by the media. If it had been possible, I would have preferred to see the men from *The Times* elsewhere, but that was out of the question. I was filled with misgivings about the kind of article Dowden was expected to write, but he assured me that anything I or my family said would be in strict confidence and that all they wanted was a description of the crowd at the gate and the general atmosphere in the village. Having thus reassured me, and given me the telephone number of his hotel in Bath, he left.

My father telephoned the local police and asked if they could do something to enable members of his family to enter and leave the house without difficulty. Chief Inspector John Maggs arrived soon afterwards and came in to see us. He had been besieged with questions from reporters as he arrived and said that they wanted to know if I would speak to them. I asked him to tell them that I would not be leaving the house and that I had nothing to say to them. I knew that they were probably determined to stay, and had no doubt been told to do so. Once again we had the extraordinary experience of seeing the result on our television.

He handled the situation beautifully. As he emerged from the house he was instantly surrounded on the doorstep by a mass of reporters. He told them politely but firmly that I was not coming out and that my father wanted them to leave his property. They duly withdrew to the gate. From that morning, for over a week, we had police officers outside the house. They kept a police car parked on the drive and patrolled the garden regularly, which was very reassuring, particularly at night. Just how necessary the police was for our privacy and peace of mind was proved several days later when most of the reporters appeared to have left and the police were withdrawn. As Flora was about to get into her car to go home at about ten o'clock at night, two men rushed up to her. It was pitch dark and their sudden appearance frightened her. They must have entered the garden as soon as the police left and been lurking near the house. Flora ran back indoors and we telephoned the police, who came straight back and continued their vigil.

The police post on the drive meant that the doorbell rang a little less frequently. Even so, individual reporters would come to the door to try their luck and, to avoid having to go to the door, we established that anyone we wanted to admit would have to ring the bell an agreed number of times. Failing to get a reply to their ringing of the bell, the reporters took to pushing notes through the letter box. I still have these and they are an interesting collection.

Media commentators continued to assert that I had broken a legal agreement and referred to the 'latest statement by Miss Keays'. One reporter had said that I had twice broken the agreement, the first time being when I had 'called reporters' to my home in Battersea. I decided to telephone Wicks and Sweet, thinking that it was time they spoke up for me. It was easier said than done. We had taken the telephone off the hook and buried it under cushions, because the line seemed to be permanently open and we were afraid our conversation would be overheard. When I picked it up to make a call I heard a voice at the other end. It was the operator, saying that the exchange was inundated with complaints that our telephone was out of order and that they had sent an engineer who could not gain admittance to the house. I apologised but said that the telephone was staying off the hook for the time being for reasons which I hoped she would understand. It was exceedingly difficult to make a call because the instant I put the receiver back the telephone would ring, but at last I managed to get through to Wicks at around 2 pm.

He said he was glad I had rung him as they had been deluged with telephone calls from the media and had a large contingent of reporters camped at their offices. He said that he had the *Panorama* people sitting in his office and that they had said they would not leave until he had spoken to me. He continued:

> "Everybody wants to place before you their particular request that you give them an interview. If I were able to say to the press today that you are going to be interviewed on *Panorama* on Monday night, that would effectively scotch everybody else and keep them away."

I thought that was a faint hope and that, far from dissuading others, it would encourage them to think that I might be prepared to give further interviews.

Wicks said:

> "I have had requests for interviews from the BBC, ITN, the *Sunday Times*, *Daily Mail*—the Editor, David English, wants you to know that he would personally handle the interview and would expect it to be conducted in the presence of your solicitors—the *Observer*, *Evening Standard*, and many others. The *News of the World* have indicated their absolute intention of calling on Jack Sweet later this afternoon and can only have one reason and that is a desire to increase their offer."

I said that I was not interested in giving any interviews or selling my story to anyone.

Wicks went on:

> Jack Sweet had Farrer on the telephone this morning, absolutely crimson with rage and he [Sweet] thinks the financial arrangements may well have gone completely up the spout.

Wicks also pointed out that Cecil was on record, on the news, as saying that he was consulting his solicitor about certain 'errors of fact' in my statement. I told Wicks that I was quite prepared to enlarge on my statement if I were driven to it and that he should so inform the press. I also told him that I wanted to scotch the lies that I had broken my word and that I had broken a legal agreement.

I sat down again in front of the television with the rest of the family to watch the Prime Minister's speech to the Party Conference. We were all waiting to see whether she would make any reference to Cecil's resignation and the circumstances in which it had occurred. We were not unduly surprised that there was none.

I still had some anxiety about the article which Richard Dowden was writing for Saturday's *Times*. I tried to reach him at his hotel but he could not be found. Instead, I telephoned Charles Douglas-Home, the Editor. I was apprehensive about telephoning him, being very wary of all newspapermen and reluctant to say anything further to anyone, but it seemed that the attacks on my character were likely to continue and I wanted to be able to defend myself if necessary. If I had to make a further statement, *The Times* was probably the best medium for it. He was most reassuring and promised that he would treat anything that I said to him in strict confidence. I said that I hoped it would not be necessary for me to say anything further, but if I were to make such a statement, I would be happy to give it to *The Times*. He said that would be fine. I then explained that I was anxious about Mr Dowden's story and that I had been unable to get through to him, but I wanted it to be clearly understood that I did not wish *The Times* to print anything in that story that was attributed to me. Mr Douglas-Home said that he quite understood and that if I cared to ring him again later he would check the story with me.

At 7.15 that evening the police posted a note through the letter box to tell me that my solicitor, Mr Sweet, wished to speak to me urgently and would I please telephone him after 10 pm.

At 7.30 pm I telephoned Charles Douglas-Home again and he read me Dowden's article. My fears had been groundless: it was a descriptive piece, and did not report anything that I had said to him earlier in the day.

At frequent intervals throughout the day, letters from television and newspaper reporters had been pushed through the letter box. All had requested interviews. I did not respond to any of them, believing that even the briefest note of refusal would earn comment of some kind.

I realised that I had spent most of the day in the same room, either on the telephone or watching television. My father and Elisabeth had been with me all day and Flora too had been with us whenever she could. The television had an awful kind of fascination for us and we had spent a great deal of time watching it and discussing what we saw. I had a feeling of unreality as I sat there and heard my words repeated and analysed time after time.

A major point of discussion by the media was whether the matter had damaged the Prime Minister. I could imagine the fury being directed at me by members of the Conservative Party and I wondered if they were capable of understanding that the Prime Minister's actions had put me in the position where I could not defend myself without causing embarrassment to the Party.

On the BBC's *Nine O'Clock News* we saw Gummer trying a rearguard action with more references to 'loyalty to friends' and saying that 'what has been a private matter has become a public one'. Did he really believe that? He did not sound at all convincing, but perhaps he thought that if it were said often enough he would eventually believe it himself.

No part of my statement was challenged, except by implication. I heard this, for example:

> His [Cecil's] friends say he strongly disputed Sara Keays' facts but was not going to say anything further in public.

Jim Prior was interviewed and said that he did not think Cecil was wrong not to have resigned earlier and a euro-MP referred to it all as a 'typical bit of British hypocrisy'.

I remembered Sweet's message via the police asking me to ring him and I did so at around 10.30 pm. I said that I had received a message saying that he wanted to speak to me urgently. I did not say that I had thought it surprising, if it was indeed urgent, that he had not wanted me to telephone him until after ten o'clock at night He said:

> "I only want to report a meeting that we had with representatives of the *News of the World*. They want an interview with you with a view to preparing a statement in a 'sympathetic and understanding way' for which they are offering you a quarter of a million pounds. We

said we thought it unlikely you would accept, but we have a duty to inform you of their offer."

I was staggered and at the same time disgusted. I told him that he was right and that I would not give them an interview. I asked him if he had been watching the news on television and what did he think. He replied: "What did I tell you? It's just what I expected". I tried to contain my anger and said, "I am talking about the references to my having broken a legal agreement. What have you done about it?". "There is nothing I can do about it" was his amazing reply. I reminded him of my instructions to Wicks earlier in the day, that they were to tell the press that there was no such agreement and that I would make a further statement if necessary. He said that they could not deal with everything that was said about me. He was openly hostile towards me. I said "Have you done any of the things I have asked you to do?" He said something about thinking that they had done quite a lot for me. I asked whether he was going to carry out my instructions and he said "I told you that you would lose sympathy". I said "I didn't ring up just so that you could say 'I told you so'. I want to know why you haven't done as I asked." He said, "If you are going to talk like that, I don't see how we can go on acting for you".

"Are you withdrawing your services?" I asked. There was a silence. He said that, he did not see how he could go on acting for me. I retorted: "I gave you a simple instruction and you have not carried it out. Now you're saying you can't go on acting for me. Are you withdrawing your services?" Again there was a silence and again I demanded: "I want to know. Are you withdrawing your services?" "Yes, I am. I don't see how we can go on acting for you". I hung up, filled with anger and despair.

When I thought of the continual struggle I had had all through the previous weeks to get Wicks and Sweet to do as I asked and not continually try to persuade me to a different course of action, I felt regret that we had not parted company sooner. Far from helping me they had in the end undermined me. I now had the added anxiety of what the press might make of it if they discovered that my solicitors had backed out. My father reassured me on that score, saying that he thought it extremely unlikely that Iliffes would want it known that they had pulled out as it would look very bad for them. But I was worried, nevertheless, that it would lend weight to the widespread belief that I had broken a legal agreement when I issued my statement. And how was I going to find another solicitor, especially over the weekend? Again my father reassured me by suggesting that I speak to his solicitor, Richard Smerdon, who was a friend of many years standing and would be discretion itself. How I wished that I had consulted him at the outset. But everything had happened so fast and I had not wanted to drag my father into it.

It was too late to ring Richard Smerdon that night and I hoped fervently that he would be at home the following morning. It was also time for Flora once more to run the gauntlet of the waiting reporters on her way home. Having listened for the sound of her car pulling out into the main road, we went wearily to bed.

More propaganda

Saturday 15 October

To my great relief Richard Smerdon was at home when I telephoned in the morning and immediately said he would do whatever he could to put me in touch with a firm of solicitors to deal with my rather unusual problem. He told me not to worry and said that he would make some discreet enquiries over the weekend and let me know what he came up with. I explained about having to leave the telephone off the hook and agreed to ring him again on Sunday. Feeling much reassured, I joined the rest of the family who were sitting in the kitchen drinking coffee and studying the newspapers.

Flora arrived and said that driving up to the house was becoming very nerve-wracking as the reporters had taken to shutting the gate, so that she was trapped for questioning. Having failed to get anything out of her, they eventually opened the gate and let her through. It was unpleasant for her and it could possibly have caused an accident. Roger solved the problem by hammering a hefty iron stake into the drive against the gate, so that no-one would be able to shut it. He told us that the reporters looked as if they expected to be there for some time, as they had kitted themselves out with camp stools and backgammon sets to while away the time. Later they even installed a brazier and litter bin.

Chief Inspector Maggs called to see us again. When he left he again told the reporters, who had remained there all night, that I would not speak to them. Still they waited.

Saturday's newspapers were dominated by reports of Cecil's resignation and comment on it in political circles. Most of them also reported that Cecil had issued a statement the previous evening, through his solicitors, as follows:

> On October 5 I issued through my solicitors a statement which had been agreed with Miss Keays and her advisers.
> In the last paragraph of that statement it was made clear that neither of us nor our respective families would thereafter answer questions concerning it.
> As I remain convinced that it is in no-one's interest that our

> differences should be discussed publicly I do not now propose to say anything further on the matter.

It is noteworthy that this statement did not say that I and my family had given an undertaking that we would say nothing, but the remarks already made by the Parkinsons and others had convinced the media that I had broken an agreement of some kind.

My relief at his announcement that he would say nothing further on the matter was to be short-lived. He had already let it be known that he disputed parts of my statement—he did not disclose which. Over the next few days this was to be done covertly, if not by him personally, then by unidentified friends and colleagues of his. It was also immediately apparent from Saturday's newspapers that my solicitors had failed to carry out my instruction and had done nothing to scotch the lie that I had broken an agreement with Cecil.

The speculation about when Cecil had seen the Prime Minister and what he had told her continued. The information being given out by 10 Downing Street was vague, if not deliberately misleading. The *Daily Telegraph* reported that:

> It was confirmed that Mr Parkinson told the Prime Minister about his affair on the evening of 9 June, General Election day. But she told him he could remain in the Government and two days later, she gave him promotion to Secretary of Trade and Industry as a reward for masterminding the election campaign as party chairman.

They avoided saying precisely when on Polling Day he had spoken to her and of course there was no mention of the fact that she had told him during that conversation that he was to be Foreign Secretary. The *Daily Telegraph* also reported that:

> The Prime Minister's aides still refuse to discuss the question asked by many Conservatives throughout the conference: Exactly when did Mr Parkinson disclose details of his affair and how much did he tell Mrs Thatcher. All that could be established last night was that he had told her sometime before she and he went to Conservative Central office in the early hours of June 10 …

He told her soon after telephoning me at 4 pm on Thursday 9 June, having said to me that he was going immediately to Downing Street and that he was already late for his meeting with her.

The *Daily Telegraph* said:

> The question over Mrs Thatcher's judgement is whether she was right to risk political controversy over Mr Parkinson's affair by giving him Cabinet promotion. But it was not known whether Mr Parkinson had told Mrs Thatcher that he wanted to divorce his wife and marry Miss Keays.

Evidently they did not believe what I had said in my statement—they were always prepared to believe him and the Prime Minister—and had tried to check my facts. The fact is that when he telephoned me later that night to tell me what had transpired at the meeting with Mrs Thatcher, he said that he had told her he would be obtaining a divorce from his wife in order to marry me.

I wondered how many of the Cabinet and other Ministers she had discussed the matter with subsequently. I am sure that she discussed her reply to my father's second letter with some of her colleagues and, no doubt, with one of the Law Officers. Some of the Cabinet must have known, having discussed Cecil's statement with him only hours before it was issued.

Michael Heseltine's comment on Cecil's resignation, according to the newspapers, was "I find it a deeply shattering event . . . I am deeply sad to see him go." When he was asked whether he thought Mrs Thatcher had been wrong not to accept Cecil's resignation at the outset he said:

> "No, I don't think so. I think the Prime Minister is a deeply loyal person to people she believes in and to causes she believes in. She felt it absolutely right to distinguish between the public and the private life approach, and she obviously has the highest regard for Cecil and stood by him as I would have expected her to do."

He also said:

> "I think it was the right judgement and I think that if she had to make it again she would make it the same way."

Mr Heseltine's Cabinet colleague, James Prior, also supported the Prime Minister:

> "I'm deeply sympathetic to the Prime Minister on this. I think she acted as I would have always expected her to act. She has been extremely loyal to her close colleagues and given them all the support she possibly could and, alas, it didn't work out. My sympathy goes out to Mrs Thatcher."

He also said that he hoped Cecil would have the chance to return to office in the future, saying "You can't just ruin a man's life on this sort of thing." But you can ruin a woman's, it seems.

Another Cabinet Minister, Tom King, was reported as saying:

> "The real test of the Prime Minister—and she has shown it on earlier occasions—is the way in which, faced with a challenge and problems, she has surmounted them. She acted very bravely indeed. She obviously felt personal gratitude for the support he had given her and she acted in an equal way."

Edward Du Cann expressed the hope that Cecil would return to the Government, saying "I hope the time will come when he can display his great talents again."

It did not seem to occur to anyone that both the Prime Minister and Cecil had acted selfishly.

There had apparently been widespread criticism of the timing of my statement, which was believed to have been malicious and calculated to cause the maximum damage and embarrassment. I suspect that similar criticisms would have been made whenever I had decided to issue it.

Saturday 15 October 1983

The *Daily Telegraph* went to great lengths to convince everyone that I had misquoted their leading article of the previous Monday, to which I had referred in my statement. The Editor, William Deedes, had written a letter to *The Times*, which was also printed in the *Telegraph* under the heading LEADER MISQUOTED, MORALITY OF ABORTION. He attacked me with the same false logic that he had used in his offensive editorial. He did not address himself, as I had done, to the *legality* of abortion, or rather, in the circumstances in which he mentioned it, to its *illegality*.

I had said in my statement:

> For the *Daily Telegraph* (Monday, October 10) "the moral logic is that a quiet abortion is greatly to be preferred to a scandal." I was not aware that political expediency was sufficient grounds for an abortion under the 1967 Act.

and later,

> According to the view expressed in the *Telegraph*, I should have sacrificed my baby's life for Mr Parkinson's career and the Government's reputation.

Mr Deedes wrote condescendingly:

> While I appreciate that Miss Keays's statement was made under emotional stress, I have to point out that by misreading the argument and then ignoring the last sentence she has drawn and attributed to us a conclusion precisely opposite to what we wrote.

I had done no such thing. His editorial had set out what he called the arguments, one of these being that the scandal could have been avoided if I had had an abortion. If Mr Deedes did not wish to be associated with it, he should not have mentioned it at all, or having done so he should have condemned it. Why did he mention it and, having done so, why did he not condemn it? All he could say was that it was 'hardly a moral advance'.

Not only could there have been no *moral* element to the 'logic' that a 'quiet' abortion would have been preferable to a scandal, an abortion would never have been a legal option. Not by the wildest stretch of the imagination could the need to avoid a scandal, political or otherwise, be considered sufficient grounds for an abortion.

In attacking me, Mr Deedes was careful to avoid that point. It was clear that he recognised its truth, or he would not have been so anxious suddenly to disown the 'argument' he had set out in his editorial. I wonder what exactly he had meant by a 'quiet' abortion anyway.

I had pointed out in my statement that at the time that I became pregnant I had believed Cecil intended to marry me. Mr Deedes ignored that point. If he had considered it, he would have been bound to acknowledge that his editorial had been most objectionable.

Stripped of all its pompous wordiness, what Mr Deedes' editorial boiled down to was that the case of Cecil's resignation rested on three things: the adultery, the fact that it resulted in my pregnancy, and his broken promise of marriage. To prove his case against resignation, Mr Deedes dismissed the first (lots of people do it, so why should Cecil be singled out), and the third (it was wrong to make the promise and right to break it), but did not know how to dismiss the second, except by suggesting that I could have prevented the scandal by having an abortion.

It seemed to me that, rather than holding forth about 'the public's prurient interest in scandalous goings-on among prominent people', the Editor of the *Daily Telegraph* should have reflected on what kind of a society it is which can talk so lightly of the taking of a human life, and treats it as if it were a kind of cosmetic surgery, available to enable 'prominent people' to keep up appearances.

By his own admission, Mr Deedes had had little information to go on other than what he had referred to as Cecil's 'unusually candid statement', but that did not deter him from holding forth on the matter. He had been quick to pass judgement on a matter about which he knew almost nothing, but showed no similar readiness to admit his error when given the facts. His editorial on Saturday showed that he had disregarded my statement and was sticking to his guns:

> ... We said at the outset that when a situation of this kind arises, a very heavy burden falls on the Prime Minister; adding that, while excitability might sweep events out of control, Mrs Thatcher was right in her first difficult judgement on the facts before her. We hold to that ... If she erred in this matter, it was not an uncompassionate error.

It was a singularly uncompassionate error, but Mr Deedes evidently believed that Mrs Thatcher did not know the whole story when she made her first 'difficult judgement'. In fairness to him, he could not have known that she had made her decision in full knowledge of all the facts and in total disregard of what my father had told her.

The *Daily Telegraph* did not content themselves with their criticisms of me that Saturday, but repeated them on various occasions, claiming that they had 'poured scorn' on the idea of an abortion. They also boasted that they had persuaded the BBC to excise from the recording of the *Any Questions* radio programme of Friday 14 October an answer given by Mrs Shirley Williams in which she referred to my statement. On what grounds the *Daily Telegraph* sought to censor Mrs Williams' remarks I do not know, but I was amazed that the BBC should have co-operated with them. Those champions of free speech at the BBC, who guard their own rights so jealously, were quite willing to censor my words. Could anyone imagine the BBC doing for me what they had done for the *Daily Telegraph* and deleting something from a programme just because I did not happen to like it?

The *Daily Star*'s comment on the matter appeared under the headline: HELL HATH NO FURY. They wrote:

> By issuing a long and detailed timetable of their affair, Sara Keays yesterday made certain that Cecil Parkinson had to go now ... her intervention could not have come at a worse time for Mr Parkinson. Her motives are her own affair. No doubt she feels she has much to be bitter about. But of all the characters in this sorry story, she may seem to be the least sympathetic.

I was not looking for their sympathy. Nor had I given a long and detailed timetable of our affair—I had dealt with events of the past five months.

Another article in the *Daily Star* quoted Edward Du Cann as saying of my statement:

> I think everybody was very surprised to hear it. I just hope it wasn't calculated to do damage.

What his Party had done had been calculated to do damage to me.

The *Daily Mail* had a long article by Gordon Greig and others. Headed THE END OF THE AFFAIR it began with a reference to Cecil being left with the 'ashes' of a Ministerial career and a 'love affair that went sour'. I'd like to know in what way it went sour. He had ended it abruptly. It had not slowly decayed. There were other headlines overleaf DARK HOURS ... AND A DESOLATE DAWN, THEY SMUGGLED PARKINSON OUT A BROKEN MAN and SARA SAW HIM ON TV, THEN DECIDED TO ACT. How could they presume to know whether I had watched television? It was clear that they too believed that my action had been that of the 'woman scorned' who sought revenge on her former lover.

> All over Blackpool as the news spread, the Tories, whether they were Cabinet Ministers, MPs or delegates from the farthermost shires, discussed the news. In the end, most of their views came down to the same thing—summed up by the Government Whip in the House of Lords, Baroness Trumpington, "I am not suprised at what has happened," she said. "After all, Hell hath no fury ..."

They reported that Cecil 'disputed much of Miss Keays' version of events' and quoted his reaction to my statement: "I gave an undertaking and I kept it. Other people can answer for their own behaviour".

Referring to Cecil's belief during the past week that he could 'ride out the storm', they said:

> But it was now becoming a media event. Sara Keays retaliated by appearing before photographers in bright and flowing maternity clothes. And the speculation mounted. Could Parkinson survive? ... The newspapers and TV were generally of the opinion that he could and, even more important, that he should.

As I have said earlier, Fleet Street can create myths simply by repetition of their 'facts'. It was now widely believed that I had invited the press to come and take photographs of me at Albert Bridge Road. I had hardly set foot outside my house yet I was accused by almost all the newspapers at one time or another of seeking publicity.

The *Daily Mail* continued:

> Just at the time his speech was on live at Blackpool, Miss Keays, deliberately it seemed, had left her father's house to walk to the cottage being converted for her and the baby. But she certainly saw an early-evening news bulletin.

Of course I went deliberately. I would hardly have walked there by accident.

> So, as the Parkinsons drank their champagne with their friends at McAlpine's party, Sara Keays began to work with senior *Times* executives who had come to the house to prepare the statement which would bring about the end of Cecil Parkinson's ministerial career.

I had not worked with the men from *The Times*. I had written the statement myself.

> It was a devastating and detailed account of their love affair and it differed from Parkinson's account in many ways.

The *Daily Mail* also said:

> Mr Parkinson is consulting his lawyers about answering her new allegations.

New? Apparently they too believed that I had said something already about the matter before I issued my statement.

The *Daily Mail* leader was headed THE REVENGER'S TRAGEDY and said:

> ... Easy now with hindsight to say that Mr Parkinson should have insisted on quitting more than a week ago. But he did not ...

Should he not have insisted on resigning in June?

> He has been destroyed by his own vacillation and by 'the woman scorned'. A politician has been broken to balance the broken heart of his lover.

The Woman's Editor, Diana Hutchinson, had her say in an article headed BIRTH OF A POLITICAL CONTROVERSY. It started nicely:

> For the last ten days handsome, clever Sara Keays has been a woman under seige.

but then:

> ... She came out briefly and tantalisingly in her brilliantly printed maternity clothes. Communication with her lover might have been broken off, but here was a signal to him that she had no intention of hiding the proud fact she was having his baby.

I had hidden the fact for as long as I possibly could and was the last person who wanted it discussed in the newspapers.

> ... After a hiatus in the affair two years ago, and then a tender reconciliation, all her instincts must have been pushing this unusually clear-headed career woman into conceiving a baby at last.

Where had she got the idea that there had been a 'hiatus' two years previously? In 1981 I had been living in Brussels, but Cecil had asked me to marry him and we saw one another whenever possible, either in Brussels, or on my visits to England.

The article also said:

> ... She has always indiscreetly waved the flag of her joy over the child to come. Her almost eccentrically bright, frankly too-large and too-soon maternity frocks have splashed the message that she is proud to be pregnant.

What drivel. I was getting a little tired of the press comment on my appearance, especially the suggestions that I sported brilliant maternity dresses in order to draw attention to my pregnancy. Either these people had been incredibly unobservant, or they chose to avoid the evidence of their own eyes, because it wouldn't have suited the slant they wanted to put on their stories. Or perhaps they hadn't even seen me and just took a look at what photographs they had and wrote whatever they thought they could get away with. I had only four maternity dresses. None was brilliantly coloured. On the contrary they were rather subdued. They were all cast-offs of my sisters. My wish to keep my pregnancy a secret for as long as possible and, after the visit of the *Daily Mirror* people in August, my fear of being followed again by reporters, meant that I was never able to go shopping for maternity clothes of my own. It was a small point, perhaps, but was typical of the general inaccuracy, and even downright dishonesty of some journalists, and revealed their bias against me.

The *Daily Express* wrote that:

> The verdict among the Tories is that Miss Keays was determined to bring Mr Parkinson down, and had the ammunition, which she used, to destroy him. If she had kept to the letter of the agreement to say no more, Mr Parkinson would still be in the Cabinet today.

If they really believed that I wished to do him down, surely I would have done so in May or June, or following the events of 1 and 2 September? If the restoration of his position had not been achieved by means of attacking my reputation, I would not have been driven to speak out. Even then, I had withheld information which would have been damaging to Mrs Thatcher and highly embarrassing to the Party. The press were not to know this of course and I hope they will realise now just how galling some of their comments on the matter were, especially the constant references to an 'agreement'.

The *Daily Express* published an atricle by Katherine Hadley, Woman's Editor—an irritating title for a post that in my opinion should not exist. If they have to have a 'Woman's Editor', why do they not also have 'Man's Editor'? Under the heading THE WOMEN WHO LOVED AND LOST . . . WHAT NEXT FOR THE REAL VICTIMS OF THIS SCANDAL? she had written a snide attack on me. For sheer arrogance, it deserves a mention. I suppose that I should have expected the *Daily Express*, like the *Daily Mail*, having nailed their colours so firmly to the Thatcher-/Parkinson mast, to attack me. Like the *Daily Telegraph*, they were unable to admit their earlier judgement had been wrong. Katherine Hadley revealed her opinion, if not her actual allegiance, in her opening paragraph:

> What Sara Keays must be feeling today is a sense of regret and desolation. Regret that she spoke so opening yesterday of her affair with Cecil Parkinson. Regret that she was so particular in describing the wrongs of the relationship that led to her imminent baby. And if she loved him at all—and obviously she did—she must feel desolation that she caused his resignation.

Here we have the argument used by so many, but predominantly by men, that if I had 'really' loved him, or loved him 'enough', I could not have 'caused his resignation'. In what way did she think I had spoken 'so openly' or been so 'particular'? It would not have suited her argument to acknowledge that my statement was far from being an emotional or detailed account of our love affair and dealt specifically with only the events of the past five months out of twelve years.

She said that I would have done myself and my child no good whatsoever and that I had 'simply smashed a political career'. Then we had the surprising assertion:

> Revenge accomplished is never so sweet as the plotting of it. Especially against somebody you have loved.

Evidently she was speaking from personal experience. She said that it was 'reasonable' to assume that revenge was 'at least part of her motivation' and that 'What really amazes me is that her family allowed her to do it.'

Referring to my having said that I had a duty to put the record straight she wrote:

> Nonsense. The record was already straight. She was, in the eyes of most humane people, wronged. He had acknowledged her child and his proposals of marriage; acknowledged himself to be a deceiver.

Nothing more could be done to help her, except marriage. It was up to him. And he decided against.
If anybody had a duty, it was her family—to stop her bringing public opprobrium on her own head at this emotional time. When a baby is imminent women are often emotional.
She needed a family to think logically about the situation for her ...
What can her father and sister been thinking of?
... Sara Keays's statement shows the less than logical state she was in.

She made it sound as if emotion was something to be suppressed, to be ashamed of perhaps, certainly not to be trusted. She was apparently unaware of the opprobrium that had been heaped on my head throughout the past week, thanks to the Party's efforts to blacken my reputation, and that it was to put a stop to it that I had issued my statement. I was indeed emotional—I was at a fever-pitch of anger, anxiety, and unhappiness, but I am very thankful that I had the strength and resolution to go through with my statement, misunderstood and maligned though I was by people like Katherine Hadley.

As each day passed and the birth of my baby drew nearer, the pressures on me increased. As for those who said that my statement provoked media attention, I would remind them that it was already apparent, and had been remarked by a number of media commentators, that the Parkinson Affair was not going to go away and that interest in both of us would continue up to and beyond the birth of our baby. I had continued to be hounded by the press in spite of my refusal to talk to them. As the tension mounted, so my ability to deal with it dwindled. I knew that it would become increasingly difficult for me to do anything to defend myself; after my baby was born it would have been impossible. For many months all I could do was look after her and regain my strength. It is only in the last year that I have been able to address myself to the task of writing this book.

As for my family, to answer the *Daily Express* woman's question, they were thinking of me first and foremost. Although the pressure on them was intense, they never complained. They backed me at every stage. They never once questioned my decision to publish a statement, but supported me completely, considering that it was something that had to be done, and the sooner the better. My father was wonderful. He never let me see that he was worried, although I knew that he must be. He was always cheerful and was my staunch supporter and ally. Throughout my hours of agonising over my statement, he was ready with advice whenever I needed it.

Ms Hadley had not done. She, too, accused me of misunderstanding the *Daily Telegraph*.

> Those around her who were not pregnant ... and not in her state of maternal anxiety, should have read the newspaper properly. And headed her off.

They did read it and they shared my disgust.

> What she has done—and fortunately for her, it will pass—is turn many people against her; people who previously felt sympathy.

What a pity that she could not see that I did not want sympathy or pity from anyone. I wanted an end to the hypocrisy and the lies about the kind of relationship I had had with Cecil.

She said:

> ... there is a reason for silence—and that reason is not just bravery or protection of a man. When you are in the public spotlight it is best to put on a dignified and brave front for your own self-protection ... Today one's heart goes out to Ann Parkinson in her silence. She has no choice but to soldier on.

And what made this woman so sure that Ann Parkinson had remained silent?

Ms Hadley trotted out the lie that I had tried to expose in my statement. She protected herself by allowing it to be someone else's responsibility:

> There are those who suggest that Sara Keays, at 36, with time ticking by and threatened by a childless future tried to catch him with a baby. But these suggestions will always remain, unfortunately for her baby, speculation.

Either she had not troubled to read my statement, or she was determined to do what she could to undermine it. Why was she so partisan, I wonder? If she could not restrain herself from comment, why could she not have been neutral?

Referring to my words, 'I could not deny my baby his right to know the identity of his father', she said:

> Cecil Parkinson has not done this. He has publicly acknowledged the child and his intention to provide for them both. There is nothing more to be done for her now.

How dared she presume to know better than I what he had or had not done or said? She did not know the events leading up to his statement. She could not know. By what right could she dismiss my statement as if it were a pack of lies? She was not qualified to pass judgement on me. She finished, in arrogant self-righteousness:

> What is important is that this baby is born in as peaceful circumstances as possible—given the hoo-ha. His mother has had her regrettable, if understandable say, and that must be the end of it for her. For the sake of the child.

As if she, or any other journalist, cared about my child.

The *Sun*'s leading article said of the Prime Minister:

> Now, when all the facts are known at last, her opponents will inevitably accuse her of a failure of judgement in not accepting Mr Parkinson's resignation last week. Yet we do not know how much or how little of the story he had told her.

I do not know either, but I do know that my father's letter ensured that she knew whatever facts Cecil had omitted.

The *Daily Mirror's 'Comment'* said:

> The end was inevitable, but Mrs Thatcher wouldn't see it. That is why the public agony of the Parkinson family last for nine days. If the Prime Minister knew the full truth about Mr Parkinson's affair with Miss Sara Keays, then she misjudged the situation. If she did not know the full truth, she misjudged the man. She had a chance to limit the damage to her party and to the Government. Instead she made it worse . . . then there was a foolish attempt to work up sympathy for Mr Parkinson. That was a fundamental mistake. No-one felt sorry for him. . . . Her defenders say she was being loyal. But loyal to what and to whom? Loyal to the party? Loyal to Mr Parkinson? Loyal to the country? Or loyal to a vanity which thought she could do no wrong?

I did not much care for the behaviour of some of the *Daily Mirror*'s reporters, but I thought their *Comment* was spot on.

The Guardian's headline was THATCHER WOUNDED BY PARKINSON HUMILIATION. In a lengthy article by their Political Editor, Ian Aitken, it was said that:

> The content of Miss Keays' statement is clearly damaging to Mr Parkinson's reputation, and in political circles it is expected that he will eventually be forced to reveal further details about his relationship with her. Her [the Prime Minister] image as a woman of firm and decisive resolve has been seriously damaged and her judgement is in question.

Another article headed COLLEAGUES SHOCKED BY RESIGNATION said:

> Miss Keays' lost some sympathy among delegates by making her second [sic] statement on the affair. One prominent Tory MP said that if she had been in Miss Keays shoes "I would have kept my mouth shut". A Tory Peer, Baroness Trumpington said "Hell hath no fury. . .".

John Selwyn Gummer, Conservative Party Chairman, was reported as having said "I think this was a private matter which was becoming so public that Cecil has decided he cannot do his job properly. I think it is much better to leave it like that." This was to be the official line: he had resigned because of the publicity.

Another article said that Cecil Parkinson had planned to retire from Parliament at the last election and give up political life, but changed his mind when, in 1981, Mrs Thatcher asked him to become party chairman. I wish he had told me.

The leading article was typical *Guardian* stuff. Under the headline WHEN LOVE GOES WRONG, NOTHING GOES RIGHT they wrote:

> For all the portentous flummery of its presentation—for all its talk of 'duty' and 'necessity'—Miss Sara Keays' statement is little more than a scream of pain. She believes she has been greatly wronged. She has

> been consumed, over eight days, by a feeling that he is getting away with it. She has made sure, now, that Cecil Parkinson got away with nothing. If revenge is sweet, then she will perhaps rest easier as she awaits her baby. The rest of us—knowing from bitter experience the impossibility of picking sides in the eternal triangle—can only tiptoe away.

If anything were portentous flummery, that was.

If only the press *would* tiptoe away, but no, the Editor of the *Guardian*, like most of his Fleet Street colleagues, trampled on, disregarding the facts, determined to score a point against me somehow. For all his high-minded talk of not taking sides, he could not resist doing exactly that.

> He resigned yesterday ... for the simplest of reasons. His private life could no longer be kept private. The possible pact of silence, and thus of eventual forgiveness, was shattered ... He was let down not by his friends, nor by his Prime Minister, nor by conference itself... But then came Miss Keays and ... the breakdown of relationship which had precipitated everything would allow nothing to fade in silence.

So it was I who had let Cecil down, not the other way round. It was the breakdown of the relationship that had precipitated 'everything'. Just what did they mean by 'everything', anyway?

The *Guardian* said:

> There can be ... no forming of outside judgements about the relationship, or its breakdown. Simply, we do not know enough to tell. ...

But they did so nevertheless. They made it plain that they believed that I had caused his downfall and that I should have kept quiet. They indulged in some high-flown speculation on the Prime Minister's role in the matter but concluded:

> Mrs Thatcher may take all manner of flak when her policies go astray. But in this case she has striven loyally—and at some risk—to help a colleague in distress. That is not much of a political hanging matter. The wreckage of the affair is strewn all around. Can it now be, at last, left to lie?

The Times published an article by Jock Bruce-Gardyne, who, as one might have expected from one of Mrs Thatcher's former appointees, supported the Prime Minister and dismissed Cecil's resignation as a victory for hypocrisy. Under the heading HOUNDED OUT BY HYPOCRISY he wrote:

> So that great British tradition, hypocrisy, has claimed another victim. [He argued that a politician can behave rashly or incompetently in the performance of his public duties and escape] without a

> word of condemnation, [but] let him be exposed in a marital entanglement ... and he is hounded out of office, his career and future wrecked.

By whom Cecil was supposed to have been 'hounded' from office, he did not trouble to say. The answer was presumably contained in the following, which appeared later in the article: '... the press has won, more's the pity.'

Mr Bruce-Gardyne supported the Prime Minister's decision not to accept Cecil's original offer to resign, saying that it was 'entirely typical of her to show sympathy and to stand beside him in his moment of trial.' He said that Cecil had 'already paid a heavy price' for his 'personal difficulty'.

The rest of the article was a eulogy to the Parkinson career, but finished by asking what chance there was of attracting men and women of the 'calibre' needed in government 'if we allow them to be hounded out by such a press campaign and innuendo.' What innuendo, I wonder, and whose?

At about 5.30 that afternoon I telephoned Wicks. It was evident that he regretted Sweet's decision to withdraw their services, but there was no point in discussing the matter with him. I was exceedingly anxious lest either of them say anything to the press and I repeated to Wicks what I had already told Sweet, that they were to say nothing to anyone about me until I had appointed new solicitors. I hoped that, at last, they would now do as I asked.

Throughout the day, the waiting reporters had pushed notes through the letter-box requesting interviews. They even asked if there were a 'spare garden shed or stable we could shelter in', saying they were wet and very cold. I did not envy them, but I was certainly not going to do anything to encourage them to stay. So that note, too, I ignored.

Later that night a note was delivered informing me that 'some clearly intimate friends of Mr Parkinson have given their answer to your statement' and inviting me to telephone the *News of the World* if I wished to know what they had been saying. I wondered which of his friends would take on such a task, but guessed I would find out all too soon.

Anonymous attacks in the *Sunday Times*

Sunday 16 October 1983

I found out just what Cecil's 'friends' had been saying on his behalf as soon as I saw the Sunday newspapers. Not satisfied with the blackening of my name that had gone on throughout the week, they were now doing their utmost to discredit my statement. Cecil had said through his solicitors on Friday that he would be saying nothing further publicly about the matter. Instead this was being done covertly by his 'friends' and 'colleagues'.

If I had ever flagged from the task of writing this book, I should have needed only to look again at the newspapers of 16 October 1983, and the *Sunday Times* in particular to steel myself to the task. What it had allegedly been told about me was a pack of lies. I had been told the previous Tuesday of the efforts being made to blacken my name and discredit me, but my informant had spoken only in general terms, having, perhaps, wished to spare me the details. It was not until several weeks later that I learned the specific lies that had been put about: that Cecil had tried many times to break off the relationship, that I had done everything I could to keep it going, that he had 'sent me' to Brussels to get me out of the way, and that it was only as a result of sleeping together 'two or three times', 'for old times' sake' in the 'early part of 1983' that I had become pregnant, and other things too vile to repeat. Only then, although I had suspected it, did I learn of the systematic briefing of the media by sources 'close' to Downing Street and Central Office, ostensibly to give reporters an 'informed' view of the matter. You do not need to work for long in politics to learn about the way in which politicians—Ministers especially—use the custom of briefing reporters 'on Lobby terms' for their own ends, to manipulate the news, pave the way for or pre-empt changes of policy, tone down bad news, and 'soften up' or colour the public view of certain events or policies. Nor are many people aware of the regular cosy little get-togethers of editors and political journalists with the Prime Minister's Press Secretary. The Lobby correspondents go along with this no doubt because they are hooked on the prestige and influence they enjoy from being 'in the know' and on the 'inside track' with Ministers. Their editors go along with it no doubt in the hope of knighthoods or other rewards from a grateful Prime Minister.

It is a deplorable practice which makes a mockery of the belief that we have an independent press, which helps to keep the machinations of government shrouded in secrecy and yet is nurtured by all the political parties, even by those who urge the need for more 'open' government and greater freedom of information. It is bad enough that this practice is used to manipulate the news on matters of public policy. It is loathsome that it is used against individuals, as it was undoubtedly used against me. And for what? To enable the Prime Minister to keep a favourite in the Cabinet? Was he so indispensable? Or was it merely that she was afraid that her first judgement of the matter would be shown to have been at fault?

I had thought, naively no doubt, that my statement would have shown how totally unfounded the rumours about me had been and show the media how they had been misled and misinformed. When I read the so-called 'exclusive' article in the *Sunday Times*, I saw what a vain hope that had been. The lies had not stopped. Cecil's 'colleagues' and 'friends' had stepped up their efforts and some newspapers, the *Sunday Times* in particular, were doing all they could to help them. The *Sunday Times* so-called 'exclusive' contained a string of vile and totally unsubstantiated accusations against me, which had been dressed up with references to unnamed Government Ministers in order to lend them authenticity. It was disgusting that any newspaper, but especially one that pretends to respectability and to a desire to seek out the truth with its so-called 'investigative journalism', should have published such an article.

No-one, Cecil included, had publicly questioned one word of my statement, nor would anyone have dared to do so. Instead they did so in the most cowardly and dishonest way possible and, what was worse, the press assisted them. Not a single one of the 'friends' and 'colleagues' to whom the allegations against me were attributed was named by any newspaper. The press act as if they have some kind of God-given right to keep secret the identity of their sources. Indeed under the Lobby system a journalist can even withhold the identity of his informant from his editor. These unscrupulous 'friends' and 'colleagues' of Cecil's were taking advantage of this convention in order to circulate blatant lies, to which they would not have dared to put their names. I despise the journalists concerned for helping them do so. Why did they not identify their sources? Presumably because they wanted to maintain their cosy relationship with the Prime Minister's Press Secretary and other influential people and of course they knew that they incurred little or no risk in doing so. As for their informants, they knew that their names would never be published and that whatever I might say, they would have achieved their object because mud sticks, especially to a 'fallen' woman.

Labelled '*exclusive*' the *Sunday Times* article was headed THE CASE FOR PARKINSON and EX-MINISTER'S FRIENDS SPEAK OUT ON SARA KEAYS.

Who these friends were, who were supposed to know so much about me and to have volunteered their information to the *Sunday Times*, the reader was never told. The whole article was written as if the unnamed people quoted had precise and intimate knowledge of my affair with Cecil. If there were any such people, they could have acquired their information only very recently and only from him or someone close to him. The article was written in such a way as to suggest that there was an army of 'friends' and 'political allies' who had rushed to give their 'facts' to the *Sunday Times*, accusing me of a campaign to 'break' my former lover and 'destroy' his career.

The *Sunday Times* must have known that none of the accusations against me could be substantiated, but that did not deter them from printing them in inverted commas to look as if they were actual quotes, even though not one of the 'Government Ministers', 'friends' and 'colleagues' alleged to have made them was identified in any way.

The article said that:

> ... Cecil Parkinson's friends yesterday rounded on Miss Sara Keays and her family, accusing her of a wilful campaign to destroy the career of her former lover. They also made it known that they did not accept significant details of her version ... and delivered point-by-point refutations of her statement. ...

A government minister 'who did not wish to be named'—how surprising—was quoted as saying 'no-one can describe her as a sweet young woman'. It was said that Cecil was taking a break after his 'ordeal', that the Prime Minister was 'deeply disappointed about his departure' and would 'still rely on Parkinson for political advice'.

The 'friends' rejected my 'claim' that the baby was conceived in a long-standing, loving relationship. 'They claim that there had been "a clear break" in the relationship lasting several years and that he had only seen her "two or three times" this year' ...

> Parkinson first proposed marriage to Keays in 1979. He did not go through with it, however, because one of his daughters was taking heroin and he feared that a divorce and public family break-up would set back her treatment.
> When the affair resumed ... [they were careful not to say that it was he who had resumed it] there was never any talk of marriage until after she had told him she was pregnant. ...

Since our affair was a closely guarded secret, how could any of his 'friends' have known what we had talked of?

> It was not until a month later, on election day, June 9, that he proposed marriage for a second time. It was also on that day he told Mrs Thatcher of the affair saying "I think I will have to marry her".

If that were indeed the case, what a pity he had not couched his proposal of marriage in similar terms.

The lies continued, this time in the mouth of another unnamed government minister who was alleged to have said:

> "It's remarkable that he kept going through the election campaign

> with that woman ringing him up twice a day and asking about the divorce. We should be grateful that he kept the flag flying.
> "Strangely enough it was Sara Keays who was then getting all the hate mail."

What hate mail? No-one other than Cecil and my two sisters even knew that I was pregnant. It sounded as if Cecil himself had received such mail at some stage. Then:

> Parkinson's friends do not excuse his behaviour in resuming the affair [what reasonable chaps they are] though they say he was amazed when she told him she was pregnant.

Amazed? Were they suggesting that he did not know how such things happened? The next lie concerned his refusal to tell the Prime Minister. His 'political allies' were said to be 'particularly furious' with me on that score:

> They say that he did not want to trouble the Prime Minister with such a scandal during the election campaign and that he learned about the baby only on the eve of Mrs Thatcher naming June 9. As soon as the election was over he made a clean breast of it.

He would not have told her anything unless he had been made to and when he did see her on Polling Day, he did not make 'a clean breast of it' as her reaction to my father's letter had shown.

The Prime Minister, according to the article, had not been happy at the prospect of divorce 'taking the view that the break-up of a marriage is more an affront to Victorian values than an illegitimate child. Her main concern was for Ann, his wife.' Lies and deceit were not an 'affront' to her 'values', presumably.

The article went on to quote Cecil as having said, when 'told by the *Sunday Times* about friends rallying to his defence' ... "I have no further comment to make. Any friend who has the interests of me and my family at heart should refrain from any further comment. They are doing me no favour".

But according to the *Sunday Times* these friends 'clearly believe otherwise. What they had to say yesterday was uncompromising and unanimous.'

Referring no doubt to Ian Gow, amongst others, the *Sunday Times* said:

> Some of Mrs Thatcher's top aides are known to have approached Parkinson, asking him to stay with his wife.

The next was of great interest to me:

> When confronted by Ann, Parkinson confessed the affair while the family were on holiday ...

That was exactly what he had told me. But who had told his wife?

No doubt quoting Mr Bernard Ingham, the Prime Minister's Press Secretary, the *Sunday Times* said:

Sources close to Mrs Thatcher say the Prime Minister was delighted when Parkinson returned from holiday to inform her there would be no divorce.

They went on to deal with the negotiations between Cecil's solicitors and mine which they said were 'tortuous and bitter'. They said that he had been 'prepared to admit that he had broken his promise to marry in 1979'—he had not been prepared to do anything of the kind—but that he 'would not agree to anything which implied that he had allowed her to become pregnant this year on the understanding that marriage would follow'. He had not wanted *any* reference to *any* promise of marriage.

Next came the various references to the 'Keays camp' and what they were supposed to be trying to achieve. It was said that:

> ... all of the Parkinson allies who spoke to the *Sunday Times* suspect that the Keays camp thought that statement alone would be enough to break Parkinson. They say there was mounting anger in the Keays camp when Parkinson survived the *Panorama* interview and ... was well-received by the party conference ... Hence the Keays statement to *The Times* that night.

How could any of these so-called 'friends' possibly know what my family had thought or said amongst ourselves during the past week—or were they saying that they had somehow managed to eavesdrop on us?

> ... There is now considerable bad blood between the rival groups of supporters in the affair. [I had no 'group of supporters' other than my family.] Parkinson's friends claim that Sara's sister, Flora, has been the main influence in urging her to take a hard line.

Cecil knew Flora, but *none* of his friends had ever even met her. And no-one, other than the Prime Minister, not even the three men from *The Times*, had been given any indication of the views of any of my family on the matter. It was said that:

> Parkinson's friends are aware that by giving their version of events, they could provoke Keays into another damaging attack. But they are anxious to set the record straight nevertheless.

I should think Cecil was indeed worried that I might say more. No doubt he hoped that I would be gullible enough to believe that he had had nothing to do with these lies.

The *Sunday Times* also published a long article in their *Insight* column. A paragraph which leaped out of the page at me was the following:

> The fact that Sara Keays had decided to break her silence—a silence Parkinson had been banking on—had been known to the Tory whips since about 8 pm. Charles Douglas Home, the editor of *The Times*,

was in Blackpool and he had alerted the Chief Whip, John Wakeham, the moment his men set off for Bath.

But it was impossible for anyone to guess how damaging the statement might be until they knew precisely what Keays had typed down.

The men from *The Times* had given me their word of honour that everything I said to them both prior to and during our meeting would be in strictest confidence. I had asked for such a pledge because I had not yet decided whether to give them the statement and I wanted to know first whether they would agree to my conditions. I was also determined that no-one should be able to prevent publication.

The *Insight* article was just as despicable as that on the front page. It too was full of 'facts' supplied by Cecil's friends. It said:

> Parkinson's supporters say that he hotly disputes some of her version of events: in particular that he knew about the pregnancy in May, when he first said he was not going to marry her. They claim the sequence was this: on May 9—when Mrs Thatcher announced there would be a June election—Keays told Parkinson she thought she 'might' be pregnant; but it was not until June 9—polling day—that Keays confirmed she was having a baby. Later that day Parkinson told the Prime Minister: "I think I'll have to marry her".

The writers made no attempt to conceal the extent of their hostility towards me. Referring to the events of polling day, they said:

> Sara Keays's version of what else happened on the day of electoral triumph is extraordinary. She claims that Parkinson found time to seek 'a reconciliation, and asked me to marry him. I gladly accepted.' She also claims he said he was about to see the Prime Minister to inform her of their relationship . . . [It may be extraordinary, but it is true.]
>
> The version of the Parkinson camp is somewhat different. They say that he saw Keays on June 8, not June 9, and did not seek a reconciliation, but to learn that the pregnancy she had first suspected in May had now been confirmed. When she told him that, he decided he would *have* to marry her.

The magnitude of these lies will be clear from what I have written of the events of May and June earlier in this book. The article continued:

> And that, allegedly, was very much his sentiment when he saw Thatcher after the polls closed the next evening. The same day, in the same vein he supposedly telephoned Colonel Keays, Sara's father, to say he would 'stand by her.'

This was extraordinary. Who could have told them of Cecil's call to my father and have put such a dishonest slant on it? Other than my father and my sisters, only Cecil and the Prime Minister knew. Was it she or Cecil who had told the *Sunday Times* informant? How interesting that they had rearranged the order of events in this way. Cecil had telephoned my father not to say that he had decided he had no choice but to marry me, but to reassure my father that he genuinely wanted to do so. When my father was sceptical about his motives, Cecil was angry and protested that he was not a 'rat' and that my father was speaking to 'your future son-in-law'. My father did *not* want me to marry Cecil, having grave doubts about the sincerity of his proposal, but suppressed his feelings because I was so obviously in love with Cecil and because I believed him. Moreover, Cecil did not telephone my father on Polling Day, but two days later, on 11 June.

The *Insight* article went on to contrast what they referred to as the 'picture' presented by my statement with that presented by the 'Parkinson camp ... of a man trapped by an unwanted pregnancy, deciding to do the decent thing'. How anyone could regard that as the 'decent thing' defeats me. It is a hangover from an age when women were regarded as both inferior to and totally dependent on men.

The 'Parkinson camp' were said to view me as a 'not very competent, but fiercely ambitious and calculating secretary to whom, in the end, he was only casually attracted and who is now motivated by vindictiveness'. The word 'secretary' seemed to have been brought in as if it too were derogatory.

In the outline of the history of the relationship, they said '... at the age of 23, she got a job in the House of Commons with the newly elected MP for Enfield, Parkinson'—I was already working there—and 'Their affair apparently started three years later'—where did they get that idea? And that, following his ministerial appointment in 1979 '... within months the relationship had begun to cool'—wrong. Much against his wishes, I had decided to leave. And 'according to Colonel Keays, Parkinson told him that the target date for their wedding was June 1983'—my father had never said anything of the kind, nor had Cecil said anything to him about *when* we would get married. And further:

> Once again, the version from the Parkinson camp is different. They say that Keays' move to Brussels marked a complete break in the relationship, and that it started again only this year.

The *only* breaks in the relationship were when I left in July 1979 and he agreed never to get in touch with me again, only to ask me three months later if I would marry him and after my return from Brussels in January 1981, when again I asked him to leave me alone. Again he came back to me several months later. Worse was to follow:

> Even then, they say, the couple slept together just 'two or three times'. [Note the use of inverted commas to give this an air of authenticity, when it was a damnable lie.] But there is no dispute that he made her pregnant [How decent of them.]

Of the negotiations between solicitors, they wrote 'Keays was determined there should be a public statement.' It was his solicitor who proposed that a statement should be made. 'Parkinson had to agree . . .' Why? He did not *have* to make a statement, or to get my endorsement of it, any more than I had to. We could each have made our own independent statements if and when the need arose.

It was then said that he wanted the statement as far ahead of the conference as possible, when it was clear to me that he only wanted it when it was feared the *Daily Mirror* and perhaps other papers would release what they knew following Gummer's appointment as Party Chairman.

The article went on to talk very knowledgeably, albeit inaccurately, of the negotiations between the solicitors. But someone had given them some information which came remarkably close to the truth. Who? Cecil? Or had one of the solicitors talked? The former seemed more likely.

Then it was said that 'Parkinson was ready enough to agree to a generous financial settlement—£100,000 was the figure being touted in ministerial circles last week, with a separate settlement for the child when it was born'. This was news to me. Evidently he was prepared to talk to his colleagues about it, but had put forward *no* figures of any kind to me. Would that he had indeed been so 'ready'. In fact the negotiations on a financial settlement did not start until after I had appointed new solicitors and were not agreed until just before my baby was born, and even then not until they had haggled to the last pound. It was only because I was under such pressure and became ill that I gave up the struggle with them. Even then they did not want the 'deal' confirmed until I had succeeded in producing a living, healthy baby. The picture presented in the *Sunday Times* and other papers was an absolute travesty of what had happened.

Referring to the piece in *Private Eye* of 5 October, the *Insight* article said:

> As soon as she heard about *Private Eye*'s story, she telephoned Parkinson, flourishing a threat he could not ignore. He now had to agree to her wording—and the implication that their relationship had always contemplated marriage—or suffer the consequences. According to the account which she subsequently gave to *The Times* Keays had told Parkinson that if he did not agree to a statement, 'then I would be obliged to defend myself'. The language she actually used was distinctly more direct: issue the statement, or I call a press conference at noon.

I had said no such thing. This passage was written in such a way as to suggest that I had lied in my statement. What I had said to Cecil was that he had until midday to make up his mind whether he was going to issue a statement, or I would make one myself. If I was motivated by vindictiveness, as they implied, my statement could have been far more specific and far more damaging to him.

The article went on to describe how he had survived the reaction to his statement, although a 'broad sample' of Tory MPs:

> ... produced an almost unanimous view that the Prime Minister should have accepted Parkinson's resignation.
> Additionally, there was Sara Keays. The deal appeared to be breaking down.

What 'deal'? They said that my solicitor had 'contacted' various 'selected' newspapers and told them I was returning to London and that 'photographs were invited'.

> Parkinson survived his first ordeal [the *Panorama* interview] answering Fred Emery with dignity and refusing to go beyond the statement he thought was meant to settle the matter once and for all.

He *did* go beyond the statement in that interview and in any case I do not know how his statement could have been considered to have 'settled' anything.

Myths about money, and more lies

Sunday 16 October 1985

The 'facts' about the relationship which had supposedly 'emerged' or been volunteered to the *Sunday Times* and other newspapers were nothing but a pack of lies. Cecil and I had kept our affair a closely guarded secret and if any of these 'friends' knew anything about it, it could only be because they had *very recently* been supplied with such information. None of them had any personal knowledge of the affair. Yet the *Sunday Times* claimed to have been told even how many times Cecil and I had slept together in 1983. How did these 'friends' claim to know such a thing, unless Cecil himself, or someone acting on his behalf, and put such an idea into their heads.

I do not for a moment believe that he talked to any of his colleagues about me *before* he decided to break with me in the summer of 1983. If he did, it calls into question the honesty of his relations with me over several years, not just the last five months. He may well have talked to all sorts of people after I became pregnant – certainly he told me he had talked to Ian Gow and Norman Tebbit.

Even if the *Sunday Times* had believed the things they were alleged to have been told by Ministers and others, how dared they print such accusations against me if they were unable to attribute them to anyone or substantiate them in any way. Their behaviour was worse than that of the 'gutter press' to whom they like to take such a superior attitude.

It was hateful to have to face it, but the inescapable conclusion was that the accusations against me had originated with Cecil. He may not have uttered them personally to the journalists concerned, but he had undoubtedly inspired them.

The press coverage of the matter that Sunday had three striking features.

The first was that the *Sunday Times* story was not an exclusive. Other papers published similar articles about Cecil's 'friends' rallying to his defence, and contained remarkable similarities, even to the extent of using identical phrases. Either his 'friends' had been very busy indeed and had contacted a number of newspapers, or the journalists concerned had attended the same briefing session.

Secondly, the *Sunday Times* was not the only paper to contain references to a financial settlement. The *Observer* alleged that such a settlement had already been made. The way in which this further piece of disinformation was presented was clearly designed to show how generously and honourably he was behaving towards me in spite of my 'ruining his political career'. Figures of £100,000 to £200,000 were bandied about. None of Saturday's newspapers had made any reference to a financial settlement, so why was the topic raised by so many of them on Sunday? Who had fed them this story—Cecil? A member of his family? Or had Cecil primed one of his 'colleagues'? The *Observer* alleged that Cecil was intending to 'stand by' the financial settlement 'he had made to Miss Keays' and that it was 'understood to be in the region of £200, 000.' The *Sunday Telegraph* headlines said: LAWYERS DISCUSS SETTLEMENT FOR SARA KEAYS and said:

> 'Provision for mother and child' may reach £100,000,

the use of quotation marks round the phrase 'Provision for mother and child' being intended, no doubt, to lend authenticity to the story. The *Mail on Sunday* headline was £150,000 PAY-OFF FOR SARA and said:

> . . . The package is said by some Tory sources to comprise three parts — provision by the shamed former Minister to Miss Keays and the child she is expecting by him, improvements to the cottage near Bath where she plans to live and a sum in lieu of her selling her story to a newspaper.

If there had ever been any question of the latter, Cecil's settlement would have to have been at least five times greater than the sum he eventually agreed. I had no doubt that the talk of money came from Cecil or someone very close to him indeed and that it was designed to swing opinion against me. His behaviour and that of the 'friends' speaking for him disgusted me. It was pitiful that they should go to such lengths to obtain the support of the media.

Thirdly, several newspapers referred quite openly to the Conservative Party's attempts over the past week to blacken my name. What I had been told on the Tuesday evening was confirmed, although none of the newspaper articles revealed precisely who was responsible for the smears. I wondered what had made them mention this at last. It was significant that it emerged only after I had made my statement. If I had said nothing, would any of the newspapers have questioned what they had been told? Did it ever occur to any journalist that much of the information about me that had been circulated at Blackpool must have originated with Cecil and that it was suspect? Even if he was not personally responsible for the smear campaign, he had made no attempt to stop it or to deny any of the allegations. His silence—if indeed he had refrained from comment to his journalist friends, which I very much doubt—amounted to an endorsement of what was being said about me.

On the front page of the *Observer* was an article by their Political Editor, Adam Raphael, which contained the same vicious accusations as were published in the *Sunday Times*. Once again, the 'friends' and 'colleagues' who were supposedly quoted were all unnamed. Take the following:

> One close Cabinet colleague of Mr Parkinson said: "This woman failed in destroying his marriage but she succeeded in ruining his political career". Rightly or wrongly the Parkinson camp [how they loved this picture of two 'camps'] believes that most of the damaging publicity could have been avoided if Miss Keays had not been intent on vengeance. His colleagues make no secret of their anger at the way in which they believe he was hounded from office.

Were they afraid, perhaps, that the same thing could happen to them? Then we have another unnamed 'colleague':

> A colleague, still shocked by Mr Parkinson's downfall, said: "It's like a Greek tragedy. Cecil was her [Mrs Thatcher's] favourite son—everything was going for him until this."

Like the *Sunday Times* 'exclusive', Adam Raphael's article went on to say that Cecil's 'friends' disputed 'many of the key aspects' of my statement:

> In particular his friends dispute Miss Keays's assertion that their relationship was a longstanding one. There were, they claim, several breaks, including one in which Miss Keays went to Brussels for a year.

I do not know how anyone could say that an affair of nearly twelve years—even with two breaks of three and seven months—did not merit the description 'long-standing'. Adam Raphael continued:

> According to this account, the affair was beginning to fizzle out when the baby was conceived which Mr Parkinson's friends allege was a deliberate act on the part of Miss Keays.

How could a supposedly reputable reporter, the Political Editor of the *Observer* no less, write such things? Even if they had indeed been said to him by 'Mr Parkinson's friends', did it not occur to him to ask himself how they could possibly claim to know anything about the affair, when only a week previously, at the time the scandal broke, it had come as a complete surprise, a 'bombshell' to most of Cecil's colleagues, and none of them had claimed any such intimate knowledge? He continued his article:

> They also blame her bitterly for provoking the avalanche of publicity. First, by insisting on a joint statement that was damaging to Mr Parkinson [it was not in my power to *make* him issue a statement] and which did not make clear that his fresh offer of marriage was only made after she told him she was definitely pregnant on 9 June. Second, by breaking her word that neither party would say anything further.

And then, to show how good Cecil was being to me and how little I deserved it:

> Despite what Mr Parkinson sees as a breach of the understanding that neither party should add to the joint statement that was issued 10 days ago, he intends to stand by the financial settlement he had made to Miss Keays. This is understood to be in the region of £200,000.

Mr Raphael also reported that Anglican bishops were to meet to establish a common reaction to the affair and that the Archbishop of Canterbury was believed to be alarmed by the statement made by the Bishop of Bath and Wells, who had said that Mrs Thatcher should have accepted Mr Parkinson's resignation when it was first offered. Dr Bickersteth was quite right on that score, but the Archbishop of Canterbury was quoted as having said 'Christians don't kick a man when he is down'. Did the Archbishop mean, I wonder, that you don't kick a man when he's down, but a woman is fair game, or is it simply that he is a sporting chap who thinks that you should give your man a chance by letting him stand up first? The article did say that the Archbishop had been in Africa, so perhaps he did not really know what had been going on, but chose, like so many others, to express an opinion nevertheless.

The *Observer* also published an article by Simon Hoggart, headed THE END OF THE AFFAIR, in which, it was said, he 'traces the personal story behind the headlines'. He too set out to show special knowledge of the matter. He did at least acknowledge the covert attempts to blacken my name, but it was evident that he had been fed the same story as the *Sunday Times*. He wrote:

> As with all love affairs that go horribly wrong, there are two distinct versions. These differ only slightly on facts but on interpretations they are entirely at odds ... it is worth remembering that they are very much the views of people who are deeply involved and emotionally committed on one side or the other. [On my side, the only facts he could possibly refer to were those given in my statement, but he proceeded to write as if he knew the whole story.] The rival versions were both circulating in Blackpool last week, and it seems to be the fact that his account was beginning to appear to gain acceptance in the papers, combined with Thursday afternoon's clapping, which made Miss Keays decide to make her statement.'

I had no 'version' circulating in Blackpool. There was no way I could have circulated any information there, even if I had wanted to, which I did not. Nor was there anyone in Blackpool (other than Cecil and the Prime Minister) who knew the facts. It was a snide and deceitful bit of writing, but it confirmed what I had suspected for the past week, that far from keeping to the much-vaunted 'agreement' Cecil or his colleagues had been busily embellishing and 'explaining' his statement. Proof that Cecil had been commenting on the matter while professing to maintain an honourable silence was contained in the next paragraph:

> As for Parkinson, he remains exceedingly bitter and speaks very angrily about her. As it happens, though, a spark of his affection does remain; last week at one point he remarked that if she needed all the publicity in order to get over her unhappiness, then he was prepared to accept it.

That remark indicated a feeling far removed from affection. He knew how upset I had been following the visitation by the *Daily Mirror* reporters and how I had detested the thought of any publicity. He must have known very well, when he said that, just how much I hated what was happening to me and my family. Hoggart continued:

> . . . However, his view is that she wilfully broke the arrangement made between their solicitors to add nothing to their joint statement.'

There was no such *arrangement*. I had refused to give up my right to speak out for myself if the need arose, and it was not a *joint* statement. It was his statement, containing his words, which he made with *my consent*, no more. In any case, couldn't Hoggart see that what I was being accused of was just what had been done throughout the week either by Cecil, or by others on his behalf?

> Some of his friends go further and accuse her of deliberately doing all that was necessary to ruin him politically. One common view in this: 'when she saw she couldn't wreck his marriage, she decided to wreck his career instead.'

Did he poach that from Adam Raphael, or had they and the *Sunday Times* journalists been briefed by the same person? He went on:

> Certainly, these people argue, she had every right to feel badly let down by Cecil. [How kind of them.] But she had no right to destroy him. [But 'these people' evidently thought that they had the right to destroy me.']
>
> They claim, too, that the affair was beginning to fizzle out when she became pregnant, and that he had only been with her three or four times in the previous year. In spite of this, they say, he was prepared to do the honourable thing and marry her when he learned that she was pregnant. However, he changed his mind when he feared that there might be catastrophic consequences for his first family if he left them.

This was an interesting variation on the *Sunday Times* theme. Either the 'friends' were slipping up or Hoggart's shorthand was not up to scratch. Why the reference to Cecil having 'been' with me (the *Sunday Times* were more explicit) 'three or four times' the previous year? They were presumably referring to 1982. The *Sunday Times* said we had only 'slept together "two or three times"' in 1983; the *Observer* believed it was only 'three or four times' in 1982, which would have put the length of my pregnancy in to the record books.

These 'friends' and 'colleagues' claimed such intimate knowledge of the affair that I am surprised that they did not also tell the press on which of these two, three, or four occasions my baby was conceived. Another claim made by these 'friends' was that:

> Having changed his mind [about marrying me] he was concerned to do the best he could by his mistress. He indicated that there would be handsome financial provision for the child, and he agreed somewhat unwillingly to her request for a joint statement, to be issued as soon as it became clear that the story was public.

What a travesty of the facts. It was he who had proposed the statement. And if he had genuinely wanted to do the best by me and, more important, our baby, he would have resigned from the Government and so spared us much of our ordeal. 'He even agreed to her wording of the statement.' He did *not* agree to my wording.

> He wanted it to make clear that he had offered marriage 'after' she had become pregnant. However, her solicitors insisted on a much vaguer form of words. This was important for the whole balance of emphasis. His version would make him look like a man doing the decent thing by a woman he had got into trouble. Her version made it appear that marriage had been under constant consideration.

My solicitors had not insisted on a 'much vaguer form of words'. I had struggled for weeks to get him to agree to admit that he had *ever* asked me to marry him. It was his solicitor who wanted the wording to be vague and all I had asked, as I have explained in describing the negotiations between solicitors, was that he should acknowledge the extent of the relationship and my belief that we would marry. The former was allowed only in the vaguest possible terms, the latter not at all. Hoggart also wrote:

> There was also an agreement—though not a legally binding one—to say nothing further. In the pro-Parkinson version of events, he stuck to this rigorously, even to the extent of pleading with friends not to give journalists his side of the story.

Did it not occur to him to ask why those friends had been given his side of the story in the first place?

> When he appeared on *Panorama* he was obliged to answer questions about the affair, but he did this in an anodyne fashion which didn't break the deal.

Again, it did not occur to Mr Hoggart that Cecil did not *have* to appear on the programme. If he had intended to keep to the agreement he should have refused to do the interview. And he did comment on the matter, misleadingly, by suggesting that the Prime Minister had been kept fully informed and that all that needed to be said on the matter had been said. It had been a public relations exercise and it had been built on deceit, with the approval and support of the Prime Minister. There was worse to come:

> He did not resign, say his friends, because Sara Keays's statement made him appear a liar or because it brought to light any new and damaging facts. [But it had done just that.] He had to go because the statement showed she would continue harrying him until he went.

He did not say in what way I had supposedly been 'harrying' Cecil. Remembering all too painfully what I had gone through on Cecil's account, I found these accusations almost unbearable. If anyone had been harried it was I. It was evident that Hoggart believed the lies that had been fed to him and that I had set out to destroy Cecil. He wrote:

> Throughout last week, she did not see Parkinson as a frightened, miserable figure, humiliated and half destroyed by his own foolishness.

He was another who believed it was all mere foolishness. Selfishness never came into it, apparently.

> She saw a man who had twice behaved disgracefully towards her and who was now going to get away with it, in part by covert blackening of her name. On Thursday night she contacted *The Times* hesitating only because of a laughable fear that she might upstage Mrs Thatcher's speech.

Perhaps it seemed laughable to him. I was motivated by deep, albeit misplaced, loyalty to the Party. I could have done more than merely upstage Mrs Thatcher's speech if I had published all the facts.

The *Observer* also published a silly article by Katharine Whitehorn and Auriol Stevens headed WHAT EVERY DAUGHTER SHOULD KNOW. They started grandiloquently:

> Behind the instant politics, gossip and titillation of the Parkinson affair, the dim outlines of more serious issues are discernible. [Whatever those serious issues were, they did not get to grips with them in their article.] In just the same way as nature's most spectacular eruptions owe their origins to slow movements in the earth's crust, so it is those scandals which reveal shifts in moral values which gain this peculiar incandescence. [Wow. What a beginning. But what have we next?]
>
> Adultery is no longer a deadly sin. That much is clear. What undid

> Cecil was the baby: no baby, no story. Mr Parkinson's sin was to give Miss Keays sufficient faith in a secure future for her to become, and remain, pregnant—something she'd refrained from doing during a long affair—and then to welsh on her.

Once again we have the casual suggestion that I could have had an abortion and the presumption that I had 'refrained' from becoming pregnant until it suited me. It was a typical of the spiteful tone of the article as a whole that they worded this in such a way as to suggest that perhaps I had become pregnant at some other time and had had an abortion. Of course, it may have been due merely to the carelessness in the use of words to which some journalists are prone. To judge from the superior and condescending tone of the article as a whole, I do not suppose that they would care much either way. They were trying to be clever and succeeded merely in trivialising their subject.

> Parkinson was either a rotter, or not, according to whether you thought he was conned into his present position by his mistress, or whether he never intended to marry the poor, swelling, pregnant innocent.

They had started by telling the reader that they were going to 'discuss the dilemma for women caused by the shift in moral values revealed by the Parkinson scandal', but—if you still had the energy after that to wade through the rest of the article—you found that all they really had to say was that it does not matter what wrong you do or how badly you behave to anyone, so long as you do not get found out. Like so many others, they seemed to believe that had I not become—and remained—pregnant, it would not have mattered how Cecil conducted his private life.

The press comment was not all so unpleasant. There were a few articles which showed understanding of my predicament and they were of great comfort to me amidst the welter of disinformation and accusations.

Alan Watkins, in the *Observer*'s *Political Diary* referred to

> ... the blackguarding of Miss Keays which went on throughout the week and which was one of the principal causes of Friday's statement. ... One hopes that Mrs Thatcher and Mr Parkinson had nothing to do with this talk and that it derived from over-enthusiastic acolytes using their own initiative merely.

One of them must have had something to do with this talk. How else would their 'acolytes' have got their information?

> ... Mrs Thatcher chose to continue to support Mr Parkinson, when she could have removed her support. She did this not because of any abstract considerations of the proper division between private and public life but because she calculated that a resignation would do the Government more damage than a period of embarrassment ...
>
> As this was by now a political matter, it was dealt with by political

> means which, unhappily, involved the blackening of Miss Keays's character. It is difficult to see how, as she alleges, Mr Parkinson breached any agreement with her by refusing to answer questions on *Panorama* and *News at Ten*. It is not at all difficult to see that she was angry at being portrayed as vindictive and calculating.

The *Sunday Telegraph* published a perceptive article by Ian Waller who asked some pertinent questions and revealed a great deal about what had been said to discredit me:

> . . . the real question-mark over the Prime Minister's judgement rests on what happened after Mr Parkinson told her of the affair and how deeply she inquired into its ramifications, albeit a delicate and distasteful task . . .
>
> It is not even clear whether he ever told Mrs Thatcher that he was going to get a divorce. His friends are saying that he only put in the one-time offer of marriage to Miss Keays in the agreed joint statement of October at her insistence . . .
>
> But how, it must be asked, could Mrs Thatcher have imagined that disclosure would prove any less embarrassing for Mr Parkinson, her Government and the Party, while he was still a Cabinet Minister—unless she hoped that, somehow, the whole thing could be swept under the table or passed off as a nine-day wonder? . . .
>
> By Tuesday at Blackpool it had become clear that a powerful defence of Mr Parkinson was being mounted—which an obviously bitter Miss Keays called in her statement 'the Government's desire to restore Mr Parkinson's position . . .'
>
> It was, as Miss Keays perceived, to be done at the expense of her reputation: a scurrilous whispering campaign that in the end rebounded badly—and deservedly so—since it forced her to issue the detailed statement that precipitated Parkinson's resignation.
>
> Miss Keays, so the word went round, had behaved badly—'moral blackmail' was one phrase I heard to describe her insistence on having the fact that he had proposed marriage to her written into the original statement about the affair. A more charitable interpretation might be that Miss Keays was anxious to make clear for herself and her unborn child that she was not promiscuous, but that her pregnancy was the product of a genuine love affair.

I was glad that at last someone had understood.

> Miss Keays, it was said, was a 'publicity seeker'—her readiness to be photographed last weekend was particularly cited although, I understand, this was on the advice of her lawyers to deter harrying by persistent photographers.
>
> Her pregnancy was 'obviously no accident' and was being used as a

> weapon to force Mr Parkinson into marriage and disrupt his family life.
>
> Mr Parkinson slowly emerged as something of a persecuted martyr ...
>
> Mr Parkinson did keep his promise not to comment, but showed no reluctance to appear on television, presenting the image for which he was originally chosen to front the election campaign—clean-out and honest ...
>
> Rarely has a woman appeared to achieve so spectacular a revenge. Miss Keays's seething anger at having her name and reputation bandied around Blackpool and in newspaper comment is all too understandable.

I had seen so many horrible things written about myself that I felt a burst of gratitude as I read this. There was so little understanding of my motives to be found in the newspapers.

In the *Sunday Mirror*, Woodrow Wyatt, whose spite and muddled thinking rate some mention, wrote:

> There was no need for Miss Sara Keays to give the interview for Friday's *Times* that finally destroyed her lover ... she makes much of her concern for her unborn child. How will that child be helped by knowing the part the mother played in ruining the father's career?

This was just the line Cecil had taken when begging me to have an abortion, saying that the child would hate me for 'destroying' his or her father's career.

> Mr Parkinson has been a vacillating fool in his private life, but what about Miss Keays?
>
> She is 36. She is a tough woman of the world ... Surely every mature woman knows it is asking for trouble to trust a married man who says he will marry you....
>
> Miss Keay's statement has made sure that poor Mrs Ann Parkinson's public suffering has come to naught. If Mr Parkinson behaved badly, so did Miss Keays. He was wise not to marry her ...
>
> It is greatly to Mrs Thatcher's credit that she stood by Mr Parkinson. It was Miss Keays, the would-be Tory candidate, who made the situation impossible.

The *Sunday Express* published a ridiculous article by St John-Stevas entitled THE SHINING LIGHT AMID THE HYPOCRISY AND MUDDLED MORALITY. St John-Stevas wrote:

> The only person who comes out of the affair with any credit is the Prime Minister ... She has been compassionate, concerned, tolerant, and Christian.

Perhaps if St John-Stevas had known the truth he might have been less fulsome in his praise. He said that a country, 'in such a state of moral confusion and so full of cant, hypocrisy and pharasaism, did not deserve the head of Mr Cecil Parkinson on a dish'. They had not asked for it nor had I. Cecil chose to resign. If there had been no justification for it, he and his colleagues could have denounced my statement and carried on as before. If the country did not deserve Cecil's head on a plate, St John-Stevas evidently thought they deserved mine and proceeded to try to dish it up to them.

> ... Nor do the other parties in this imbroglio with the notable exception of Ann Parkinson emerge with any great credit.
> Miss Keays has been wronged but must have known that her statement in *The Times* on Friday would destroy the political career of the man she claimed to have loved.

St John-Stevas is evidently one of those who believe that a woman should put up with whatever a man does to her—he can behave towards her as badly as he likes and do whatever damage to her he chooses: if she dares to criticise his actions or to protect herself from their consequences, she cannot really have loved him. It was significant that St John-Stevas had nothing to say of how Cecil's actions reflected on the love he had 'claimed' to have for me for so many years.

> Mr Parkinson is shown as being weak rather than wicked ... But he has purged any guilt by the dignity of his public demeanour and the magnitude of the penalty inflicted upon him.

So you can earn absolution for your sins by giving a good performance on television and at Party Conferences. What a novel idea. Mr St John-Stevas should propose it for the rest of the nation. And what is this penalty 'inflicted' upon Cecil? No doubt it was I who was supposed to have 'inflicted' it. Did he not bring it on himself? What a pity that I too could not earn such tolerance and forgiveness. But if I had appeared on television to try to win the hearts of the media commentators and the public, I would have been accused of a publicity stunt and Mr Norman St John-Stevas would no doubt have been amongst the first to criticise me. He concluded with the following:

> Had Cecil been able to survive, a major chunk of the national vice of humbug would have gone and Britain would have been a better and more civilised country to live in. As it was, the Prime Minister failed, but I for one, applaud and bless her for having tried.

Mr St John-Stevas' article was as good a display of the 'national vice of humbug' he professes to deplore as any I have ever come across. Why had he expressed an opinion at all when he, like so many others, was so ignorant of the facts.

And the *John Junor* column had the following:

> If Miss Sara Keays' purpose was to destroy the career of Mr Cecil Parkinson she has succeeded brilliantly. But could we not at least have been spared the cant that she issued her statement to *The Times* out of a sense of 'public duty'. And now that she has wreaked her vengeance, may we expect a period of silence? Or will a continuing devotion to public duty prompt Miss Keays to take the matter further by publishing her memoirs either in *The Times* or some other fish and chip newspaper?

If the author of this nasty little piece was so stupid as to be unable to understand then why I considered it a public duty as well as a duty to my family to issue my statement, I do not suppose he will understand now, but that will not be any great loss.

It was interesting to see how the propaganda machine had changed tactics to deal with the awkward questions thrown up by my statement. Only a few days ago the press had been led to believe that Cecil's 'wish to marry' me had been something that he had fallen prey to long ago, but had got over, and that it was not until much later that I had become pregnant.

Now, because of what I had said in my statement, it was being put about that Cecil had not learned until Polling Day that I was definitely pregnant, that he had reluctantly decided that he would 'have' to marry me—to do the 'decent thing' by me, and that in any case my pregnancy was merely the result of our meeting 'two or three times' after the affair had fizzled out. It was loathsome and I did not know how to deal with it. There were such powerful forces lined up against me, people with constant access to and influence with the media. I had no-one, other than my family, to give me any assistance or advice.

Flora arrived with a message from Richard Dowden asking me to telephone him. Instead I rang Charles Douglas-Home as I wanted an explanation for the *Sunday Times* report that he had told the Chief Whip at eight o'clock on Thursday evening that I was issuing a statement. It turned out that the message I had received had been garbled and he wanted to speak to me himself, to find out if I wished to say anything following Sunday's newspaper comment.

I explained that if I did decide to say anything further, I could do so through the medium of *The Times* only if I felt I could trust him and that I had been very concerned by the report in the *Sunday Times* that the Tory Whips had known since around eight o'clock on Thursday evening that I was considering issuing a statement, Charles Douglas-Home having 'alerted' the Chief Whip. He assured me that the report was totally untrue and recounted to me the chain of events in Blackpool from the moment he had been informed by his staff in London that I was considering issuing a statement.

In spite of his assurances, privately I was still worried. If the *Insight* report had been correct and the Chief Whip had indeed known at eight o'clock, it could only mean one of two things: either that what Charles Douglas-Home told me was untrue, or that my telephone was tapped—something I had long considered a possibility. It was also possible that the *Insight* piece was a typical piece of careless journalism, but it did nothing to ease my nervousness and anxiety that morning.

As for the *Sunday Times* 'exclusive', I told Douglas-Home that I hadn't made up my mind, and would be taking legal advice about certain matters. I told him what I thought of the *Sunday Times* articles and the 'official' attempts to discredit me, but said that I did not intend to be stampeded into responding to these unattributed allegations. I did not tell him that I no longer felt I could trust him, or anyone outside my family, that my solicitors had withdrawn their services and that in any case I did not know how to deal with the problem without being dragged into a degrading tit-for-tat with Cecil, from which the only people who would benefit would be the newspaper publishers.

On top of all that, I was utterly exhausted and feeling rather unwell. I wished that I could shut my mind to it all and just go to bed and sleep for a week. However, I still had the problem of finding another solicitor and had arranged to telephone Richard Smerdon that evening.

Norman Tebbit accuses 'pygmies'

The *Sunday Times* and *Observer* articles were not all that we had to endure that day. There was an infuriating interview with Norman Tebbit on the television programme *Weekend World* at midday. He said that the Prime Minister had been in a 'no win' situation, no doubt to gloss over the fact that the Prime Minister could have avoided the whole mess by telling Cecil that there would be no place for him in her Government until after I had had my baby and any scandal had subsided.

Where he was really unscrupulous was in the following remark:

> You will recollect that an agreement was made, and it was published, between Mr Parkinson and Miss Keays that they would neither of them comment any further upon the matter.

I am quite sure he knew perfectly well that there had been no such agreement—he must have been party to the Cabinet discussions—and his assertion that such an 'agreement' had been 'published' was a deliberate attempt to discredit me and cover up for Cecil. After all, Norman Tebbit knew a lot of the facts, Cecil having discussed the matter with him in June, when he did not want to marry me and did not want to tell the Prime Minister.

Brian Walden put in, "But they did didn't they?" and Tebbit replied:

> "They did indeed. Now had that agreement been adhered to, I think we would have been in a slightly different position."

What he should have said was that, if Cecil's colleagues had refrained from attacking me, I would not have been driven to defend myself. He went on:

> "Politics is dangerous. [How right he was.] And sometimes you have to take risks, if you want to do what is right and I think it would have been right for Cecil Parkinson to have been in the Cabinet today. I wish he were, not only for reasons of personal friendship but because of his ability and because I think it is a tragedy when what I regard predominantly as pygmies can bring down a man like Cecil Parkinson."

That prompted a burst of laughter from all the family, it being clear from his earlier remarks that I was one of those 'pygmies'. If I were a pygmy, he was positively Lilliputian. On his own he was a mere irritation, but he and the rest of the army of 'friends' and 'colleagues' were trying to tie me down with a web of disinformation and downright lies. What made his utterances so nauseating was the knowledge that Cecil had confided in him and that Tebbit had told him not to 'sacrifice' his career for me. I wondered how much Tebbit really cared about Cecil and how much his remarks now were due merely to the need to support for the time being the leader he hopes one day to supersede.

When he was asked if the handling of the affair had been botched, he said:

> "I think it does damage to the Government temporarily, yes. But I suspect that even more people feel that with a little more understanding, not least from some of those who were writing without too much thought of the glass houses in which they have lived for many years, with a little more understanding from them and Cecil Parkinson could still be standing in the Government today."

It seemed to me that the one thing Cecil could not complain of was that he had not been shown understanding. If anything, he'd been shown too much understanding, certainly by me. Tebbit was careful not to identify those he was criticising. If he was saying that the press brought about Cecil's downfall, then he was talking nonsense. The press had largely been won over to the Government's view that it was 'private' and not a matter for resignation.

Tebbit's interview was repeated time after time on news programmes, as was Cecil's statement to the media around midday when he emerged to pose for cameramen with his wife and children (if I had left my house that day I would have been accused of a publicity stunt, but no such charge was made against him) to tell the waiting reporters that he was staying on as an MP. Then Cecil made the following remarks:

> "I don't intend, as I said in my statement, to make any further comment and people calling themselves my friends who wish to express an opinion are not speaking for me. And I just hope that whatever their motives are, they will follow my example, refrain from comment and let us get on with our lives."

I thought that was pretty rich, considering that anything his friends were saying on the subject they must have learned from him. Cecil told reporters that he wanted to 'underline' the point and said:

> "I don't intend, whatever the provocation, to say anything further and I hope friends of mine won't be provoked into saying anything further."

He meant, presumably, that my statement was the 'provocation' but that he was going to do the decent thing and keep quiet in spite of it. Referring presumably to the 'friends' mentioned in the *Sunday Times* article, he said

'Anything they may have said to date has not been said with my approval or at my request.' Thus did he disclaim any responsibility, appear to be maintaining a dignified silence, while at the same time conveying the impression that what they said was perfectly true. He did not denounce anything they had said, but merely wished they hadn't been provoked into saying it.

It never seemed to occur to anybody that if, at any stage, he had truly wished to make no comment, he would have remained silent and out of sight. It was, like the other instances, a calculated public relations exercise. I felt embarrassment for him that he should go to such lengths and at the same time felt exceedingly angry with him.

That day was one of the worst I experienced in the whole ghastly business. I had been dragged into this appalling situation simply because of his and the Prime Minister's determination that he should remain in office. As if the publicity were not enough, the most damaging accusations had been made against me.

I wished I had held nothing back from my statement and that I could fight back. But I felt unable to prepare another statement and no longer sure that I could trust *The Times* any more than any other newspaper. I should have been able to ask my solicitors to help me, but they had deserted me. Even had they stayed, on past record it was likely they would have refused to do what I wanted or would have worn me down with argument.

I told myself that I would have to be patient and that I would find a way of dealing with the accusations. I did not. I would have had to do something immediately, that Sunday or the following day, and I lost the opportunity. By the time I had appointed a new solicitor it was too late to do anything without stirring up renewed attacks on me and in any case I was feeling less and less able to cope with the problem as each day passed. From time to time I felt very unwell. My sisters were worried about me and telephoned our GP to ask if he could come and see me.

I was not too happy about this, believing that the press would find out who he was and start speculating about why I was seeing a doctor. However, he anticipated that problem. He left his black bag tucked out of sight in his car, concealed the items he needed in his pockets and told the throng of reporters who followed him to the door that he was a friend of the family, as indeed he is.

He reassured me that the baby was doing well, urged me to relax and entertained us all with a description of the scene outside the house.

Elisabeth then said that she was very anxious for me to get away and proposed that I accompany her when she went back to Muscat in a few days' time. At first, I was not keen on the idea—I did not relish the thought of any journey and especially if I was to be escorted by reporters—but my doctor thought I ought to consider it and said he would come back in two or three days to see how I was, when we could make a decision.

Late that afternoon, Roger told me that he had had a telephone call from Wicks who said that if I wished to make another statement, the *Panorama* programme (which could promise me a 'quiet and generally pleasant atmosphere'), the *Daily Telegraph* (as she 'got them wrong', they would be 'most happy to assist her'), and the *Daily Mail* (the man himself, Sir David English, would 'meet her personally and handle everything himself most sympathetically') were all asking for interviews. It infuriated me that, having refused to issue my statement and then having withdrawn their services, Iliffes should contact me with such a suggestion.

That evening I telephoned Richard Smerdon who told me that he had made some discreet enquiries and come up with a firm who sounded just right. He proposed that I ring him again the following morning, by which time he would have made contact with the appropriate person.

On the news we learned who had been favoured in Mrs Thatcher's Cabinet reshuffle. Norman Tebbit's comment on his appointment to Cecil's post as Secretary of State for Trade and Industry was that he was 'just sad that it became vacant in the way it did' followed by a repeat of his *Weekend World* reference to Cecil having been brought down by pygmies. In all the comment I saw on the matter, I never saw it suggested by anyone that he had brought his downfall on himself.

As I lay in bed that night trying to get to sleep, from time to time I heard car horns blaring and angry shouts. It sounded as if some motorists passing the house were expressing their disapproval of the reporters waiting at the gate. It was an extraordinary situation.

Friendly words amidst continuing propaganda

Monday 17 October 1983

When I came downstairs in the morning there was a large bundle of letters waiting for me on the kitchen table. I had received many letters over the past week or so, mainly from relatives and friends but also some from total strangers. I was amazed by the number I received that day (and for months afterwards) from well-wishers, some containing moving accounts of their own unhappy experiences and wanting to reassure me that the difficult times would pass and that my baby would bring me joy. They were very touching. I also received many that were critical of me, often enclosing extracts from the more virulent attacks on me in the press, and also some anonymous letters of the 'poison pen' variety.

The communication which made the greatest impression on me that day was a Telemessage signed merely 'Punch'. To this day I do not know his or her identity. I would be very interested to know who sent it.

It read as follows:

> TREAT WITH CONTEMPT ST SPLASH. PARK PHONED EXPOTTER DIRECT NEWED NEAL SLAGGING YOU NONSTOP ALSO SUGGESTING PEOPLE TO MAKE ANON APPROPRIATE QUOTES. PARK INSISTED ON PARASTATING PARK MADE NO COMMENT AND NEAL DID SUMEDS. JOURNALISTS FURIOUS AT UNETHICAL DISHONEST DESPICABLE DECISION. APOLOGIES FOR ANONYMITY BUT WILL KEEP YOU INFORMED AND SELFDECLARE ASWHEN VERY BEST WISHES
>
> PUNCH

My first reaction was one of disbelief. I did not want to believe it. The *Sunday Times* article had upset me very much and I knew in my heart of hearts that some, if not all, the unattributed accusations against me must, at the very least, have been inspired by Cecil. Even so, I did not want to believe that he would do such a thing. I tried to persuade myself that it was merely another attempt by a journalist to 'smoke me out' and provoke me into saying something more to the press. Try as I did to dismiss it in this way, I could not shake off my doubts and these were heightened by an article in *Private Eye* later that week, which said much the same thing as the 'Punch' telemessage.

Eighteen months later, I read Henry Porter's book, 'Lies, Damned Lies And Some Exclusives'. This confirmed that the *Sunday Times* article was inspired by Cecil, whom he referred to as 'the master of the planted rumour and the judicious leak'.

He wrote:

> After the unceasing public discussion of his infidelity, the ex-minister showed no particular inclination to respond in detail to Miss Keays's allegations. However, the new editor of the *Sunday Times*, Andrew Neil, decided to chance his luck by sending a hand-delivered letter to Parkinson's home, suggesting that he put his side of the story in the *Sunday Times*. A reply did not come until well after midday on Saturday, by which time the political staff and a news reporter had put together a story consisting mainly of unattributable and vaguely sympathetic quotes from the cabinet-colleagues. Parkinson telephoned Neil and gave an extensive interview on lobby terms and on the express condition that the paper would disguise the contribution ... When this appeared there was, to put it mildly, a good deal of unease in the *Sunday Times* newsroom. Reporters pointed out that the piece was almost entirely based on quotations and information attributed to supporters of the ex-minister. The truth, of course, was that these, almost without exception, were supplied by Parkinson himself.

Mr Porter did not know, apparently, that the Editor of the *Sunday Times* also wrote to my solicitors to ask if I would agree to an interview with his paper, 'to amplify her statement in today's *Times*.'

I was not aware of Mr Neil's letter at the time and did not see it until long afterwards, when I eventually saw Wicks and Sweet's file.

Andrew Neil's letter makes interesting reading, especially in the light of his approach to Cecil the same day. He wrote:

> We would be prepared to pay a substantial sum ... The main reason why we hope she would talk to us, however, would be to ensure that her full story is told in a discreet and tasteful way. As evidence of our good intentions and sympathies I would point out last week's editorial.

Monday's newspapers showed that the rest of Fleet Street had picked up the allegations made in the *Sunday Times* and the *Observer*, though they did not go into the same detail.

The *Daily Telegraph* reported on its front page that:

> Mr Parkinson will be going away on holiday with his family to give himself time to ponder his future. He leaves a trail of bitterness and claims and counter-claims between his political friends and Miss Keays and her family.

His friends, described by the *Daily Telegraph* as having 'leapt to his defence' were indeed making all sorts of claims, but there were no 'counter-claims' made by me or by any member of my family, then or at any other time.

The same article said:

> Many of Mr Parkinson's Westminster colleagues believe that many people have received a one-sided picture of his affair [referring presumably to my statement] and he can expect warm support on the backbenches when he returns to the Commons.

I am sure he could. No-one was speaking up in my defence, so whatever lies anyone cared to circulate were doubtless swallowed whole by his colleagues, including no doubt those who had once professed to be my friends.

Several papers referred to the claims made by his 'friends and colleagues' over the weekend and that, when asked about his reaction to my statement, he had said that he did not intend to say anything further 'whatever the provocation'.

The *Guardian* contained some interesting information about the *Sunday Times* 'exclusive':

> 'In the first edition the story, by-lined by Michael Jones, the paper's Political Correspondent, quoted friends as being 'at pains to throw new light on his (Parkinson's) unstated account of events'.
> The final edition version, which had no by-line and was labelled 'exclusive', quotes Mr Parkinson, on being told that 'friends were rallying to his defence,' as saying: 'Any friend who has the interests of me or my family at heart should refrain from any further comment.'

The reference to Parkinson's 'unstated account of events' was dropped from the later edition. Was this because it showed that he was the source of the information?

A classic example of the way newspapers present fiction as fact was an article in the *Mirror* headed SARA 'TRIED TO BUY FLAT NEXT DOOR' which said that I had 'considered moving in next door to Cecil Parkinson a year ago' and alleged that I had spoken to neighbours and told them that I was Cecil Parkinson's secretary. It said 'She did not tell them her name, but when her picture appeared in newspapers last week they recognised her. Miss Keays did not buy the flat.' I did not even look at it or any other flat and I had not been his secretary since 1979. They must have been really desperate to write something about me to have cooked up such a story.

The *Sun* had a headline BREAKING OF CECIL. Presumably, like so many others, they considered that I had done the 'breaking'. They too had apparently been told about a financial settlement and said:

> Mr Parkinson had been expected to hand over up to £150,000. [Oh really?] But he is furious that Sara spoke about their affair to *The Times*.

The *Daily Star* had an thoroughly unpleasant article which suggested that I had been 'moved to want motherhood because of the pregnancy of a best friend', that 'The baby was no accident' and which repeated the lie put about by the 'friends of Mr Parkinson' that 'the baby was born out of "two or three" meetings spread over months'.

The same article went on to say why (according to the *Star*) I had issued my statement, alleging it was because 'news interest in the affair was slipping . . . no statements were being issued, Mrs Thatcher had said: "No question of a resignation". Then on Saturday 8 October, Sara suddenly appeared in public for the first time, wearing a maternity dress that emphasised her pregnancy.' In what way it 'emphasised' my pregnancy they did not say. It went on 'She smiled happily at photographers as they took her picture entering her father's house'—actually it was my sister's house, my father's house being 120 miles away, but why should the *Star* trouble itself with little details like that? And then: 'TV news bulletins showed her in her scarlet-coloured dress time and time again.' Again they would not trouble themselves over such a trifle as the colour of my dress, and no doubt they picked the colour scarlet from their fertile imaginations to fit with the brash, unashamed image of me that they wished to convey to their readers. As for the news coverage, it was no fault of mine if the television companies wanted to keep showing their film.

However, paragraphs in that article which most aroused my ire were those dealing with Cecil's proposal of marriage on Polling Day. The 'friends' had clearly been busy again:

> On 9 June, Cecil Parkinson's standing was at dizzy heights. He and Mrs Thatcher had led the Tories to an amazing election victory. His messy private life had remained a secret.
> So, in that spirit of euphoria, Cecil Parkinson promised Sara Keays that he would 'do the right thing' and marry her. He told her father, Colonel Keays, not to worry.
> Parkinson then told the Prime Minister. He was able to tell Sara all about their meeting, that Mrs Thatcher said it was a private matter for him. And that he would be a senior Cabinet minister.

This was a repeat of what was said in the *Insight* article, a calculated distortion of the facts. Either the *Daily Star* reporters had lifted it from the *Sunday Times* or they had spoken to the same 'friends'. Nor was *The Times* above publishing unattributable smears, as its front page article showed.

Perhaps *The Times* had decided that I was no longer a source of information or news and they might just as well publish the 'official' line. In any event, it seemed to me that they were going to run with the hare and hunt with the hounds and I was glad that I had not given them any additional information. No doubt the reaction of the Conservative Party leadership to my statement had been such that *The Times* decided to protect their relationship with them, which I dare say they considered to be of far greater importance than their brief encounter with me.

Under the headline THATCHER'S KEY ROLE ON PARKINSON MARRIAGE, an article by their Political Correspondent, Anthony Bevins 'explained' the Prime Minister's decision to refuse Cecil's resignation and their anger at my statement. They also published an article headed 'OUR MAN MUST STAY' SAY VOTERS in which they reported that enquiries had revealed that Cecil had the sympathy and support of the majority of his constituents and that 'Most people ... apportioned blame for his embarrassment equally between the media and Miss Sara Keays.' Apparently it occurred to none of them that his embarrassment might be, at least in part, self-inflicted. This article, however, did at least identify the people it quoted. The front-page article by Anthony Bevins, did not trouble itself with such niceties. He wrote:

> The Prime Minister played a key role in persuading Mr Cecil Parkinson not to marry Miss Sara Keays ...
> Mrs Thatcher's views on divorce are particularly strong [but obviously not strong enough to prevent her from marrying a divorce] and when Mr Parkinson first told her on 9 June of his secretary's pregnancy [I had not been his secretary for almost four years] and his view that he would have to marry her, it is understand that the Prime Minister advised caution and further consideration.

From whom was this 'understood'? The Prime Minister herself? Her Press Secretary?

If the Prime Minister had indeed 'advised caution' and if Cecil had indeed only proposed marriage because he felt he had to do so, his, and the Prime Minister's subsequent conduct is even more deplorable. Why did he not say so to me straight away? Did it not occur to either of them that I deserved to be told that he was giving the matter the 'further consideration' she had advised? His 'friends' had made much of his doing 'the decent thing'. The decent thing would have been to tell me straight away that his heart was not in it.

> It is also understood that Mr Ian Gow, then the Prime Minister's Parliamentary Private Secretary and a friend of Mr Parkinson, became active in reinforcing that strong and influential advice.

It was this delightful man who had said, according to Cecil, that if I had really loved him I would either have had an abortion or have gone abroad and started a new life without him.

We were then told that Mr Gow 'is said by some informed sources to have played the role of link man, working behind the scenes to ensure that Mr Parkinson's career and marraige were protected from the impending scandal.' I wondered what exactly Gow had done to prevent a scandal. Short of finding someone to persuade me, where Cecil had failed, to have an abortion, I do not see how he or anyone else could have hoped to avoid at least some scandal when my baby was born. And how much more interesting this story would have been if these 'informed sources' had been identified. Was it Gow who had provided Bevins with his information?

There was more explanation on the way:

> Mrs Thatcher's positive stand during June, July and August and Mrs Parkinson's decision to stand by her husband explain the change of mind and the secret September 1 meeting. [For explain read justify.]

The one thing they do not explain is why no-one thought it necessary to tell me until then. Evidently it did not matter that throughout those months of Mrs Thatcher's 'positive stand' I believed that Cecil was going to marry me. Perhaps they all wanted to keep me in the dark for as long as possible and he was obliged to tell me of his change of heart only because of the *Daily Mirror*'s arrival on the scene.

The Prime Minister's 'positive stand' and 'influential advice' were supposed to justify everything that followed from it.

Mr Bevins reported that Ministers had been 'dismayed' by the media interest in the matter,

> But they have been even more dismayed by Miss Keays' refusal to remain silent in the face of their attempts to save his career. Those attempts explain the reports, which first emerged at Blackpool last week, that the baby had not been conceived 'in a long-standing, loving relationship'.

Further confirmation of the smear campaign that had been going on in Blackpool. They tried to 'explain' those 'reports', but they could never justify them. And where did these 'reports' originate?

> It has been stated on Mr Parkinson's part [once again we are not told by whom] that the relationship began to peter out as far back as 1980, the year after Mr Parkinson first asked Miss Keays to marry him.

Bevins continued: 'Some of the bitterness felt by Mr Parkinson's friends was made public yesterday by Mr Norman Tebbit' and went on to quote Tebbit's allegations about an 'agreement' between Cecil and myself having been 'published'.

I think the friends' bitterness stemmed more from the fact that, having carried the Parkinson banner during the past week, they had been made to look foolish, a distressing experience for a politician.

So *The Times* was no better than any other paper. It was just as willing to be used by its unnamed sources as a vehicle for their campaign against me. If anything, it was worse than the rest for allowing its substantial reputation to be used in this way. Perhaps the practice of publishing unattributed smears has long been established in the British press. I had had no cause to question their impartiality or integrity until that fortnight of torment. I was astonished that they should be so easily manipulated, so willing, apparently, to be the tool of the Government.

As for the politicians for whom the press were so ready to speak, I was not so naive as to think that they were the dedicated idealists they would have us believe them to be. I knew many of them well enough to know that they are as good, bad, or indifferent as the rest of the nation. Where I was naive was in my belief that the Party leadership upheld the standards of honour and integrity that are supposed to be part of the tradition of public life in this country. I was appalled that they should resort to such means to justify an unwise and selfish decision.

My honour had been impugned by the anonymous accusations of Cabinet Ministers and others. They had been helped in their smear campaign by the so-called reputable press, who saw nothing wrong in disseminating such accusations on behalf of people too cowardly and dishonourable to identify themselves. I had tried to put a stop to the smears and had succeeded only in increasing the determination of the people responsible for them. Some people said later that I had brought such attacks on myself by rocking the Establishment boat and that I would have done better to remain silent. It was evident to me that whatever I had done, whether I had issued my statement or not, Cecil's 'friends and colleagues' would have kept up their campaign and had he succeeded in remaining in office, they would have redoubled their efforts to deal with the publicity attendant on the birth of my baby.

There was some good news for me that day. Richard Smerdon turned up trumps and put me in touch with Allan Hughes, of Payne Hicks Beach, who took over as my solicitor that day. It was indeed a turning point in my fortunes. He came to see me the following morning, undaunted by the throng at the gate, and I soon found that I had not only a first-class lawyer but a wise, understanding person to advise and help me.

Life became a little more tranquil for all of us. We had adapted to our strange circumstances and on Tuesday afternoon Elisabeth announced that she was going shopping for presents for her children and she was confident that she could do so without the press observing her. This was important as they were quite capable of mistaking her for me and following her about in a pack. She went out of the back door, through the kitchen garden, climbed over the wall and ran across the field and down to the lane below the village where Roger was waiting with the Land Rover. She hid in the back and he drove through the village followed by Flora in their car. Some distance from Marksbury they stopped and Elisabeth emerged from the Land Rover, covered in bits of straw. She then took the car and went off to Bath while Flora and Roger returned home.

Part Six

No respite

Attempted escape from the press

Allan Hughes reported that Cecil had gone away on holiday and suggested that I do the same. I was worried about my father being bothered by the press while I was away but Flora and Roger announced that they were going to move into Winsbury House and begged me to leave everything to them and to have a complete break.

I decided to do as Elisabeth had suggested and go with her to Muscat. She proposed that we leave as soon as the coast was clear but by Thursday it was beginning to look as if the reporters would never go. They had continued to stand guard at the gate, day and night, regardless of the cold and rain, huddled round their brazier. They looked set to camp there for the winter, but gradually their numbers dwindled.

On Saturday my doctor pronounced me fit to travel and provided me with a certificate to that effect lest the airline feared the birth was imminent and refused to take me. Flora went to the chemist for anti-malaria pills and all that remained was to pack the coolest clothes I could find which still fitted me.

There was a flight to Muscat on Sunday evening and Elisabeth was determined we should catch it. I was still nervous about being followed and did not want to go until all the reporters had gone. On Sunday morning Flora and Roger and the children moved into Winsbury House. Roger reported that only two reporters were in sight and they were sitting in their cars in the lay-by. By early afternoon they had gone. We left immediately. William drove us to Heathrow and we arrived with only a little time to spare. We had not made reservations, not wanting to alert anyone to our depature, and were very lucky to get seats as the flight was almost full.

Towards the end of the flight, when I was sitting in silent torpor and longing to get to our destination, I became conscious of a voice at my side saying "Miss Keays?" It was the British Airways steward who wanted to know when I was planning to return to England and whether I would like any help with the arrangements for my journey. I had believed that we had got away unnoticed and was somewhat startled to have been spotted. He explained that he had seen my name on the passenger list. I had not given a thought to when I would return and in any case was very reluctant to tell anyone what my plans were. My response must have sounded rather ungrateful, but a little later he came back and handed me his card. When he had gone I turned it over and found a charming message on the back, wishing me good luck and giving me the name of the British Airways official at Muscat who could help with my return journey.

We arrived in Muscat early on Monday morning, 24 October, to find Richard waiting for us. It was so hot after England that I quailed to think what it must be like in the summer. It was thrilling to be there. Everything about the place seemed so exotic: the hot dusty smell in the air, the brilliant early morning sunlight and the desolate rocky hills shimmering in the distance. The anguish of the last few months dropped away and I looked forward eagerly to seeing my nieces and nephews and to having a wonderful holiday.

I spent most of my first day in Muscat either sleeping, or sitting on the balcony of Richard and Elisabeth's flat, gazing at the spectacular view of the horseshoe bay, with its rocky cliffs stretching out on either side into the ocean, dominated by two massive, ancient fortresses. The light was brilliant and the sea shimmered and sparkled in the heat. Even the breeze off the sea felt hot. It was wonderful to be there and a great relief to have escaped the press.

Thursday 25 October 1983

I should have known it was too good to last. On Tuesday evening Allan Hughes telephoned me to say that the Press Association had asked him for confirmation that I had gone to Muscat. He had neither confirmed nor denied it, but it was just a matter of time before they tracked me down. Flora had had a similar enquiry that morning from a *Daily Star* reporter who said that Elisabeth and I had been spotted by a reporter at Heathrow airport. The same evening the British Council in Muscat informed Richard that a reporter had telephoned from Abu Dhabi, asking for his home telephone number. They had not given it.

From that moment the pleasure started to go out of my holiday. Richard assured me that no-one would be able to get hold of me and that in any case reporters would find it very difficult to obtain visas at short notice to enter Oman, but I was distressed by the thought that constant enquiries from the press would be a nuisance to the Embassy staff and an embarrassment to him. Where I had felt safe and secluded, I now felt conspicuous. I wished that I had stayed at Marksbury. Richard told me to banish such thoughts from my mind and just enjoy my visit but from then on I could not help feeling anxious whenever the telephone rang.

Daily Express libel

Friday 28 October 1983

At about 4.30 pm on Friday—twelve thirty in the afternoon in England—Flora telephoned. Elisabeth answered and I knew immediately that something was wrong. Flora was dictating something to her. It turned out to be a piece from the William Hickey column of the *Daily Express*. It was the principal Hickey story and was headed MISTRESS SARA MAKES A RETURN TO WESTMINSTER. Not only did it allege that I had been at the House of Commons on Monday—when I was already in Muscat—it said, in the most repulsive terms, that I had gone there with the aim of embarrassing Cecil and his colleagues.

It began by saying that while Cecil was on holiday 'recovering from his political downfall', I, 'his spurned mistress' had 'stunned MPs by turning up in the House of Commons as Parliament reopened for business this week'.

It said that Cecil was with his wife on a 'holiday of recuperation and reconciliation' and that he would not appear in the House until next month. I, on the other hand, was supposedly making an exhibition of myself in the House of Commons:

> But the moment the House was open for business, there was the heavily pregnant Miss Keays, standing for all to see in the Central Lobby, waving at friends. Standing beneath the effigy of Mr Gladstone—himself something of an expert in fallen women—she quite unrepentantly displayed that if Mr Parkinson was not there when Parliament re-convened, she for one was not going to miss a moment. Pregnant or not.

The article went on to speculate whether it would not be 'embarrassing for the former Trade and Industry Secretary when he gets back to work—clearly Miss Keays has no intention of staying away . . .'. Finally, presumably to give credibility to his story, *Hickey* alleged that I 'held one conversation with the affable Murdo Maclean, the private Secretary to Chief Whip John Wakeham'.

The wording of this piece of fiction was repellant. The writer—and, no doubt, the source of his information—evidently thought there was something disgusting about my condition. Not only was I portrayed as a 'fallen' woman who was without shame, but a whiff of something even worse was brought into the story with the reference to Gladstone.

Contrast the language used about me with the references to Cecil. According to *Hickey*, Cecil was 'recovering', on a holiday of 'recuperation and reconciliation'—the victim, licking his wounds and staying discreetly out of sight. He would, of course, get 'back to work' in due course. I, on the other hand, was portrayed as shameless and calculating, flaunting my pregnancy 'for all to see', showing that I 'was not going to miss a moment. Pregnant or not.' While I was portrayed as unscrupulous and disreputable, my behaviour an outrage and an embarrassment, Cecil was the unfortunate victim, trying to 'do the right thing'.

One of the most objectionable features of this article was the reference to my having spoken to Murdo Maclean. I knew that the *Daily Express* would not have published a story which relied for its air of authenticity on the reference to the Chief Whip's Private Secretary, without first checking on its accuracy. They must have checked with Maclean and he knew me quite well enough for there to be absolutely no question of his being able to claim that he had mistaken me for someone else. Why, therefore, had he not denied the story when asked for confirmation? Furthermore, it was apparent from the calls Richard had received from the press in the past three days that other newspapers knew where I was. It seemed hardly credible that the *Daily Express* should not also have known. Like the quotes from 'Cabinet Ministers' and 'colleagues' in the *Sunday Times* and the *Observer*, the reference to the Chief Whip's Private Secretary had been made to lend authenticity to the story and would not have been made without his knowledge. I was terribly upset by this loathsome story.

It is distressing enough, having become pregnant, to discover that the father of your child has ceased to love you. To find that he is not only prepared to put you through prolonged and awful publicity, but actually will encourage, even perhaps initiate, a smear campaign against you is a terrible experience. The totally groundless and unprovoked attack launched by the *Daily Express* was the last straw.

I had tried very hard to shut my mind to the awful things that had happened and to think only about my child. I had partially succeeded, until the *Daily Express* published these lies. I cannot express the feelings that I suffered at being portrayed as I was in the Hickey story. I felt that there was an army of people ranged against me. It seemed that there was no limit to their malice and that there was nothing they would not do to damage me.

As for the writer of the William Hickey column, I wonder about the attitude towards women generally of a man who can write in those terms of a woman who is pregnant and about whom he knows nothing. He was, presumably, fed the 'facts' of my mythical visit to the House, but the phraseology and terms of the story must have been the product of his own unpleasant imagination.

Flora told me that she had spoken to my solicitor about the *Daily Express* story and that he would telephone me in about two hours' time—it then being lunch-time in England.

Allan Hughes telephoned me at 7.30 pm to say that he had drafted a letter to the Editor, demanding an apology. It would be delivered to the *Daily Express* office that afternoon. He said that I could sue them for libel, but that Fleet Street would, of course make the most of the story. We agreed that initially he would demand a full apology and retraction to be given equal prominence to the original story.

An apology would be of little comfort to me. No doubt everyone who had read the story would have been taken in by it. How many of them would see the subsequent apology?

Allan also said that he had received a telephone call from someone who identified himself as 'Punch', the person who had sent me the telemessage the previous weekend. I had told Allan about this before I left for Muscat and had asked Flora to send him a copy. He had not yet received it and had therefore made a somewhat non-committal response to 'Punch', who said that, if I had not taken my solicitor into my confidence, then neither could he, and hung up. I was disappointed, as I should have liked to know who he was and why he had telephoned.

At nine o'clock, Allan rang me again to get my approval of the wording of the apology we would require of the *Daily Express* and said that he would report back to me the next day.

The Government Chief Whip ignores my plea

I discussed the matter at length with Elisabeth and Richard. I pointed out to them that the *Daily Express* would not have published the story without first speaking to Murdo Maclean to satisfy themselves that it was true. I proposed to telephone Maclean and demand an explanation and a public denial of the story. Richard did not wish me to suffer the indignity of a conversation with the man and insisted that he should telephone for me. I gave him the direct line telephone number to 10 Downing Street and told him to ask to be put through to the Chief Whip's Office at 12 Downing Street, where he would be most likely to find Maclean on a Friday afternoon. If that failed he would try the number of the Whips' office in the House of Commons.

At nine-thirty that night—five-thirty in the afternoon in London— Richard spoke to Maclean and and asked why he had lent his name to the story, knowing it to be untrue. Maclean's explanation was that he had apparently been seen talking to a lady in Central Lobby on Monday, that of course it was not me, but when William Hickey telephoned and asked him to confirm or deny the story, he had thought it better to give a 'no comment' type of answer. He had seen the article but thought it was best to ignore it. Richard told him that he could not just ignore it and that he must issue a denial of the story to the press. Maclean's response was that he did not talk to the press and that, as a civil servant, he could not issue such a denial. Richard disagreed and insisted that Maclean was honour-bound to deny the story, but Maclean said he would have to take advice. That meant he would have to consult the Chief Whip or 10 Downing Street.

Maclean's words were astonishing. With his job and his political experience in the House of Commons, he must have known perfectly well what would be the result of a 'no comment' response to such an enquiry, if indeed that was all that he had said. It was significant that the newspaper had made no attempt to verify the story with me, my family or my solicitor. Either they were very confident of its truth, or they had believed they ran no risk in publishing it. Whoever had inspired the story must have been very convincing. It was highly unlikely that the journalist had dreamed it up all by himself. It was much more likely to have originated amongst those in the Conservative Party who had been blackening my name throughout the past fortnight.

As for Maclean's assertion that he did not talk to the press, it was nonsense. Of course conversations between the Whips' Office and the press are not acknowledged, being 'on Lobby terms', and of course most of them are conducted by the Whips themselves rather than their minions, but the idea that Maclean never spoke to the press was ridiculous. I had myself seen him in conversation with journalists when I was working in the House. Furthermore, the fact of his being a civil servant would not prevent him from issuing a denial to the press in a matter of personal honour or to prevent damage to someone else.

There was obviously no point in trying to get Maclean to do anything and I decided to telephone the Chief Whip, John Wakeham. Elisabeth did not wish me to do anything that would upset me any more than I already was and Richard again asked me to let him handle the matter for me. He rang 12 Downing Street and asked to speak to John Wakeham, to be told that he had an appointment in Colchester until about 7 pm and would not get home until about an hour later. Richard was given Wakeham's home telephone number.

When Wakeham got home it would be around midnight in Muscat. Elisabeth and I waited up for Richard to make this call. At his first attempt, Richard spoke to Mrs Wakeham who told him to ring again in about an hour. It was nearly one-thirty in the morning for us when he finally spoke to Wakeham. I listened to the conversation. It was obvious that Maclean had spoken to Wakeham following Richard's call. Wakeham was very much on the defensive. He said that the reason for Maclean's response when asked for confirmation of the story was that Maclean 'couldn't talk to strange people over the telephone who said they were ringing from the *Express*'. He said that Maclean had subsequently spoken to the *Daily Express* lobby correspondent, John Warden, and denied the story. Wakeham said he had himself 'taken steps' to ensure that the Deputy Editor knew the story to be a fabrication, only to find that my solicitors had been in touch with the *Daily Express* and were discussing what should be done. He said that he had done all he could do in the matter.

Two important points emerged from this conversation. First, Maclean could not have spoken to Warden until *after* the story had appeared, or the *Daily Express* would not have published it. Second, Wakeham's 'steps' had been taken only as a result of pressure from us. Wakeham would undoubtedly have been informed of the piece in the *Daily Express*, if not by his office at 12 Downing Street, then by the Whips' Office in the House of Commons. He could not have been unaware of the story and indeed it is highly likely that he knew about it the previous day, as Maclean would almost certainly have told him about the call from William Hickey. By Wakeham's own admission, he had not telephoned the Deputy Editor of the *Daily Express* until Friday afternoon—how else would he have known that my solicitors had been in touch with the paper? In all probability he rang the Deputy Editor only after Richard's call to Wakeham.

What it boiled down to was that Wakeham would have done nothing about the story, but for the presure from us. The story did him no harm and no doubt he was content to let it stand, even though its credibility rested on the mention of his Private Secretary. As far as I was concerned, Wakeham's call to the *Daily Express* meant nothing if he was not also prepared publicly to dissociate himself and his office from the story. I could not help imagining what it would have been like if I had been in England when the Hickey story came out. How much more difficult it would have been for me to get something done about it. I dare say that that thought had been in the mind of the person who had inspired it.

Saturday was blighted by the Hickey business, as indeed was most of my holiday. The time difference meant a long wait to hear from my solicitor, who eventually rang at about 4.30 in the afternoon to say that the *Daily Express* had not been able to publish an apology because there was no *Hickey* column on a Saturday—which seemed a feeble excuse to me—but in any case, they said they had to check the source of their information fully and were having difficulty in doing so. It seemed to me that any agrument over who supplied them with the story was irrelevant to an apology. There could be no argument whatsoever about its being a total fabrication.

Allan told me that when his partner, David Leverton, had been speaking to the Editor's Secretary the previous afternoon, she had told him to hold because they were talking to the Prime Minister's office, which cast an interesting new light on the business. Allan agreed that it was important that we press the Chief Whip for a statement disowning the story. He said he thought it was strange that the story had come out on the Friday, when it concerned an incident that had allegedly occurred on the Monday, especially as it was known in Fleet Street from Tuesday onwards that I was in Muscat. To my mind it meant that the source of the story must have been very credible indeed and it also cast doubt on Maclean's assertion that he had said merely 'no comment' to the *Daily Express*.

At a quarter past ten on Saturday night I rang John Wakeham. Richard wanted to make the call for me, but I insisted that I must speak to Wakeham myself. After all, we were acquainted with one another. No doubt he recalled the occasion some years before when he had asked me to work for him. I dare say he regrets it now. I probably still have the two letters, he wrote, the first telling me what a wonderful and well-paid job it would be, the second expressing his great regret that I had declined his offer. I had had no shortage of job offers in those days and was confident of my good reputation in the House of Commons.

I told Wakeham that my call was nothing to do with the fact that I had demanded and expected to receive an apology from the *Daily Express*. I said that my call concerned the political aspects of the matter, that I had been appalled to hear that Murdo Maclean had not immediately denied the story outright, but had merely refused to comment. I pointed out that no attempt had been made to verify the story with me, my family, or my solicitor and that the newspaper's decision to publish rested solely on their confidence in Maclean's involvement.

He repeated what he had told Richard of the call to the Deputy Editor on Friday afternoon, but I said that, while I was glad he had taken that action, it had been ineffective and the appearance of authenticity which the story derived from its association with his office still survived.

I asked that he issue a statement, dissociating his office from the story. He said "But Sara, my dear, the Whips can't talk to the press". 'My dear', indeed. And did he really expect me to believe that the Whips couldn't talk to the press? They do it all the time. I said, "That's nonsense and you know it".

He then had the nerve to say that he could not see what the fuss was about. He said "No-one will believe the story and in any case I can't see what harm it has done you". Whether he intended to be offensive or simply couldn't help himself, I wasn't sure. I asked him how he would like it if a newspaper article were written about a member of his family in such terms. Would he not be disgusted and think it extremely damaging? He said nothing.

I said that he knew perfectly well that it had damaged me, that the story was believed and that it was the mention of his office that made it credible. I told him that I was again being hounded by the press, some of whom wanted to know my opinion of the story and the way it had arisen. He expressed surprise and said that the press had not been in touch with him about it. I did not bother to ask him why, if the whips never talk to the press, he would have expected them to try to speak to him.

I said that I expected the Government to wish to dissociate itself from this libel, that the paper's apology to me was a separate issue, and that if the Government did not publicly disown their apparent connection with the story, there was only one conclusion to be drawn: that they wished the story to stand, and were content to be associated with it and to give it credibility. I said, therefore, that I expected his office to issue a statement to the Press Association without further delay.

Wakeham repeated, somewhat lamely, the line he had taken earlier, about the Whips' office not speaking to the press. I urged him to reconsider his position. He said that he would 'have to see', that the matter would require 'further consideration', by which I suppose he meant that he would have to consult 10 Downing Street. I suppose I should not have expected any more from him, in view of what had gone before.

The *Daily Express* did not publish an apology on Monday. When David Leverton rang me late on Monday night it was to say that he had had a 'battle' with the *Daily Express* solicitor and that they had agreed to print an apology in Tuesday's edition. The explanation given by the *Daily Express* for the story was that the information had been fed to them by a lobby correspondent as a 'leg-pull'. I thought that was baloney and said that it was inexcusable that they had not printed an apology straight away, regardless of who had pulled their legs and why. Leverton said that the excuse given by the *Daily Express* for their delay in apologising was that 'it had all happened on a Friday and it was difficult to get hold of people over the weekend'. I dare say that the difficulty lay in their dealings with the Government Chief Whip's office. The *Daily Express* would no doubt have liked to lay the blame at someone else's door and Wakeham would have been determined that their apology would not put his office in a bad light.

Leverton said that all that remained was the question of damages and costs and that he would report back to me on Tuesday when he had taken expert advice on that aspect of the matter.

The *Daily Express* did not publish their apology on Tuesday. This time they put forward some feeble excuse about a break-down in communications in their office and it having been too late to reset the Hickey page. It was sickening. They'd known for five days, if not longer, that the story was a damnable lie and still they had not apoligised. Nor had Wakeham or any other member of the Government made any public denial of their connection with the story.

I told Leverton that I did not believe the string of excuses we had been fed by the *Daily Express*, which were totally unconvincing. I also said that, in view of Wakeham's failure to dissociate his office from the story, I wanted to issue a statement to the Press Association denouncing the appalling behaviour of the *Daily Express* and exposing the failure of the Government to dissociate itself from the story. He insisted that he should do this for me.

On Wednesday 2 November the *Daily Express* published their apology, at last. It was an insignificant little piece compared with their libellous story, which had been prominently displayed, with a large, eye-catching headline. The Government Chief Whip kept silent. My solicitors' statement to the Press Association was too bland and attracted little attention from the press, although I gather it caused a flutter of anxiety in the offices of the *Daily Express*.

I was persuaded to accept £5,000 damages from the *Daily Express*, plus my legal costs, although I was told that I could have got considerably more if I had taken them to Court. I was so sickened by the publicity I had received already that the prospect of a court case in about two years time and another going-over at the hands of the press was more than I could face. I was also told that damages would be reduced considerably because I had already 'lost my reputation' as a result of the recent scandal.

It was another pointer to the double standards applied by our society in such matters: a 'fallen' woman suffers permanent damage to her reputation, while a man's can make a substantial, if not complete, recovery.

The *Daily Express*'s story ruined my holiday. The whole week had been taken up with it and it had been very difficult to deal with the problem when I was so far away. From then on I was worried about what might happen next. I spent only another five days in Muscat.

Return to England

I took the 3.50 am flight to London on Thursday 10 November. Elisabeth had insisted that I get two or three hours sleep. When she woke me at 1 am, I was plunged into gloom. I felt that I could not stay any longer in Muscat, but going back to England meant facing up to other problems. Richard drove me out to the airport. Thanks to the British Airways official in Muscat—I had taken the advice of the steward on my outward flight—I had a very comfortable journey and was even able to lie down and sleep for the greater part of the flight. Even so, my hands and feet had swollen considerably by the time we arrived at Heathrow seven hours later. I had rather unwisely removed my shoes and could scarcely get them on again.

Heathrow looked exactly as it had two and half weeks earlier, except that then it had been evening and represented escape and excitement. Now it was seven in the morning and very cold after Muscat. But it was crowded and anonymous and there was not a photographer in sight. I tottered out to the taxi rank—my shoes were now so tight that there was no way I could have endured a walk to the tube—and was soon on the familiar route into London. It was a beautiful, crisp, sunny morning and London looked very attractive. My spirits rose. There was no-one lurking outside the house in Battersea.

I rang my father, who had heard from Elisabeth that I was on my way home. He said that William wanted to drive me home and proposed coming up to London that afternoon.

The prospect of being driven home rather than having to catch a train, or even perhaps stay a night in London was wonderful. I decided to make the most of my short time in London and to get my hair done. Harvey Nichols' hair salon said Yes, Margaret could do my hair if I came straight away. When I arrived, I was surprised to be greeted by the manager with the suggestion that I have my hair done in a private room off the salon. Maragaret explained that not long after the story 'broke' the press had discovered that I had my hair done at Harvey Nichols and had beseiged the salon. She had been completely booked up with new 'clients' wanting her to do their hair. She was offered large sums of money for information about me. She had taken a couple of days off and when her new 'clients' were told that someone else would do their hair they cancelled their appointments. However, there were no reporters or photographers in evidence now and it was a great treat to have my hair done, not having been able to go to a hairdresser for months.

In the afternoon I went to Lincoln's Inn to see Allan Hughes. He wished to discuss the draft of a letter he was proposing to send to Farrer following their first meeting. He also reported to me the latest offers he had received from newspapers for my story, but I said that I did not intend to accept any of these.

William was waiting for me at Albert Bridge Road when I got home from my meeting with Allan Hughes. Once again, he drove me home—this time without a press escort—and brought me up to date with what had been happening while I was away, describing the continued visits and telephone calls from reporters and the idiotic questions they asked.

It was a great relief to get home to Marksbury. I had only been away for two and a half weeks but it seemed like months. Flora and Roger were still living at Winsbury House, fending off press enquiries and opening my mail. Amongst the many letters awaiting me was one which deserves a special mention. It was signed Christopher Wilson and in brackets underneath the signature 'or Wm Hickey, for it is he ...'

This was the man who had alleged that I had 'stunned MPs by turning up in the House of Commons as Parliament reopened for business', and who had written about me in such loathsome terms. This man, to whom I was a scandalous and unrepentant 'fallen' woman, had written to apologise:

> Dear Miss Keays,
> I have made some mistakes in my time, but never such an appalling one as I managed to perpetrate in the William Hickey column last Friday.
> ... I feel I owe you a personal apology, which I here present. I have very much admired your personal courage and decorum, and would not wish to misrepresent you in any way ...

I would have liked to feel that his apology was genuine and totally sincere, but I found it hard to reconcile his protestations of admiration for me with the horrid things he had written about me. Even if he had been fed a pack of lies and had genuinely believed that I had been in the House, he need not have chosen to write about me in the terms that he did.

He concluded his letter by expressing the hope that he hadn't spoilt my holiday, which he undoubtedly had. The episode had turned what should have been a complete rest into a most upsetting and exhausting time. What people like him always seem to forget is that their lies do lasting damage. I do not suppose that all the people who read the article also saw the apology—which in any case was not published under the same kind of shouting headlines as the original piece. Mr Wilson and others who play the same game should realise that they can't wipe the slate clean simply by apologising.

Perhaps the most galling aspect of the whole episode was that some of the people who saw or heard about the *Hickey* piece, not only believed it without question, but were outraged by it. For some time afterwards people commented on it. One person actually said 'What on earth was Sara playing at, going to the House of Commons? How could she have done such a thing?'. Evidently the very idea that I might have gone to the House was shocking.

No apology and no amount of money can undo that kind of damage. Many people, although they do not remember where they picked it up, have acquired the idea that I have sought publicity.

It was further evidence of the double standards in our society that there was no public criticism of Cecil's decision to continue with his political career, but the very idea that I should even show my face in the House of Commons was outrageous.

Had Cecil not asked me to give up my job there, in order to keep my pregnancy a secret and so protect him, and had I not had a loving family to help me, I should have been obliged to go on working at the House of Commons for as long as possible before my baby was born. I had no wish to do so, life having become quite difficult enough for me already, but had I not had a loving family to help me and had Cecil not promised to provide for me, I would have had no option but to continue working. Indeed, I would have had the right by law to ask for my job at the House to be kept open for me to return to after maternity leave.

Also waiting for me in the pile of mail were a number of letters from literary agents and publishers, enquiring whether I wished to publish my 'story'. I had no wish even to reply to them and I had so many letters to answer by then, that I could reply only to those from friends and relatives. The rest had to remain unanswered.

The following day, the *Daily Mail*, published an article by Robin Oakley, whom Cecil had known from some years, headed PUBLIC GIVES VERDICT ON MINISTER'S LOVE AFFAIR and CECIL PARKINSON 'SHOULD BE CALLED BACK'. In the centre of the article was a photograph of me with the caption 'Sara Keays ... She comes out of the affair with little sympathy'. Reporting the findings of an 'exclusive survey of opinion conducted for the *Daily Mail* by NOP' he wrote:

> The way should be open for Mr Cecil Parkinson to resume a Cabinet career after a discreet interval, according to public opinion

and revealed that

> There is little public sympathy for pregnant Miss Keays, the former secretary whose revelations forced Mr Parkinson's dramatic resignation.

This was insignificant compared with some of the things the *Daily Mail* wrote about me over the ensuing months, in which they emerged as a kind of pro-Parkinson, anti-Keays broadsheet, with articles by Robin Oakley trumpeting the return of the hero and vicious pieces by Nigel Dempster intended to show me as scheming and money-grubbing.

Burglary

Thursday 17 November 1983

A week after my return from Muscat I went to London to have a scan at St Thomas's Hospital. It was extraordinary to be able to see a picture of my baby on the screen beside me and to watch it moving about in response to the slight pressure of the scanning device. Feeling very thrilled I went to see Mr Kenney who said that the pregnancy was proceeding just as it should. We then talked about the arrangements for the birth and he proposed that I go not to St Thomas's, but to a smaller hospital where it might be easier to keep my presence a secret and to fend off unwelcome visitors. He suggested St Teresa's Hospital in Wimbledon. He also proposed that I be admitted under an assumed name. Finally, he said that the best way of keeping the event secret from the press would be by choosing the time of the birth, in other words by inducing it, rather than waiting for nature to take its course, and that a good date would be New Year's Eve, when journalists might have better things to do than try to find out where I was having my baby. I was only too happy to go along with these arrangements and when the time came I was very grateful indeed that he had suggested them.

That afternoon I telephoned Allan Hughes, who wanted my approval of a letter he was sending to Farrer. I returned to Marksbury that night hoping that I would now have some peace and be able to concentrate on getting my cottage ready to move into before my baby was born. Once again, my hopes were short-lived.

Sunday 20 November 1983

At 2 am on Sunday 20 November, Flora woke me to say that Keynsham Police had telephoned to ask me to contact Battersea Police because Elisabeth and Richard's house in Battersea had been burgled. I did so immediately. The Inspector who took my call said that the burglars had broken in through the kitchen window, but that it appeared that nothing had been taken. I asked if the safe had been tampered with. After a moment or two spent in conversation with someone else, he told me that the safe was intact, but that my filing cabinets had been smashed. He said that they did not consider that it was a run-of-the-mill burglary and that it appeared that the burglars had been after something out of the ordinary.

How thankful I was that I had, at the last moment, removed from the house everything I could think of that concerned Cecil and myself. In fact I was not particularly concerned about the safe, as the items I had left there were less important than those I had removed. I was impressed that the police had already been over the house and should be able to tell me already that it appeared that no valuables (in the usual sense) had been taken. The Inspector said that the house was insecure at the moment and asked for my authority to get the window boarded up. I said that I would be very grateful if he could arrange that for me. He also wanted to know when I could make my own check on the house and I agreed to do so the following afternoon.

I repeated the conversation to Flora and Roger, who were aghast. We were all thinking the same thing. If it was, as the police suspected, an out of the ordinary break-in, who was responsible and what were they looking for? My father's correspondence with the Prime Minister? If that were the case, then I would have expected the break-in to have been at Winsbury House. Had they been looking for my letters from Cecil, or something else concerning him?

It was appalling even to suspect such things but my feelings then were nothing compared to those I experienced the following afternoon, when I arrived at the house with William, who had insisted on driving me up. I had told Battersea Police when I would arrive and there was a sergeant waiting outside the house. The scene that met my eyes when I opened the front door took me aback, and that was only the hall. Apparently one of the burglars—it was assumed that there had been more than one—had cut himself and had bled copiously. However, to avoid dripping blood on the carpet and furniture, he had hauled out some sheets and towels from the airing cupboard and had draped them around the hall and sitting-room.

We went downstairs into the kitchen. I remembered that when I had last been in the house, three days before, the internal lock on the kitchen door had jammed when I had locked it behind me just before leaving for Marksbury. The burglars had broken into the kitchen, only to find that they had to break out of it into the passage. They had tried to force the lock back with a kitchen knife, which was lying on the floor with its blade snapped off. That was presumably how one burglar had cut himself.

The kitchen was a shambles. My two filing cabinets, which I had installed in the corner of the room until they could be moved to Marksbury with all my other belongings, had been broken open. The drawer which had contained my personal correspondence had been ripped out and its contents spilled onto the floor. The other three drawers which contained only political papers, such as Conservative Party briefing material from Central Office, and an assortment of correspondence and other general filing, were apparently untouched. One of the lights, which had a long flex and had been hooked up to the ceiling, had been pulled down and left hanging low over the table.

We had only been in the house a short time when CID officers and forensic experts arrived. They joined us in the kitchen. The detective-sergeant in charge of the on-the-spot investigation amazed me by saying—no doubt to reassure me—that 10 Downing Street had been informed and had ordered a news black-out, and that the matter had been referred to the Commissioner of the Metropolitan Police. He added that it would be helpful if I kept the matter to myself. I said that I had to inform my insurers and he suggested that I delay doing so for a few days. When I asked the reason for the news black-out, he said that there was a suggestion that it was a security matter. I wondered who had introduced this extraordinary idea and I said that they had better get it quite straight in their minds that there was absolutely no question of any matter of national security being involved.

I certainly had no intention of broadcasting the fact that my sister's house had been burgled and the last thing I wanted was to attract the attention of the media, but I could see no reason why the matter should be kept secret, unless the police hoped that, if papers had been taken or photographed and information about them appeared in the press, they might be able to track down the thieves.

I did not believe that it was my interests that 10 Downing Street had at heart when they imposed a news-blackout of the burglary. What interest could 10 Downing Street have in the matter, other than my father's correspondence with the Prime Minister? There was nothing else that could have concerned them. If the burglars had found Cecil's letters to me, or photographs, that could cause us both embarrassment and distress, but no more than that, surely?

The CID officers accompanied William and me round the house, while I checked every room. We went upstairs to the sitting-room. Just about everything in the room appeared to have been moved, but apparently with care. My stereo had been lifted off a chest and rested across an armchair. The canteen of silver cutlery which had been hidden in the chest had been taken out and opened, but the contents left untouched. The dresser had been opened, but none of the china, some of it quite valuable had been taken. Pictures had been taken down and left leaning against the wall.

It was the same in each room. It appeared that a very thorough search had been made, but nothing had been taken, not even cash from the desk in my bedroom, although that too had been searched. The receiver had been lifted off the telephone and left lying on my bed. All the matresses had been lifted and the bedclothes torn back. On the top floor, the burglars had managed to set off a fire extinguisher, so that the whole house was covered with a fine whitish powder, which took weeks of vacuuming to remove. The mess was indescribable, particularly in my bedroom, but little damage had been done.

As nothing appeared to have been taken I wondered whether the intruders had perhaps left something behind instead. After all that had happened so far, I was beginning to think that anything was possible. The police obligingly examined the telephones to see whether they had acquired any additions, but said they thought they were alright, adding that it was exceedingly difficult nowadays to detect listening devices.

We returned to the kitchen. I could not tell, without going through them very carefully, whether any of my personal papers had been taken. They were in such a mess that the only thing we could do was bundle them into a cardboard box to take back to Marksbury, where I could go through them at my leisure, if I ever got any.

It was then that I remembered that I had had some of my diaries there. I had taken some of my possessions to Marksbury, where they were still packed up in boxes, but a lot remained, some still unpacked, at the house in Battersea. The five months since I had moved from Temple West Mews had been so hectic that I could not remember what I had done with them. However, at least one diary appeared to be missing, possibly two. The thought that they might have been stolen was horrid.

Eventually the police completed their examinations and left. William and I then packed up as much of my china and other valuables as we could get into the car and drove wearily back to Marksbury.

Monday 21 November 1983

I telephoned my solicitor and told him about the burglary and what the police had said. He said that I was obliged to inform my insurers and should do so straightaway.

That afternoon I had a telephone call from a Detective Chief Inspector at Battersea Police Station, who was at some pains to play the burglary down. He said he thought we were reading too much into it and that it was probably just a routine break-in after all. I said that if that were the case, it was very strange that the burglars had taken nothing.

He left me with the distinct impression that the officer who had been in charge on the spot the previous day had been talking out of turn. I hoped the Chief Inspector was right, but it was hard not to be alarmed. If it was just a 'routine' break-in, what had the burglars been looking for? Why had they not taken any of the valuables in the house? And why had all the police officers I had spoken to hitherto said that it was an unusual burglary? It was not I who had read anything unusual into it, but the police, although I readily agreed with them when I saw the house. And I had never heard of burglars being careful with the householders possessions and putting down towels to keep bloodstains off the furniture.

Weeks later I discovered something even more peculiar. The burglars had prised off the front of one of the loudspeakers attached to the stereo and had partially cut through the material inside the speaker with a very fine knife or razor-blade. They had then put back the outer cover and I did not discover what they had done until I tried to use the stereo and found the speaker no longer worked.

Tuesday 22 November 1983

On Tuesday I called on my father's solicitor, Richard Smerdon, and asked him to make notarised copies of my father's correspondence with the Prime Minister. I then lodged the originals and the copies at separate addresses for safe-keeping.

It may seem strange that I should have gone to such lengths to preserve my father's correspondence with the Prime Minister, but it had become very important because of what had happened since Polling Day. My feelings about this correspondence had changed dramatically because of those awful experiences. In June, when I learned that my father had written to the Prime Minister, I had been distressed and embarrassed. Now I was very glad that he had done so, as I could produce it, if necessary, to corroborate what I had said in my statement to *The Times*.

The idea that that correspondence was likely to be stolen may now seem far-fetched, but then it seemed a real possibility and I was anxious about it. So many alarming things had happened, on top of all the unpleasantness with Cecil. There had been the sinister letter from the ex-mercenary, the blackening of my name that had gone on since publication of Cecil's statement, the anonymous telemessage, and now the alarming break-in at Elisabeth and Richard's house. I wondered what awful thing would happen next.

There had been no let-up in press interest. Although we no longer had reporters camped on our doorstep, they called at the house or telephoned us, and other members of the family, almost daily. I went out very little, and only when I was sure there were no reporters lurking in the neighbourhood. I could not bear being followed about and questioned. I felt very conscious of my appearance and hated being photographed. If I wanted to go and talk to the builders at the cottage, I checked first that the coast was clear. Reporters called there regularly offering large sums of money for information and permission to take photographs inside the house. They got short shrift from the builders, who became thoroughly irritated by their persistent and idiotic questioning. A smartly dressed pair from a Sunday newspaper had followed one man about, brandishing a wad of banknotes and asking questions, one of the most memorable of which was 'Does she look like the kind of woman who would have an affair with a Cabinet Minister?'

Not all the reporters who flocked to Marksbury behaved badly. Some of those who succeeded in speaking to members of the family were very polite and apologetic about troubling us. They would say that they knew what the answer would be, but they had been told that they had to try, and having done so and failed they would apologise and depart. It was a waste of their time and ours and all it achieved was to keep me anxious and on my guard, so that I never answered the doorbell or the telephone, unless I was alone in the house and obliged to do so.

I was becoming very impatient to move into my cottage. I felt that I was a burden to my family and a constant cause of anxiety to them. I thought, mistakenly as it transpired, that if I moved into my own home, they would not be bothered continually by reporters.

However it was looking increasingly as though the cottage would not be ready before the baby was born and in any case, the media were doing everything they could to find out where and when the birth would take place. I agreed with my family that when the time came for me to go into hospital, it would be much harder to give reporters the slip from the cottage, which is at the end of a cul-de-sac, than from Winsbury House, which it was possible to leave, as Elisabeth had found, by other routes than through the main gate, although I did not relish the thought of being driven over a bumpy field in a Land Rover when the birth was imminent. All Mr Kenney's carefully-laid plans would go awry if I went into labour when I was a hundred miles or more from the hospital.

The propaganda continues

Thursday 24 November 1983

Various newspapers telephoned seeking confirmation of a story published that day by the *Daily Mail* who had informed their readers that my baby would be a boy. This was news to me. As neither I nor my doctor knew whether I would have a boy or girl, how could the *Daily Mail* know, or were they claiming a divine source for their information?

In due course I saw the *Daily Mail* piece. It was the principal item in Nigel Dempster's *Mail Diary*. The claim that I was expecting a boy was only a minor irritation compared with the rest of the article. Headed KEAYS TO THE COFFERS, it was written in such a way as to suggest that Cecil was not nearly as well off as was generally thought and was being taken to the cleaners by a woman with whom he had merely whiled away his time on two or three occasions. It pretended to know details of the financial settlement which Cecil would have to 'stump up' as the price for his 'dalliances'. It began:

> The final bill facing the former Trade and Industry Secretary for his 'two or three' dalliances this year with Sara Keays will be considerably less than the sum of £200,000 that has been mooted ... His family worth is less than £1 million.

If the last sentence were true, then he must have suffered a recent dramatic decline in his financial circumstances.

Although I was not surprised that the *Daily Mail*, which has never been renowned for its impartiality, should show such bias, I could not inure myself to their spite. Time after time they repeated the lie that Cecil had merely 'dallied' with me.

Did they merely poach this from the *Sunday Times*, or was it fed to them direct? Why was it that such people disbelieved what I had said in my statement to *The Times* yet published as fact allegations by people who were not prepared to be named? I felt utterly powerless against such attacks and as the birth of my baby drew nearer, I found them increasingly distressing.

I wondered who had prompted Dempster to write the article. It struck me as significant that just at the time when Cecil was at last addressing himself to the matter of financial provision for me and my baby, disinformation about his financial circumstances was being put about Fleet Street.

Dempster went on to suggest that he had discussed the matter with my solicitor, to whom he attributed a remark which Allan Hughes assured me he had not made.

Dempster said that I had 'had a scan which shows her baby to be a boy'. How did he know I had had a scan, or was this just guesswork dressed up to look like fact? In any case the scan had not revealed the sex of the baby.

Not one of the reporters who telephoned or called at the house that day had questioned any part of the Dempster article other than the reference to the baby. No doubt that was because they believed everything else. I wondered how many other people believed that my pregnancy was the result of Cecil having merely 'dallied' with me 'two or three times' and that I was using it to get money out of him.

Dempster's article ended with the following:

> Other matters under discussion are the boy's surname, but matters are not expected to be sealed until the baby's actual birth.

This was another figment of Dempster's fevered imagination. There was never any question of my child taking any surname other than Keays.

A week later, the Associate News Editor of the *Daily Mail*, Garth Burden, wrote me a 'letter of introduction' in case I ever wished to contact his newspaper. He told me that 'the *Daily Mail* would treat any picture or interview with the greatest respect' and that 'We do have a reputation in Fleet Street for fairness and sensible reporting'. He could have fooled me.

Thursday 30 November 1983

I went to London for one night, having an appointment with Mr Kenney the following morning. While in London I spoke to Dr Tom Stuttaford, Medical Correspondent of *The Times*, whom both Cecil and I had known for a number of years, having first met him when he was a Member of Parliament. I had not spoken to him for some months. He told me of the disinformation campaign that had followed publication of Cecil's statement. He told me that all the major newspapers, *The Times* included, had been briefed 'off the record' by 10 Downing Street on the background to Cecil's statement.

The most significant of the 'facts' fed to editors and Lobby correspondents by 10 Downing Street were the following: that Cecil had only seen me two or three times that year, that we had had intercourse 'for old times sake' as a result of which I had unfortunately become pregnant, that the relationship had already ended, that Cecil had not seen me while I was in Brussels, that it was he who had ended the affair and I who had tried to keep it going. As to the precise source of this information, Tom said that Charles Douglas-Home had referred to its having come from 'the fountain head' which could only mean either Mrs Thatcher herself or her Press Secretary.

On Friday morning Sidney Young of the *Daily Mirror* rang to ask if it was true that the house in London had been burgled a fortnight ago. Rather than risk him writing a sensational story based on pure speculation, I had a brief conversation with him and confirmed that there had been a break-in, but that nothing appeared to have been stolen. He asked if any documents had been taken and I said that it was a possibility, but that I was still checking.

Within a few minutes of that call, I received another from Tony Frost of the *Sunday Mirror*, who had considerably more information than Mr Young, saying that he understood that my filing cabinets had been broken open and that papers and photographs had been scattered on the floor. Naturally, he did not say where he had obtained this information, although it seemed it could only have come from the police. That night Flora and Roger were inundated with calls from press, radio and television reporters asking for confirmation of a story being carried by the *Daily Mirror*.

The following morning the burglary was mentioned on several *BBC* news bulletins, but by lunch-time the story had apparently died and apart from one or two calls from reporters on Sunday who would have got very carried away with the story if we had given them a chance, that was the end of the matter, or so I hoped. The really surprising thing about the story was that it had not got out sooner. The news black-out which the police told us had been ordered by 10 Downing Street had been very effective. I wonder what other, more serious, things are concealed from the unsuspecting public in this way.

More legal negotiations

We were into December, the birth of my baby was only four weeks away and still Cecil had put forward no proposals for a financial settlement, even though he had promised these at the beginning of September. My solicitor had written to Farrer, asking for confirmation that Cecil would pay the costs of my confinement and the sum towards the improvements to my cottage which he had promised in June, most of which I had already paid for, and also asking for Cecil's proposals for what he and other people had described as the 'full and generous provision' he would make for me and my child. It was particularly tiresome that he had as yet paid nothing towards the improvements to the cottage when he had urged me to get the work done and had promised to pay for them. When he changed his mind three months later about marrying me, I was left with the bills.

On 6 December, Allan Hughes rang me to say that he had received a lengthy reply from Farrer. He was sending me a copy but we would need to meet to discuss it, so two days later I went to see him in London. Any financial provision was to be strictly controlled:

—the money Cecil had promised for the improvements to the cottage to go not to me but into a Trust for the child;
—he would pay for education up to the age of 18 (his other children had the benefit of further education);
—the maintenance was to be fixed at £3,000 a year as 'in the early years savings can be made for the child to be available thereafter', and was to be done under an Affiliation Order for his tax purposes.

I was not exactly qualified by experience to judge whether £3,000 per annum was adequate provision. Nor did I anticipate that this would result in a blaze of unpleasant publicity when the Affiliation Order was made in a West Country Magistrate's Court. It also meant, of course, that the maintenance would be paid net of tax and I would have to reclaim it each year.

As for the payment in respect of the loss of my career, not only was the figure proposed less than three years of my salary at the House of Commons, but they were proposing that the whole financial settlement should be conditional upon my not accepting any payment from the media, directly or indirectly, for my 'story'. I told my solicitor that if Cecil thought he could buy my silence, he could keep his money. I found all the arguments over my 'worth' and my entitlement insufferable, especially as I had expected Cecil at least to wish to provide as well for his child by me as he had for his other children. It was as if he and Farrer considered that they should decide my standard of living and that it should remain at whatever arbitrary level they chose.

If I had been the money-grubbing and unscrupulous woman I had been made out to be, I could have turned my back on these negotiations, waved goodbye to my solicitor and accepted any one of the countless and staggering offers I had received for my 'story'. It would have been a very easy way of assuring myself and my child of a comfortable life, free from financial worry.

I was very tired and decided to stay the night in London. Feeling a great desire for some light relief I went out for supper with two very good friends, both of whom worked as secretaries in the House of Commons and whom I had not seen for some time. We had a very enjoyable meal in a rather crowded restaurant but were aware of a group of people at a table nearby staring at us and evidently discussing us. A little later I saw a young woman get up from the table and go out of the room, returning after a few minutes. I thought nothing more of it until we were leaving the restaurant. As we crossed the threshold we were dazzled by a camera flash and found ourselves waylaid by a reporter and photographer. It was very tiresome. It was the first time I had been out for a meal for months and I immediately regretted it.

I went home for five days of comparative peace at Marksbury. Flora and Roger continued to fend off reporters while I thought about wallpaper and tiles and kitchen equipment for the cottage. My sister-in-law, Georgina, returned from Lagos with the good news that my brother Tom would be joining her in ten days time and that they would be able to stay in England until after my baby was born. Elisabeth rang up from Muscat to say that she too was coming home and would be arriving on Boxing Day or the day after. I was very happy that all my family would be around me to celebrate the arrival of my baby.

On Wednesday 14 December, Flora drove me to London for another check-up by Mr Kenney on the Thursday morning. We returned to Marksbury to learn that reporters had been much in evidence again, trying to find out when the baby was due. My father said that he had been inundated with telephone calls, including one from an American television company. I hated being the cause of these continual invasions of his peace and privacy, but he was very cheerful and amusing about it, making light of it for my sake.

Friday 16 December brought another shock. The house in London had been burgled again during the night and was apparently in a terrible mess. The Inspector at Battersea Police Station to whom I spoke on the telephone said that he did not think it was a professional job like the last occasion, but a 'typical Battersea break-in', probably by youths, who had gone to the drinks cupboard and got loaded and then turned the place upside down. He said that the police would do their best to make the house secure, but they could not give it full-time protection. I agreed to meet the police at the house the next day.

That afternoon a freelance reporter telephoned to say that he wanted to do a story for *The Times* on the burglary in November. He said that since the news of this was given out on 3 December, he had been puzzled by the absence of any further news about it or any details of the burglary itself. He wanted my permission to research the matter and in particular wanted to know what was stolen, or what was not stolen, whether it was possible to tell what the burglars had been looking for and what the police had done about it. I too was puzzled by the matter and would have liked to know myself what the burglars were after, but I could not face the thought of any more problems or publicity and I told him that I did not wish him to pursue the matter.

There were two weeks to go before the birth of my baby. They seemed interminable, although they were very hectic. On Saturday I went back to London with William and Flora and we spent the whole day clearing up the mess and arranging for Banham's to make the house burglar-proof. It was very tiring and I felt that I had had just about all I could take. However, there was still the matter of the financial settlement to be dealt with.

On Tuesday 20 December, ten days before I was due to go into hospital, I received a copy of Farrer's reply to Allan Hughes. Cecil had made little or no alteration to his earlier proposals and had the nerve to press for agreement before Christmas. Considering that I had had to wait weeks for him to come up with any proposals, it was really rich that he should be pressing me to agree them when the birth of my baby was only ten days away.

Cecil had, however, promised to pay for the costs of my confinement. At least I could go ahead with the arrangements for the birth of my baby, knowing that I would be able to pay the bills.

The following day I went to London again to see Allan Hughes, who had already drafted a letter to Farrer for my approval, protesting that Cecil's delay in dealing with these matters should have put me in the position of having to make decisions on them when the birth of my child was imminent, and stating categorically that I would not make my 'silence' a condition of the settlement.

The following morning, Thursday 22 December, I awoke feeling very unwell. A friend drove me to see Mr Kenney, who ordered me to rest and expressed strong disapproval of my being pressed for such important decisions when the birth of my baby was imminent. He put me on antibiotics and said that my blood pressure was up and that if I did not rest I would have to go into hospital early. He said that it was important that I should be well before I had my baby and that I should get as much rest as possible. That was easier said than done. I went back to Albert Bridge Road to where Banham's were making the house secure, having undertaken to do the work before Christmas, in spite of the short notice. To my great relief, my brother Tom arrived from Nigeria and took charge of the situation. I was able to go to bed and Tom divided his time between supervising the workmen toiling in various parts of the house, answering the door to reporters, and providing me with delicious meals and amusing conversation. I was feeling very unwell indeed and would have found it extremely difficult to cope on my own. Not only did he deal with all the problems, but he cheered me up enormously.

Allan Hughes rang me yet again about the financial settlement. He said he thought we had reached the end of the road in the negotiations. I certainly had. One of the most insufferable aspects of the discussions of the settlement was that I had had to list in detail anything and everything that I had in the way of financial assets, which were paltry in any case, but Cecil never had to specify what his financial circumstances were.

I told Allan that I could not take any more arguments and that the whole business sickened me. But for his and my family's insistence that I must stick out for some provision by Cecil, I would have washed my hands of the matter long before. I told him what my doctor had said and that I felt that I could not cope with any more discussions. He was very sympathetic and said that he was well aware of the demands that were being made upon me. He had to consider whether it was better to postpone a decision until after the baby was born or to try to settle the matter now. He had discussed the matter with his partners and it was generally felt that it would be in my interests to settle now, if possible.

He proposed to have a further discussion with Farrer and to report back to me the next day.

Friday 23 December 1983

Allan Hughes rang me to say that he had had a discussion with Farrer over the telephone, that there had been some improvement in what Cecil was offering.

Farrer had again tried to raise the question of my continued silence, but Allan had refused to give any such undertaking. He wanted to know whether I would agree to the 'package' that he and Farrer had discussed. I said that I could not think about the matter any more, that I was grateful to him for what he had achieved and said that he could inform Farrer that I agreed. Finally, Allan said that Farrer wished to know when and where the baby was to be born. I was reluctant to let them know anything but decided that it was only fair that Cecil should know when the baby was due. However I told Allan he should not be told which hospital I was going to.

We had a brief respite from the press that weekend because of the Christmas holiday, but on Tuesday 27 December the enquiries started again. On Wednesday the telephone rang repeatedly with reporters asking for confirmation of the report in the *Western Daily Press* that I had gone into a London clinic, that the baby was expected on New Year's Day and that if it was a boy I would name him George. Flora fielded all the calls, saying that the story was pure speculation and that she was not prepared to discuss the arrangements for the birth.

My GP called to examine me and said that the press had been asking whether I was to have my baby at Keynsham Hospital. He had had to say definitely that I was not in order to prevent further nuisance to the hospital staff. That evening Elisabeth arrived from Muscat and caused a certain amount of confusion amongst the reporters who called at the house the next day, one of whom thought she was me and that I had already had my baby.

On Thursday the *Daily Mail* was at it again. On one page they reported that Mrs Thatcher was 'being urged to make Mr Cecil Parkinson a Common Market Commissioner at around £60,000 a year', referring to his political career being 'temporarily becalmed by the revelation that his former secretary is expecting his child', while their *Diary* page claimed that I was booked into a private London nursing home and that my baby might be born before New Year's Day. They referred to me as:

> Former Commons secretary Sara, 36, who dallied just 'two or three times' with the then Secretary of Trade and Industry this year at the end of an eight-year affair.

I rang Allan Hughes and told him about the *Western Daily Press* and *Daily Mail* articles. As no-one outside my family, other than Allan and Mr Kenney, knew when I was having my baby, we wondered where they had got their information.

Part Seven

Scapegoat

New life

Friday 30 December arrived at last. I had had a bad night and felt very tired. I was longing to get to the hospital, but was very apprehensive about the journey. So many reporters had called at the house and been seen roaming about the neighbourhood that I was convinced that I would be spotted leaving the house and pursued up the M4.

Elisabeth and Flora told me to relax and leave the worrying to them. They were going to take me to London and stay as long as necessary. They had arranged for a friend to come and look after the children while Flora was away. Elisabeth said she was going into Bath to hire a car and returned with a very luxurious-looking limousine, which she parked on the lawn at the back of house, where it could not be seen by anyone coming to the house or waiting at the gate.

There was no let-up in press enquiries in the afternoon and I became increasingly nervous. I was due at the hospital by six that evening, which meant leaving by four o'clock at the latest. I decided to delay my departure until after dark.

Shortly after six o'clock, I kissed my father goodbye and went into the kitchen, where Flora was seeing to last-minute arrangements for her children while she was away. "I'll be back soon, darlings", she said to Lucy and Emma. Then she and Elisabeth and I walked out of the back door to the car. Flora had no idea that she would be away for nearly a fortnight.

Elisabeth kept the car in darkness until we reached the gate, when she switched on the headlights and drove off fast. Fortunatley there were no reporters waiting and we made our escape without being followed. There was a slight disagreement amongst us as to the best route to Wimbledon from the M4, with the result that Elisabeth took a wrong turning and got lost. I thought that if any reporters had been following us, they would have been mystified by all the stopping and starting and doubling back on our tracks. When at last we arrived at the hospital it was after eight o'clock and I was feeling slightly hysterical, a state of mind which was heightened by the barely suppressed hilarity of my sisters.

At last I was installed in my room. It was a wonderful relief to be there and to know that my whereabouts were a secret. Even at the hopistal my identity was known only to the Matron and two or three of her staff. Elisabeth and Flora unpacked my things while I ate a delicious supper. A nurse came in to say that various things had to be done to prepare me for the morning and Elisabeth and Flora said they would go.

In no time at all I was being told that it was time to go to sleep. I felt incredibly wide-awake and said that I would watch television for a little while. That was a mistake. I switched straight into the Jasper Carrott Show to hear him cracking a joke about Cecil and me. I did not know whether to laugh or cry. It gave the final touch of unreality to an extraordinary period of my life.

It had been a singularly unhappy year, but I had been carried through the worst of it by my pregnancy, which was taking me irrevocably forward to a new life and new happiness. It was in keeping with previous events that the last day of the year should also be something of an ordeal.

It was a very long day indeed. There were times when I wondered whether the clock on the wall facing me was actually working. I felt almost no pain during my labour, having had an epidural anaesthetic, and my sisters were with me almost the whole day. They arrived in the morning, looking very cheerful, and entertained me with a description of their adventures after they left me the previous night. They had gone to Albert Bridge Road, confident that our departure from Marksbury had gone unnoticed and that they could safely stay the night at Elisabeth's house. Within minutes of their arrival but, fortunately, before they had turned on any lights other than the one in the hall, someone rang the doorbell. They stood transfixed and heard people talking outside. Someone rapped on the door and a few minutes later banged on it thunderously. Elisabeth and Flora waited in silence. A voice outside said, "They can't be here. That light's been on all week". A few minutes later the people outside withdrew, the gate squeaking behind them. Elisabeth and Flora sat on the stairs, waiting until they felt confident the coast was clear, then hurried out of the house and back to the car. There was nothing for it but to go to a hotel.

I was very pleased to have Elisabeth and Flora with me. They were very amusing and light-hearted, encouraging me and behaving as if it were the most normal and delightful way to spend a day. Elisabeth tried to divert me by reading aloud from 'The Dynamiter' by Robert Louis Stevenson, but I kept dozing off and Flora said she was beginning to think it would take dynamite to get things moving. I was watched over throughout the day by Mr Kenney and ministered to by a charming Irish midwife, but by the evening I was beginning to wonder if the ordeal would ever end. Mr Kenney expressed some concern at my slow progress and by about ten o'clock that night he said that he would have to deliver the baby by Caesarian section. I was very upset and said that I wanted to see my baby born. Mr Kenney hastened to reassure me that I would, that I could have another epidural anaesthetic and that it would all be over in no time at all. He also said that my sisters could be with me and so it was that Elisabeth and Flora, gowned and masked, were sitting one each side of me when my baby was lifted, crying, into the world. A moment or two later I was holding her while she peered silently up at me out of dark, inky blue eyes.

Afterwards I stopped concentrating on what was happening and was scarcely aware of being taken up to my room. Flora and Elisabeth came with me and I remember them bending over me and kissing me and saying "Well done! And Happy New Year!" They telephoned my father from my bedside, while I lay with my eyes closed and listened happily to them saying what a lovely baby I had and how thrilling it had been to witness her birth.

All that remained was to let Allan Hughes know, so that he could in turn inform Cecil's solicitor as promised. Elisabeth duly rang him and then she and Flora left, promising to return the next morning.

Besieged again

I believed that having got to hospital without the media finding out, my whereabouts would remain a secret until I went home. I had two days of comparative peace before our troubles started again. Elisabeth and Flora arrived early each morning and remained with me until late at night. I was in considerable pain and incredibly tired, but elated and thrilled with my beautiful baby. I slept off and on throughout the day, while she slumbered alongside me. If I needed a reminder of my peculiar circumstances, I had only to look at the card at the head of her cot, which displayed my assumed name. I announced to my sisters that I was naming her Flora Elisabeth.

On Tuesday morning a woman walked into my room unannounced and said that she was taking photographs of all the New Year babies to raise money for the hospital. Could she take a picture of my baby. I said hastily, 'No. I'm afraid not.' But she advanced into the room, looking at my sisters and saying 'May I just take a look at your baby?' The nurse at my bedside, sensing my alarm, stepped forward and told her to leave, but she continued towards me and I saw that she was looking not at the baby but at the name tag on the cot. The nurse ushered her from the room, leaving my sisters and me feeling somewhat anxious. The nurse reappeared and assured us that the woman did indeed take photographs regularly in the hospital but said that she was not meant to barge in unannounced. The woman's visit may have been perfectly innocent, but it was hard not to connect it with what happened later. In any event, from that moment we were on the alert for trouble and it was not long before it arrived.

That evening the night sister came to my room to say that a woman had rung through to her asking to speak to me. The caller claimed to be a friend of mine but gave a name I did not recognise. I said that I had never heard of her and that in any case none of my friends knew where I was. I knew then that the press had tracked me down. It was very upsetting. The thought of the press descending on me again was more than I could stand.

Elisabeth rang my father who said that he had been inundated with calls in the past hour or so from reporters wanting confirmation that I had had my baby. He would have liked to take the telephone off the hook, but wanted to be available in case we needed to speak to him. I rang Allan Hughes who said that he had heard from Farrer that reporters were gathering outside Cecil's home. I agreed that a statement should be made to the Press Association, announcing Flora Elisabeth's arrival, in the hope of putting a stop to media enquiries. A faint hope that was.

During the course of the next day, reporters started to gather outside the hospital. I dreaded the thought that they might find out which was my room and come barging in. From that morning I always had one or both of my sisters with me or sitting outside the door of my room, from the moment visitors were allowed into the hospital each morning until the doors were closed at night. I was even afraid to let baby Flora out of my sight and from then on she remained with me all the time, except when she was taken away to be bathed or examined by the paediatrician.

That afternoon Allan Hughes telephoned me to say that he had had a call from the Administrator of St Teresa's who said that visitors to the hospital were being pestered by the waiting reporters who wanted to know if any of them had been to see me. He was afraid this would upset other patients and thought it was necessary to say something to the media, either to confirm or deny my presence in the hospital. He also told Allan that he felt that my sisters' presence was probably encouraging the attentions of the reporters. Allan said he was obliged to let me know about this as no statement could be issued without my consent. It was most distressing. The incident with the photographer on Tuesday had shown that the hospital could not stop determined visitors from walking into my room. The nurses were very busy and could hardly stand guard over me. The only people I could rely on to protect me from intrusions by the media were my sisters and I resented any suggestion that they were encouraging media attention. Elisabeth and Flora, who were of course with me at the time, agreed that their presence was essential for my security and peace of mind.

I felt quite wretched about the problems my presence was causing the hospital and telephoned Mr Kenney. I said that I could not bear these added difficulties and I wanted him to arrange for me to be moved to another hospital. He came to see me shortly afterwards and said that I was to stay where I was and that in any case I was in no fit state to be moved. In due course the hospital Administrator came to see me. He proposed issuing a statement to the media and wished to discuss its wording with me. Shortly afterwards he gave out a statement confirming that I was a patient in the hospital and asked the media to respect the privacy due not just to me but to all the patients.

The following morning, the ward sister came to tell me that a Dr Stuttaford was downstairs, asking if he could come and see me. A number of friends had called at the hospital that day, but had been told they could not see me. I told the sister that Tom Stuttaford could come up. It was good to see him and to hear his praise of my baby. My sister Flora had met Tom on a number of occasions, but Elisabeth had not. We were all interested to hear his comments on recent events, given his own connection with Fleet Street. I did not take much part in the conversation, feeling somewhat limp, but enjoyed listening to it. Tom did not stay long, saying that I needed to get plenty of rest.

The next three days were fairly uneventful, except that when Mr Kenney called in the morning he closed the curtains over my window and said that we would have to keep them drawn for the time being. The reporters waiting outside showed no signs of leaving and had ascertained which room I was in. He did not wish any of them to have an opportunity of spying on me. Elisabeth and Flora were with me most of the time, withdrawing to the passage outside my room when I drifted off to sleep. The Sisters and the hospital staff could not have been kinder. There had been the momentary difficulty because of the press, but now that we had all come to terms with their presence outside I was very relieved that I was at St Teresa's. Elisabeth and Flora did a great deal to raise my spirits. There were occasions when they made me laugh so much that it hurt and I would beg them to stop.

On Sunday 8 January my brother Tom brought my father to see his youngest grandchild. She remained oblivious to their admiration and slumbered on. That evening Elisabeth returned to Muscat. I wished that she did not have to leave, but she had to get back to her family and in any case they would all be coming home in less than six months' time for a holiday.

The following day I decided that I too must go home. Flora needed to get back to her children and I could not expect her to stay with me indefinitely. The reporters continued to wait outside the hospital and evidently would stay there until I left. They had been sending letters and messages up to me daily, asking for my permission to come and photograph my baby. I did not want any of them to come near her, let alone taking photographs of her. I longed to be rid of them. Most of their letters were very polite, expressing their good wishes and their regret at bothering me at such a time, but one or two were extraordinary. One in particular, written by Clive Limpkin of the *Daily Mail* on behalf of a number of fellow reporters, deserves a special mention.

He had the nerve to suggest that 'it might be more civilised' if I could tell them when I was proposing to leave the hospital so that one of them might photograph the occasion 'with your co-operation' on behalf of the rest. He went on to say:

> This would avoid the present situation where your continued presence is an embarrassment to the hospital administration, an inconvenience to neighbouring residents, and prevent any unseemly scenes that might occur when you depart.

Evidently he considered I was to blame for the embarrassment, inconvenience and unseemly scenes. Mr Kenney had urged me to stay in hospital at least until the end of the week, but that afternoon I told him I wanted to go home the next day.

On Tuesday morning, 10 January, my brothers arrived to take me home. I was in no hurry to face the the waiting reporters. During the morning Mr Kenney came to say goodbye. I was deeply grateful to him for everything he had done for me, not only in delivering my baby safely into the world, but through all the difficult months of my pregnancy.

Flora packed up all my belongings, and William and Tom loaded up the car. The hospital authorities did not wish to call the police, but had put up a rope across the car park and the reporters had agreed to remain behind it so as to avoid crowding me when I left. I was not confident of their ability to exercise such self-control and was glad that I would have William and Tom escorting me to the car. One of the nurses dressed little Flora and wrapped her up against the cold and then we were ready to leave. When we emerged from the lift at the ground floor I was surprised to see a mass of people waiting inside the hospital. They were other patients and hospital staff who had come to see me off. However, I scarcely had time to take them in, being rather preoccupied with the horde I could see through the glass entrance doors.

At the entrance the Deputy Matron handed baby Flora to me. I thanked her warmly for all that staff of St Teresa's had done for me and then someone opened the doors and we stepped out to face the media. The noise was extraordinary. They were all talking at once, firing questions at me while their cameras clicked and flashed from all directions. Most of them were still behind the rope. All I could think of was getting to the car without looking as if I would like to make a run for it. It was only a few yards from the hospital entrance, but by the time we reached it, some of the crowd had broken through and others were shouting at them "Get back!" and "You're breaking the agreement!" Some man came up and asked me if Mr Parkinson had been to see his daughter. I turned my back on him and got into the car. William shut the door and turned to help my sister into the front seat. By then the car was completely surrounded with photographers pressing their cameras to the windows and exhorting me to show them my baby's face. The noise was considerable and the car was shaking. William was trying to get the front passenger door of the car open and had to brace himself against the car in order to hold off the mass of people behind him and pull the door open so that Flora could get in. A moment or two later he was at the wheel and we were away. Tom was right behind us, driving my car, and we made our way in a slow procession to the motorway. I put my baby into her carrycot beside me and leaned back, feeling enormous relief that we had got away without a worse ordeal.

By the time we reached Marksbury it was nearly dark and I said with relief as we came along the dual carriageway "I don't think there's anyone waiting." In the same moment we saw all the cars parked along the road and the crowd of people standing at the gate. Fortunately the police were there as well and held the crowd back otherwise I think someone might have been hurt as we turned into the drive. A brilliant light was shone at us just as we turned across the main road into the gateway. I was completely dazzled. I do not know how William managed to see anything at all. I could hear someone, a police officer presumably, shouting "Get back!" to the reporters. Even so they surged forward and nearly blocked our path. Then we were home at last and in no time at all Flora was installed in her cot in my room and we were both sound asleep.

I awoke next morning to find Winsbury House once more under siege by reporters. They were waiting at the gate and in the lay-by at the end of the paddock, from which vantage point Roger said they were peering at the house through binoculars. Others roamed about the village in search of something that might make a story.

The requests from the media for photographs of my baby had started before she was born. I had had a steady flow of letters from them while in hospital. After I returned home I was inundated with them. My solicitor reported that he had received a similar flood of requests. The line taken by all of them was that I could get the media off my back once and for all if I would only allow a photographer to come in and take photographs, which would be published exclusively by the lucky applicant and distributed to the rest of the media the following day. For my first week home I was so exhausted I was scarcely able to think about these requests, let alone decide what to do about them. I was suffering considerable pain and realising just how much I had depended on the nursing staff at St Teresa's to help me look after Flora. She was very good and absolutely adorable, but waking at three-hourly intervals during the night to feed her was quite an ordeal. My sister Flora was marvellous and frequently came in to see me in the middle of the night offering to help and assuring me that I would soon find it much easier.

The day after I came home, Tom Stuttaford rang me to say that he had written a piece for *The Times* medical page the coming Friday. He had been to see me the day before I left St Teresa's and had said that he was proposing to write an article about Caesarian birth under epidural anaesthetic and wanted to mention that that was how I had had Flora. When he telephoned me I was horrified to find that he had written a lengthy article about me. I had thought he intended to write a general article in the course of which he would make only the merest reference to me. Apparently, he thought that I had given him permission to write about Flora's birth in some detail. When I questioned him about his article and realised just what had happened I was aghast. I begged him to change it. He explained that he had unfortunately already given the story in, but said that he would see what he could do and would have a word with the sub-editor. I was very embarrassed and upset at having to ask him to do such a thing and angry that he should have put me in such a position. He had been a good friend over many years and it was dreadful to have such a misunderstanding. Perhaps I was unduly sensitive about it because of my state of health and because it was less than a fortnight since Flora's birth. I began to worry about what I had said to Tom when he visited me, but my sister Flora who had been present on both occasions, reassured me that there could be no question of my having given permission for an article to be written about me and certainly not as an interview. It looked very much as if the newspaper were taking advantage of his friendship with me. I felt very uneasy and hoped fervently that he would be able to sort it out and spare me any embarrassment.

The following day, Thursday 12 January, I was appalled to find that *The Times* had a notice on their front page advertising the story as an interview with me. In a box headed 'THE TIMES TOMORROW' was a photograph of me taken as I left hospital with Flora in my arms, with the caption 'Babe ... Sara Keays talks to The Times Medical Correspondent about the delivery of her baby.' In no time at all the telephone and the doorbell were ringing, and I was being bombarded with requests from reporters saying that they understood I had given an interview to *The Times* and hoping that I would do the same for them.

I had given no interview. I had seen Tom as a friend and if there had been any question of his expecting an interview I would not have allowed him to come and see me. He knew that, of course, and I suspected that the matter had been taken out of his hands. Whether it was just a misleading bit of headline-writing by *The Times* or whether they had persuaded him to write his story as an interview I do not know. I telephoned Charles Douglas-Home and said that I had no idea that Tom had been intending to do anything other than merely mention me briefly in a general article about epidural anaesthesia in labour, and that I had seen him only because he was a friend. I said that there had been no question whatsoever of my having given him an interview and any suggestion to the contrary was an abuse of personal trust. I strongly objected to the trailer on the front page of that day's *Times*.

Mr Douglas-Home was sympathetic and assured me that there would be no question of the article being presented as an interview. He apologised for the misleading advertisement. He said that the article had already been amended, that he had it in front of him and would be happy to check it through with me and make further amendments as I thought necessary. I was grateful, although I was inwardly seething at having been put in the position of having to make such a call. It was embarrassing and very exhausting.

It was a most unfortunate episode. It was hateful that I should have become so cynical and distrustful that I should find myself doubting the motives of a close friend. It was upsetting to have had to beseech Tom to change his article. I did not want, in my turn, to harm his position in *The Times* and I was only too willing to agree with Charles Douglas-Home that the whole episode had sprung out of a very unfortunate misunderstanding. I hoped that both he and Tom would understand why I felt as I did about it.

The article was published the following day and I was relieved that it was just a straightforward and factual account of the event. It had caused me anguish, but its message was constructive, being intended to encourage other mothers who had to have a Caesarian delivery to opt for an epidural anaesthetic. I had been thrilled that I had not needed to have a general anaesthetic but could be awake for Flora's birth and able to hold her immediately afterwards. It meant a great deal to me not to have missed that wonderful moment.

The clamour for photographs

While I was in hospital I had looked forward to going home to peace and quiet and being able to devote all my time and energy to looking after Flora and getting my strength back. I longed to settle down to a normal and tranquil existence and just to be able to enjoy my baby. I had been home for three days and the pressures were just as bad as before.

Not only were decisions required on such things as the apology to be published by *Private Eye* for their libellous article of last October, and the finalisation of the financial settlement to be made by Cecil, but the media were pressing very hard for photographs of Flora. Reporters and photographers still had the house staked out and we had to keep the curtains drawn in all the rooms in which we might be visible from the road. Roger said that some of the reporters apparently thought I might appear at any moment pushing a pram, which raised a laugh all round, as it was as much as I could do to go downstairs, let alone take my baby out for an airing.

Allan Hughes reported regularly on the visits and calls he received from newspapers, who wanted to know whether I would be likely to agree to photographs being taken for publication that weekend. I said that I did not know what to do and that in any case I did not feel well enough. Perhaps they would give up after a few days.

The following week we were still under siege. Still I resisted the idea of having photographs taken. Then we heard that someone in the neighbourhood who was a good amateur photographer had been offered £5,000 for a picture of Flora. He would not oblige them but others might for that kind of reward. I discussed the matter with my family and we came to the conclusion that someone would be bound to get a picture eventually, unless I remained hidden away indefinitely and that if anyone was going to benefit from such photographs it should be me and my baby. If I allowed some photographs to be published, it might deter other photographers from trying to sneak pictures and touting them round Fleet Street. I rang Allan Hughes and said that I would agree to whichever of the proposals he had received he considered the best, provided that the newspapers concerned agreed to certain strict conditions, principally that there was to be no story about Cecil and me and no sensational or embarrassing presentation. I was also very anxious that whoever came into my father's house should not write about any of us afterwards or pass on any information for publication elsewhere. He said that he would draft a contract that would cover all the essential points.

In due course I agreed to a joint arrangement with the *Observer* and the *Sunday Mirror*. However, having given my consent, I did not feel well enough to go through with it that week, with the result that the photographs were not taken until the following Wednesday, 25 January.

In the end, it was not as much of an ordeal as I had feared. I was afraid that Flora would get very tired and upset by it, but she seemed oblivious to the cameras. The biggest difficulty for the photographers were getting a picture of her with her eyes open as she spent most of the time either yawning or fast asleep. She was very tranquil and did not cry at all.

Both newspapers were to publish their photographs the following Sunday, 28 January. On Friday afternoon I telephoned Allan and asked him whether he thought we ought to warn Cecil that the pictures were coming out, as the press would very likely try to get a reaction out of him. Allan agreed and said he would telephone Farrer.

Not long afterwards the telephone rang and my sister Flora answered it. A moment or two later she came up to my bedroom to say that the telephone call had been from Peter Simmonds of the *Mail on Sunday*. He had asked to speak to me and she said that was not possible as I was attending to my baby. He had then said that he understood photographs had been taken and wanted to know whether there was any possibility of his paper having some. She declined to comment. He said he did not know what to do, adding after a pause 'Well, do we get the photographs, or shall we do a story about how much your sister is getting paid for them?' She said she was sure he would do whatever he wanted and hung up.

I tried to telephone my solicitor, but he was out, and decided to disconnect the telephone to avoid similar calls from other newspapers.

On Saturday Allan reported that he had had a call from the *Sunday Express* who wanted to know if it was true that I was being paid £25,000 for the photographs. Naturally he had told them nothing. Later that day my father took a call from the BBC who said the *Mirror* had told them about the pictures and could they interview me and take some film? He told them they could not. We disconnected the telephone again.

On Sunday the photographs appeared in the *Observer* and the *Sunday Mirror*.

The *Mail on Sunday* carried a malicious article headed: SARA SHOWS BABY OFF FOR £25,000. It said:

> Sara Keays, jilted mistress of ex-Cabinet Minister Cecil Parkinson, has put their baby on public show for £25,000

and that I

> went down market to pose with Flora Elisabeth for today's *Sunday Mirror*.

Then unnamed 'friends' were brought in to attack me:

> Her extraordinary move left friends of Mr Parkinson saddened and angry that she could 'exploit' the baby. ... One said: 'It merely confirms our view that she was out to get Cecil all along'.

Once again a newspaper had printed fantasy as fact and attributed to unidentified and no doubt non-existent individuals the defamatory remarks they wished to make about me.

Peter Simmonds had pestered me time and again for an interview and photographs of the baby. Both I and my solicitor had received numerous letters and calls from him. On the morning of 30 December, the day I went into hospital, he had called at the house and had been so persistent that I eventually spoke to him briefly on the telephone and said that the past behaviour of his paper towards me, like that of the *Daily Mail*, was such that I did not believe them capable of dealing fairly with me. However, he continued to write both to me and to Allan Hughes, and said that he was sure that the only way I would get the press to leave me alone was by agreeing to have photographs taken of Flora.

Yet, here was his newspaper accusing me of putting my baby on 'public show' and of 'exploiting' her.

The article was written by David Rose, but I felt sure that Simmonds had had a hand in it. It was pure spite. I suppose I should have known, from a letter he wrote to me a few days earlier, just what this particular worm would do when he finally turned. Delivered by hand to Winsbury House on Friday 13 January, it had said:

> It's me again. The Political Editor of the *Mail on Sunday*, wondering why on earth he got involved on a quiet Friday before the New Year in driving down the M4 trying to discover whether you wanted to talk or have pictures taken.

He said that he had done as I had suggested and spoken to my solicitor, Allan Hughes, 'a lovely man no doubt but unfortunately unable or incapable of telling me whether or not you are interested in talking, having pictures taken etc. on your terms.'

He said he was looking forward

> with a desperation I cannot describe to the resumption of Parliament on Monday so I can at least tell myself that there is too much going on at Westminster to drive down the M4 yet again.
> Or you telling me to drive back up the M4 sharpish.
> Or you inviting me in to talk ...

I had been out of hospital less than three days when I received this communication and was lying in bed feeling rather unwell and trying to shut out the sound of the reporters outside, and the frequent ringing of the doorbell and telephone. When Flora brought the letter up to me I had a great desire to send a very rude answer down to Mr Simmonds. You would have thought from his letter that it was my fault that he was tearing up and down the M4 and that it placed me under some obligation to respond to his messages. I asked Flora to tell him that whatever chance he may have thought he had of an interview or anything else, he had scuppered it with his letter.

Some time later he delivered a card in which he said that, as his efforts 'both with formality and informality' had failed, he sent his best wishes to me and my daughter for the future. I had wondered if perhaps he had not intended his letter to be as rude as it sounded. His telephone call to Flora confirmed that my first opinion had been correct.

He and so many of his fellow-journalists were incapable of understanding that I wished to have nothing to do with any of them because whatever I said or did, even if I found momentary favour with one, I would incur the wrath of the others. And they have ready means and opportunity to exact their revenge, as the *Mail on Sunday* had shown.

Simmonds had urged me to spare myself further media harrassment by having photographs taken—for which his newspaper was prepared to pay me a substantial sum of money—but when another paper got the photographs, his accused me of exploiting my baby. It was perfectly acceptable for his newspaper, or any other, to make money out of photographs of my baby, but outrageous for me to do so. I wonder what prompted them to say that I had been paid £25,000? Or did they simply think of their own offer and treble it?

Their story resulted in a call from Cecil's solicitor to mine, suggesting that I had somehow behaved improperly. Allan Hughes pointed out that Cecil had had an article published in the *News of the World*, for which he had no doubt been paid handsomely.

Needless to say, the *Mail on Sunday*'s malicious remarks were repeated and embellished by other newspapers. Ian Beales of the *Western Daily Press* wrote:

> . . . by reaching a deal in which money changes hands, Miss Keays has changed the nature of her relationship with the media and the rest of the world.

I was not aware that I had any 'relationship' with the media or with 'the rest of the world'. He went on:

> Her pleas for privacy will no longer be heard with quite the same sympathy now that she has made herself and her daughter public property.

When had I ever made any such pleas? And what was this sympathy I was supposed to have been shown? He said that privacy

> should not be negotiable at a price. . . . If you accept money, you accept the role of public peep show.

It was the media who did the peeping and who put people on public show.

The hypocrisy of such people was staggering. If he did not think Flora and I should be peeped at, why had his newspaper been so anxious to secure the photographs? How could Mr Beales pretend outrage at a 'deal in which money changes hands' when that is exactly what happens every time a newspaper is sold. He saw nothing wrong in the newspapers selling the photographs to the public.

His Assistant Editor, Peter Gibbs, had delivered a letter to me at Winsbury House on the day I came home from hospital, asking permission for the *Western Daily Press* to take photographs of me and Flora that evening. He urged me to consider them as 'a special case', being the only local morning newspaper in the area, and said they would supply any such photographs to the rest of the media 'and thus, hopefully, free you from some of the media pressure.' Perhaps they would have been less spiteful if I had allowed the whole ravening horde into my father's house, so that each of them could exploit my baby and my circumstances in his own particular way and they could all have made as much money as possible out of us.

The publication of the photographs did indeed have the desired effect and reporters and photographers vanished from our gate. At last my family could go out without being followed about and pestered for information about me.

I had received a reminder from the Registrar in Merton that the time limit for the registration of Flora's birth would soon be up. I did not relish the prospect of being followed to Bath Registration Office and thought I would get it over with while the coast was clear. Even so it got a mention in the press.

I thought that my life would settle down at last, but not a bit of it. In no time at all, reporters were rootling about again, trying to find out when Flora would be christened. I had not even had time to think of it until the press reminded me. I made up my mind that whatever else might happen, they would not intrude on that occasion and that I would put if off until the summer, when Elisabeth and Richard would be home from Muscat and the media might have lost interest in us.

However, there was still something for them to get their teeth into. Thanks to Cecil's insistence on paying Flora's maintenance under an Affiliation Order, which was done solely for his tax purposes, there was plenty more publicity in store for me.

In due course the media found out that the hearing would be on 29 February, at Radstock Magistrates' Court. Although it was very brief and fortunately neither Cecil nor I had to attend, the Court was swamped by reporters, and this momentous occasion was the cause of major televison and radio news items and banner headlines in the newspapers. It was trumpeted as an act of magnificent generosity on the part of my baby's father, with headlines like PARKINSON'S PAY-OUT and LOVE CHILD FLORA TO COST HIM £54,000 and £54,000 BABY BILL FOR CECIL. The *Daily Mail* article, which was headed £3,000 A YEAR FOR BABY FLORA said that:

> Mr Parkinson has accepted full responsibility for his daughter's future . . .

I do not know what possible grounds they could have for such a statement, even if, as I suspect, they measure a man's responsibility for his child in purely financial terms.

The Parkinson reinstatement campaign

In the months following Flora's birth, it became apparent that the media thought there was still plenty of mileage in the Parkinson/Keays Affair. They were encouraged in this view by the strenuous efforts made by the Party to persuade the public that he ought soon to be brought back into Government, indeed that he should never have left it. The Party's determination to play the scandal down and so justify the Prime Minister's handling of the matter ensured that the story was kept alive.

The result was that I was constantly being questioned by reporters. Whenever there was any talk of Cecil being brought back into the Government, or whenever he made any public appearance or gave an interview, I was immediately telephoned or visited by reporters seeking my comments. Although I refused to be drawn and did everything I could to avoid them, nothing would put them off and they continued their efforts for months, throughout the whole of 1984 and well into 1985. It made no difference that I refused to talk to them; they still pestered me and invariably mentioned me in their articles and interviews, often in very derogatory terms.

Cecil, on the other hand, apparently made no attempt to avoid publicity, but seemed indeed to be encouraging the attentions of the media. I never once saw any criticism of him for doing so. It was taken for granted that he would continue in the public eye. It was also taken for granted, apparently, that I should hide myself away. It was put to me that I should allow a 'decent interval' to elapse, to allow people 'time to forget', when in fact neither I nor my family was to be allowed to forget anything. As if that were not injustice enough, the Party, willingly assisted by the media, busily rewrote the story. At times it seemed that I might just as well never have issued my statement.

The campaign for Cecil's reinstatement began soon after the Party Conference. Within weeks of my baby's birth it was being conducted with renewed vigour. It might have been tolerable had it not required the propagation of the lie that our affair and my pregnancy were a mere 'blunder' and had it not excused his role in the matter but condemned mine.

Media discussion of the affair continued to be very biased. Some journalists pretended impartiality, but could not resist a spiteful remark or two, like the woman who wrote in the *Guardian* on 12 January 1984 of my 'dreadful pregnancy pictures ... with her ordinary face, boring haircut and absurd multi-coloured maternity frocks.'

The writer, who was not named, expressed some sympathy for me and a grudging admiration for my having tried to defend myself, but went on to reveal a positive dislike for me, or perhaps it was jealousy. Most of the article was devoted to an account of her own difficulties as an unmarried mother and the implied comparison with me was intended to be derogatory.

I was surprised at the number of women journalists who wrote about me in such condescending and disparaging terms, their 'compassion' well watered with spite. How they contrasted with the women, and men, total strangers, who wrote to me from all over the world, who were truly sympathetic and wanted to reassure me about the future. Their generosity and sympathy was very touching and helped me to shut out some of the malicious things that were said and written about me.

It was evident that many journalists had swallowed the Party's propaganda hook line and sinker. Some made no secret of their belief that Cecil had suffered cruelly at my hands. Countless newspaper acticles were written about his 'plight', urging his reinstatement in the Government. He was referred to in glowing terms, as a 'favourite' of Mrs Thatcher's whom she sorely missed.

I suppose that it was not surprising that the media took the line that they did, in view of the propaganda exercise that had been mounted in October 1983 and appeared to continue unabated throughout 1984.

On 8 February Nigel Dempster's 'Diary' in the *Daily Mail* had a large headline REHABILITATION OF PARKINSON above a photograph of Cecil with Denis Thatcher and a lengthy article predicting Cecil's return to public office by 1985.

> The rehabilitation of disgraced former Cabinet Minister Cecil Parkinson continues apace and in the early hours of yesterday he was feted like a hero at the Tory Party's Winter Ball ... enjoying the patronage of the Prime Minister and Denis Thatcher.
> ... Cecil, 52, has of course, done no public harm in the eyes of Mrs Thatcher—she bemoans his fall from grace and still contends that the ill-advised affair with his secretary was a 'private' matter.

The 'ill-advised' affair—which lasted nearly twelve years—is dismissed as a trifling event.

Punch of 15 February 1984 contained an article by Simon Hoggart about Cecil's misfortunes, in which he referred to him as having

> clearly been made rather more miserable in the past four months than most people are in a lifetime...
> Mr Parkinson believes that Sara Keays agreed to have pictures of herself and baby Flora published ... only as a means of further tightening the emotional screw...

And at the end

> Perhaps worst of all, his family have made it clear that he must never even meet his youngest child. Sara Keay's radiant face glows at him out of the newspaper photographs, her triumph deriving almost wholly from his despair.

What triumph? Evidently Mr Hoggart believed, like so many others, that I had planned the whole thing and enjoyed every moment. Furthermore, it was Cecil's own decision, as he told me himself, that he would never have anything to do with his youngest child. But such facts would have spoiled Mr Hoggart's story and that would never do.

Four days later, Woodrow Wyatt held forth on the subject in the *News of the World*, with an article headed FAIR PLAY FOR CECIL, which he said that the two newspapers which published photographs of me and my baby 'got a rough response from their readers', claiming that they thought Cecil had 'suffered enough'.

He said:

> If Mrs Thatcher wants to employ him again in a few months there will be no public outcry worth bothering about ...

and

> Mr Parkinson has behaved honourably in providing for his child ...

Honour, it seems, can be satisfied by money.

Evidently Woodrow Wyatt thought Cecil had done something exceptional, when it was surely his duty, if not his wish, to provide for his child.

I suppose this is the sort of article one should expect of a man pompous enough to describe himself as 'The Voice of Reason'.

Later it was said that the Prime Minister too believed that Cecil had behaved 'honourably' in making such provision and I learned that colleagues of his in the House of Commons had been told that he had made a 'magnificent' settlement on me and that I was living in the lap of luxury—enjoying the spoils of my vengeance.

A magazine called *Options*, the Assistant Editor of which had written to me on the day Cecil's statement was published, inviting me to give them an interview, published an 'Options Special Report' in their March issue, entitled BABY POWER: IS IT BIGGER THAN ALL OF US? The blurb alongside said 'Tiny, helpless, totally dependent, babies can and do change lives. they can wreak havoc or work wonders—and they start to do it before they are even born. Penny Vincenzi explores a mystical and manipulative power.'

A number of women were mentioned in the article and some were quoted, talking about the effect their pregnancies and their babies had on them, to demonstrate the author's belief in the power of babies to 'work wonders'. The antithesis, the idea that babies can 'wreak havoc', she expounded as follows:

> Babies have great power, too, in the smaller field of personal politics. The ultimate gift of love they may be, but they can also be used as the ultimate weapon, and the ultimate tool in manipulation. Sara Keays used her baby as a weapon in many ways. As a statement of her love, a staking of her claim, a bid for status and a cry for help. All she has achieved is a wedge of bitterness driven between many unhappy people which will follow them down the years.

She made no secret of her admiration for all the other women she mentioned in her article, whom she referred to as being 'very serious about motherhood.'

Why did she single me out and accuse me of using my baby as a 'weapon'? Was it by any chance because I would not co-operate with the magazine, and they thought they would get their own back? Or did she really believe the nonsense she had written about me? If she did, then presumably she also believed that I should have put aside my 'weapon'—by having an abortion—so as to spare the 'many unhappy people' she referred to but did not identify. And presumably by 'wedge of bitterness' she meant by baby.

The same magazine published an interview with Cecil several months later. By way of introduction it said,

> The last year has seen Cecil Parkinson transformed from shamed politician to glittering public figure, bestowing his charm and considerable talent on all he chooses to favour.

The questions were more significant than his answers, for what they revealed of the interviewer's attitude to the affair. The first question referred to his having resigned 'after your affair with Sara Keays was made public', as if its having been published were nothing to do with him. He was asked:

> Do you feel a sense of injustice about the fact that you did the 'right' thing and stood by your family, and yet still had to take the punishment for that?
>
> Are you surprised that you had the strength of character to pull yourself through?
>
> Despite your problems over the past year, you have become increasingly popular. Why do you think this is?

On 11 March, the *Sunday Times* published a long article about the Chancellor of the Exchequer, Nigel Lawson, in whom Cecil was said to have confided his troubles. It was said that:

> When Parkinson was considering resigning from the cabinet [sic], believing that could put him in a freer position to answer allegations about to be made against him, he discussed it with Lawson, who helped him clear his mind. Lawson apparently argued that his was a private matter: "For God's sake. A fair number of the cabinet are divorced. Yet you're proposing leaving cabinet because you're not

> going to divorce your wife. This is a funny old world we live in."
> Lawson went to see Mrs Thatcher to tell her how he felt about it. Throughout the entire episode he was a staunch friend to Parkinson.

This was interesting for two reasons. First, for the reference to 'allegations about to be made' against Cecil. The reader was not told whose this idea was, but it was reasonable to infer that it originated with Lawson. It implied that Cecil had been considering resigning, not because of the imminent scandal, but because I was believed to be about to make various groundless accusations against him.

Second, Lawson was quoted as saying that Cecil had been considering resigning because he was going to stay with his wife, when in fact Cecil had promised to marry me and had assured both my father and my twin sister of his good faith. This was the fundamental point in my statement in *The Times*: what Cecil told the Prime Minister on Polling Day was *not* that he had decided to stay with his wife, but that he was going to marry me. At least that is what he told me and allowed me to believe for the next three months.

Even if he had told Lawson something quite different, Lawson knew from my statement that Cecil had deceived me for three months. Lawson apparently saw no wrong in that and even wanted to do his bit to discredit me. Indeed, that would appear to be the only reason for his mentioning Cecil at all in the interview.

In all the endless newspaper comment on Cecil's 'misfortune' and the Prime Minister's sad loss of her 'favourite', I never saw it suggested that both he and she could have avoided the scandal, had they not been determined that he should remain in office. Apparently it did not occur to the media commentators that not only could embarrassment to the Party have been avoided, but my family, and his, could have been spared a great deal of suffering if he had resigned after the General Election.

There were continual references to his ordeal. The *Sunday Express* was as spiteful about me as ever, 'Crossbencher' having taken up the campaign. On 25 March, the 'Crossbencher' column was headed CECIL AWAITS THE CALL with an article about his dreadful experience and his hopes of a return from his exile on the backbenches, reminding the reader of 'that awful night in Blackpool when that wretched girl issued her statement to *The Times*.'

Cecil even gave interviews to the press on the subject, one particularly worthy of mention appearing in the *Daily Express* on 27 March.

The writer of this piece, one Ross Benson, gave a wonderful gloss to the events which had led to Cecil's resignation:

> He stood on the heights of a brilliant political career—and watched helplessly as his life and his life's work toppled over the precipice into ruin.

Helplessly? He makes it sound like an act of God. There was more in the same vein:

> His secretary announced that she was carrying his child. He acknowledged that he was the father but had decided to stay with his job. In the subsequent furure of charge and accusation, the man tipped as future Prime Minister found himself ignominiously and reluctantly drive from his job.

I was not Cecil's secretary, and I presume the reference to my having 'announced' that I was carrying his child was intended to give the impression to the reader that it was I who had made the matter public. And what was this 'furore of charge and accusation'? My statement to *The Times*?

Anyone reading this fiction would have thought that this disaster had befallen Cecil without warning, that he had been sailing through life without a care until I suddenly appeared on the scene and destroyed it all. Certainly there was to be no question in the reader's mind that Cecil might have brought it on himself.

As for Cecil, he was reported to have said:

> I won't pretend that it was the happiest period of my life ... It was an experience I wouldn't wish on my worst enemy ...

But he inflicted it on me, when we could both have been spared had he refused a post in the Government in June 1983.

The *Daily Express* article went on to refer to '... back bench calls for his reinstatement to the Cabinet, even to the elevated position of Deputy Prime Minister ...', to Mrs Thatcher being 'in regular touch with him', to his being 'feted like a hero' at the Winter Ball. ... 'None of this has been in any way orchestrated, as is sometimes suggested ...' If you believe that, you will believe anything. 'It is as if the past and Miss Sara Keays had never happened—which is the way Mr Parkinson wants it.'

It was also the way the Conservative Party wanted it. while treating him like a hero recovering from the wounds of battle, they removed my name from their Approved List of Parliamentary Candidates. It was not enough to have used the media to discredit me. Some time between Cecil's resignation and the beginning of 1983, they decided that I must not be allowed to apply for Parliamentary constituency vacancies, although I had been on the Candidates' List since November 1982.

Conservative Central Office did not trouble to notify me of their intention, or even to discuss the matter with me. When I demanded an explanation, they refused to give one. They tried to have it both ways: they claimed that my name was still on the List, presumably because they were afraid of any publicity, but ensured that I was never again allowed to apply for any constituency vacancy.

Conservative Party machinations

When I attained the dizzy heights of the Conservative Party's Approved List of Candidates in November 1982, I was immediately asked to pay a subscription to cover the cost of being notified of constituency vacancies.

In accordance with a recommendation in 1972 of the Party's Review Committee on the selection of parliamentary candidates—and I quote from a letter I received from the Secretary of the Standing Advisory Committee on Candidates in November 1982—

> ... all persons on the approved list should be circulated with the names of constituencies about to select a parliamentary candidate. It was agreed that, combined with this circulation of constituencies to potential candidates, there should also be an undertaking by each person concerned to become a subscriber to the Party's literature service.

The Secretary therefore urged me to pay the sum of £25 to the Director of Finance as soon as possible 'so that Candidates' Department may add your name to the list of those who receive vacancies'.

I paid my £25 and started to receive notification of vacancies, and the Central Office literature, both of which are sent out by a computerised mailing department at Reading. After the General Election in June 1983, there was only one by-election, in Penrith and the Border, which had become vacant following William Whitelaw's elevation to the peerage. Like everyone else on the Approved List, I received notification of the vacancy.

It was the last such notification I ever received.

Three months later the scandal burst around Cecil and myself. From then on Central Office behaved in the most curious manner towards me. They would not acknowledge that they had removed my name from the List, but were determined that I should not be allowed to apply for any constituency vacancy. Interestingly, they asked me to renew my subscription to the service for notifying vacancies and providing candidates with literature. They were not above taking my money, and continued to send me the monthly packages of literature, but the constituency vacancy notifications, which are sent out on the same mailing list, ceased altogether.

In March 1984, a by-election was held in Chesterfield, followed by three more in May: Cynon Valley, Stafford, and Surrey South-West. I was not invited to apply for any of them. Then came the three by-elections in May, the Writs for which were moved early in April. Applications from the Candidates' List would have been invited at about the same time, with a very short deadline. I received the usual bundle of literature from the Party, but no notification of these vacancies.

The rules concerning the Candidates' List are that all candidates remain on it until they either get adopted by a constituency, or ask for their names to be removed. Not only had Central Office stopped notifying me of vacancies, they had said nothing whatsoever to me on the subject and had been quite prepared to ask for renewal of my subscription. In the meantime, the other party to the scandal continued to enjoy the patronage of the Prime Minister, to be feted by the Party and championed by the media.

Once again, I decided to give them the benefit of the doubt—it was the last time I did so—and wrote to David Hunt MP, who had taken over from Sir Anthony Royle as Vice-Chairman responsible for Candidates, asking why I was no longer being notified of constituency vacancies. I had to wait two weeks for his reply. In the meantime, it was announced that a by-election would be held in Portsmouth South, following the death of Bonner Pink MP.

David Hunt's reply was dated 10 May, but postmarked 14 May. I received it on the morning of 16 May. It said:

> Dear Sara,
>
> Thank you for your letter of 2nd May, and may I please hasten to reassure you that you are on the Approved Candidates List. I will check with our records department at Reading to ensure that you are notified of any vacancies. Apart from the recent By-Elections, there have been no Constituencies seeking applications.

There was no apology and no explanation of their failure to notify me of the four 'recent By-Elections'.

He went on to say that he wished to give me 'advance notice that we shall shortly be circulating the vacancy in Portsmouth South, following the sad death of Bonner Pink'. Enclosed with his letter was an application form, with the deadline heavily underlined, 'return to arrive *not later than the first post on Wednesday 16th*'.

Far from giving me 'advance notice', the letter had arrived too late for me to apply. Why had it not been posted until 14 May, although the letter itself was dated 10 May? And why had the form not been sent out in the usual way, from the Reading Office?

On 20 May, I wrote again to David Hunt, requesting an explanation. His reply showed that he had no intention of answering my questions.

Dear Sara,

Thank you for your letter of 20 May, and there have obviously been a series of misunderstandings of which I have been unaware. The only fact of any real importance is that you have certainly not been removed from the Approved List.

As to the other points you have made, would you like to come in and see me when you have a moment.

Yours sincerely,

David

His assurance that I had not been removed from the List was not worth the paper it was written on, because I never received a single notification of a constituency vacancy from that time. He gave no explanation, not even for the strange delay of his last letter, and no apology. He was not prepared to commit any explanation to paper nor, as I found later, was he prepared to do so orally. I wonder what he meant by the 'series of misunderstandings'? It was the kind of woolly phrase so often used by politicians when they wish to avoid answering a question. I wrote back to him asking what useful purpose would be served by my going to see him when he obviously had no intention of answering my questions. He did not bother to reply.

If the Party thought I was unfit to be a Candidate, why did they not have the courage to say so? Could they not at least try to live up to their professed principles and traditions, rather than down to the worst accusations of the Opposition?

In the meantime, the Bring-Back-Parkinson campaign continued unabated. In mid-May it was reported that Conservative Central Office had held a party for Cecil, at which he had been presented with a miniature Commons despatch box to mark his 'triumphant' years there. The Prime Minister was present to applaud him and demonstrate her special regard for him.

On 4 June, the *Daily Mirror* reported that Cecil was 'quietly but effectively rehabilitating himself in the eyes of those Tory ladies who were less than pleased when he wavered off the straight and narrow with Miss Sara Keays'. I thought 'wavered off the straight and narrow' was a remarkable euphemism for a love affair of so many years.

On Saturday 16 June, Tony Frost of the *Sunday Mirror* rang me to say that he had heard that Flora was to be christened the following Sunday and that the paper would like to report the occasion and take photographs. I had done everything I could to keep the occasion a secret and was very irritated that a newspaper should have found out about it. I said that I was glad he had telephoned and that there was no point in his coming to Marksbury on 24 June as I would change the date.

On the assumption that the press would expect me to postpone the event, I brought it forward to Thursday 21 June. Although the rearrangement meant that some relatives and friends could not come, at least we managed to keep a very special occasion private and it was two weeks before the press caught up with it.

On 8 July, 'Crossbencher' wrote of THE PROBLEM WITH CECIL, claiming that the Prime Minister was 'tempted' to bring him back into Government, but for the tricky question

> Can Miss Sara Keays really be relied upon not to speak out again if Mr Parkinson is restored to favour? Mrs Thatcher cannot rely on it. She may want Cecil back. She may feel she needs him back. But she has not the slightest intention of allowing her Government to become a hostage to the whim of Miss Sara Keays.

As all the political snips in 'Crossbencher' are prompted by gossip or by deliberate 'leaks' by MPs and others in political circles, I wonder who prompted this article? I dare say the Prime Minister wished it to be believed that it was merely a 'whim' of mine that had caused her troubles, but it was interesting that I was believed to have it in my power to hold the Government 'hostage'.

On 3 August, it was widely reported that Cecil might be recalled to Government, the Prime Minister having made it plain that she wanted him back in her Cabinet and did not 'rule out' bringing him back in the lifetime of this Parliament. As usual, this caused a flood of telephone calls from journalists hoping that I would comment on her remarks. They did not always require such prompting, but would telephone to ask if Cecil had seen his baby yet, which of her parents she most resembled, and other maddening questions. That they never got any answers did not appear to put them off in the slightest.

On 5 September Cecil was interviewed on the BBC Radio Four *Midweek* programme as their birthday guest, having celebrated his fifty-third birthday on 1 September. He was treated with deference and sympathy. He referred to the past year as having been 'traumatic'. He said 'One has one's life mapped out and then all of a sudden the blackboard was wiped clean and at 52 one had to make a fresh start.' He avoided mentioning me by name—'One regrets the unhappiness one has caused a lot of people'—but his questioners were not so squeamish. He was asked if it ever occurred to him and worried him that he had been treated 'slightly like a criminal' and that he would 'always be shadowed by the memory of Sara Keays and her baby'.

He was asked if he thought that one day he would 'have to set the record straight'. Clearly the questioner thought that he had been unjustly treated and ought to say so, but Cecil said "I made that statement. I would not make any further comment and that is my position". Once again there was the suggestion that an agreement had been made that we would not comment, that I had broken it, but he was not going to do so. He added "I do not feel under the slightest obligation to tell my story or anything of that kind."

He was asked if the past year had been difficult, if he had been "fighting back private fury" and 'When all that came to an end did you resent what happened?' And 'Do you long to return to Government?'

These exchanges were most interesting for what they revealed of the interviewers' misconceptions of the affair.

The following day the *Daily Mail* reported Cecil's interview under the headline A TRAUMATIC YEAR SPENT PICKING UP THE PIECES, BY PARKINSON. Gordon Greig, Political Editor, who wrote the article described Cecil as:

> The MP for Hertsmere who was Mrs Thatcher's favourite Minister until he resigned last October after his secretary Sara Keays announced she was having his baby.

What fondness such people have for re-writing history. By now it was universally believed that Cecil's 'secretary' had 'announced' that she was pregnant and so caused his downfall. He said that 'Parkinson fans have been hoping that he might now be brought back' and that he 'can expect' to be back in the Cabinet, although not in that autumn's reshuffle.

As the 1984 Conservative Party Conference—and the anniversary of Cecil's resignation—drew nearer— so the media renewed their efforts to obtain a story from me. By the end of September I was receiving frequent telephone calls from reporters and the more determined of them called at my house. The line most of them took was: 'We wondered if you would be interested in doing an interview, Miss Keays. Of course, we know you don't want to talk about private matters, but perhaps you could tell us how you are spending your time, what your plans for the future are? And how is your baby?'

Of course, there was nothing remarkable, they said, about the timing of their enquiries. It was pure coincidence that they should ring me just before the Party Conference started. I refused to give any interviews, but photographers called hoping to get a picture of Flora. I could just imagine the accusations of publicity-seeking and wishing to embarrass the Party that would be levelled against me if they succeeded. I decided that the only way I could avoid the problem would be by going away for a few days.

On my return, I found a letter waiting for me from Candidates' Department at Conservative Central Office, saying that if I did not reply to their letter of 6 August (I did not receive this letter and I do not believe it was sent) they would 'presume that you do not wish us to process your application at this stage, and please let us know as and when you wish your application to join the List to be considered'.

I had made no application to *join* the List. I had been on the List since

November 1982 and David Hunt had assured me that my name had *not* been removed.

Two days later, *on* 24 October, I had a telephone call from John Roberts of the *Daily Express* who said that he had heard that I had been dropped from the Conservative Candidates' List and that I was 'angry' about it. I asked him where he had got hold of the idea that I had been dropped from the List, but of course he could not possibly reveal the source of his information. When I pressed him he said that it came from a 'private source', adding that he thought it had come from Central Office originally but he really couldn't tell me definitely.

I said that as far as I was concerned I was still on the List and that all I could tell him was that I was in correspondence with Central Office about it. I didn't trust his newspaper for a moment, remembering the disgusting article the Hickey column had produced the previous November while I was in Oman and the attitude they had adopted towards me generally—like many other papers they have a marked tendency to support the 'official' line. I said that I did not wish to discuss the matter with him and hung up. He rang me back a moment or two later and said "We got cut off". "No we did not", I said, "I hung up on you. I do not wish to talk to you." I told him that I had no confidence in his newspaper's ability or wish to get anything right in view of the way they had behaved towards me previously. He said that they were going to write a piece anyway and wouldn't it be better if I talked to him about it. This is another line often taken by reporters. A subtle form of blackmail—'We are going to write something about you anyway and it will be your own fault if we don't get it right'. I hung up on him again.

Sure enough, the next day there was a piece in the William Hickey column of the *Daily Express*. It was headed ANGRY SARA GETS THE PUSH FROM TORIES and contained the following interesting passages:

> There has been considerable speculation about her former lover's comeback into the political arena, since Parkinson is still considered to be one of the Tories' brightest stars. So to have Miss Keays, now a busy mother to their 10-month old daughter Flora, as a candidate either now or in the future would be a considerable embarrassment . . . Many Tories close to Margaret Thatcher would love to see him back—but imagine the difficulties if she were to pop up at the next General Election.

The article also quoted a Central Office spokesman as saying that Candidates stay on the List until they ask to be taken off, but "If they've been on there a long time, they just drop off."

I had not dropped off: I had been pushed.

As my correspondence with David Hunt had got me nowhere, I wrote instead to John Selwyn Gummer, the Chairman of the Party. Two weeks later I had still not had a reply. In the meantime, it had been reported in various newspapers that the process of selecting a Conservative Candidate for Southgate, the late Sir Anthony Berry's constituency, was well advanced. In spite of David Hunt's personal assurance in May that he would ensure that I was notified of any future vacancies, I had not received an application form for Southgate. I wrote to Gummer again, asking why I had been yet again denied the opportunity of applying for a constituency vacancy.

At last he replied. As I should have expected, he did not answer any of my questions, but could only 'urge' me to go and see David Hunt. He ignored my reference to the Southgate vacancy and I realised later that he had probably delayed replying until the Southgate selection was out of the way.

I was left with no option but to see David Hunt, although I considered that any explanation that he was not prepared to put in writing was probably not worth having. I knew that if I did not go and see him it would be put about that I had refused to discuss the matter with them and they would use that as justification for removing me from the Candidates' List. I telephoned Central Office and was given an appointment for 3 pm on Tuesday 27 November.

The day before I was due to go to London I received an enquiry from the *Daily Mirror*. Was it true that I was going to Central Office? I could hardly deny it, but refused to say when I was going. I drove to London that night. The following day there was a piece in the *Daily Mirror* about the meeting. Within a matter of hours the press had tracked me down and I was inundated with calls from reporters. I refused to discuss the matter with them. Conservative Central Office, however, had no such scruples. That evening a reporter from HTV News rang to ask for my comments on a press statement that had been put out by Central Office. He wanted to know why I had asked for a meeting with David Hunt.

I said that I had not asked for the meeting, but was going to Central Office at the specific request of both Hunt and Gummer and that was all I was prepared to tell him. He read me the press statement issued by Central Office, which had clearly been intended to convey the impression to the media that it was I who had asked for the meeting, that I wanted to talk to Hunt about applying to become a candidate, and that he had agreed to see me.

The press release was downright dishonest. There had been no need for Central Office to tell the media anything and they could have had only one reason for doing so—to embarrass me and pre-empt my questions.

It had just the effect that Central Office must have wanted. I was reported in the press as having gone to London, demanding to see Hunt about my wish to become an MP. My family told me that there had been an item on the television which had referred to my 're-opening old wounds'. I was inundated with telephone calls that evening and the following day from television, radio and press, with such questions as why had I decided I wanted to become a candidate, and wasn't I going to cause embarrassment for the Party by doing so? Other than saying that Central Office's statement was misleading and that they had asked for the meeting, I refused to comment. Nor would I tell them when the meeting was to take place.

The greasy pole

Tuesday 27 November 1984

I realised that, if Central Office were going to indulge in that kind of dirty trick, it was essential that I have a witness of the meeting. On Tuesday morning I telephoned my sister Flora and asked if she could accompany me. She caught the next train to London and we set off together to Smith Square. Someone must have told the press when the meeting was to take place as there was a group of reporters waiting for me outside Central Office.

The staff at the reception desk had evidently been told to get me away from the press as quickly as possible and were waiting outside to usher us into the building. Without ado we were taken up to Hunt's office on the first floor.

Eighteen months had elapsed since I was last at Central Office. Everything seemed just the same, except the response from the inmates. Where before I would have been greeted with friendly smiles, now there were just cold stares. We were ushered into what used to be Anthony Royle's office on the first floor. I remembered it from the few months in 1981 when I had worked for him. Cecil's office had been just along the corridor.

As Flora and I entered the room David Hunt leaped to his feet and came round the desk, all smiles of welcome. "Sara, my dear, how good to see you again!"

I introduced my sister but before he gave me a chance to say why I had brought her he was ushering her to a chair saying "Of course! Do sit down." He carried on as if it was the most normal thing in the world for me to have brought Flora with me, when of course the normal thing would have been for him at least to question her presence, if not to refuse to allow her to attend the meeting. He did not even express surprise, but of course there was nothing normal about either the circumstances or the purpose of the meeting. He said to me, "Why don't you get off your chest what you want to say and then I'll deal with the points I want to make."

I was determined that he should acknowledge my reason for asking Flora to accompany me and I told him that, in view of his extraordinary behaviour in issuing a deliberately misleading statement in advance of the meeting, I had no confidence that he would deal honestly with me and therefore wished to have a witness to our conversation. Flora had already taken her pen and notebook from her handbag and was recording in shorthand everything that we said.

He attempted to justify their press statement by saying that Maurice Romilly, their Press Officer, had advised him that they *had* to say something to the press. It was pathetic that he should put the blame on a member of his staff.

He said, "We had a number of calls about it during the weekend and then there was something in the press on Monday morning and Maurice Romilly thought we would have to tell them something".

I said "So you told them a lie. You said I had asked to come and see you, which you know is untrue."

He must have been expecting me to complain about their press release because he had a copy of it in front of him and he set about trying to justify it.

I said "You implied that I had asked to come and see you and clearly the media believed you. You did not *agree* to see me. I agreed to *your request*, and Gummer's—you *urged* me to come and see you. Clearly it is going to be a complete waste of my time."

"No, no. I want to sort this out," he said, but proceeded to try to steer me away from the subject of our correspondence. I would not be diverted. I said that I wanted answers to the questions I had put to him in my letters and that I thought seven months was long enough for him to have decided what to say.

His manner was nauseating. He tried to ingratiate hismelf with me, talking as if nothing had happened and making such remarks as 'this is not like the Sara I knew of old'.

"I want to know why I wasn't notified of *any* of the by-election vacancies this year. You *say* that I am on the List. You gave me your personal assurance that you would see to it that I was notified of future vacancies. Why wasn't I notified of the Southgate vacancy?"

"We didn't circulate Southgate", was his reply. He then said that he had felt so cut up about Anthony Berry's death in the Brighton bombing that he couldn't bring himself to circulate the vacancy, that they had simply sent the List to the constituency association and asked them to say who they wanted to interview. I didn't believe him and said so. (I was told some weeks later that Central Office had received approximately 270 applications for the vacancy and therefore they must have notified at least that number of candidates, if not the whole list. How could those applicants have met the deadline if Central Office had not informed them?) When I pressed him again about Southgate he changed tack and said that my name had in fact gone forward, that he had personally sent it in. It was so obviously untrue that he must have had a low opinion of my intelligence if he expected me to believe him.

I repeated my earlier question and said "If you think I am unsuitable, the honest and straightforward thing would have been to say so straight off".

"We don't think you are unsuitable" he said and was saved by the telephone from having to say more. Flora and I sat in silence for some minutes while he said Yes and No to some talkative individual at the other end of the line. When he hung up he said "I've got coal now, you know" (referring to his recent appointment to the Department of Energy) and it was clear from the look on his face that the prospect of dealing with Arthur Scargill and Ian MacGregor gave him greater pleasure than the matter in hand..

He then gave a somewhat rambling account of how, when he came in as Vice Chairman in charge of candidates about a year previously the Standing Committee had decided to cease having one long list of candidates all the time, that they would terminate the continuing list and have a new list for each General Election with a ten year rule (that anyone who had not fought a constituency in ten years would be dropped from the List) and that everyone would have to go through a Parliamentary Selection Board. I pointed out that I had only been on the List for two years and that I had been approved by a Parliamentary Selection Board.

Again I said that I wanted to know why I hadn't been notified of *any* of the by-election vacancies this year.

"As far as I am concerned you are on the list and still receiving notification. At a meeting earlier this year I asked whether Sara had signified her intentions."

"You knew my intentions from my letters to you."

"Let me finish', he said, 'You seem to have misunderstood things about me personally."

"You are someone else's tool in this matter as far as I am concerned", I retorted.

He did not deny it, but launched into another rambling explanation of the problems they had been having with the Reading office which sends out the notifications of vacancies to Candidates.

"Are you trying to say that this was all due to computer error? What about Portsmouth South?" I asked, referring to the by-election vacancy which had occurred shortly after my first letter to him.

"No, I am not saying it was computer error," he said, "and I sent you Portsmouth South."

"And ensured that it arrived too late for me to meet the deadline for applications. Why was your letter delayed?"

He made some half-hearted and unfinished reference to his having been very busy "You know what it's like." [I'm beginning to know, I thought.]

"Why wasn't I notified of Portsmouth South by the Reading office in the usual way? Why was it you who sent it to me?" I asked.

"There have been a whole series of errors and problems," he said, "and in any case at Portsmouth South they did consider your name because I sent it to them."

"How dare you submit my name without my permission?" I demanded, "And why didn't you tell me in your reply that you were putting my name forward to Portsmouth South? I don't believe you. And when John Gummer replied to my last letter, why didn't he say that my name had been put forward to Enfield Southgate as you say it was? I just don't believe you."

He didn't answer but said that he wanted to know whether I wanted to be included in their new Revised List. I said that I would hardly have come to see him if I had not wanted to be on the list. I reminded him that he had asked me to come and see him so that he could answer my questions and I was still waiting for those answers. They were not forthcoming. So I asked him again, "If I am the embarrassment to the Party that others say I am, why don't you come clean and say so?"

"I could not have asked you to come in here if you were an embarrassment." he said.

"Well, tell me why I wasn't notified of any of the vacancies this year?"

He did not give me an answer, but tried a different ploy, saying, "There were other people who didn't get notified, you know."

"Who?" I asked. "How many others?"

"I will check the files and tell you."

"I want the names of those people."

"I can't tell you their names. That is confidential information."

"If you can't tell me their names how can I believe you?"

"I will have to write to them and ask them if I can give you their names."

"Do that" I said.

"I want to talk about the future, what is good for Sara Keays", he said.

"I am the best judge of what is good for Sara Keays and my future is built on the present", I retorted. His habit of constantly referring to me in the third person, as if I weren't present, was extraordinary.

"That you are on the new List is the most important thing."

I asked him what guarantee I would have that I would fare any better on his 'Revised' List than I had on the other. I said that it was all very well him assuring me that I was on the list if I was not then allowed to apply for vacancies. I said, "I know about the discussion that took place and the decision, at a very high level, that I must be got off the list, out of the way. What are you going to do about that?"

There was a silence, and he looked down, avoiding my gaze. After a pause, he said: 'I got Sara Keays in today because I wanted to talk to Sara Keays about her future.'

The discussion was so futile that I almost felt sorry for him. He was, I felt sure, acting on instructions and was clearly not enjoying the task he had been given of seeing me and trying to fob me off.

He said, "I tend to regard people on my Candidates' List as my candidates."

"Then why haven't you treated me like other candidates?" Again I repeated my earlier questions.

"When I became Vice Chairman there were a whole lot of errors."

He opened a file on his desk and said: "It is not on the record that Sara Keays is in any way unsuitable. You got some of the highest marks that anybody ever got at a Parliamentary Selection Board. This note here says 'Extremely pleasant, will make a good candidate and should have no difficulty in getting selected'."

His condescension was very irritating. I was not going to be bought off with flattery and tried again to bring him back to the point.

He said, "You have my complete undertaking that you will be considered for the new List."

"Just now you said that I was on it. Are you now saying that, within two years of being approved by the Selection Board, I have to be reconsidered?"

He said hastily, "I want to put you on the new list. I want to get this resolved. I am about to give up this position because I have got coal."

For skill at avoiding answering questions, you'll take a lot of beating, I thought. You and Scargill should have a lovely time together.

I said, "If you can't say any of this in writing, there has been no point in my coming. My exclusion from the list and the things that have been said on the subject in the press have cast a slur on my character. I want your answers to my questions and your written assurance that I am on the list."

"You will have it", he said.

What he said next astounded me; I never thought I would ever hear anyone say such a thing, least of all a Vice-Chairman of the Conservative Party.

"I am going slowly up the greasy pole. The higher I get, the more influence I have. I will see that you get on to the new List. I want to settle this thing before I go off to see Scargill. As far as I am concerned you have always been on the Approved List and I wish you to be on the next Approved List", he said. "I believe you would make a first-class MP. I an very sad there has been this disruption in our relationship. All I wanted to do was to get you in to see me."

"You got me in to see you to give me the answers that you had not given in your letters."

"I will write to you", he said.

I had had enough of this futile conversation and got up to leave. He was immediately concerned about what I was going to say to the waiting repoters.

I said "I have managed to get through this past year without giving interviews to the press, as have all my family, in spite of extreme provocation, and we don't have a Press Officer or other staff to hide behind. If they ask me about the meeting, I shall say that I repeated the questions I had put to you in correspondence and that you have undertaken to write to me. I trust that you will add nothing to that." He gave me his assurance that he would not.

He accompanied us to the head of the staircase and repeated his promise that he would write to me.

His promises proved worthless. Central Office put up another smokescreen, informing the media that the purpose of the meeting was to discuss whether I wished to be considered for the new Candidates' List.

On 3 December, David Hunt wrote to me:

> Dear Miss Keays,
>
> Following our discussion on 27th November, I am just writing to confirm that I am making a number of further enquiries so that I can respond fully to the points you raised both in previous correspondence and during our meeting.
>
> I shall write to you again as soon as possible.
>
> Yours sincerely,
>
> David Hunt
> Vice Chairman
> Candidates

I never heard another word from him. He had assured me that my name was on the Candidates' List, that it would be added to the new 'Revised List' and that he would see to it personally that I was notified of future vacancies. At the end of 1984 Central Office asked me to renew my subscription. I did so, but was never again notified of a single constituency vacancy.

Hunt's assurance was as empty as his promise that he would write to me. Soon afterwards he was replaced as Vice-Chairman in charge of Candidates by Tom Arnold MP. No doubt Hunt will try to use that as an excuse for not writing to me, if he is not too busy climbing his 'greasy pole' to comment, but I do not suppose that a little thing like a broken promise means any more to him than it does to Mrs Thatcher.

I was widely criticised for having 'sought' a meeting with David Hunt and was told that my timing was 'unfortunate', that I should allow 'a decent interval' to elapse before pursuing a political career. Others regarded my meeting with Hunt purely as publicity seeking on my part, an event which I had engineered in order to embarrass Cecil and dash his hopes of an early recall to the Cabinet.

The *Sunday Express* referred to me as 'popping up in the newspapers at every possible opportunity'.

Following my meeting with Hunt I was inundated with requests from television, radio and press, to be interviewed about my 'political ambitions'. I declined them.

I know that some journalists will argue that, if I wanted to refute the allegations that were made against me, I should have taken advantage of any one of the numerous requests for interviews with which they had plied me since October 1983. However, most of them had shown such prejudice against me and such disregard for the facts that I had provided in my statement to *The Times* that I had no confidence in their wish, let alone their ability, to report my views accurately.

Moreover, I was sure that any interview would lead to further criticisms and renewed efforts to discredit me. I would then be asked to comment again and if I were to decline, it would be tantamount to admitting defeat or conceding the points made against me. Perhaps that was how the media interpreted my refusal to respond to the accusations that were made, or perhaps they believed—as had been suggested at the outset—that my silence had been bought.

In any event, I suspected that where the media were concerned, I was probably beaten before I started. Any political party and especially the party in government, has the kind of media coverage available to it with which a private individual cannot hope to compete. In addition, the Government can always resort to their secret weapon, the Lobby—that obliging group of journalists to whom they can pass whatever 'facts' they would like to see published, confident that they themselves will never be exposed. Nor do they have to worry unduly if a particular 'fact' is not actually published, as they will have done something to colour the view of the reporter concerned, and so have prepared the ground for the next planting of propaganda.

It is well known that Fleet Street, once enamoured of a particular view is reluctant to be parted from it. I knew that those journalists who had swallowed whole the 'facts' with which they had been spoon-fed by the 10 Downing Street spokesman and others would hardly want to acknowledge that they had been gulled.

Perhaps it is for the same reason that the Conservative Party has continued to apply such blatant double standards in their judgements of Cecil and myself. Either they had fallen for their own propaganda, or they had nailed their colours so firmly to Cecil's mast, alongside those of the Prime Minister, that they dared not take them down.

In any event, they were at pains to demonstrate publicly their support for him. The monthly magazine issued by Conservative Central Office displayed photographs of him as Guest of Honour at Party functions. Far from diminishing his reputation, the scandal seemed if anything to enhance it; at official Conservative Party functions up and down the land he was received like a hero returned from battle. The media picked up the Party's theme and trumpeted his return to office, giving him star billing and treating him with special deference.

Not only has no such sympathy or understanding been shown towards me by the Conservative Party, but they sought to discredit me and even put pressure on other members of my family. Where they led, the media obligingly followed and since October 1983 I have been regularly denigrated and vilified in the press. Journalists whom I have never even met have displayed extraordinary personal animosity towards me and have subjected me to the most vitriolic attacks.

Not only is Cecil referred to in glowing terms, by political colleagues and the media alike, but he has been able to continue both his political and his business careers. What was to be only a minor setback to his career was to be disastrous for mine.

Not one Conservative MP ever spoke out publicly on my behalf then or at any other time. Not one of the many who knew me ever defended me against the dreadful things that were said about me. But there were many, Ministers and Backbenchers, who volunteered their support and approval for Cecil.

The only politician's voice ever raised on my behalf, was that of Tony Banks MP, a Labour Member, who asked the following Parliamentary Question during Prime Minister's Questions on 20 December 1984:

> When the Leader of the House next sees his right hon. Friend the Prime Minister, will he ask her to drop her personal veto against Miss Sara Keays being included on the Conservative Party list of approved candidates? Such a veto is a discrimination against both women and single-parent families.

The Prime Minister was spared from having to answer this question herself, being abroad at the time. The Leader of the House, John Biffen MP, who was answering Questions on her behalf, ducked the issue with the following reply:

> That really tells us more about the hon. Gentleman than it does about the Conservative Candidates list.

I never imagined that I would be the subject of a Parliamentary Question, or that it would be left to a member of the Labour Party to champion my cause. It was deeply disappointing that not one member of the Conservative Party spoke up for me on that occasion or at any other time.

Mr Banks could have added that Mrs Thatcher's veto was also a discrimination against unmarried mothers. Is it not interesting that you never hear of unmarried fathers, only unmarried mothers; or of men having illegitimate children, only women; that you do not hear of 'fallen men', only 'fallen women'?

The only means by which I could hope to cut through the propaganda and the prejudice was by setting down the facts in the form of a book. At the beginning of December 1984 I commenced the task.

Scapegoat

In 1985, the campaign for Cecil's restoration to the Cabinet was stepped up, with the Prime Minister letting it be known publicly that she wanted to bring him back.

By then the propaganda had been so effective that the scandal was generally identified with my name rather than his:

'Crossbencher' of the *Sunday Express* on 21 April 1985 referred to John Selwyn Gummer as having been appointed Party Chairman in Cecil's place

> to clean up the party's image after the Sara Keays scandal. And he has scrubbed it as spotless as a convent floor.

On 10 June 1985, the *Daily Mail* had a front-page banner headline: CECIL MUST RETURN and reported that:

> Mrs Thatcher is expected to bring Cecil Parkinson back into her Cabinet despite opposition from senior colleagues ... With the Government slipping in the opinion polls, the Prime Minister feels the need of Mr Parkinson's star quality and communication skills at the Cabinet table.

The Prime Minister was quoted as having said of him in a television interview with David Frost: "He was a quite outstanding Minister and we miss him very much. He was also a very good communicator, very good on the media."

By the time the House of Commons rose for the Summer Recess the media had become convinced—encouraged by 10 Downing Street— that she would restore him to the Cabinet in her September 1985 reshuffle.

On 26 August 1985, the Editor of the *Daily Telegraph* asked his readers to consider the matter and, naturally, to share his view that Mrs Thatcher 'should stand her ground' and bring Cecil back into her Government. The article, which he headed THE PRODIGAL SON?, was sprinkled with references to such interesting concepts as 'the more sophisticated moral argument', and 'political forgiveness'.

He wrote:

> ... Some say that it is possible to exaggerate Mr Parkinson's talents. But it is possible to exaggerate most things, ... it is hard to resist the conclusion that his return would be a conspicuous benefit.

Turning to the 'moral aspects of the matter', he said that 'Mr Parkinson allowed himself to be beguiled by one of the strongest of human passions'.

Beguiled? For twelve years? And which particular passion did the Editor have in mind? Why so coy about it?

He continued:

> Having wriggled indecisively on the dilemma which adultery so often produces, he made the right Christian decision to go back to his wife and family and to do everything in his power to discharge his obligations to the mistress he was to desert. Human nature being what it is, this is not a uniquely bad performance, and it is one which might be expected to evoke the particular charity which the New Testament enjoins for such offences ...

What were these 'obligations' and how has he discharged them?

Of the 'more sophisticated moral argument ... that the public delinquencies of public men, and any tolerance which may be seen to be shown to them, undermine morality', Deedes wrote, 'Political forgiveness to a reformed adulterer, after a suitable lapse of time, does not seem to us to come into this category'.

Much of the press comment could be put down to kite-flying by the Prime Minister's office in an attempt to find out whether there would be any public outcry if Cecil were reinstated.

By the end of August, the media, the press in particular, had worked themselves into a state of some excitement about the reshuffle and in particular about the much-debated question of whether or not he would be included.

The resuffle was to be announced on Monday 2 September. Twenty four hours earlier, Downing Street took the unusual step of announcing that the Prime Minister had decided, with regret, not to recall Cecil to her Cabinet. There were widespread expressions of surprise and disappointment; also an unusual reticence on the part of the media. They did not, apparently, want to find out *why* the Prime Minister had taken this decision. At least, they did not press her for an explanation, but supplied their own hypotheses. No doubt they had been primed by 10 Downing Street: the Prime Minister had wanted to bring Cecil back and badly needed his advice and guidance, but could not 'rely' on Sara Keays to keep quiet. Once again I was to be the scapegoat. Whatever happened, I would be in the wrong. It was to be my fault that the Prime Minister had not recalled him and if I did anything to defend myself, I could be accused, once again, of embarrassing the Government.

It was said that the Prime Minister had excluded Cecil from her reshuffle because the risk of adverse publicity was too great. Some were quite specific and said that the risk of such publicity lay with me. The Deputy Editor of the *Observer* informed television viewers that Cecil was 'in the power of Sara Keays'. Did it occur to him that if what he said were true, he was saying in effect that the Prime Minister was 'in my power' too?

Paul Johnson wrote in the *Daily Mail*:

> The resignation of Cecil Parkinson was an odd event in the first place.
> The decision to continue his exclusion from the Government, after two years of sackcloth and ashes, becomes more and more peculiar.

He referred to it as a 'case of double hypocrisy, not easily understood in terms of conventional moral theology'. The first 'hypocrisy', according to Johnson, was that Cecil was 'hounded' out of office because he had stayed with his wife rather than marry me. He said that 'the truth of the matter is that what caused his downfall, and still makes it seem inexpedient to bring him back into the Cabinet fold, is the child in the case'.

He was wrong on all counts. Cecil was not 'hounded' out of office. He got himself into a mess of his own making and tried to brazen it out. When I revealed a very little of what had really happened, the barrage of questions from the media about his conduct threatened the Prime Minister's position to such an extent that she was obliged to part company with him. She knew that there was much more that could be revealed that would be damaging to her.

It was not the publicity that made him resign, though the Prime Minister would like everyone to believe that it was. It was not, as Johnson and others have claimed, the 'child in the case' that made the Prime Minister decide against recalling him to her Cabinet. The reason she did not reinstate him is quite simply that the facts—which she had had in her possession since June 1983—had not been made public.

Shortly after announcing her Cabinet changes on Monday 2 September, 1985, the Prime Minister was asked by a television interviewer why she had not included Cecil in her reshuffle.

She replied:

> "You know I have a very high regard for Cecil's abilities, but I have many things to consider, many many things, and I came to the conclusion which I think was the best one. When I telephoned Mr Parkinson, who was abroad, he quite understood why I had made the decision, although he would have come back had he been asked to."

Few questions can ever have been fudged so skilfully. The Prime Minister has never been asked publicly to say what the 'many things' were that brought her to her decision.

Why she encouraged the media to believe that she intended to bring Cecil back into the Government when she knew that any member of my family might be driven to publish the facts, I do not know. I can only imagine that it was simply because she had gone so far along that road that she dared not turn back.

The essential facts that have not been revealed are as follows:

—For two and a half weeks, from the moment I told him that I was pregnant, up to Polling Day, Cecil refused to warn the Prime Minister of the likely scandal and put great pressure on me to have an abortion.

—He informed the Prime Minister on Polling Day only because my family had insisted that they would be obliged to inform her if he did not.

—It would appear that on Polling Day he asked me to marry him either because he believed the Prime Minister would expect him to 'do the right thing', or because he hoped to buy time for himself until he had secured a post in the new Government, or both.

—He told me that he had told the Prime Minister 'everything' and that she was appointing him Foreign Secretary. It is apparent from her response to my father's letter, which she received some time during the ensuing 24 hours, that Cecil had not told her the full facts. It would seem that he told her only that he was going to marry me, but not that I was pregnant.

—From my father's letter the Prime Minister learned of Cecil's original proposal of marriage, my pregnancy, his pressure on me to have an abortion and his refusal to inform her of the matter. She decided that he could no longer be Foreign Secretary, but that he could become Secretary of State for Trade and Industry.

—Even if his proposal of marriage on Polling Day were sincere, some time between then and 23 August he decided that he was not going to marry me. However, he did not inform me of his decision until 1 September.

—If the 'informed sources' quoted in the media at the time were to be believed—and these sources were recognised by the media as speaking with the knowledge and authority of the Prime Minister or members of her Government—the Prime Minister knew long before I did that Cecil did not intend to marry me. Even if she did not, she certainly knew the facts from my father's second letter to her dated 2 September. In any event, she was in possession of all the facts when she took her decision to sustain Cecil in office.

—Following publication of his statement, the Prime Minister's office announced:
 —that it was a purely 'private' matter, even though they had known since 24 August, when Cecil informed them, that at least one national newspaper had the story;
 —that the question of resignation 'does not and will not arise', even though the Prime minister knew that his ability to remain in office must depend to some extent on me and my family.

—Amongst the mass of dishonest and conflicting information fed to Lobby Correspondents by 'informed sources' were the following points:
 —that Cecil had informed the Prime Minister 'immediately it was confirmed'

that I was pregnant—a lie designed to convey the impression that he had readily informed her and that he had not known of my pregnancy until Polling Day.

—That what he told the Prime Minister on Polling Day was *not* that he was going to marry me, but that he had wished to do so at one time but had changed his mind and was remaining with his wife. Either he lied to me, or if, as I believe, he did indeed tell the Prime Minster he intended to marry me, someone 'close' to the Prime Minister lied to the media.

—Following publication of my statement these 'informed sources' were saying that what he told the Prime Minister on Polling Day was that he supposed he would *have* to marry me. If he did say that, again she knew the truth of the matter from my father's letter of 2 September. At best, she tolerated his deception of me and my family; at worst—and it is hard for us not to believe this—she connived at it.

—Furthermore, these 'informed sources' were quoted as saying that the Prime Minister had told Cecil that he could have the post of Secretary of State for Trade and Industry *only* if he remained with his wife.

—They were also quoted as saying that when he spoke to the Prime Minister on Polling Day and said that he supposed he would 'have' to marry me, she 'advised caution' and told him to reconsider his proposal.

If the last two assertions are true, the Prime Minister encouraged him in his deception of me and was party to it. Even if they are untrue, she learned of that deception from my father's letter of 2 September 1983 and took her decision to sustain Cecil in office in full knowledge of it.

At the very least, the Prime Minister's conduct towards me and my family fell far short of the standards expected of her office; at the worst, it would appear that she allowed the authority of her office to be used to propagate lies in the media in order to conceal the true facts from the public and to discredit me. I wait with interest to see whether any of the Parliamentary Lobby Correspondents have the courage to identify publicly the 'informed sources' who were quoted in the press against me.

What would the Prime Minister have done, I wonder, if Cecil had *not* told her on Polling Day—if my family had not made him tell her—and she had appointed him Foreign Secretary?

What would have happened if I had waited until after the election to tell Cecil that I was pregnant, or if I had not become pregnant until some months later; what would have happened, in other words, if the problem had arisen after he had become Foreign Secretary? Would the Prime Minister have insisted that he should remain in office and have announced that it was a purely private matter?

What would the effect on the General Election campaign have been if I or my father, outraged at Cecil's behaviour, had spoken to the press in May 1983? Did the Prime Minister consider such questions, I wonder, when she chose to disregard the contents of my father's letters and to reply to him as she did? Perhaps those who accused me, time and again, of being calculating, vindictive and destructive, will ask themselves why I did not act accordingly on one of the many occasions when I could have done so to great effect.

The Prime Minister is on record as saying that she does not like people who say one thing in private and another in public, that she likes people who talk straight. I wonder how she squares such views with her conduct towards my father and me.

When I said in my statement to *The Times* that I had both a public duty and a duty to my family to put the record straight, it was because I believe that integrity and honour are as important to public office as they are to private life. If honour has ceased to be necessary to public life in this country, then is it not time that politicians stopped using the titles Honourable and Right Honourable?

Just about everyone who could possibly have had reason to comment, and many who had none whatsoever, have expressed their opinions of the Parkinson/Keays Affair. All of them did so knowing that they lacked the full facts and that such information as they had been given ought to be regarded as biased, if not totally suspect.

The moment Fleet Street got word that I had written a book, journalists rushed to attack me. It seems that everyone may comment on the matter except me. Jean Rook of the *Daily Express*, who styles herself 'The First Lady of Fleet Street' was driven into a paroxysm of rage and an outburst of singularly unladylike language:

> How can an MP's former secretary be allowed to make a fool of a Cabinet Minister, an ass of politics, and a vengeful bitch of herself?

There was much more in the same vein.

It was remarkable that any newspaper should publish an article written in such terms.

Paul Johnson 'explained' Cecil's exclusion from the Cabinet reshuffle by making me the scapegoat:

> Miss Keays is not a lady who forgets or forgives easily ... if Parkinson were restored to prominence and glory, who can say that she might not think it her right and duty to intervene again—this time with little Flora at her side?

I wonder if Johnson or Rook, or any of the other journalists who have vented their spleen on me would remain silent in the face of such odious and unfounded attacks. How would they feel if they were vilified, their families insulted, their integrity called into question? Would they remain silent?

Why should I have any reason to suppose that such people would *ever* allow me to forget, that they would ever cease to make such undeserved and unprovoked attacks? Do they really believe that I do not have a right—and indeed a duty, for my daughter's sake—to protect myself when my reputation is blackened?

If they must pass judgement, let them do so on the facts rather than the Conservative Party's propaganda and the supposition and gossip of the media.

Index